The Crypto Man

By the same author

Assassination Day
Man on a Short Leash
The XYY Man
The Concrete Boot
The Miniatures Frame
The Satan Touch
The Third Arm
Channel Assault
The Stalin Account

The Crypto Man

Kenneth Royce

STEIN AND DAY/Publishers/New York

First published in 1984
Copyright © 1984 by Kenneth Royce
All rights reserved, Stein and Day, Incorporated
Designed by Terese Bulinkis Platten
Printed in the United States of America
STEIN AND DAY/*Publishers*
Scarborough House
Briarcliff Manor, N.Y. 10510

Library of Congress Cataloging in Publication Data

Royce, Kenneth.
  The Crypto man.

  I. Title.
PR6068.098C78 1984   823′.914   84-40250
ISBN 0-8128-2988-3

Prologue
France 1944

Stacey fingered his identity tag and shivered. It was freezing in the prison, and outside the wind was blasting against the old walls. The snow had stopped falling but snowflakes covered the area for miles, adhering to the dirty prison windows like goose down and reflecting an ethereal glare into the crowded cells.

Stacey glanced around at his fellow prisoners. For once the overcrowding offered an advantage, although it was almost impossible to appreciate. Bodies gave warmth. But the benefit in a draft-riddled cell was minimal. The five men huddled in the confined space. No one spoke. Dubost had been taken from the cell early that morning. Now, almost midday, he still had not returned and his absence preyed on the minds of his friends; he had been gone too long and the resistance leader was not in good condition anyway. They all had the same thought though no one voiced it; they would not be seeing the gutsy, cheerful little Frenchman again. And they knew that they could be next. A spate of executions was due.

Those who possessed special knowledge could only wonder whether the Germans fully knew the vital information they had in their hands. Sooner or later, after constant deprivation and torture, someone would talk. The morale of the prisoners was low. And so it would be out there in the streets of Amiens and beyond, among leaderless groups of ardent patriots seeking some direction and aware that key members of their far-reaching organization were now captured or dead.

Not only French resistance leaders had been rounded up. There were British and American agents among them who knew too much. And women, too.

Stacey was an American who had been separated from his French and British contacts. Fair-haired and blue-eyed, his immediate colleagues had at first thought him to be a Nazi plant, particularly as he spoke fluent German. In fact, his ancestry was Danish and he was a third generation American. The whisper from those who had worked with him soon circulated; if he was a German, then he had taken a strange delight in killing his compatriots. It was only a matter of time before the interrogators would work on him in full measure. There were hundreds of prisoners, and Stacey had been picked up only three days ago. He had yet to be tortured, but had seen the results on some of those who had been, like Dubost. He ceaselessly wondered how he would stand up to it. If he did half as well as the Frenchman, it would be difficult for his companions to complain.

By some oversight, Stacey still had his wristwatch; it would not be his much longer, but meanwhile he kept it out of sight. He glanced at it now. It was 55 minutes after eleven on the morning of February 18, 1944. And at that moment he heard aircraft engines. So did the others in the cell. They glanced at each other, puzzled by the increasing throbbing so unbelievably low. The noise grew above the blustering sound of the wind.

The planes seemed at rooftop height. What was so important in Amiens to justify such risks? It took a few seconds for them to realize that the answer might be within themselves.

The drone increased to thunder. They heard the ack-ack and then the first of the bombs. The old walls shook. The explosions, like enormous thunderclaps, were difficult to place but they could well be around the German barracks. Sirens added to the great confusion of noise.

By now the five men had risen to their feet, backs against the walls. Snow and ice packed the prison into a tight cocoon but failed to muffle the blasts. Reverberations ran the length of the buildings, sending up tremors like an earthquake as planes roared away after dropping their bombs.

Shouts came from the corridors. Running footsteps of guards were muted by hasty commands in German. And then the scream of bombs came nearer, very brief on such short drops, and the explosions started around the prison itself, rocking the walls and moving through the foundations in waves.

The men squatted again, realizing their danger. As the bombs came nearer the prisoners sometimes heard a secondary scream before an explosion, as if the bombs were skidding on the ice before striking head-on to set off the detonators. The walls trembled and then began to crumble. Debris came hurtling down and the men crouched at the door.

For the next few minutes the prison took a pounding as waves of aircraft flew over, aiming their bombs directly at the walls. The whole place was shuddering, and Stacey, with his back to the door, suddenly felt it move as brickwork and plaster crumbled around its frame. He shouted to the others just as they were all blown flat by an enormous blast that seared their sight and created a painful pressure on their eardrums. They instinctively covered their heads and tried to ball up as the outside wall came crashing down.

Dust, mortar, and rubble flew into the air, carried by a wind that cut through the thin clothing of the prisoners. They peered through the dust haze to the gaping, ragged hole in the prison wall. The sound of bombs and guns continued, with the roar of aircraft intermingled with the increasing volume of a yelling multitude, the frantic bellowing of commands in German, and the subdued and erratic crack of small-arms fire trying to make impression against the general uproar. People could be glimpsed, momentarily, running in every direction; then they were screened by the rising palls of smoke.

With almost a simultaneous shout of glee, three of the men dived for the breach in the wall, shaking off brick dust and snow as they moved forward. Stacey was with them when he noticed that the fifth man did not move. He hesitated over the body, removed some rubble. The man was dead, his head smashed in, snow turning the blood to pink streamers. There was nothing to be done. Stacey peered through the hole. There seemed to be hundreds of escaping prisoners, a seeming handful of soldiers chasing them, but it was a token chase. There were far too many escapees even for armed men to cope with, and Stacey glimpsed at least one soldier attacked by a mass of prisoners who beat him down with his own gun.

As he was about to duck through the gap, loose masonry fell from above to strike his head, and he collapsed on the rubble. He came to with a pounding head and a sense of panic; he was not sure how much time he had lost and his watch was now broken. The prison yard was empty and he could see through the huge rupture of the outer wall to the Route d'Albert. The sound of firing was more distant and the bombing had stopped.

He glanced back at the door, which was now hanging from its hinges. Blood was trickling down his neck. Stacey stepped through the door into a rubble-strewn corridor. There was nobody in sight, as if the prison were empty. He knew where he wanted to go; the office where he had received a preliminary interrogation. At that time his identity tag had been the cause of the postponement of a real torture session. He had stuck to the story of being a United States Air Force captain, shot down over northern France and trying to evade capture for the last two months. He claimed he had stolen the French clothes he wore. In the short term, the rank, name, and number on the tag around his neck had supported his claim.

He ran lightly along the corridor, skirting piles of rubble, and continued around the corner. There were no guards in sight. Mounting the stairs two at a time, he rounded a bend on a landing to find half the outside wall blown to bits. Spread-eagled on the landing was a German officer, arms hanging through the gap.

Stacey took a quick look. The man was dead, an oberleutnant. He had to think quickly. But for prisoners still trapped in their cells the upper floors would almost certainly be empty. Prison staff would either have run for the comparative safety of the lower floor or be out chasing prisoners. The oberleutnant was bigger than Stacey; it was better than being smaller. The American raised the corpse in a fireman's lift and continued up the stairs. At the end of the upper corridor he found an empty office. He entered and closed the door.

Stacey started to strip the German. He had great difficulty in pulling his own clothes over the larger frame of the officer and split the shirt and pants. He quickly dressed in the uniform, which was loose; the jackboots were too big as well. It did not matter.

He went to the Governor's office. The door was wide open and there was a strong smell of burning. The empty drawers of the filing cabinets were hanging out, and Stacey quickly realized what had happened. While he had lain unconscious, someone else had done what he had come to do. Prisoners' records and card indexes had been piled onto the office floor and been burned; they still smoldered behind the desk. He quickly checked the desk drawers; they too, had been ransacked. He turned toward the door as he heard footsteps.

The Sturmbannfuhrer who faced Stacey showed total surprise. His uniform was dust-caked and bloodied down one arm, and he bore the look of a very worried man. He had expected the office to be empty and he did not recognize the young oberleutnant who was on the wrong side of the desk. Had he been less confused, he would have acted more quickly. Stacey grabbed the Luger he had placed on top of a cabinet, cocked it as the Sturmbannfuhrer, eyes widening with enlightenment, went for his own holstered gun, and shot him dead.

Was there anyone outside the door? Gun in hand, Stacey stepped around the desk, peered into the empty corridor, and ran as fast as he could. Reaching the ground floor, he dived through the nearest gap and fled across the churned up snow to get as far away from the prison as he could.

He headed south across the river Somme and past the Gare du Nord. As he continued, he realized he was close to Gestapo headquarters, on the corner of the rue Dhavernas and the rue Jeanne d'Arc. Would the uniform protect him? The streets seemed empty, yet he was sure he was being observed. Crazily he continued on until he reached the old building. The front door was wide open. With gun in hand he went in. It was difficult to believe the place was empty, but it was. Everybody was out chasing hundreds of escaping prisoners.

Stacey found a big man lying on his face with blood on his back where he had been stabbed. In Baumann's office, the head of Gestapo, an old safe lay ransacked, its back ripped open; filing cabinets were open and empty. Everything told the same story as the one in the Governor's office in the prison. Only a smoldering pile of ashes remained of the prisoners' files. The Gestapo records had been destroyed. But when he searched the desk he found a card index with photographs stuck to one corner of each card. There was no time to examine or burn them now, and Stacey quickly stuffed them inside his jacket and left the deserted building.

He continued on. A police car went howling past, but nobody in it took notice of him. He guessed that prison escapees had scattered everywhere. There were distant shapes ahead, but he could not determine who they were. He swung wide of them, stumbled, and then fell over some scattered masonry. A stray bomb had partially demolished an outbuilding.

As he climbed up, Stacey noticed a group of figures lying still and flat in the snow. Six men and one woman, all dead, presumably shot by soldiers. On impulse he searched for identity tags and found that three of the men were wearing them. He tore them off and pocketed them so the Germans would not be able to identify those they had killed.

There was nothing he could do for the dead. Only yards from him there was a sudden wail and a long gasp of agony. He stepped over the rubble and entered a two-sided room—the other two walls had been destroyed. The ceiling hung precariously, and a trickle of rubble and plaster cascaded down. Something moved above, and the ceiling tilted more ominously. In the far corner of the room, sheltered and partially hidden behind the debris of smashed furniture, were two huddled women. One of them was moaning.

Stacey's approach did nothing to reassure them, and they glanced up in fear. One woman held the broken leg of a table, ready to strike out at him if he came nearer. He belatedly realized what scared them.

"I'm American," he explained in French. "I took the uniform off a dead German. Look, see how badly it fits."

They were not quick to believe him. He undid the jacket neck, pulled out his I.D. "You want to look?" And when they did not reply he added, "Okay, I'll push off, but first what's your problem?" He addressed the woman crouched awkwardly with her back to the wall.

8

"She's in labor."

"Oh Christ." In the freezing snow and ice, barely under cover, with no hot water, sanitary arrangements, or clean towels, neither mother nor child could survive.

"Isn't there somewhere we can take her?"

"She cannot walk."

As he scrambled nearer, Stacey could see that they were very young. Their heads were bare, faces haggard, clothes flimsy and inadequate. He unbuttoned his tunic, retaining the gun, and placed it over the swollen stomach of the mother to be. He tried to cushion her head with his arm. And then he recognized her. She was no more than twenty, but her reputation as a resistance worker was already renowned. If he was not very much mistaken, he knew who the prospective father was. But where was he? Dead? Escaped?

And then Stacey and the other girl, who called herself Jeannette, were far too busy delivering the child to think of anything but the problem at hand. The big danger was noise. The woman who Stacey knew as Paulette Dumain was in agony. He gave her his belt to bite upon and encouraged her, sometimes warning her about the noise. Jeannette, without experience, did the midwife's job of delivery. As the baby's head emerged, Stacey looked around desperately for something to wrap the child in. He crawled across the floor to the remnants of a table, and from the pieces of wood and brick and dust, pulled out a tablecloth. He shook it as best he could and folded it to size. Behind him the child made its first cry, and Jeannette quickly cradled it to stifle the sound.

Stacey struggled back with the cloth and Jeannette folded it around the tiny, wrinkled figure that was already striving to live. Stacey looked around for something warmer for the baby. He gazed at the tilting ceiling. If there were a bed up there, there would be blankets. The stairs were in a bad way, but he believed he could manage them. Could the already dangerously poised upper floor take his weight? The two girls were in the best position for safety. Anything sliding through should fall away from them, unless the whole ceiling came down.

Time was against them. The longer they stayed too near to the prison, the less would be their chance of escaping. He could not leave the girls and the baby now being cradled so lovingly. He glanced at the young mother. Paulette appeared to be near to death. Her face was as white as the snow, her breathing very shallow. He adjusted the jacket around her and noticed the blood between her legs. He stroked her face, took the belt away, and strapped it around his waist, leaving the holster flap unbuttoned. The intense cold bit through his shirt.

He reached the stairs and started to climb their weakened and littered treads. Halfway up they began to shake. The bannisters and handrail were already broken so he kept to the wall, which itself was split right down. The whole building was in a state of near collapse, and it was a wonder the wind had not finished the job.

Suddenly he stopped, awkwardly balanced. There were footsteps outside. More than one set. Someone was climbing through the rubble. Stacey tried to turn, pulling out his gun as he did, but he was obliquely placed when he saw the first man enter; then another and another, and others were moving outside. From the way they were dressed, they were clearly French, and the German arms they carried had probably been picked up from dead soldiers, victims of the air raid.

The first man was climbing through the wreckage toward the girls, closely followed by the second. The third man, not far from the foot of the stairs, heard Stacey turn, looked up, saw jackboots and breeches and a loosely held Luger, and fired without hesitation. Stacey crashed down the stairs.

Stacey was lying with his legs up the rickety stairs and his head on the floorboards when he realized he was still alive. His body felt like an ice block with the exception of a small fire somewhere inside him. As his mind cleared, he knew that he had been hit at least once. His head ached, and when he moved his eyes he could see his own blood on the floorboards only inches away. There was movement outside again, so he remained quite still, although he doubted that he could have moved just then. There were voices: German, and very near.

He lay there hazily thinking that if his wounds did not kill him, the cold most certainly would. His outstretched hands were frozen stiff. He believed that whoever was outside was examining the bodies he had found earlier. Fleetingly, he was glad he had

10

removed the identity tags. If he survived, he would report back the I.D. details he had in his jacket pocket. With a flurry of panic he remembered that he was not wearing the jacket. No wonder he was so cold. *Why wasn't the baby crying?* He lifted his head involuntarily and the pain shot through him. Blood drifted into his eye. He did not believe he had been shot in the head; he must have cracked it open in the fall.

The voices and the footsteps moved on. No one entered the building. In great pain and with enormous effort, Stacey dragged himself face downward until he was flat on the floor. He gazed over to where the girls should be, but the debris obstructed his view, and he had to torture himself to rise to his knees. The men had gone. And Jeannette. And the baby.

Paulette Dumain was there, though, his jacket still partly covering her. It took a great effort for him to crawl across, and periodically he had to stop to clutch at his stomach. He began to understand that some time had passed since he had been shot. It was still daylight, but he guessed he had been unconscious for a while. He fingered his head; the blood had largely congealed, and it covered one more area of pain. He wiped his eye with stiff, cold fingers, and continued on. They should not have left Paulette behind.

As he reached her, he guessed the worst. They had not even troubled to close her staring eyes. Stacey did so now with difficulty. She would not feel the icy touch of his fingers. He touched her face, so cold and hard. Twenty, he thought, if that. She had really never seen the baby. He did not know whether she had been religious, but he stumbled over a crude prayer he made up as he went along, ill-phrased but sincere.

For a while he stayed there, saddened, as he tried to gather strength to make a move. He must get away from here, no matter how difficult it would be. Whatever his suffering, it would be better than being in the hands of the Gestapo.

He had placed the index cards beside her body at the time he had taken his jacket off. They were no longer where he had put them. He searched around, lifted the jacket to peer beneath. It was then that he saw the bullet wound straight through her heart. The shot had been fired through the jacket, and he could now see the small rent.

Stacey sat back sickened, for the moment forgetting his own pain. He accepted that Paulette might have been shot out of compassion. She had been in pain and it was extremely doubtful if she would have survived, even with full medical help. The chances were that she would have died in pain and without any kind of warmth, deprived of the comfort of friends. Even so, it seemed to be so coldblooded. He apologized to her there and then and cursed the war and life itself. But life had to go on, and the war would not go away.

He retrieved the jacket, put it on his shivering body with difficulty, and buckled the belt over it, the holster now empty. He made another search for the cards. And then he groped in one of the jacket pockets for the I.D. tags. They, too, had gone. He turned out the other pockets and realized that whatever they might have contained had been taken. He had no idea of what might have been in the pockets, but there would certainly have been an identity card. So he never learned the name of the man whose uniform he wore.

Somebody knew. Somebody had taken the cards and tags. And somebody had shot Paulette and had left himself for dead. And that same person and the others with him had taken Jeannette and the baby with them. Deeply bitter, Stacey began the difficult and painful journey to the door, unsure of reaching it and not contemplating what lay beyond. What point was there? He did not rate his chances further than each agonizing step. He was not to know that the daring R.A.F. Mosquito raid had accounted for at least fifty dead Nazis, some French Gestapo, and eighty-five prisoners. There were also some seventy Germans and about eighty of the prisoners wounded. Over seven hundred prisoners had broken out and some four hundred were to remain free.

But all Stacey could think of as he tried to reach the door was a young dead mother behind him and the tiny, struggling baby she had never suckled, who was soon likely to join her.

Present-Day England

1

BROOKS ROSE TO THE SOUND of the bell and stepped bare-footed into a pool of blood. He recognized the tackiness before looking down to see it. He yelled as Naylor sat up in the bunk above him.

"For Christ's sake, Brooksie. Cut the noise."

"Bugger you. I'm standing in blood." Brooks tried to follow the line of blood but it had spread everywhere, even under the cell door, and it was still creeping. "God Almighty." He had just realized its source. "Chesfield's topped himself."

"*What!*" Naylor leaned further over. "Jesus. He's slashed his wrists." He swung his legs over the side of the bunk and they dangled near Brooks' head. "Call a screw. For Christ's sake hurry."

But Brooks did not want to move. "I can't get around it."

"Then step through it, you bloody fool. You're already in it. Bang the door."

But Brooks could not take his eyes from the body of Chesfield, who lay in the opposite lower bunk, a mass of red blotches where the blood had spurted from the artery in his right wrist, which was half across his lifeless body. The left arm, its wrist also slashed, was mainly responsible for the blood that had oozed to the floor. The whole bunk was saturated.

"Move, damn you," Naylor yelled.

"*You* bloody well move." But Brooks stepped forward slowly, as if by the careful lowering of his feet he could avoid the mess. He reached the door and started to hammer it, yelling at the top of his voice, reaching a point of near hysteria.

The more controlled Naylor stayed where he was, feet well clear of the floor, and gazed critically at and around the body of the wretched Chesfield, who had never been able to adapt to prison life, even for the short time he had been there.

The cleanup was inevitably messy; mops and buckets and rubber boots. The makeshift knife was found when the bed was stripped and the blankets rolled into saturated red balls. The "knife" had been made from a small piece of plywood. In spite of the fact that the "blade" had been filed down to a cutting edge, by normal standards it would be considered to be blunt. The wrists must have been hacked at in order to cut deep, and the pain must have been excruciating. It could only have been the act of a man totally without hope, the final gesture of a despair so deep only death could cure it.

The usual inquiry followed the tragedy. How had Chesfield obtained the knife? A laughable question to most of the cons. In the first place, Chesfield had been working in the carpentry shop, and there were always ways to obtain illicit items. Had the two prisoners sharing the cell with him heard anything? No they had not. A full Home Office inquiry was satisfied. Suicides showed a lack of vigilance on the part of the prison staff, and sections of the press would feast upon it. Some would obliquely suggest that certain of the staff turned a blind eye. But the realists knew that there was no system that could prevent a determined man from killing himself.

There was another aspect the press used in varying degrees, but in no way significantly. Chesfield had been a highly educated man. Harrow and Oxford. He had not been short of money, had been a member of Lloyd's, and had other profitable interests as well. His friends had been, as would be expected, moneyed people. Some were in the public eye. Among those who were becoming increasingly so was Walter Clarke, Foreign Minister in Her Majesty's government. They had been about the same age.

Walter Clarke, when interviewed, spoke highly of Chesfield. They had not been close friends but had been at Oxford together; they had largely drifted apart since graduating. Politics, and finance in its many forms, did not always mix. But Clarke had possessed great respect for Chesfield; the man had been brilliant, his future virtually unlimited. Who could know what brainstorm had turned him into an accessory to premeditated murder, a murder that was still without a known motive and whose secret Chesfield had taken with him to a premature grave. He had been in his early forties. His torment had clearly been unbearable.

But nowhere did the unfortunate episode make big news. Chesfield stirred little interest. He died in almost as self-effacing a manner as he had lived. Until his death he had been one of the great unknowns to the general public, who were not unduly roused when he ended his life. Various rumors circulated, and people who liked mysteries put their own interpretation on his motive. The rumors lasted less time than was generally taken to recall his name, which slipped into obscurity even before the Home Office inquiry findings were made public. But in certain quarters he was never to be forgotten for one reason or another, and none of the reasons was so self-obliterating as the man himself had been.

Detective Superintendent Alfred George Bulman crossed Pall Mall without apparent concern for irate drivers who slowed or swerved to avoid him. His chunky, hunched figure mounted the canopied steps, and he pushed the huge doors to enter the club. He went straight to the desk attendant to ask for Sir Stuart Halliman. Halliman stood waiting at the rear of the long vestibule. On seeing Bulman he came forward.

"Hello, George. I almost didn't recognize you."

Bulman turned; the eyes smiled in the rough face as he gazed up at the tall figure. "I'd always recognize you, Sir Stuart. It is good of you to see me."

Halliman took Bulman's arm and propelled him to the downstairs bar. When they had their drinks, they went to the quietest corner table. "You've thickened out and you've lost some hair," commented Halliman as they sat down.

Bulman fingered his rapidly thinning dark hair. "Have to comb it forward these days or you wouldn't see it at all. You don't look any different."

"You were always a flatterer. I understand the Chesfield business worries you."

"I don't believe he topped himself."

"The coroner did. And the subsequent inquiry."

"Oh, I know all that. That's why I wanted to see you."

"But the police are satisfied, surely? They'll go along with the findings?"

"I should think so. But my chief doesn't and neither do I. We have never been satisfied about the Chesfield affair; there's much more to it than has come out. I believe you can help."

Halliman was thoughtful. He had a great deal of respect for Bulman as a detective. Much of the brusqueness had gone and his manner was easier than Halliman remembered. Perhaps Bulman had stopped going around upsetting people. "Are you still playing loose head with the MI5 pack, George? Isn't Sir Lewis Hope your chief?"

Bulman smiled. "Even you use the obsolete name for the Security Service. I'm nearer to them than the Met. I sometimes wonder why I'm kept on as a copper."

"No you don't. You're in too useful a position. Free of the formalities of Special Branch and clear of the bureaucracy of the Metropolitan Police. You used to love it. What can I possibly do that Lewis Hope cannot? You know very well I've been retired these last few years."

"Retired from office, you mean?"

"No. Retired. Period. But how can I help an old friend?"

Bulman sat forward, spatulate fingers clasped. He appeared to be uncomfortable in his chair. "I don't think there's been a whitewash. As you know, in top security prisons it's usually one to a cell, but there have been renovations going on at Hull. With trouble at some of the other prisons, as a temporary measure, some cells are being shared. It's gone on longer than planned, but these things always do. There were three men in the cell but no obvious reason why either of the other two would want to kill Chesfield. But I believe one or both of them did."

"Motive?"

"Money."

Halliman did not move. At that moment his eyes were cold. "Paid to do it? By whom?"

"Directly, it could have been anyone. I can identify the most likely cons who could have been used as paymaster. Indirectly, by whoever did not want the motive for Chesfield being guilty of murder coming to light."

Halliman stared. "A political motive?"

Bulman shrugged. "Who knows? It's a gut feeling."

"A very strong one for you to seek me out. You still haven't told me why."

"Bear with me a little. The police have got nowhere. The coroner is satisfied, the subsequent inquiry uncovered nothing."

"Perhaps there was nothing there." Halliman interrupted. "Why can't you accept matters as they are? You're not a stirrer. Is there something you're not telling me?"

Bulman rubbed an ear and looked apologetic. "I *know* nothing. But I believe we haven't heard the full story. The police won't get anywhere with the cons, and if I show my face there'd be a wall of silence. Someone who knows them, someone who has been inside and who they trust, might just ferret something out. From someone. Anyone. Not necessarily from those directly involved."

Halliman sat back and crossed his long legs. Understanding touched the cool eyes. "Now I know why you're here, but you're going too far back, George. It's years since I used him. He will have lost his old contacts a long time ago."

"Maybe. Maybe not all. He's the sort of character people don't forget."

"Evidentally. We both know who we're talking about and yet haven't mentioned his name. Did he ever get around to marrying that very lovely girl, Maggie Parsons?"

"I don't think so, although I believe they are still together."

"That doesn't surprise me; they were made for each other, and I'm no romantic." Halliman's eyes misted. "Willie 'Spider' Scott. A character indeed." Halliman switched off the reverie. "He won't help you."

"I know. He hates my guts. With reason. But he might help you."

"Ah! You're wrong, George. Willie would hate me just as much. And he certainly wouldn't trust me. Lewis Hope should approach him, if he's the man in control."

"Sir Lewis doesn't stand a chance. He's the wrong type. Willie doesn't know him anyway, and would show him the door."

The two men smiled a little bitterly. "He's always respected you, though," Bulman insisted. "He would listen to you."

Halliman considered the point. "After all this time he would immediately be suspicious. And rightly so." After a long pause Halliman asked, "Do you really consider it to be so important?"

"Would I have asked you otherwise, Sir Stuart?"

Halliman fingered his mustache. "There might be a way around it. Chesfield's father is an acquaintance of mine and a member of this club. Understandably he's not happy with the outcome of his son's death either. Give me a day or two to think it over. If I can help, I will, of course. But we both know that Willie Scott is not the easiest man to handle."

Willie Scott locked up his offices just off St. Martin's Lane as a cab pulled up to the screech of peak London traffic. Scott turned his back to glance up at the repainted sign above the shop windows. Scott Travel Ltd. Nothing dramatic. Certainly not as eye catching as the previous name: XYY TRAVEL. It was a few years now since he had changed the name. It had reminded him too much of the past and, anyway, he now considered the chromosome theory of what made for villains and villainous tendencies as a load of rubbish. There were too many medical controversies. And he had proved them all wrong. Show me a scientific expert, he reflected, and I'll show you muddle and contradiction.

The strong autumnal nip in the air suggested that winter would be early. Scott strode toward Trafalgar Square and wondered what Maggie would cook for dinner. The cold made him feel hungry. He drifted easily through the home-going crowd and suddenly felt his sleeve being tugged. He turned, quickly placing a hand over his wallet, wondering if a pair of pickpockets were trying the knock and snatch routine; it was a habit born of long experience.

A short, plumpish, well-dressed elderly man retained a hand on

Scott's sleeve and was breathlessly trying to smile. He had clearly been running. "I'm so sorry. I saw you leave the travel agency as my taxi drew in. Are you Mr. Scott by any chance?"

Scott gazed down; the man could be in his seventies. "Take it easy," he said. "You'll bust a valve. Yes, I'm Scott." He had an unmistakable London accent.

"Thank God. I'm sorry I'm so late. The traffic . . ." He trailed off as he fought for breath. He noted Scott's concern. "It's all right. Really. Shouldn't run at my age. Could I speak to you for a few minutes? Back at your office?"

"I'm closed. Won't tomorrow do?"

Disappointment covered the plump face. Scott noticed how sad were the pale blue eyes. The lips moved to speak but instead opened wide to suck in air. The two men were an island on the pavement, streams of people hurrying around each side of them.

"If it's about travel, I'm afraid it must wait," Scott added. He felt sorry for the old boy but the number of times he had fruitlessly stayed late in an effort to please people could not be counted.

"It's not travel. Something else. Private. Very personal."

Scott grinned. It was an infectious, warm action that spread to the wide-spaced eyes. "You sure you've got the right bloke?"

"Oh, yes. It won't take long." The plump man hesitated, not sure whether what he was about to say would be offensive. "I'm quite willing to pay for your trouble."

Scott saw the uncertainty. "I don't charge for listening, old son."

"No, of course not. I'm sorry. Well shall we . . . ?"

Scott took him by the elbow and escorted him back to the office. "What's your name?"

"Chesfield. Sir Richard Chesfield. I mention the title only so that should you later wish to check on me, you can find the detail in Debretts."

The name stirred uneasily in Scott's mind. As he turned the key in the lock he felt less amiable, but he would not let the old boy down now. He would listen. But he could see no point in entering his office screened behind the travel counter. There was a long, low table covered with travel brochures near the suspended travel literature racks. "Take a pew," he said, as he led the way to the chrome and plastic chairs that he secretly detested.

Sir Richard Chesfield puffed his way across the shop floor to the small reception area.

"Shall I take your topcoat? We do have a coat rack." Scott, over six feet in height, towered over the portly figure.

"Thank you, no. I think your heating is off."

Scott made no comment about the quantity of natural insulation Chesfield carried over his frame. The two men sat across the table from each other. Chesfield undid the buttons of his topcoat, and his chins wobbled below the rosy moon face. He laid his hat carefully on the chair beside him, revealing a crop of dark hair with no gray in it and presumably tinted. Vanity came in many forms, Scott reflected.

Chesfield produced a cigar, and Scott hoped that he would not still be sitting there by the time it was finished.

"I don't smoke," said Scott as Chesfield held out the case and scanned the table for an ash tray. Scott pushed one across, observing that now that they were here, Chesfield was already avoiding the issue he had called about.

"My son committed suicide," Chesfield at last blurted out. "Quite recently."

Scott's memory stirred and produced recollection and a warning. "Hull prison, wasn't it? I read about it. Sad business. I'm sorry." He wanted to hear no more, but Chesfield was suffering now that he had spoken. His face was sagging and suddenly he looked much more tired, his face seemingly less florid. He gazed at the glowing tip of his cigar, then at the passersby beyond the windows, as though afraid that they could overhear. "I think it was murder," he added abruptly.

Scott said nothing. What was there to say? And what the hell was it to do with him?

Chesfield gazed across the narrow table. "Doesn't that surprise you?"

"Death in prison is often followed by that kind of assertion. Guards beat up a prisoner and there's a big cover-up, that sort of thing. Sometimes it's true. Perhaps it's natural for a father to think that."

"Don't be so damned condescending, young man. I'm not a fool."

"Time to go," Scott said standing up. "I don't know where this is leading and I don't want to know."

"I'm sorry," Chesfield pleaded. His eyes were tear filled. "I shouldn't have said that, I know. But I had to identify him and to attend the inquiry. It was bad enough him being in prison at all. But to hack his wrists with a piece of blunt wood . . . I . . . can't . . ." He broke down and lowered his head. A tear dropped on a travel brochure and spread over the colored print.

Scott, seeing the obvious distress, sat down again. It was as though the old boy's guts were being torn from him. Maybe he had nothing left to believe in. Perhaps he had doted on his son. To be convicted of murder and then to have finished as a bloodless corpse must have hit the father like a multiheaded bomb. Gently, Scott said, "I really don't see what this has to do with me. Who sent you here?"

Chesfield gathered himself. "It's disgraceful to behave like this. I'm not normally an emotional person. Financiers seldom are." He dabbed his eyes with a folded handkerchief. "The tears were not for myself, Mr. Scott. I hate to see a life end like that without apparent reason. He should have had everything to live for."

"You haven't answered my question."

"I was recommended to you by a friend."

"Who is he and for what reason?"

"I'd rather not say who."

"Do I know him?"

"I believe so. Perhaps I should have said a mutual friend."

It was difficult to believe. "I doubt that we move in the same circles. I still need to know who and why." Scott glanced pointedly at his watch.

Chesfield moved uncomfortably as Scott prodded, "Were you warned not to pass on the name?"

"I saw it as a confidence. It's really irrelevant. I need—"

"It's relevant to me, cocker. Now let's have it or you leave now."

"Sir Stuart Halliman."

Scott sat back as the years rolled away. Sir Stuart Halliman. Fairfax, the code name Scott first knew him by. Jesus Christ, it was like a spirit from the grave, one that brought unpleasant memories. And fear. And anguish. The respect had come much later, but it had never brought with it a sense of trust. After all, Halliman had used him and might have been willing to see him put away for life to save a politician's face. He felt shaken and uneasy and wanted Chesfield out of the office.

"I haven't met him for several years." Scott's voice betrayed his anxiety, and he was disgusted with his own reaction.

"So I understand. But he has never forgotten you. He has the highest regard for you, particularly for your integrity."

"I suppose to a man who has none, even the smallest quantity would be noticeable in someone else." That was better.

"He has it too."

"You could have fooled me. Now we come to the why."

Chesfield puffed slowly at his cigar as he collected his thoughts. He was easier having crossed a bridge relatively unscathed. "I thought you might have guessed. I need your help."

"In what possible way?" Scott was irritated and disturbed.

"To find out who killed my son. And why."

Scott stared across the table and met the mild expression. Chesfield had regained his full composure; he was now negotiating, which was something he fully understood.

"You're off your rocker. I'm a travel agent, not a bloody copper. You go to the police."

"You've had experience with these things. Halliman would not have recommended you otherwise."

"Experience with what? I've never investigated a bloody murder in my life. *Or do you mean I'm familiar with murdering?*"

"No. No. Forgive me. You must know what I mean."

"You mean I'm an old con? A one time recidivist? A creeper? A cat burglar to you. You think that qualifies me to check on your son's death? For God's sake, even if it did, do you realize how long I've been out of touch?"

"I understand that, Mr. Scott. I don't think Sir Stuart had in mind your past profession. I am sure he fully appreciates the time lapse. It is clear that he recognizes qualities in you that you do not, or that you refuse to acknowledge. Only you and he know what has happened in the past between you. It left a deep impression on him."

"It left a deep impression on me, too, mate. Tell him he's lost

24

touch, too." Scott suddenly leaned across the table. "Look, I've not always seen eye to eye with the fuzz. There are some I wouldn't touch with a barge pole. But there are others I've developed a begrudging respect for. Damn it, there's been a Home Office inquiry into your son's death. What more do you want? Are you suggesting there's a cover-up?"

"Not in the inquiry. I think it was open and honest in so far as investigation is concerned. I don't think the truth came out, but I'm not suggesting that it was withheld by members of the inquiry."

"Well then, take your suspicions to the police. They'll deal with it."

Chesfield hesitated. He glanced quickly through the window.

"I already have. My title opened doors to the right man; an assistant commissioner. I was referred back to the findings of the inquiry. And there the matter rests unless I can produce new evidence."

"Which you can't?"

"I've no evidence at all. My son might well have had weaknesses. Cowardice was not one of them. He would have faced up to prison as terribly distasteful, as it must have been for him. He suffered hell there, but he would have stood it."

"A character reference is not evidence. If the police can't find any with their resources, just what do you imagine I can do? I'm sorry. I appreciate your confidence. I can hold my tongue. But there's no way I can help you."

"Sir Stuart described it, I think, as it being impossible for you to rat on anyone. I don't think I would be insulting you at this stage if I mentioned that money is absolutely no object. Write your own check. Secure your future."

Scott smiled resignedly, "That's my trouble. You spotted it. I'd undercost myself."

"Then let me do it for you. In many ways I may be ruthless, I may be mean, but in this I could not possibly be. If you had kidnapped my son, what would I be prepared to pay out in ransom? That's the sort of figure I'd contemplate, Mr. Scott. I want to clear his name on at least one issue."

"I'm not in the ransom business. Anyway, with this recession things are risky. I can't afford to neglect the business."

"I could buy you another one."

Scott sighed wearily. "It doesn't even tempt me. You've got me all wrong. I could fleece you and come up with nothing. But Sir Stuart might also have told you that for an ex-villain I've got my own brand of honesty. It's no use. I wouldn't know where to start."

"You won't sleep on it?"

"There's no need. I know my limitations. I'm getting married soon. I won't let anything get in the way of that. And there's another thing." Scott looked Chesfield directly in the eye. "You frighten me. You haven't once suggested that you want the truth. What you want is proof that your son was murdered. Right or wrong."

Scott had considered it many times; if he had to select one outstanding physical attraction in Maggie Parsons he would choose her eyes. Blue, green, they could change with the light or her mood and could reflect everything about her. And then he would consider her skin, which she had always cared for; it was like touching the softest velvet. If he considered her physical defects he usually came up with her eyebrows; for some odd reason, they virtually did not exist and she had to pencil them in.

Her most irritating foible was her intermittent insistence on covering perfectly natural deep auburn hair with a similarly colored wig. She would usually explain that her hairdresser had cut her hair too short and she preferred it long. He never understood why this was allowed to happen in the first place, but he had learned not to question it. Maggie did her own thing, and he had no complaints. And she had kept her figure.

Maggie Parsons shared the same kind of sensitivity as Willie Scott, and she also shared his sense of humor. But she was strong-willed. Had she not been, their relationship would have broken up years ago. She had endured constant pressure from her middle-class and reasonably wealthy parents to break away from Scott.

Scott himself had supported the parents' view. He understood their feelings and had never wanted to bring Maggie down to what he saw as his level. Which was why he had not married her. Maggie saw it differently. She had learned that she could not change him and now understood that if she did he would not be the man she loved. She wanted Willie Scott just as he was, whatever he did, whatever his past. And it had worked.

It was a few years now since Scott had felt one of those impossibly strong urges to do a job, if only for the challenge. Life could never be dull with him; he would always find outlets for his irrepressible nature, but he now found them within the law. Which was why, after so long, they had decided to get married, if only to keep her parents quiet. More important, Maggie was pregnant.

Maggie had, for the past few years, taken up her old job at the United Nations branch in London. She was an excellent linguist but had enjoyed no luck in passing on her ability to Willie, who had always claimed that he had enough problems with his own language.

Their love for each other ran very deep. Few associations could have endured the earlier crises that had confronted them. At one time Scott had been used ruthlessly for one reason or another. His special talents had been exploited and, but for his own guts and wit, he would now be in prison as an innocent man. In those days his partnership with Maggie had somehow thrived on the dangers flung at them, their bond extraordinarily strong.

It was with these recollections that Scott went home that night after leaving Sir Richard Chesfield. The meeting had put back the clock for him, and he suffered an odd kind of despondency. In truth, he had been partly attracted to the proposition. It was an old, almost forgotten feeling that frightened him, for he had believed it had gone forever. But there was no way he would let Maggie down, not now, not ever, deliberately.

They lived in an apartment in North Kensington. He went up the stairs, thoughtful and saddened by Chesfield's position but fully aware that Chesfield's convictions could simply be wishful thinking. He had met other Chesfields who had climbed down their social ladder to plead with him for some reason or another. They had never worried him. The person who did was Sir Stuart Halliman; his presence, even by proxy, was sufficient to make vibrations of the wrong kind.

Scott let himself in. Maggie called out from the kitchen, and they met halfway across the drawing room and embraced like new lovers.

"You'll squeeze our baby to death." Maggie pulled back her head, eyes mischievous, arms still around his neck.

He placed his hand over her stomach. "He's not even a contour yet. Unless he's a flathead."

"It's a she. Come on, I'm cooking."

He followed her into the large, ultra-modern kitchen. Their finances had improved over the years, and most of their money went to their home and collecting antiques and objets d'art. He poured them a whisky each; lots of ginger ale in hers, water in his. No ice.

"Cheers."

"Cheers. What's on your mind, Willie?" She always knew when he was troubled.

"We always have a Scotch."

"Not this big." She returned to her pots, her back to him.

He told her what had happened and saw her stiffen. Did the incident revive the same sort of memories in her? He did not intend to ask.

They spent a quiet evening together, holding hands on the sofa and watching television. But it was not the silence of contentment; too much was left unsaid between them. Maggie prayed that nothing would upset their plans. They were due to be married in a month's time. It had taken years to reach this point in their relationship; she was now where she wished to be. Willie had said that he had quite forcibly rejected Chesfield's appeal for help, and she believed him. As with Scott, it was Sir Stuart Halliman's oblique involvement that concerned her. God, it had been so long ago. But the time factor did not ease the qualms.

Scott put his arm around her. "Stop worrying."

"I'm not." But because he had voiced the need to stop, she knew that it was on his mind too. So she worried the more. For him.

Three nights later Scott went home to find Sir Stuart Halliman drinking champaigne with Maggie. His first reaction was one of shock; he had not seen the man for so long. The second was surprise that Maggie seemed to be so much at ease with him. She rose now, champagne flute in hand, and crossed the room to give him a warm peck. "Look who's here," she said, as if Scott would somehow miss the visitor. She gave Scott a wink, but he was not sure how he was supposed to interpret it. She slipped an arm through one of his and led him to Halliman, who was rising from an armchair.

"My dear Willie. How nice to see you." The tall, gray-haired soldierly figure came forward to shake Scott warmly by the hand, using both of his. "My God, you haven't changed at all."

"And I'd be a bloody fool to believe that you have either." But Scott could not help grinning. He could see that physically, Fairfax had changed little. He was older, as they all were, with slightly less hair and a lean face, more lined than he recalled. The eyes were still clear and diamond sharp, teeth still his own, and he had not put on weight. His suaveness he would take to his grave; he could not be anything other than eternally polite, and there was still a misleading openness about him that accurately reflected a part of him. Much would always be hidden.

Scott could not help being pleased to see him, even if he had no reason to trust him. It was one of those gut acceptances. In spite of himself, Scott liked the man. But he could not understand why Maggie was so composed. He glanced at the bottle in the ice bucket, at the flutes. They had not drunk so much that she would be influenced.

Halliman reached for the bottle and poured champagne into the third flute. "We should have waited for you." He passed the drink over. "But Maggie was so upset at seeing me that I felt she needed a quick one. Your good health, Spider."

"Cheers. Maggie doesn't like me being called Spider. Reminds her of the bad old days."

"I'm sorry." Halliman turned to Maggie. "You should have told me, my dear."

"I thought you knew," Maggie said sweetly.

They seated themselves and Halliman gazed slowly around the room. "You both always had good taste. You really have some very nice pieces. Those bronze plaques, the porcelain looks early English. And the furnishings . . ." Halliman gazed quizzically at Scott and murmured, "You didn't by any chance . . ."

"No, I didn't. You want to see the receipts?"

"God forbid. I was pulling your leg."

"You've come about Chesfield," Scott said bluntly.

"Just as direct, Willie. I've explained to Maggie. The silly man pushed you too far. He told me what he asked of you. It was ridiculous."

"Yet you recommend him to see me."

"Of course. Not for what he suggested, though."

"Fairfax, you're a crafty bastard. You always were." Scott gave Maggie a quick, warning glance not to intercede.

Halliman sat back unabashed, legs crossed. He smiled reflectively. "You haven't even changed your vocabulary. And Fairfax, I'm afraid, is no longer applicable to me. I retired some five years ago. I have no official status." He raised his flute. "That should put your mind at rest."

"It should. But it doesn't. You've put yourself out to come here. You've got reason."

"Naturally. Dick Chesfield has used my name improperly. It requires explanation. These days I have time on my hands, and I liked the idea of seeing you both again."

It was as though nothing had ever changed. Scott could see that Maggie was fractionally uneasy at his being so coarse to Halliman, but Halliman needed that sort of direct talk, and Scott knew that he could not match Halliman in the diplomatic game. They were opposites and they understood each other.

"The champagne is good," observed Scott. "What else could it be from you? Let's see if your line of bull is up to the same standard. You seem to have conned Maggie."

"Oh, Willie, Willie." Halliman put down his drink. He wanted to smoke a cigar but knew that neither of his hosts smoked, and he could not see an ashtray in sight. "Maggie is relieved because I'm retired. Out of the game. Out of touch. Nobody wants an old boy in my old line of work. Methods change. I'm outdated. She also knows that what Chesfield requested was far beyond my understanding. I merely told him that if he was so convinced his son was murdered, I knew a man who might possibly be able to find out."

"So what's so different? That's what he asked me."

"I understood he asked you to find out who the murderer is. Quite different, surely?"

Scott studied the still handsome face. Nothing was to be learned from it. He turned to Maggie. She seemed to be a little embarrassed. "It *is* different, Willie." From Maggie? What else had Halliman told her? He turned back to his visitor. "I think you're splitting hairs. How am I supposed to do that when a Home Office inquiry failed?"

"Willie, you surprise me. Prisoners close ranks against the police. They might be more honest with you. Enough to give a pointer."

"You mean I go up to Hull and ask around the boys?"

"Not quite so simple. But if there is word around you might well pick it up. Not who, but whether or not it happened. And that would be the end of your involvement."

Scott shook his head in despair. "Fairfax, I told Chesfield. Like you, I'm out of touch. I don't know any of the old crowd any more."

Halliman appeared to give it some thought, but Scott was satisfied that the wily ex-intelligence chief had done all his thinking long before he called.

"I can probably get a list of the present inmates. There must be some still there you used to know better than others. They would not have forgotten you; you underestimate your reputation." He turned to Maggie. "Forgive me for that, but it's true."

"I thought you'd retired. Getting a list like that needs high connections."

"I can still ask a favor." Seeing Scott's suspicion, he added, "I really *have* retired. It was published and it's checkable. This is a favor for a friend. He's probably wrong anyway, but at least he'll know that inquiry has been made through nonofficial channels."

Scott did not reply. He looked to Maggie, who uncomfortably avoided his gaze, which was not at all like her. This was the effect that Halliman always had on them; doubt, suspicion, uncertainty clothed him like an aura, yet his own appearance always belied it.

"Look," Halliman continued. "No pressure." He spread his hands. "What possible pressure could I exert? If I get a list and there is nobody on it who you feel you can approach, then we'll forget it. If you go, just one visit. Then whatever the result, a magnificent wedding present. That's the least Chesfield could do."

So he had even wheedled out of Maggie their wedding plans. Perhaps that was why she appeared so guilty. Scott did not blame her; he knew how adroit Halliman could be.

"Incidentally," Halliman added, "I was more than thrilled to hear that you two are at last getting married. Marvelous. Absolutely marvelous."

You crafty bugger, Scott thought, but for Maggie's sake he did not voice it. "I'm an old con. I have to get Home Office permission to visit. It's doubtful that they'll give it to me."

"That can be arranged."

What have I said, Scott reflected. I almost conceded. He wished he had more active support from Maggie, who would normally have backed his refusal to the hilt. He turned to her. "What has he said to you? Why are you putting up with this?"

Maggie returned his gaze. She was a little drawn and thoughtful.

"I know what you're thinking. But he's not going to leave us alone, is he? Or even if he does, we're going to reproach ourselves for letting him down. If it's as simple as he says, one visit and finished, then you've done what you can. As a favor. We want nothing from it except peace of mind. But only you can judge if it's as simple as he says. And I go along with whatever you decide. What I don't want is it hanging over our heads, some sort of regret." She spoke as if Halliman were not present.

Halliman observed quietly, "Would you rather I left while you discuss it?"

"Would it make a difference? Stay where you are. Let me think."

"I *am* being honest with you," Halliman prompted.

"Part of you is. It's the other part that worries me. If you can get a list of prisoners, I'll look at it. If there is someone on it who I think might help, I'll talk to him if you can fix it. And that's as far as I'll go. Chesfield can stick his money and his wedding present. This is a favor to *you*. That way, what morality you have should come down on my side."

Halliman finished his drink silently. "I'm not offended by what you say. I understand perfectly. I can ask for no more." He turned to Maggie and took one of her hands. "Do you really think I'd do anything to upset you two? After so long, and on the brink of getting married?"

Scott knew that Halliman already had. Even if he himself had refused to help, the upset would still be there.

When Halliman had gone, the remainder of his champagne was there to remind them of him. They clung together as if they were about to part from each other for a long time. It was not simply an old and precious love that united them like that, but a renewed need; they had been here before.

"Why didn't you stop me?" Scott whispered in Maggie's ear.

"Because you want to go. I've suffered it before. And so have you. Get it out of your system, Willie. It can't be as bad as the other times. Your restraint was much better, and you'd have said no had I insisted. That's a big step, isn't it? A big step."

2

SCOTT DROVE UP TO HULL in his ten-year-old 4.2 liter Jaguar. Home Office permission had come through remarkably quickly; Halliman knew how to pull strings. The weather was chilly, but Scott still preferred to have an open window. He left the radio off. Driving to him was a single-minded occupation. During his last stretch in Dartmoor, he had been offered a job as driver for the Reisen mob, to be effective immediately on release. It was a backhanded compliment he did not need, and turning it down had been a tricky business.

Scott had always been a loner. Only once or twice had he used help during his old jobs. Nor did he use fancy or heavy equipment. He had worked on his personal skills. For such a big man he had been amazingly agile and had been able to climb a rain stack at great speed. Nor had alarms worried him, but his approach to them had been simple and basic. Why risk cutting wires when the bloody siren and bell could be choked with foam?

The very act of driving up the road to Hull prison brought back memories of some of the capers he had enjoyed. It also brought back memories of a few of the villains he had known. When studying Halliman's long list, he had been staggered by the number of names he knew. Old mates. Old enemies. He had then made Halliman check on the four names he had selected to discover which block they were in. That was important in a top security prison. He had then selected one name.

Scott glanced at his speedometer. He was doing a ton. Thirty miles an hour over the 70-mile speed limit. He glanced at the mirrors, maintained speed. As a traffic cop had once explained to him, "We don't nick you for speeding. We get you for driving without due care and attention." Which meant that you had been stupid enough not to notice the fuzz noticing you. Slow down, acknowledge you've been seen. It was like doffing your cap to them. They appreciated that.

Old memories. Many of them sweet. Old urges. And it was this that worried him most, and what Maggie had so quickly perceived. True, his very first reaction was to get rid of Chesfield. But the problem had begun to tug at him, and his reason for getting rid of him had changed before he left. At the time it had been difficult to define, but now he could clearly see that he was beginning to be tempted and not because of the money. His concern for Maggie had saved him. Then. He hoped to God that he had more control over himself now. He had shown *some* control. The years had honed him down, but how much? In some respects Halliman knew him only too well. He must prove him wrong, for Maggie's sake.

He made one brief stop en route and had an early light lunch in a roadside cafeteria. Then he continued on. He wanted to get it over with. He smiled to himself as he strapped up again. He wanted to get there. That was different. By the time he crossed the Humber River and drove into the chewed up edges of Hull, his feelings had changed. When he finally pulled up opposite Hull prison, he found that he had to park across the street. To be so close to the prison was having a strange effect on him.

He looked across the street at the huge gates flanked by the squat Victorian towers, and at the adjacent graveyard. To his surprise he found he was sweating a little. Now that he was here he did not want to go in. He knew the security by heart. Twenty-foot walls wired and with arc lamps and television scanners brooding over them. Fifteen feet inside was an equally high wire fence, set with alarms, illuminated, and televised. And inside that were dogs and handlers with two-way radios. The recollection was bitter.

36

Scott locked the car and shakily crossed the wide street. A group of visitors was already waiting in the cold, mostly women to see husbands or sweethearts. They went through the series of safety locks as if they were visiting wild animals in a game park.

The visitors' room was like a cafeteria, tables and chairs quite well separated and a small soft drink bar at one side. Scott selected a table and sat down nervously. He was reliving a life of incarceration. If he needed deterrent, it was here all around him. He fought down the urge to run out; he was a visitor now, the other side of the fence. The realization did not help much. He had been in this room before as a con. And he knew that the prisoners would enter the door facing him at the farther end of the room. Guards were not too evident, just one at each end of the long room. Authority tried to achieve an informal atmosphere.

Tables were filling up, and Scott became nervous that another visitor might be forced to sit next to him. If that happened, it would be impossible to say what he wanted to. And then he rose as he saw Lennie Peel being ushered toward him. He was shocked at the sight of the old forger; the man had aged almost beyond recognition. The short, hunched figure was ashen and appeared to be ill. The only hair he had left hung about his large ears in dirty white tufts.

Yet Lennie recognized Scott at once. A smile broke over the prematurely aged face. He shuffled forward hurriedly as the guard dropped back. "Spider. Me old mate. Where the bloody hell have you been?"

The two men shook hands vigorously. As Peel sat down Scott said with feeling, "Great to see you, Inky. Tea or coffee?" He went to the bar and bought tea and biscuits and put a steaming cup in front of Peel, who placed stiff hands around it for warmth. Scott noticed the stiffness of the swollen fingers.

"Arthritis," Peel explained, noticing Scott's glance. "Murder, in my game. I do get a bit of painting done in here, but it's hard, Spider. Bloody hard."

Peel had been a fine artist until he found easier money in forgery, and he had been an artist at that, too. If he could not use his fingers, there was nothing left for him.

They talked of old times, better days. There was much to laugh about and Scott was glad to see Peel respond so easily. Scott was the first visitor Peel had received in five months, and in his dejection and the effort he made to repress it, Scott saw all too clearly what could have become of himself.

Time was trickling out when Peel asked, as Scott knew that eventually he would, "So why have you really come, Spider, as much as I'm pleased to see you?"

"I had to see you like this so that no eyebrows would be raised. Just an ordinary prison visit." Scott lowered his voice. "What's the inside word on Chesfield?"

"Chesfield?" Peel went blank-faced. "The bloke who topped himself?"

"Did he?"

"Did he what?"

"Inky, it's me, your old mate, Spider, you're talking to."

"For a minute I thought it was the fuzz. What's your game? You crossed over?"

Scott laughed. "You know better. How could I do that?"

Peel gripped his empty cup, his fingers trembling slightly.

"I dunno. You got up to some funny dodges a few years back. A bloody hero, the papers said."

"Come on, that was ages ago, and it was nothing to do with the police. I don't want detail. Just the whisper. As a favor to me. I'm acting for a friend who is definitely not fuzz."

Peel surreptitiously peered around the room. In the far corner a prisoner was fondling a woman quite openly, and the nearby guard was trying not to look, knowing there would be a point at which he would have to intervene. Peel turned back. "You wouldn't believe it's his wife would you? It's time for me to go, old mate."

"There's money in it. In a bank or to relatives. Could be used for little extras in here."

"This isn't like you, Spider."

"I'm not trying to finger anyone."

"Money? How much?"

"I can't give a figure. It's not mine. You can trust me, though. I'll see that you're more than fairly paid."

Peel appeared subdued. He gazed across the table, still gripping the cup. "If you're the old Spider, I know you will." He paused for a long time. Some visitors were already leaving, but Scott remained patient. Peel said, "I'd have to be alive to enjoy it."

38

Scott observed carefully, "We'll be guided by you. We won't make the payments obvious."

Peel was clearly nervous. He thought carefully, weighed up friendship and money. Scott had helped him many times in the past, but honor among thieves was a load of rubbish, with just a few exceptions. He said slowly, "I don't want the same thing happening to me, Spider."

Scott accepted the allegory in the way it was intended. Inky Peel had come as close as he intended. "Why?"

"That's not on the agenda, brother."

"You don't know?"

"I don't want to know. The guy topped himself like they said, OK? You read the papers."

The room was almost empty, the two guards restless. "Sure. I understand." And then, Scott added, "An act of God, then? The outside universe or inside the pearly gates?" The riddle would be understood by Peel, who could honestly say that he had openly betrayed nothing.

Suddenly one of the warders called out to Peel, who rose at once. He smiled wanly. "There's no God in here, mate. Except in the Governor's office. I believe you've got one your side who spreads the word. Nice to see you, Spider. Really nice."

The two men shook hands and Inky Peel shuffled down the aisle to the room beyond for a routine search.

Scott and Halliman sat in a quiet corner of the latter's club. They each had a cognac on the low table in front of them.

"You're reading an awful lot into it," Halliman observed.

"No. There are times when a villain prefers to talk in parables. I've had friends telling me about jobs they have done, but they don't describe the actual job, just something akin to it. So that the confession is not quite there. What did you expect Inky to say? 'I don't want the same thing happening to me.' That means it happened to Chesfield. He was topped, all right."

"And you're saying that the instructions came from outside?" Halliman drew slowly on his cigar.

"That's what Inky implied."

"Can we get more from him?"

"No. I doubt that he knows more. It's a whisper that spreads among the cons. Innuendos. Insight. An understanding."

"But it's not evidence and could be utterly misleading." Halliman frowned, dissatisfied with what Scott had told him.

"Not something like this. There would be foundation. Take it or leave it."

Halliman inclined his head, eyes sharp as he looked at Scott. "Not much to tell Chesfield, is it?"

"He doesn't need convincing. He's already sold on the idea. I'm satisfied that Inky's satisfied that Gordon Chesfield was killed in his cell."

"Which means it was Naylor or Brooks or both."

"That's right. They're not going to confess to it, are they? They need only to keep their nerve and keep quiet."

"And you think someone contacted them from outside?"

"Either that or one of the barons inside was contacted, and he in turn chose his moment. The inducement would have to be substantial. A bent screw might have been contacted."

"Why?" asked Halliman, but he was really asking himself.

"Chesfield must cough up for Inky. I can fix the method. Inky must not appear to be suddenly flush."

"I'll attend to it. If Chesfield is satisfied."

"Not if *he's* satisfied. Because *I'm* satisfied. OK?"

"Touchy, Spider. Not like you."

"It's a point of honor."

"Do you know Naylor or Brooks?"

"No. I could ask around, but it won't help."

"Well, that seems to be that. I'm not entirely satisfied. The whole thing seems ambiguous."

"Let's put it this way," Scott smiled. "You thought enough of me to put me on the job, so you'll have to think as highly of my findings. I haven't even charged for expenses. But if Chesfield welches on Inky, then I'll have to raise the money from press articles."

"That's blackmail."

Scott rose and then drained his goblet. "That's right. You know my motto. Never make a threat unless you mean it. Cheers, Fairfax. I've kept my word, you keep yours."

Scott bawled out, "Maggie. I'm home."

40

She entered the drawing room from the kitchen, her expression guarded.

"We're going out," he said. "I've got rid of Fairfax."

"It's over?"

"It's over."

Maggie twirled, skirt billowing. She spun to face him again. "Willie, I'm *so pleased*. In the old days you'd have found an excuse to go on with it. Thank you, darling."

He caught her hand and pulled her to him.

"The old days have gone, love. I told you."

Sir Richard Chesfield was not alone in thinking that his son had been murdered. Walter Clarke at the Foreign Office also had his suspicions. He shared Sir Richard's belief that Gordon Chesfield was not the type to commit suicide. It was easy to take such a view, but it was firmly founded on his knowledge of the man.

Chesfield had been able to maintain silence in any situation, whatever the pressures, if it concerned someone close to him. He could be utterly relied upon. And he had possessed his own cast-iron brand of justice. He would willingly have served his prison sentence for someone else if his belief in the other were sufficiently strong. He would have endured the downgrading of his own standards and would have accepted public findings regarding his own guilt. Chesfield's weaknesses were abysmal, but he possessed immense and unusual strengths and loyalties. It was not the kind of personal assessment that had any value in law.

Sir Richard Chesfield and Walter Clarke met briefly at the funeral that had been delayed by the inquiry. They did not know each other well and did not discuss their personal beliefs. Even if they had been closer, it was doubtful whether they would have discussed the matter. Their reasons would have been quite different. Both men were strong-willed. Ambition was another common denominator, but Sir Richard's had waned somewhat of late. Age had little to do with it; it was simply that he could see fewer mountains to climb.

Walter Clarke, on the other hand, was at the pioneering stage. One day, not too far distant, he wanted to be Foreign Secretary to Her Majesty's government. At the very least. He was already Foreign Minister. He was young and there were colleagues who objected to his whiz-kid attitude. But notoby, not even his political enemies, could deny his ability. Walter Clarke was brilliant and sufficiently sensible to keep within the bounds of personal integrity. He paid his taxes and had no secret bank accounts in the Channel Islands or elsewhere. He was going places. And few doubted that he would get there.

On that chill autumn morning, as Clarke watched the coffin being lowered into the ground, he could not help reflecting that he was responsible. Not directly, of course. But he had some knowledge of what had led up to it. He felt deep regret as his one-time friend disappeared forever. And he was left feeling worried for himself. Something had gone radically wrong.

There were a good many people at the funeral, including Sir Stuart Halliman, who stood back from the rest to get a better view of everyone. Halliman was aware that there were onlookers some distance away; they could have been passersby attracted to the event and the massed colors of the flowers and wreaths. Behind them he thought he detected Spider Scott.

There was to be no reception afterward. Sir Richard, a widower these past few years, saw nothing in the tragedy to drink about, not even with relatives. When he was driven off toward London in his Silver Cloud Rolls Royce, he was unaware that he was being discreetly followed. Even Halliman did not realize it, with so many cars at the funeral.

Nobody followed Walter Clarke on his way back. Not on this occasion at least. And nobody followed Sir Stuart Halliman, although he had been recognized in certain quarters.

Walter Clarke drove himself in his new Daimler sedan. Above middle height, he had a strong face, keen, searching eyes, and dark, thick hair that he allowed to drop noticeably over one eyebrow, a characteristic the political cartoonists were quick to pick up, as he had intended they should. It was difficult to know that he was worried. His face was grim, but so had been the funeral he had attended. Behind the severe mask, his fertile mind grappled with his problem. He would solve it for sure. He had striven too hard to let anything interfere with his future. Brave, determined thoughts. So what was making him feel so physically sick?

The offices of the First Chief Directorate of the KGB had been moved to the new building off the circumferential highway just outside Moscow in 1972. General Anatoli Rogov had not liked the move from the outset. Even though, during that time, he had improved his rank and status to chief of foreign operations, and his personal office was now sumptuous compared with the previous one, he still preferred the old offices in Dzerzhinsky Square. At least from there he had been able to look through his window, small as it had been at that time, and see something of Moscow life. He loved the city.

Here, where he now sat, there were no such distractions. In spite of its size, fashioned as it was on the lines of the CIA buildings in Virginia, it was for him too clinically isolated. He was unrelentingly surrounded by his own profession, which was fine for work, but not good for the spirit. Distraction could sometimes stimulate the mind and, therefore, work could benefit. His office was an island in the huge network. When he had been a colonel, mixing with colleagues was a daily routine. Now all he got was deference, hypocrisy, and sometimes obsequiousness. He was astute enough to detect these defects, but at times he yearned for a common chat with old friends. He was intolerant of "yes men," which made life difficult for some. His position demanded respect from subordinates, and he could not allow himself to slip.

Rogov was young for his position. At forty-eight he supposed that he might be considered *too* young by some. So he had grown older and more serious too soon. As he studied the report in front of him, he did not miss the fact that his comparative youth, in terms of success, was something he shared with Walter Clarke, M.P., in London. It seemed, too, that Clarke shared his strength and some of his ruthlessness. The similarities provided interesting speculation.

Rogov had already absorbed the Home Office findings on the death of Gordon Chesfield. They were thorough and long-winded, like all official inquiries. He had no comment to make on them. What interested him was Sir Richard Chesfield's reaction to them. Without actually having direct access to Sir Richard's dialogue, the indications were that he was restless about the way his son had died.

The reemergence of Sir Stuart Halliman was also interesting. When Yuri Andropov had been chairman of the KGB, long before his ascension to the ultimate pinnacle of power as Secretary General to the Soviet Union, he had told Rogov many stories concerning Halliman; and he had clearly retained a respect for him. But Halliman had retired, and sound checks confirmed this. There was a four-year gap between Halliman's retirement and Rogov's present appointment just over a year ago. Prior to that, Rogov had mainly been in the field and largely in the United States, so his knowledge of Halliman was mostly secondhand. Reputations had a habit of sticking. Halliman still retained the aura of a legend. A pity he was not Russian.

And now a new personality had entered the ring. Rogov saw many of his forays as being encompassed by ropes; he had at one time been the Red Army middleweight boxing champion. A mister Willie "Spider" Scott. Rogov had been surprised to find that Scott was already in his files. A thief. Apparently one with scruples. An old-fashioned thief then? But still a thief. He read the dossier with interest, wondering how much had been omitted to cover the failings of the "resident" in London of the day, Colonel Kransouski, now a colonel general. Rogov instructed an aide over the intercom to bring the colonel general's file.

When Rogov had the file he studied it closely. He could not be expected to remember all those under him, even the higher ranks. His organization was vast. It seemed that at one time Kransouski was thought of highly. His decline stemmed from his period in London, and it would seem that the common thief Scott was involved in the matter.

The more Rogov studied the files the more he became convinced that Scott had been used, and was therefore disposable by Halliman, and that Kransouski had perhaps been too harshly treated on his return to Moscow. He checked Kransouski's present posting to discover he had only five years left before retirement was due. Kransouski was with the eleventh Department of the First Chief Directorate, and was now in Bucharest keeping a fatherly eye on Rumanian intelligence. Rogov picked up a telephone and ordered Kransouski's return to Moscow. Perhaps the colonel general should be given the chance to go out in a blaze of glory.

3

SCOTT WAS NOT SURE WHY he went to the funeral of Gordon Chesfield. He hated funerals, particularly when they were so far away. He was more sure of why he had hung back from the crowd, and he guessed that Halliman might have seen him. Maggie knew why he went. She understood his impulses better than anyone. Much better than he did himself.

Anyway, he learned nothing by going and saw nobody he knew other than Halliman and the elder Chesfield. So it had been a waste of time.

Chesfield, through Halliman, had accepted Scott's findings, unfounded as they were. An arrangement was made to see that Lenny Peel received some benefit. Now that it was over Scott felt empty of purpose. The business was not doing well in the face of recession. The holiday season was over and business travel was slack. Many of the villains, some extremely wealthy and with large legitimate interests, who had booked through him, had drifted away for one reason or another. The business continued routinely, and they relied too much on Maggie's job at the United Nations. When the baby became imminent, that income would stop.

Scott recognized that he was working up to turning to other

interests. The old urge had been dormant, not dead. He was satisfied only in that he knew that there was no risk of him returning to crime. Maggie would not have to worry about that again. But she would detect his restlessness and that would worry her sick, because she knew where it could lead. With a baby on the way, Scott could not let that happen. It was with considerable effort that he hid his feelings from her.

When Sir Richard Chesfield called two nights later, it was to repeat his original request that Scott find out who murdered his son and why. Scott's reaction to the idea had undergone a definite reappraisal. The days had passed and the urge had slowly built up in spite of all efforts to stem it. Resolve was eroded like the inevitable encroachment of rust on exposed metal. It had taken longer than it used to, and he clung to this. It was improvement. But after so long he now had to face the fact that whatever the time lapse, there would be occasions like this; the tremendous urge that bedeviled him would carry through his life. He wept inside as he realized the effect this would have on Maggie.

To his credit, he fought off the offer, still refused if shakily, and then he seized on one disturbing aspect of what Chesfield was telling him across the desk.

"You say you went to the police again?" Scott asked.

"I told them what you had discovered."

"You brought *me* into it? I've a record."

"It did no harm. I explained the position."

Scott's gut tightened. "You didn't mention Lenny Peel by any chance?"

"Well, I had to give credence to what—"

"You bloody fool. If the police make inquiries at Hull the guards will soon know what it's about. If your son *was* killed, you could have killed Lenny, too. They'll get him if they think he's talked."

"Surely not? He made only innuendos, which you interpreted."

Scott rubbed his face. He felt sick. "I'll have to speak to Sir Stuart. We've got to get Lenny out of there. Poor sod."

Chesfield could not believe it was so bad. Still obsessed with his own problem he asked, "Will you help?"

"Not now, you bastard. I don't trust you." But the shock also brought him back to earth. Even if he wanted to, what could he do? Men like Naylor and Brooks would never talk.

Colonel General Kransouski had the bearing of an aristocrat, which had an anachronistic effect on some of his colleagues who could easily believe he had stepped straight out of the czarist days. He was tall and elegant and moved with a quiet air of purpose. He dressed well and imparted an unconscious aura of propriety. Over the last few years he had grayed considerably, but this merely added dignity. He sometimes carried a cane and swung it as it should be swung. And yet there was nothing of the dandy about him.

Those who really knew him feared him. Those who did not know him so well usually soon learned. It was true that some of his power had ebbed and that in his present post his long experience and ability was largely wasted. This had made him bitter and more dangerous to those who worked for him. The system understood this, for failure could be turned to advantage with the right move. There was no way that Kransouski would tolerate failure from those he controlled.

When he was instructed to return to Moscow, he did so with a degree of indifference. He knew his true value and that everything was under control. He caught the Aeroflot flight to Moscow without misgiving.

General Anatoli Rogov received Kransouski warmly. He knew how to deal with older men, men who might believe they had been passed over, and he could sometimes detect their hidden resentment. Kransouski showed none of this as he shook hands, but Rogov could have sworn there was a speck of disdain in the cold, gray eyes. After the greetings, Rogov asked, "How's Bucharest?"

The green-topped desk was like a small field at the end of which sat Rogov. Kransouski gave Rogov the answer he already knew. "Restless. We will always need to be there." After his own small office in the Soviet Embassy in Bucharest, Kransouski felt he should raise his voice in order to reach Rogov behind the jungle of telephones and intercoms.

"Do you think it's time you had a change?"

Kransouski was wary. "Are you offering one Comrade General?"

Rogov smiled. "Relax. I'm merely sounding you out about a return to London."

"London?" Kransouski stiffened. He had not expected that and there would be a reason, not necessarily to his advantage.

"Does it appeal?"

"London certainly appeals. I speak fluent English, perhaps a little rusty now. I had a good network there, but it broke up. It would depend on what is required. If you are ordering me, then there is nothing more for me to say."

Rogov sat back and eyed Kransouski easily. "No order. I don't like ordering men with your experience. You've been at the game far longer than I, and your record is largely impressive. I've studied your file. It was right to bring you back at the time but not to let you stagnate where you are. You're a field man, not a nursemaid to a dissident satellite."

Kransouski was fully aware that Rogov was in no way involved in his recall from London. "Could I know what you have in mind? I can then give an honest appraisal. I know London better than anywhere."

"I know." Rogov turned a page of the file in front of him. "Does the name Scott mean anything to you?"

"In London? Scott. Willie Scott? The burglar?"

"It's good that you remember him. Tell me more."

Kransouski cupped long-fingered hands. As he gazed over them at Rogov, he was annoyed to see the tremor in his fingers. But he kept his hands there knowing that Rogov would already have seen his reaction. His usually tidy mind was in turmoil. The name Scott was like a trigger word under hypnosis. He took his time.

"He's not a man to forget. He was called Spider because he could climb like one. The first time we met was soon after he had been released from prison. S.I.S. used him to burgle the Chinese legation, and incredibly he managed it. But he had been set up by S.I.S. It was intended that he should return to prison, or better still be killed. What he stole attracted the attention of all the big agencies. He survived them all."

Rogov glanced at the file. "He made rings around everybody?"

Kransouski shook his head slowly. "I doubt that even Scott

would claim that. He was in deep trouble. He wormed his way out. A question of survival. And he had luck. A lot of luck."

Rogov goaded once more, trying to widen the scanty sectors of the original report. "And the rest of you had none?"

Kransouski shrugged, slightly ruffled. "He took us by surprise. He was unorthodox. The Americans would offer the same opinion."

Rogov laughed quietly. "I believe their man finished up in Ecuador." He did not know this, but was giving Kransouski the doubtful comfort of believing that banishment did not only apply to him.

"It could not happen again. Scott, too late, became predictable. Had the matter dragged out a little longer, results would have been quite different."

"I'm glad you said that. You might have another opportunity to get him. Would that appeal to you?"

Kransouski quickly saw that he had trapped himself. It did not matter. He replied truthfully and in a cold, even voice, "Yes, it would. I believe in paying debts."

"Good. It may amount to nothing, and if so I shall have wasted your time. But you will not be returned to Bucharest. I want an eye kept on Scott. Sir Stuart Halliman, who's retired, by the way, has, I believe, seen Scott. I simply want to know what Scott is up to. We can give it a month. If after that time it's obvious that he's leading a normal life, then we'll drop it."

"How do you want me to operate?"

"Obviously, you won't follow him personally. You will become a Polish national and you will arrive in London from Warsaw on a trade mission to link up with a delegation already there. Poland is in such a bad way that almost all their intelligence strength is at present centered on home ground. You will operate through the Polish Embassy in London. Discreetly. I'll arrange for them to have personnel available for you."

Rogov pressed a buzzer and a secretary came in. He raised his brows at Kransouski. "Coffee? We've much to talk about afterward. I want your briefing to be thorough. And you'll be answerable solely to me."

Kransouski held up a hand. "One question, please. Is Scott still with a girl called Margaret Parsons?"

Rogov referred to his files. "There is mention on the original file. The recent notes are understandably scanty as we are not yet sure of Scott's interest. Is she important?"

"Extremely. If they are still together." Kransouski uncrossed his long legs. "Perhaps I'm being carried away. A long time has passed, but it was no casual affair. They had a deep dependence on each other. Opposites, but with a common core."

"They were in love," prompted Rogov with a smile.

"A special kind of love. There were social factors involved. Everyone was trying to tear them apart."

"I can see your interest. You'll know when you get there."

"He refuses to help. I upset him by mentioning that forger chap to the police." Chesfield was petulant, one fat leg pulled over the other.

"I'm not surprised. It was an indelicate thing to do. Scott's had a word with me, and I've already had a word with the Home Secretary. I don't want the police tramping all over Lenny Peel just to show they're willing to help a cause they don't believe in. You have to understand people like Scott. He gave his word."

"Well, I'm damned if I like the way he spoke to me."

Halliman laughed softly. "I've suffered it too. Often." His eyes were reflectively amused. "And I can't think of a single occasion when I hadn't asked for it. Position means nothing to him. You have to earn his respect."

"You suggest he's worth it."

"Oh, he's worth it. I like him. And I trust him. Which is far more than he would say for me."

"You'd still use him, though?"

"I keep telling everybody, I'm retired. But you know, really, he's the sort of person who gets used, sometimes quite unintentionally. He's been through a long, quiet spell. When he stirs things seem to happen to him. Don't push him any more. If he wants to help, he'll surface. He might even do a little on his own account. But I want an understanding from you, Richard, that if anything happens to him arising out of this, you'll damn well see that Maggie Parsons is cared for."

Chesfield lowered his leg with difficulty and sat forward.

"What are you talking about? Why should anything happen to him? Is there something you are not telling me? Is that why you've tried to help me?"

Halliman was watching the smoke spiral of his cigar drift and intermingle with that of his host. "Not at all. But somehow things happen to Scott, usually unpleasant things. And you don't believe there's a simple answer to your son's death any more than I do."

Someone was tailing him. After all this time. Bloody hell. Scott had been followed so many times in the past, and he had become so used to it, that it had never before worried him unduly.

He continued walking toward his offices. By the use of shop windows, parked car mirrors, and reflections on moving buses, he located one man. A short burst of window shopping confirmed his opinion. He located another man across the street, intermittently on view through the traffic gaps. And now he believed he had spotted one ahead of him.

The familiar stirring raised his adrenalin. It could not be coppers, no, not "old bill," he had been clean for too long. Even the half forgotten terms were entering his mind, probably out of date now, but he was thinking like a villain again and this both worried and stimulated him. He entered the already open shop door.

Charlie Hewett, the office manager, threw out an automatic greeting as Scott moved behind the counter where Charlie stood checking the morning's mail and went into his office. As he sat at his desk he could see Charlie's shadow against the translucent glass partition. From the cell next door came the sound of Lulu clacking at her typewriter.

Scott sat quite still. It was a long time since he had thought of Lulu's tiny office as a cell. What was happening to him? He picked up his direct line telephone and dialed the number Halliman had given him. It rang so long that he was in the act of hanging up when he just caught Halliman's answer. He pulled the instrument back to his ear.

"You took your time."

"Good God, Willie, I was in bed."

"*Now* I believe you're retired. There's a team on my tail."

"A team? Professional?"

"They'd think so. I don't think they are police. Thought you might have an idea."

"Nothing to do with me. Anyway, I haven't that kind of pull anymore."

"Balls. But I'll believe they're not yours. So whose?"

"Can you handle it or do you need help?"

"I can handle the tailing, but I don't know how far they've been told to go. Can you raise somebody to see where they drift to when the shifts are changed?"

"I'll ring you back. Oh, and Willie. Don't be overconfident. It's been a very long time." Halliman hesitated before using Scott's own jargon, but by so doing strengthened its impact. "Be lucky."

Scott put down the phone. Halliman hated criminal slang. To use it as he had endorsed the concern behind it.

Walter Clarke idly watched the captions go up on the screen in the visitors' restaurant of the House of Commons. He was entertaining a striking beauty whose posture and clothes sense suggested that she might be a model. Many eyes turned their way; beauty was not all that usual in the restaurant, or elsewhere in the House for that matter, and as Clarke was considered to be one of the most eligible bachelors in London, polite speculation ran high. They made a splendid couple.

Clarke enjoyed the company, and he quietly reveled in the pockets of envy scattered around the room. But all good things must come to an end. He had to be available that afternoon; the opposition had a question on the floor that he must answer in the absence of the Foreign Secretary.

After he had escorted his attractive visitor out, he returned to the lobby, where he bumped into the fair-haired Tony Marchant, an undersecretary in the Home Office. The two men walked down the corridor together.

"You knew Gordon Chesfield, didn't you?" queried Marchant.

"Enough to go to his funeral. We were at Oxford together."

"Strange development. The 'old man' has been asked to transfer one of the prisoners in Hull because of him. Apparently, this old con was visited by another old con in connection with Chesfield."

"That's odd. What's it about?"

"Haven't a clue, though the 'old man' thought sufficiently of it to action the transfer. I believe he was nudged by the Security Service."

"What's his name?"

"Whose?"

"Well, both. I don't suppose it will throw any light, but you never know."

Mildly surprised, Marchant glanced at his colleague. "If you're really interested I'll let you know if you give me an introduction to the dish you had lunch with. She raised a few temperatures, I can tell you. Certainly mine. Anything serious?"

"With Sue? No. Not really. Her personality doesn't live up to her looks. You might be disappointed."

Marchant grinned. "In the long term, perhaps. The short term could be quite interesting, though. Come on, let's go to the office. Confidential, mind. Although I don't think it's meant to be too big a secret."

Scott walked to Charing Cross underground station as he always did. He was now absolutely certain of being followed and did nothing to show that he knew.

When he opened the apartment door to call out to Maggie, who was invariably home first, he felt more relaxed. He could cope. The television was on and he stood watching it for a while. He turned to see Maggie standing in the doorway, a cheerful apron on, and a wooden spoon held high in one hand.

"You going to clobber me with that?" he asked with a smile.

Maggie lowered the spoon. "Are you going to take your coat off?"

They embraced and as they broke away she said, "It's starting again, isn't it?"

He noticed her anxiety, led her to a chair, lowered her into it, and sat opposite, topcoat still on. "Do you think I've forgotten what you put up with? Do you believe I could ever forget your suffering?"

Maggie knew then that she had been right.

"I've no regrets, Willie. But it's different now with a baby on the way. And you can't be as agile as you were. I just don't want it to start again." She sat with the wooden spoon held in both hands between her knees in a kind of innocence that always pulled at Scott.

"I was tempted, Maggie. Not as much as before, but I'd be a liar if I said I wasn't. But I did turn Chesfield's offer down. Twice. So far as that's concerned, it's over."

Maggie waggled the spoon, blue, green eyes on him. "But," she prompted.

"I'm being followed."

"Oh, God." Her knees closed, and the spoon was now gripped tightly between them.

"I've asked Fairfax to look into it for me."

Maggie gazed at him wondering whether she could endure it all again.

"It's not like before," he tried to explain. "This isn't because of something I've taken on. Don't worry, I'll find out."

"*Don't worry.*" Maggie shook her head in despair. "*Don't worry.* Just like that." The spoon dropped to the floor, but she did not notice.

The telephone rang and Scott rose to cross the room. After giving his number, he simply listened, avoiding the temptation to glance at Maggie. He put the instrument down and braced himself. "Fairfax," he said, "just to say he had managed to arrange a check. It's not the police, anyway." He watched Maggie groping for the spoon and lied, "He'll let me know when he knows something definite."

Maggie rose. "I'd better get on with dinner then." She stopped halfway to the door. "Don't try to protect me, Willie. I love you too much. Don't lie to me."

He dropped his gaze. "I'm sorry. One man has been traced back to an apartment used by the Polish Embassy." He held up his hands, palms outward. "For God's sake, don't ask me why because I've no idea."

Maggie's hands crept down to her stomach. She pressed slightly as if to reassure the embryo inside. "But you're going to find out." It was a statement.

"What else can I do?" he pleaded. "I haven't asked for this."

"Well, take your coat off first. Dinner's almost ready."

He did not like her stiffness; Maggie was so essentially warm. Oh Christ. Where had he gone wrong?

"They were cooked in the Marmitout," she explained when they were eating. "The vegetables. No water; their own juice."

"Terrific," he said. But his appetite had gone.

She gazed at him across the table, her lips trembling. How could anyone with his record convey such wide-eyed innocence? At the moment he was like a little boy; it was no act. And she knew how worried he was for her. Being followed did not trouble him; her reaction to it did. "I love you, Willie," she said simply. "Nothing can change that. I shall never fully understand why these things happen, but I'm with you all the way. It's all right. I'm getting over the shock."

It was cold on the flat roof. He had put his topcoat on. He walked across to the parapet and peered down into the street. Car roofs reflected like oil patches. Doorways slunk back in the shadows, but Scott could dissect shadows into various shades. He located movement in one of them. And the interior light of a stationary car came on for a second. It was too cold for lovers. And too public.

The modern block of apartments on whose roof he stood faced older buildings across the street. Small balconies went down the front of the block; there was one attached to their own apartment. He wondered if he could still climb down, balcony to balcony. Would his muscles stand up to it? A cigarette glowed in the car. Bloody amateurs; he felt affronted. For Maggie's sake he decided to leave it for tonight, but if Fairfax did not come up with anything concrete by tomorrow, then he would act himself.

Walter Clarke's apartment was large, expensively furnished, and located in fashionable St. John's Wood. He also owned a small country estate in his Wiltshire constituency. He rose, showered, and shaved, and afterward gazed through the large windows to Regent's Park across the street. Some people were already walking their dogs. It was a sunny, crisp morning, and Clarke had slept well. But for one minor, niggling problem, he felt good.

He went into the hall, said good morning to the ebony blacka- moor who stood perpetually smiling by the door, arms outstretched to hold a silver card tray, and bent down to collect his mail. His official mail went to the House of Commons; this address was not publicized, the telephone number unlisted.

He entered the kitchen, placed his mail on the coffee bar, and switched on the coffee maker. The letter that so dramatically changed his mood and took the blood from his face was the fifth one he opened.

Walter Clarke held on to the bar and retched. The envelope fluttered to the Italian tiled floor in lazy movements, as if to taunt him. After forcing himself to straighten, he gazed again at the contents of the envelope. But he had to lay the paper down flat, his hands too unsteady to hold it. It was a photocopy.

He could not think straight. He had believed it to be over. Finished and dead. But here it was again, threatening his whole future. There were no demands; they would come quite separately; the dreadful thing was that he would not know when. The longer he was kept waiting, the worse it would be.

Clarke groped for a bar stool and eased himself onto it. He poured some coffee. He was forcing himself to do these things. He was still shaken but he had to think, and that meant no panic.

He folded the sheet to envelope size and slipped it in his dressing gown pocket. Even now he could not really grasp that he was the subject of blackmail. He had done nothing morally wrong in his life, not that he would consider to be wrong, anyway. Nothing corrupt. And yet his whole future was threatened unless he could somehow solve the problem.

The main threat came from what was in his pocket. There seemed to be a second threat developing, although it was difficult to take seriously, and he could not really see how it could lead anywhere. He had learned from Tony Marchant that an ex-burglar named Scott had been to see a prisoner in Hull about the way Gordon Chesfield had died. There was nothing directly to threaten him there; he himself was puzzled by the death. Still, the action niggled at him. Someone was stirring, and although he could not see how he could be affected, he would much prefer that the death remain the way the official inquiry found it.

Clarke sipped at his coffee, steadying the cup in both hands. Nobody was going to blackmail him, even if there were justification, which there was not. He needed help, though. And there was no official channel to which he could safely turn, even with his top-level contacts. On the contrary, those kinds of contacts must never know his problem.

4

WILLIE SCOTT, EVEN WITH MAGGIE now reluctantly accepting what he must do, still avoided distressing her as much as he could. He waited until he reached the office before calling Ray Lynch, and when he did he had to endure another frustrating hour before he could reach him.

"A voice from the dead," he announced at last. "Your angels protect you well, oh father."

"Balls. Spider, my God, I thought you were dead."

"Stop talking to yourself, cocker. I need to see you."

"You only ever saw me when you brought trouble with you."

"Since when has good news been of use to a newspaper man? Anyway, you did well out of it."

"Time for me to pay my debts, then?"

"Come off it. When and where?"

"Twelve thirty, my office." Lynch changed his tone. "Nice to know you're still around, boyo. It's been too long."

Ray Lynch was average height and slight of build, with fair hair short on top and tidily long at the back. It was the impression of general neatness that took Scott by surprise. Although he had briefly seen Lynch about two years ago, it was the image before

59

that that always stuck in his mind. Lynch had then been a failure, on the booze and heading quickly for skid row. Now he was almost a picture of health, or as much as any journalist could be.

Lynch, after his unrestrained friendly greeting of Scott, took him to the Cheshire Cheese in Fleet Street. It was obvious from the moment they sat down that Lynch had not given up drink or cigarettes, but it was equally clear that he now controlled his intake.

As the pie arrived Scott said, "I heard you could have been editor of the *Mail?*"

Lynch raised his wine. "I prefer my column in the *Express*. I'm a journalist, boyo. The best since Chapman Pincher. And I like it."

Scott said, "Sally will be pleased?"

"Who?"

"Oh, hell." Scott concentrated on his food.

Lynch smiled. "Don't worry, boyo. I divorced her four years ago. She was sleeping around." He looked up over a forkful of pie. "Made a play for you once, didn't she?"

"If she did, she didn't get anywhere."

"Same old Spider. Straight down the line. So how can I help? If you're on the run, forget it."

"What do you know about Gordon Chesfield, the bloke who topped himself?"

Lynch was surprised. "Not much. Not newsworthy until he committed murder. Know more about his old man; rich, ruthless bastard."

"Can you look through your files? Give me what you've got?"

"No need." Lynch waved a fork. "Don't want the pie to get cold. Wait till coffee."

They had the cubicle to themselves. Scott ate slowly. He gazed around. Dickens had eaten here. And Boswell. Perhaps it was part of the reason it drew journalists. He was glad that Lynch had pulled himself from the rut; sometimes it was difficult to equate the man eating steadily opposite him with the one who had helped him before under a shroud of alcohol.

When the coffee was in front of them, Lynch gazed at the ceiling reflectively. "Gordon Chesfield. Poor bugger." His gaze switched to Scott. "You going to tell me why you want to know, boyo?"

"Usual terms. You'll be the first if there's anything to it."

"An enigma. Some thought he was gay, but there was never any direct evidence. Seemed to be under the strong arm of his father, who's into tax avoidance up to his hairline, if he has one. Quiet, retiring bloke, self-effacing, good at finance. Few friends, so far as is known, but strongly loyal to those he had. Mixed with, but had no reputation for, women. Could have been that he had tendencies he managed to subjugate."

Lynch pulled out a pack of cigarettes, lit one, knowing better than to offer the pack to Scott. "His short life might well be described as a continuing innuendo. But nobody really cared, he was too back seat to rouse journalistic passion."

"Until he sanctioned murder."

"Is this what you're after? Why he did it?" Lynch eyed Scott thoughtfully. "If it is, there's a lot more to it than it would seem." He called for two cognacs. "Don't worry, I know you too well to try to trap you. The truth is, boyo, nobody has a clue why he did it. And once he'd made up his mind to keep quiet, there was no way to find out."

Lynch pushed his empty cup away. "How do you intimidate someone who puts up no defense? Makes no denial? Offers no protest on getting life? Okay, he might have been out in ten years, less even, but with his lifestyle that would have been sheer purgatory. I can understand why he . . ." Lynch trailed off as an idea struck him and asked, "You think he didn't . . . ?"

Scott did not answer.

"Maybe that's answer enough, boyo. Jesus. In prison?"

"*I* came to ask the questions. I didn't follow the trial because I wasn't interested at the time."

"Well," said Lynch, cupping his brandy balloon, "it seems that he wanted this character knocked off. Knowing that he was incapable of managing it himself, he hired someone who could. He was right out of his depth. As clever as he tried to be, he left a trail that no experienced copper could miss. He finally hired a guy who did the job, crudely, six shots all over the body. The victim died more from multiple wounds than from any particular shot. In fact, he was still alive when they found him, but too far gone to speak. D.O.A. at Charing Cross Hospital.

"The hired killer was a ham, a braggart, probably his first job.

Chesfield had paid him so well that he couldn't keep the money in his pocket, nor the liquor from his guts. He hadn't even fixed an alibi. The trail really led from him back to Chesfield. Anyway, he's in Parkhurst doing life."

"So if Chesfield had been more careful in his selection of hit man, he might have got away with it?"

Lynch threw up his hands. "Willie, the whole thing was a complete cock-up. Unbelievable. The blind leading the blind."

"But the job was done just the same."

"Chesfield would have done better firing the bloody gun himself. Motive was never established and never will be now. The killer—Bert Smith, really, I ask you—killed for money. That, and the fact that the other guy was dead were the only established facts. Boyo, I'm telling you that it was the most unprofessional killing of all time. The only thing that kept it going was Chesfield's part in it, rich upper class, and the mystery of why. The only thing that can be said for it is that because it was so cut and dried, the trial was brief and therefore saved the taxpayers money."

"Who was the character who was killed?"

"Nobody of note. Duncan Seddon. Had a small pad in Kilburn. Shady but no record. Unemployed. The best part about him was his name. It was a nothing crime committed by nothing men on a nothing victim. There was no motive at all that came to light."

"Blackmail? You suggested that Chesfield might have been gay."

"That was fully gone into. At one time it seemed the only hope of getting anywhere. But it was completely dead end. Seddon was straight, in fact his only claim to local fame was his interest in women. He had no money. That theme was pursued so much that Chesfield came out of it quite well, whatever his inclinations might have been. Funny business altogether."

"You say Smith's in Parkhurst?"

"You'll get nothing from him. You could read a transcript of the trial, but I don't think you'll get any more than I've told you. You sure you're not in trouble, boyo? You sound like a bloody dick instead of an old con."

Scott laughed. "I'm clean. Have been for years, Ray."

Lynch called for the bill. "You're up to something. Make it a good one for me."

Scott did not tell his old friend that he had been followed here, nor that he would be followed back.

Scott left the Cheshire Cheese and walked slowly down toward the Strand and Trafalgar Square. It was a reasonable route to take to return to his office but a fair walking distance with cabs and buses available. He did not hurry. When he reached the Civil Service Stores in the Strand, he pulled out his wallet, checked the number of notes in it, then took out a slip of paper and read down it as if it were a shopping list. He entered the store unhurriedly, holding one of the doors open for a couple who were leaving.

Once inside he moved at rapid speed through the departments, left by the side door in Agar Street, and headed the short distance north. He was already out of sight by the time his tail had entered the store. He knew that someone would wait at the entrance and that there was probably a standby car, but unless they were familiar with the store, it would take them time to discover where he had gone.

He moved very quickly now, using the back streets to Shaftesbury Avenue before cutting up to Dean Street into strip club land. Soho had always been cosmopolitan, but it had changed for the worse. Some of the character remained, its restaurants and coffee houses were institutions, but hard porn was openly gnawing at its core.

He turned off Dean Street. The once-faded sign had been considerably improved; the whole facade recently painted. The upper windows, though, were still opaque. Gainboy Studios. Well, well. Some things do not change, but this studio was one that should have a long time ago. Scott rang the bell. There was an entry phone now and it crackled. "Who is it?"

Scott smiled to himself. That plaintive whine could be from only one person. "Bluie. It's Spider. Open up."

"Spider? *Spider?* My dear boy, what a time to call. I'm in session."

"I can wait, but let me in."

"Are you alone?"

"Aren't I always? Come on, Bluie, open up. The fuzz are beginning to eye me."

There was a buzz and the door clicked. Scott pushed it open and went up the expensively carpeted stairs. The address was the same, but Bluie's fortunes had definitely changed for the better, mused Scott. He could smell perfume in the air and the quality of that seemed to have improved since the last time he had called here.

At the top of the stairs was a door marked studio and a notice that said, "Please Ring." Scott rang.

The door opened and at first Scott did not recognize his old acquaintance. Bluie Palmer had lost all his hair, but he did not look his age, his face virtually unwrinkled, even without makeup. Bluie beamed at Scott, who could see a girl dressing over the shorter man's shoulder. For a moment Scott believed he was about to be embraced, but Bluie remembered in time and settled for preening himself. "It's so lovely to see you, Willie. Really, after so long. You look just as gorgeous as ever." He wore tight jeans and a loose jacket with a turtleneck shirt beneath.

Scott was used to this from Bluie, so nicknamed because of his pornographic film making. As Scott followed Bluie in, the girl was slipping into a bra. A well proportioned blonde, she knew she had nothing to fear from Bluie, but when she saw Scott, her expression of indifference faded quickly and she dived behind a screen.

The studio was larger than Scott recalled, and he guessed that another room had been opened up. As he stepped over cables and props, he noticed the quality of the equipment; arc lamps, cameras, backcloths, an open wardrobe of deviationist apparatus, and the inevitable bed. The sad thing to Scott was that Bluie was a brilliant photographer by any standards and could have been successful by being straight. Scott had never understood why Bluie had gone the way he had, but he had a few things going for him, and, like the dead Chesfield, loyalty was among his pluses.

They crossed the wide, littered floor and as they passed the screen Bluie called out, "See you next week, ducky." The girl did not reply or respond to Scott's wicked grin above the screen.

The living room was fussy with flowers and tassels and a color scheme of mixed pastels. Bluie poured two large whiskies and passed one to Scott.

Bluie sat on the arm of a massive settee. "Well, darling, I don't suppose you've come to see me for my own sake. Cheers, just the same."

"Cheers. You remember this bloke Chesfield who was up for murder and slit his wrists inside?"

"Ghastly business." Bluie shivered and half finished his drink. "Was he gay?"

"How should I know, lovey? There are a lot of us. There are gay clubs all around the country."

"That's just it. He was a Londoner. West End. Okay, your lives were quite different, but wouldn't monied men be attracted to monied clubs? I mean, is there a social status among you? Would you and he frequent the same sort of club?"

"I've never thought about it."

"Think about it now. Where would a man like Chesfield go?"

Bluie gave it some thought. "I think you're up the wrong tree, ducky. It's true that some of us would avoid certain clubs. Not all gays go to clubs. I haven't heard of him as being gay. If he was, he was getting us all a bad name."

"So you don't know whether he was or not?"

"No."

"You all have an affinity. There's a natural magnetism among you. You're not holding out, Bluie?"

Bluie could be serious when he wanted to be. He dropped the pose that everyone expected of him, and even his voice lowered a tone. He displayed a toughness he was usually careful to hide. "I wouldn't handle you this way, Spider. You and I were good pals a long time ago. I know you don't care for the way I make a living. But it's easy, and I'm very lazy."

Scott gazed around him at the obvious affluence.

"I don't know how you've got away with it for so long without finishing in stir. Look, can you make a few inquiries for me? It's something I want to clear up. It could be important."

"Sure. I'll pass the word around. It won't guarantee a correct answer."

"If he was gay it will come out one way or the other. Oh, and it's not information I intend to publicize. I think he suffered enough."

"Then I will try. That's it I suppose? After so long?"

Scott rose. "No. Have you got a small cardboard box and some paper I can wrap the box up in?"

Back at the office Scott placed the wrapped box Bluie had supplied at the back of the desk. He rang Halliman's club. "Can you produce that prison list again?"

"Possibly. Why?"

"Are there any strong Commies on it? I mean, if I have a red tail, there must be a reason."

"I already made notes on that. I have one or two names."

"Dammit, you didn't tell me."

"It was sheer routine."

"Anyone significant?"

"Willie, you should know better than anyone the types that go to prison. There's almost bound to be some political bods. Terrorists, I.R.A. The extreme left and right. It was not the obvious ones I was looking for. Not the paid up members or the bombers. I found two who were known to be active sympathizers without carrying a card. I won't give you names now; I'll drop them in this evening."

"I reckon you topped him," Brooks accused Naylor.

Naylor, sitting on the opposite bunk, plate in one hand, fork in the other, looked across the steaming stew. "What you on about, sunshine?"

"Chesfield. I reckon you topped him in the night."

Naylor's vicious eyes became stone hard. "With you in here? You've lost your marbles." And because he believed he should have said more, added, "What made you say a crazy thing like that?"

The cell door was open. All cells remained open from the time of slopping out to nine in the evening, when the inmates were locked in again. During the day prisoners could come and go as they pleased, mix in the cells, or go to the workrooms or television rooms. The top security was outside and the comparative inside freedom of dangerous and long-term prisoners helped to stave off gate fever and ease the burden of overcrowded cells.

Naylor and Brooks had only just got their cell back. Police forensic had been crawling all over it; then it had been sealed off for a few days.

"Why did they move Lenny Peel? In a hell of a hurry. Nobody knows where he's gone."

Naylor had recovered from the first shock. "What's he got to do with it? Up and about in the middle of the night looking through closed grilles was he? What's got into you?"

Brooks would not be put off. "The whisper is that Lennie had a visitor who wanted to know what inside opinion was."

"There's only you and me for Christ's sake. How could anyone know anything apart from us? Chesfield topped himself. Now shut up, you're spoiling my grub."

"The whisper now is that there was a third person. Someone you know."

"In here?" Naylor waved his fork angrily, his plate tilting. "You're a nutter. *I'll* close your mouth if you go on with this crap."

Brooks produced his ace. "You could, too. I'm no match for you. But you can't get away with it twice, and you wouldn't be so bloody stupid to try. You know I'm a heavy sleeper. When I hit the deck I've gone."

"So while you were asleep I hacked his wrists and he let me? Be your age."

"You gagged him, maybe with your own pillow, and then you held him. He'd have struggled, but you're plenty strong enough. And the struggling would soon have eased."

"Okay, sunshine. Have it your way. I slashed his wrists. How did I avoid the blood? It spurted all over the place."

"I thought about that. Not easy. You might have half suffocated him first. You might have thumped him one. And you'd have worked from behind his head. One wrist at a time. You probably stripped off afterwards. When the screws came I fetched up in the bowl. There was a trace of blood on the rim. Not much but enough. The blood I took over with me was on my feet. My hands were clean. I reckon you dipped your fingertips in the water jug and stirred them around. I used some of the water anyway, and the mess I left would have confused anyone."

Naylor carefully put his plate down on the bed and balanced the fork across it. He eyed Brooks thoughtfully, his expression chilling. "Will you be sleeping heavily *tonight*, sunshine? Can you chance it?"

Brooks tried to keep his nerve. He had built up a case, more than half believing it but never quite sure. Naylor was tough and extremely cunning. Chesfield would have been no problem to him. Now Brooks was almost a hundred percent sure, and the man opposite frightened him considerably. He was sorry that he had started it. "Like I said," he managed nervously. "They'll never swallow it twice."

"You've spoiled my bloody dinner, Brooksie. I'll get you for that alone. Anyway, you're talking through the back of your head. Going to tell the Governor are you? Implicate yourself? Nobody will believe you were asleep if you spread that kind of bullshit."

"I don't intend to tell anyone."

"You've told me. And I'm the last person you should tell. Dear, oh, dear. Poor Brooksie. Tell me though, why did I do it?"

"Money. Someone here put you up to it. And they'd have paid you well. Very well considering the risks."

"And you want your share?"

"Not of yours. You've earned it. But whoever's footing the bill can pass some my way. You're out in nine months. There's no way you'd have done it for peanuts."

Naylor picked up his plate again, forked some food into his mouth, then threw the plate down angrily. "It's gone cold. Sod you, Brooksie. But if you pass any of this on I'll get you. And I'll know before they come for me. I know you inside out. You won't be able to hide it. If they get me for one, it might as well be for two."

"I'm not screwing you, for chrissake. Just pass the word. I don't expect what you got. They should have brought me into it in the first place."

Naylor nodded slowly in agreement. He sighed, hands clasped between the legs that overhung the bunk. "You're right, Brooksie. They should have. I'll see what I can do."

Brooks did not like the way it was said. Naylor was even trying to smile at him, but his eyes stayed the same, matching the cold cell walls.

Mervin Soames saw Naylor at the nonfiction section and sensed trouble. Although they had first met in the prison library, Naylor was rarely seen there. He was standing in front of the biographical shelves. That Naylor would be interested in anyone else's life was in itself a giveaway. Soames edged himself nearer to Naylor. His prison clothes hung like a sack on him. Bony and lanky, he had an awkward frame mounted by a hungry, thin face with bright brown eyes that seemed always to appear feverish. He ate like a horse but never put on weight, and in spite of his sickly appearance, he rarely reported sick. His wispy hair was combed forward to suggest that there might be some degree of vanity in him. That small giveaway was the tip of the iceberg. Soames was immensely vain and described himself unflinchingly as an intellectual. He was in prison because society was not yet ready for him. More realistically, he was found guilty of repeated fraud.

"Try Frank Costello," he suggested as he sidled up to Naylor. "It's up your alley." He was not even sure that Naylor could read; certainly the book Naylor had pulled out was being held upside down.

"There's trouble with Brooksie," Naylor said. "He wants a cut."

"There was always that risk. Perhaps we should have included him at the beginning."

"That's what he said. But he'd have chickened out. You'll have to see that he gets something."

"That's no problem. But he'll have to be patient. I've got to wait for a visit. And then it will have to be sanctioned."

"It didn't take you long with me, Soamesy."

"That was an emergency."

"So is this. If he opens his mouth, so do I."

They moved down the row of shelves, occasionally eyed by a guard, but they were well practiced. They conversed like two aspiring ventriloquists, lips barely moving, voices pitched just sufficiently for each other to hear.

Soames smiled nastily. "You can open yours as wide as you like. You'd never prove a thing. But don't worry, I'll take care of it. Keep him happy meanwhile."

"How much shall I say?"

"A couple of hundred?"

"You're kidding. We're talking about a topping."

"Tell him four figures then, but no specific amount. But

remember this; the longer he keeps quiet, the more difficult it will be for him not to."

The two men shook hands without warmth. The third secretary of the Soviet Embassy in London was called Nicolai Gorkin; he was the KGB "resident" in the United Kingdom. Of peasant stock, he was of medium height and muscular, as if he had literally fought his way up the tree, which was not too far wrong. In his fifties, he had occupied his position for only the last four months, since his predecessor had been declared *persona non grata* by Her Majesty's government.

This fact tied his hands and made it necessary for him to keep a low profile. Technically, as "resident," he was Kransouski's superior officer, though of lower rank. Yet it was not that that caused ill-concealed friction between them. Kransouski was on a special mission under the direction of General Rogov. Gorkin, therefore, would be wise not to interfere. And yet they would get nowhere without cooperation. Even this delicate balance was not the cause of their immediate distrust of each other.

They were opposites, their backgrounds quite different. Men like Gorkin would always suspect men like Kransouski, who sometimes flaunted their aristocratic bearing and higher academic education. It might have been easier for Gorkin had his wellborn compatriot been a theorist or even a planner behind a desk, but Kransouski had long since proven his value as a field man, with all the ruthless toughness that implied. He had held Gorkin's present position when he was still much younger than Gorkin was now.

They were, of course, polite to each other. They were in Gorkin's office at the Embassy, and now sat amid the utilitarian surroundings of office equipment. It did not prevent them from drinking together, and they each nursed a generous vodka.

Before leaving Warsaw it had been suggested that Kransouski change his appearance by using hair dye and cheek pads and strips behind the ears to push them out. Spectacles could also make a difference to appearance. As it had been some years since he had operated in London, and because he had returned to Moscow under something of a cloud, it was decided that disguise was not really necessary. He had aged anyway, though his bearing was the same, and it was acknowledged that even KGB men sometimes moved to other work, the supreme example being Andropov. Also, his mission was limited and largely exploratory; no state secrets were involved.

To Gorkin's annoyance, Kransouski sat cross-legged with the quiet air of a man who owned the place. There was no deliberate arrogance, it was simply something about him, a self-assurance Gorkin knew he could not emulate.

It was Gorkin who was uncomfortable in his own office. By comparison with Kransouski he was a bulldozer, though a highly discriminating one. He pushed things through. After the too polite generalities, punctured too often by short, awkward silences, he stated what was on his mind.

"We could do the job. What is there to it? I don't understand why you should be sent over here. With all due respect."

"It's simply that I knew the man. Quite intimately at one time." Kransouski smiled an actor's smile. "He's a slippery customer. Perhaps the good General Rogov understands my value."

Gorkin moved awkwardly in his chair and was reminded of his colleague's apparent comfort. "Even so, so trivial a matter."

"I agree," Kransouski said. He had made Gorkin uncomfortable; it was time for work. "Look at yesterday," he continued. "Scott is lost in a London store. Panic. He is next seen much later, heading toward his office from the direction he had been originally traveling, with his purchase under his arm, apparently unaware of the commotion he had caused."

Gorkin picked up the innuendo of criticism. "Are you trying to say something?"

"I'm saying that I've been handed a bunch of amateurs. Scott knew what he was doing. But where did he go that he found it necessary to shake off my men? The newspaperman I knew about. It's the one I don't know that concerns me."

"Couldn't the men simply have slipped up? It's difficult in a foreign country to get the right help."

"That's what I mean about knowing Scott. He's probably been aware of being watched since the beginning. He decided that this time he did not want to be seen."

"And the shopping?"

Kransouski laughed. "Typical Scott. He has some nice touches. That's what I mean about knowing him."

"But you saw through him. Apparently."

Kransouski ignored the innuendo. "He doesn't know I'm here. Colonel Gorkin, I'm now satisfied that Scott has something to hide from us. And that's what I was sent to find out. If he knows he's being followed, then he'll know by whom. For the moment he'll believe the Poles are behind it, but that won't last for long. I want two things from you. First some decent men. There used to be a first-class detective agency that could handle this sort of thing. Expensive but good. I shall drop my present crew and use the agency. Secondly, I need advice from you on what exactly this is in aid of."

"Your instructions were to watch this man Scott."

"It's moved on a stage. I can't run blind."

"Then you must refer back to General Rogov. I have no authority to inform you." At last Gorkin was enjoying himself; he was cracking the whip.

Kransouski finished his drink slowly, allowing the silence to build up around the small action. He eyed Gorkin passively before putting down his glass on the desk. "So you won't help me?"

"I can't help you. Not without Moscow clearance."

Kransouski nodded slowly. "I'm beginning to wonder if you know any more than I." He rose, bowed politely. "Then I'll do it my way, Colonel. I'll log this conversation."

Gorkin rose too. "By all means. But you can always have a copy of my own tape."

5

"FULLER, CLITHEROE, SOAMES, MCWATT," Halliman read out. "McWatt you can pretty well rule out." They sat around the kitchen table, each with paper and pen, and the coffee maker was within Maggie's reach.

"He was suspected of letter bombs but nothing was proved. He's capable of setting something up, but his aims are so obscure that ultimately he would be a risk."

"Clitheroe?" Scott asked. "I vaguely knew him once."

Halliman arched a critical brow. "I had a friend look into the dossiers of these four before calling here. They're all political and all extreme left. I've excluded the extreme right because of the Poles. I don't think Clitheroe has the stomach for it. He'll organize muscle at pickets, and he's a great stirrer, but I can't see him having the nerve for organized murder. Our best bet is Soames or Fuller. Both nasty pieces of work. Hate each other's guts, incidentally." Halliman looked up from his list.

"How can we put a watch on Soames and Fuller's visitors?"

"I'll have to seek more favors, Willie." Halliman leaned back and the kitchen chair creaked.

"Wouldn't Special Branch throw a helping hand?"

Halliman inclined his head. "I've considered various options. In the end it comes down to judgment. I have a feeling that the fewer people who know about this the better. It's by no means easy to hide a murder inside a prison. There must be a lot of money involved, but to take the risk in the first place suggests a very serious issue."

"Perhaps the Poles are involved in the murder," Maggie said.

Halliman rubbed his temples. "If they are, then it's something really big for them to stick their necks out like that. And in that case I very much doubt that it's the Poles themselves."

Maggie's hand crept into Scott's. "Can't you give Willie some protection? They'll know you've been here."

While Halliman searched for a reply, Maggie added. "What's wrong with you two? All this is supposed to be to help Sir Richard Chesfield discover whether his son was murdered or not. So let him foot the bill. We need help." The two men did not argue.

Claude Denise switched off the television and went to gaze out of the big Victorian windows of his Baywater apartment. It was evening and motorists were jockeying for parking spots.

In his early forties, the Frenchman was slimly built and wore a loose turtleneck pullover that betrayed no bulges. His lantern features carried deep lines to the jawbone, giving him a half-starved look; his dark brown eyes had a bright feverishness about them. He wore old jeans, and, generally, he gave the impression of being slightly down at the heel.

When he pulled his sleeve back to observe the time, a question mark immediately hung over him. The watch was eighteen-carat gold, but more important, so was the heavy strap. He was wearing over a thousand pounds worth of chronometer on his sinewy wrist. And below the near shabby jeans were handmade turtleskin shoes.

These points raised the question of why he was currently living in a low-class apartment rather than a good hotel. Money was not his problem, and the quiet confidence of the man supported this.

He was restless at the window, and a powerful nervous energy began to show. Yet he could control it, or find harmless outlets for it. He had entertained many women in the apartment and had always been attractive to women from his early teens. It was not something he boasted about, he simply accepted his luck without humility, a word he did not really understand. When it came to the important issues, he could pace himself, whatever his urge. Nervous energy would never pester him to deviate from the course he had carefully reasoned out.

Above all things, Claude Denise liked money and possessed a good deal of it. But there could never be enough, and he used its power with expertise and a sadistic delight when he could wield it to make other rich men squirm. He accepted that there was power without money, but he knew that with money it was yet more formidable. He was a loner, not a company or committee man, qualities he shared with Willie Scott, a man he had not heard of.

He returned to the divan and pulled a flat document case from under the mattress. It was no hiding place against professionals, but he would not expect professionals to find sufficient pickings in a place like this. He laid the contents out on the coverlet. The originals were in a safe deposit box, and he had created a death trail before and after obtaining the documents now before him. Killing did not worry him.

He had two main ambitions: to be master of his own destiny and to work from his system a hatred that governed most of his actions. Claude Denise, when in his early twenties, had been interned in a criminal asylum in France after killing his half sister. It was during the years of his imprisonment that he had learned to control his reactions. He had never gone back after doctors had proclaimed him cured. And he never would again.

He gazed down at the items on the bed and thought about Walter Clarke, Her Britannic Majesty's Foreign Minister. Clarke had surprised him considerably. He now knew what he was up against; Walter Clarke would go all the way to protect his own position. It was worth knowing, for Clarke was the only person who could produce deep loathing in him. When he thought of Clarke, he could control his feelings only with enormous effort, and he would need calm and wit to destroy the man.

Denise cared nothing about the death of Duncan Seddon. Nor for that matter about the sad fate of Gordon Chesfield. But he was worried about the *way* Chesfield had died. And he guessed that Walter Clarke might be too. For once in his life Denise had qualms as he realized the magnitude of the power he was up against. The Soviets were formidable, and cunning like himself. But qualms did not induce fear; they merely increased the flow of adrenalin. When all was said and done, he had forced the issue, forced everyone concerned to show his hand. *But they had no idea who he was.*

At moments like these, his feeling of total power exhilarated him. He was not the worried party. Not being worried was not the same as not being concerned. He knew what he was up against. He must be careful. But there was no way he could lose. Precautions had been laid a long time ago. Let Clarke sweat. And let the Russians too.

"You give him complete control of the funds. Open an account he can draw on."

"Stuart, you can't possibly be serious. A burglar?" Chesfield was appalled at the idea.

"An ex-burglar," pointed out Halliman. "Your money will be a damned sight safer with him than with some of your investment companies. He cannot possibly do it alone."

"How much have you in mind?" Chesfield's flabby features expressed truculence.

"A few thousand."

"*What?*"

Halliman's good-mannered poise faltered. "You'd better make up your mind whether you want anything done or not. If you do, fund Scott."

"But you already know who's the murderer."

"We think we do. That's as far as it goes. We have no idea what's behind it. With your help we might find out." Halliman waved a warning finger. "And if we do, you might not like what we find. It will be then up to you whether we sit on it or pass it over to officialdom. It could be a big advantage to you."

"Will he spend this money on detective agencies or something? Dammit, I can do that myself."

"Not without showing your hand. It might be unwise to do that. Richard," Halliman implored, "I'm no longer part of the service. There's a limit to the help I can raise. Trust Scott, you'll find no one better." And thus Halliman avoided answering the direct question about using a detective agency. He dare not tell Chesfield how he thought Scott might spend the money.

"Will you underwrite me, then?"

Halliman laughed quietly. "Sometimes I think you really don't deserve help. Rich and mean. Surely you'd prefer a better epitaph? Make it about three thousand to begin with. That's petty cash to you." And then, pointedly, "Expenses, not fees. Those will come later, if Scott succeeds. If it goes bad for him, then I'll remind you about looking after Maggie Parsons. You have my own services free of charge. Think what you're saving on that."

Chesfield nodded slowly. "All right. I don't begrudge fees. I've already told him that. It's free rein on my money for expenses that frightens me. You'll keep me in touch?"

"Of course. But this is not like instant coffee. We'll have to stir a lot more before we recognize the brew. And that could turn out to be cyanide."

When Sir Stuart Halliman requested the favor from old friends that he be supplied with a list of future visitors to Hull prison, he was surprised at being refused. He could understand the reticence toward invasion of the privacy of the visitors, but his reasons for wanting the list were anything but flippant. When he pushed a little harder, he was able to discover that the blockage was directly with the Home Office, and he wondered why.

Willie Scott knew there was a difference the moment he left the apartment complex. Until then he had been quick to detect his immediate tail and had not worried too much. Now he was not sure. Either he was no longer under surveillance, or a new and better team had been put on. If that were the case, then they had known he was aware of them. He walked to the subway station as usual, but it was not until he was striding up St. Martin's Lane from Charing Cross that he was really sure he had company.

This lot are good, he thought. He did not accept that he was rusty. Over the last few days, all the old instincts had returned. He had not forgotten anything. After entering the agency, he greeted

Charlie Hewitt and Lulu and nodded to a youngster Charlie had taken on. He sat at his desk listening to Lulu clacking next door while she gossiped to a temp.

He had to have freedom of movement without arousing suspicion. It was far from easy, if possible at all. He rang Bluie Palmer and cut the protest short. "I'm not chasing you about Chesfield. Listen. I want some mug shots of the visitors up at Hull. Name your price."

"Ducky, I'm too busy. Besides I hate prisons, even the outsides."

"Give me a figure, Bluie. If you can't do it, I want someone who can. Someone who doesn't speak in his sleep."

Bluie thought for a moment. "How long for?"

"Every day for a week. Everyone who goes in. If they're missed entering, I want them coming out."

"It can't be a stand up job. People would hide their faces. We'll need a van."

"Just give me a figure and ring me back when you've fixed it. Today, Bluie."

"There's a woman. Did a turn in Holloway, but *very* good with a camera."

Scott had no time to express surprise. "I want the pictures sent to me daily. First class."

"She can develop in the van."

As an afterthought, Scott said suspiciously, "On her own, Bluie. I don't want anything else developing in the van."

Scott then rang Rex Reisen. Reisen was the active side of a two-brother crime syndicate. The ferret-eyed Reisen had recently left jail after a five-year stretch, less parole. Five years was nominal for a man with his crime record, but like so many gang leaders, he was difficult to pin down on actual charges. Normally Scott would never have contacted a man like Reisen, whose turn of mind could be deadly; he was too finely balanced. A pat on the back could be a death sentence.

As he announced himself and waited for Reisen to come on the line, Scott knew that this was one contact he dare not tell Maggie about. He would have had greater qualms himself but for one thing. Reisen was a strange phenomenon; a highly placed criminal who was also a staunch patriot. He was the only villain Scott knew who had a Union Jack on a chrome stand, rumored to have been

78

changed to solid silver, permanently on his desk. Scott had once convinced Reisen, at considerable risk, that a job he was asking of him was for the government. Intelligence. It was the only way through to him. But it was fortunate that Reisen wanted to believe it. And that Fairfax supported the illusion by offering expenses.

Reisen came on the line. "*Spider?* I don't bloody believe it. Where've you been?"

It was where Reisen had been that had broken some of the sequence, but Scott was not fool enough to say it. "Life's been quiet, Rex." Scott felt obligated to swap notes; Reisen was nobody's fool and could not be rushed. He was also unpredictable in moments of uncertainty, and could be so unstable under stress that he saw the easiest way of solving problems as literally being to remove them from the face of the earth.

Scott was careful. "Remember that caper some years back? You did the old country a service then. You're on record for it."

"Spider, they gave me five, the cheeky buggers; if it hadn't been for my help then, it would have been ten, I'm telling you." Reisen would believe it.

"That's what I heard, too," Scott lied. "There's something similar going on now. I need a little help."

"What sort of help?" Willingness for queen and country did not remove suspicion.

"I had some pirates following me from one of the embassies. Their pudding faces were like a string of Sputniks. They've wised up to it and put the McCoy on. Pros. Local, I would say. Can you spare one of your long service boys to wander down while I'm still in the office."

"You want them sorted out? That'll cost you."

Christ no. "Nothing like that. Your bloke might see a face he knows. Long shot, but you never know."

"That all?" Reisen sounded cheated.

"For the moment. I don't want to show my hand."

Reisen chewed it over. "I'll do what I can. I've lost a lot of good boys. Some went inside with me, some are still there. Things aren't what they were, Spider. The finesse has gone out of the game. You sure it's for Her Majesty?"

"Absolutely."

"I've got a big portrait of the queen behind the desk now. Oil.

Drop in and see it. Be nice to see you, boy. You were a bloody good artist yourself once. A craftsman."

Scott found he was sweating slightly when he put down the phone. The bonhomie from Reisen meant nothing. Like a gun with a hair trigger, he could explode at any time. But when Reisen did a favor, he would see that the job was done properly. Some of his men had been at the game for a very long time. And his well-guarded offices were not more than a twenty-minute walk away.

Reisen rang back before lunch. "No problem," he announced. "There were two my boy picked out. One is an ex-Flying Squad sergeant he picked out straightaway. The other one he doesn't know, but he reckons his beady eyes are fastened on your place, and he's stamping his size tens through standing around too long."

"Does he know who they work for?"

"Sure. The ex-Sweeney is called Barber. Tough sod. He works for the Hammerton Agency, off Bond Street."

"Thanks, Rex. I'll call in to toast the queen and to salute the flag."

There had been no problem in drilling a hole through the side of the van nor in mounting the camera inside. The worst part was the tedious drive to Hull. Parking on the opposite side of the street was fairly easy, as if nobody wanted his vehicle to be seen immediately outside the jail.

Kate Mooney was a striking looking brunette with sparkling blue eyes and a surprisingly clear skin, considering the hours she kept and the smoke-filled cellars she helped prop up. Her figure fitted the requirements of her part-time job of luring wealthy married men from bars to boudoirs. She rigged her own hidden cameras, which cut expenses and left all the profit hers. Her blackmail was one shot, quick return with the negatives handed over for a one-time payment. She took the view that she was an indispensable asset to married women, for after one misdemeanor with her, husbands clung fearfully to the straight and narrow.

She was a superb photographer or Bluie would not have used her. She also did photography for cookbooks, which these days required the highest standards. Kate Mooney was well off, but she could not resist working or compromising. She had vaguely heard of Willie Scott, but as she was only twenty-six she had been too young to pick up the full legend about him.

The battered van was blue, with the white painted inscription of Jessop's Collection Service on both sides. The hole had been drilled in the first O of the second word. Kate knew all about prison visits. She had a telephoto lens mounted, and reasoned that her best shots would be when the visitors left the prison and would be facing the camera. With her long legs now encased in slacks, she crouched behind the camera and waited. She would do a good job. She always did. Her main problem was fear of being noticed by the prison staff when the gate was opened. If she were seen in the same position for a week, it might arouse suspicions. So she varied her parking as far as possible, and sometimes it made her shots more difficult. But nothing was simple. She did not complain.

Willie Scott climbed into his track suit and zipped up the front. Maggie eyed him in alarm. "Oh, no," she protested, hands going to her mouth. "Willie, please, no."

He had been expecting her reaction. He could have slipped the track suit out to the office and told her he was working late, but that would have raised other problems. "It's all right, love. Stop worrying. I'm only doing a casing."

She shook her head, and ran a long-fingered hand through her hair. "I've been dreading this," she burst out. "It doesn't even fit you anymore. Look at it."

"It'll be better when I've covered a few miles. The pounds will drop off. Stop worrying I'm not sticking my neck out for Chesfield."

Maggie was close to tears. She had not anticipated that the clock would be put back so far. "You're going to break in," she said simply. "It's as though the past few years have no meaning. We're right back where we started."

He placed his hands on her shoulders, but she backed away shaking her head miserably. Then she turned and disappeared into the bedroom. He had the sense not to follow. There was nothing he could say that would reassure her; she knew him too well. He should give up the whole business now. Maggie needed him, and she wanted their baby to have a father. Yet the hook was already in him. Not only was there his immense need to finish the job, but right outside, this moment, were men waiting to take up his trail for a reason he did not yet understand.

He called out, "Maggie, I can't go up to these jokers and tell them there's no need to follow me anymore, I've packed it in. They won't believe me." He could have added that it might even make them desperate. Detective hire on this scale was costly, and that meant there was something to protect at any price. "I won't be long. Okay?" He closed the door, feeling wretched.

He took the elevator to the basement and went behind the boilers to see if the old racing bicycle was still there. The frame was cobwebbed and he roughly cleaned it down. The lamp worked by a dynamo turned by the wheels, and he hoped it would still operate. He pumped up the flat tires and slung the cycle over his shoulder to mount the stairs to the ground floor.

It was quite dark outside, street lamps coyly reaching too high to be effective. But he accepted that he would be seen and made no attempt to avoid the issue. He sat on the saddle, finding it hard after so long. The drop handlebars were now difficult to reach, and he felt the strain on his back. He moved off and the light flickered on, throwing a shaky beam that improved as he picked up speed. A car started up, and footsteps rushed toward it as he continued down the street between the two rows of parked cars. He wore a woolen hat on his head.

He ignored the car behind and was more concerned with the rising ache in his legs; his spine felt as if he had pulled it. I'm in my early forties and I'm already like an old man, he reflected. He increased speed. If he could not ride a cycle without discomfort, how could he expect to scale a wall?

It was just after eleven P.M., and he kept a steady pace. Thickening traffic headed toward him from the West End. His legs were moving better, but they were still painful on the upper thighs. His speed was steady but awkwardly slow for the following car. And then he suddenly lifted his front wheel, crossed the pavement, and sped up a narrow alley between two blocks of stores. The lamp picked out bins and empty crates, which he skirted around. He began to feel at ease. The car would circle around to try to pick him up the other end, but he knew that it would be far too late and he was too fast for anyone on foot.

When he reached the West End, he made a careful check to ensure that the car driver had not been lucky. He took the long way around to Bond Street. No longer familiar with police patrols, he wanted to get his bearings and to get the feel of the place again. Bicycles stuck out in so wealthy an area, but in his track suit, and on a racer, he raised no eyebrows. A patrol car passed him, and his only worry then was the possibility of a stop and search. He passed two overweight joggers and waved to them.

He turned into Maddox Street and then turned left after a short distance. This street was virtually empty. Someone was paying off a taxi, the yellow sign visible above the car line. He passed the Hammerton Detective Agency, its sign still on until the time switch would douse it at midnight. He traveled the length of the street, sat, waited, listened. The noise of traffic filtered from Bond Street. Footsteps approached, uneven and sometimes unsteady, and sometimes stopping. Lovers. He did not need to see them.

Scott turned around and cycled slowly back. He dismounted outside the agency and was alarmed to see a high-class fur shop two doors away; that would be on the police rounds for sure. The Hammerton Detective Agency occupied offices above street level, although the sign gave an illusion of ground-floor premises.

He propped his bicycle against the short inside railings leading to the door, then examined the door itself. Solid pine; there was no sign of an alarm. Who would want to burgle a detective agency? But there were two security locks.

Scott carried a variety of security key heads that he could fix in turn to a specially made shank he had designed himself. At home he also had a full set of antique pick locks, but there were so many, the thin shanks so long, and the ring that held them so large, that they were really impractical to carry. They had been made by a crafts-man well over a hundred years before. Scott had chosen a few that had general use, and had recast them onto much shorter shanks, but he still kept them at right angles to the key head instead of using the usual straight-on design. He carried no more than six of these dispersed around his waistband.

Unknown to Maggie, he had sprayed his fingers with "New Skin" before leaving; he had always found it difficult to work in gloves.

It took him longer than he remembered to find the right key heads, and he had to admit to himself that the gift of instinctive choice had rusted. The delay created danger because he was on view, and the streets were quieting around him. Each approach of footsteps or car became an increasing threat, and he would huddle down in the doorway until the danger had passed. His build-up of tension concerned him. Perhaps it was impossible to put the clock back; he was taking too long to get in.

At last the tumblers moved, and the second lock opened more quickly. He pushed open the door, could just see the stairs ahead, then wheeled the cycle into the small hall. Resisting the urge to use the main lights for fear of them showing under the front door, he used the limited beam of a pencil flashlight and went up the stairs, keeping to the outer edges, where the creaking would be minimal.

By the time he reached the landing, he was feeling a little shaky, and for a few moments he leaned against the wall, reflecting on the slowdown of his skills, and wondering whether his nerve had gone as well. He was glad that nobody who knew him in the old days could see him now.

Of the two doors facing him one was marked *Inquiries*; it took him little time to open it. He felt better after that. He entered the inquiry office, plush armchairs and small tables with up-to-date magazines on them. He used his flashlight carefully; the walls were hung with crime prevention posters. He went past the switchboard and entered an unlocked general office. Well-spaced typists' desks with hooded machines formed three neat rows.

It was in one of the four private offices that he found the clients index. He used a pick lock to open this and then faced the long job of finding the name of the client who had authorized his tail. He had nothing to work on. He opened another cabinet and found a cross-index. Under his own name was a reference to the main file and a Mr. Peter Goring. He returned to the first cabinet.

There was a time log detailing each day and the number of men assigned to the case. A 24-hour watch, a team of three from eight A.M. to midnight, after which one man coped. The change of shift was every four hours, except for the night man. The names of all the operators so far used were meticulously listed with a time check.

Scott sat behind the desk to study the file. They had done a good job. It knocked any complacency from him. Even an agency this size could not employ the fifteen men so far used for a single job of surveillance. They must have access to ex-policemen who were willing to operate on a standby basis. But the cost would be considerable. He made a note of Mr. Peter Goring's Kensington address, then carefully returned the file and relocked both cabinets.

He locked up as he went. At the bottom of the stairs he opened the front door slightly, listened, took out the two key heads he had used to get in, then stepped out, pushing his cycle before him.

6

W HEN CHARLIE HEWITT RANG THROUGH to Scott's office to advise him that a Mr. Bulman had called to see him, Scott suffered the strong sensation of sitting in a prison cell. The feeling was so real that for several moments he sat staring into space, seeing his past. From a distance Hewitt's voice kept nagging at him, and Scott suddenly realized he was holding the phone away from his ear.

"Send him in," he said hoarsely. He was standing when Bulman entered the office, and at first Scott did not recognize him.

Bulman came forward and held out a hand. He had changed, fattened out, a broad smile indenting a melon face. And because he had put on weight, he seemed to be shorter. His dark hair was now sparse and brushed forward. The small eyes were bright and without malice. "Hello, cocker," Bulman said pleasantly. "Long time no see."

As Scott took his hand, surprised by the warmth of the grip, he haphazardly recalled the number of times Bulman had tried to put him away. But Bulman was not acting like an old enemy, and that worried Scott even more.

"All right to sit down?"

Bulman being polite? Scott indicated a chair and slowly sat down himself, wary and highly suspicious.

"You've worn well, Spider." And then Bulman spoiled it by saying with a grin, "But I'm forgetting you started young."

Scott was not used to this type of bonhomie from Bulman and did not know what to make of it. "I can't say it's nice to see you, because you would know that I'd be lying through my teeth."

Bulman laughed. "Well, some of us change a bit, don't we? Mellow with the years." He beamed. "I know I did a lot of things to you I shouldn't have done, but you didn't make it easy for me, did you?"

That was true. Yet it still could not be a social call. Scott remained wary. "Coffee?"

"Why not? You've got suspicion written all over your mug. Never seen a villain who gives his feelings away so much."

Scott ordered the coffee by shouting through to Lulu. "Ex-villain. Still in the force?"

"What else could I do?" Bulman asked reasonably. "Detective Superintendent now. A lot of water under the bridge."

"Congratulations. Local?"

"Yard. Been there for five, six years. Special Duties."

"Which can cover anything?"

"More or less. Nudges toward the political, but I'm not with Special Branch."

"They'd tie you down too much." Scott was sorry that he said that, but Bulman took no notice.

Lulu flounced in with coffee in plastic cups, and gave Bulman a quick look as she left. Lulu made up her mind about people after one glance, but Scott learned nothing from her about Bulman.

"I've called about your visit to Hull," announced Bulman as he sipped the hot coffee. "You saw Lennie Peel. Old Inky. How was he?"

"Aging and arthritic. I should think his forging days are over."

"Sad in a way. Ever see any of his copies of the masters? Thank God he didn't sell them; they'd have caused havoc in the art world. Murder Squad don't rate your conclusions, Spider."

"Murder Squad can get knotted." Now that Scott knew why Bulman had called, he was more at ease.

"I mean, Inky would say anything."

"Not to me, he wouldn't."

Bulman rubbed the corner of an eye. He was thoughtful. "Anything else you can tell me?"

"Are you investigating Chesfield's murder, then?"

Bulman did not reply immediately. He noted that Scott had not lost his knack of nailing coppers to the post with directness. "I just told you, we don't see it as murder. Not without something else. I saw your name on the report, thought it would be a good idea to say hello and ask you what you're up to."

"You haven't answered my question."

"I'm not in Murder Squad. I'm merely doing a little liaison for them."

Scott accepted that. Bulman was clever; sometimes in the past too clever. "I've nothing to add. I went up as a favor to Sir Richard Chesfield. I've received no fee. I made one visit. It means nothing to me personally how Chesfield was killed."

"I suppose Sir Stuart Halliman put his fellow knight onto you."

"It'll be in the report."

Bulman put his cup down on the edge of the desk and peered across at Scott with a half friendly, half serious expression.

"Will you believe I'm here to help you?"

Scott could not resist a smile. "That'll be the day."

"Do you *really* think Chesfield was topped."

"Yes."

"You wouldn't know why?"

"No idea."

"I believe you. Did you know that Kransouski's in town?"

Scott froze. It was like stepping in and out of a time capsule. His fingers were stiff on the desk. "That's interesting. But it can't be anything to do with me."

"Maybe. Thought you'd like to know. He came in as a latecomer to a Polish trade delegation. It was a lucky sighting. Sickness in immigration brought in one of the old boys as a replacement. Kransouski could be genuine, of course. These characters get shifted around if they cock something up. We didn't kick him out at the time. He was recalled."

Polish delegation? The word rattled in Scott's head. *Polish.* "Are you watching him?"

"On and off. He's with the delegation a lot. Nothing to shout about so far. Coming in openly like that, he's probably clean."

"Where does he hang out?"

"You want to drop in?" Bulman laughed again. "Kensington, where most of them hang out."

"He used his own name?"

"Apparently. It's more Polish than Russian, anyway."

Kensington. "Do you know his actual address?"

"I couldn't give it to you if I did."

"If you're here to help me, you could."

"Come on, Spider. Unless you've something to trade."

"I'll find out the hard way. What happens now?"

"Not much. Anyone tailing you?"

"Me? What the hell for?"

"I thought I recognized one of our old boys hanging around outside."

"It's a free country. There's nothing on me. I'm clean and I'm straight."

"Glad to hear that, Spider. More than you think." Bulman finished his coffee and rose. "So you've nothing else to tell me about Chesfield?"

"He's dead," Scott replied.

"Seems so." Bulman pulled out a card and laid it on the desk. "If anything crops up. You know." He held out a hand again. "Nice to see you, Spider. Come and have a drink in the canteen sometime."

Scott said that he would. They both knew that the invitation was dead. It would take more than a drink to entice Scott into any coppers' nick.

They studied the photographs, placing them face down as they finished. "Anyone?" Scott asked.

Halliman went through them again and picked out one of a bespectacled man, innocuous in appearance, medium height, and fair-haired. "Not a man to catch the attention," Halliman pronounced. "But exceedingly dangerous, notwithstanding." He turned to Scott. "I have to be sure. May I borrow this?"

"You want your old friends to run it through?"

"I also want to know who he visited. My guess is Mervin Soames or Garry Fuller. As the Home Office has become so unhelpful, I must try elsewhere."

"Try Bulman. He called on me today."

"I thought he might. He's been in touch with me, too. I'd rather leave the police out of it for the moment. If they were hooked on the murder possibility it might be different, but as things are, they could be obstructive." Halliman paused. "They could even be behind the Home Office's reluctance to help." Halliman slipped the photograph into his pocket. "This Kate Mooney, she'd better finish the week. Did Bulman tell you about Kransouski?"

"Yes. It shook me. Why would he come in so openly?"

Halliman buttoned his coat as he rose. "All sorts of reasons. He may have nothing to hide, in general terms. I think he was originally Polish, or his parents were. If he disguised himself and was spotted, he would be out on his ear." Halliman became pensive. He gave Scott a strange look, part quizzical, part warning. "Or, quite simply, he was ordered to come here openly. I can't see him as a trade delegate, so he'll be here for a specific purpose as opposed to overall stirring. And the way he's been set up could mean that after the event, Moscow would not be too concerned about what happened to him."

"Can you find out where he lives? I have an address but I haven't the time to stake it out myself."

Walter Clarke stared at the blackmail letter and the accompanying typesheet. He sat down well away from his window, as if by finding the darkest corner of his room, he could hide everything, including himself. He was glad now that he was unmarried. In this bachelor apartment he did not have to hide his feelings from anyone. He could openly show his fear without worrying about being observed.

After a while he rallied, as he always did. Hooking one leg over the arm of his chair he read the demand again. No money was involved; it would be much easier if it were. And then the accompanying threat. It was an article set out in French for the French press with an attached English translation. The torture was to be slow. Publication in some obscure French magazine that might take time to be picked up by the larger newspapers, at which point it would find its way over the various borders and across the Channel to Britain. And all he would be able to do would be to wait for it to happen. The threat, though, carried no deadlines, as if the blackmailer knew that Clarke would not panic, that he would hold out in the belief that once the material was released, the threat, and, therefore, any gain from it, would no longer apply.

Clarke recognized the flaws in this strategy. Money could be obtained for the article, so the blackmailer would not entirely lose. And the cat and mouse game would have to end sometime. There would come a point when Clarke's nerve would snap, or he would stand off once too often. Either way he would be finished. So he needed judgment as never before. And he desperately needed to know who was sending the threats.

In all these careful deliberations, Clarke never once considered calling in the police. He could have obtained priority attention, but the possibility never even entered his mind. When he knew the contents of the sheets by heart, he considered burning them; then he saw the possibility of their being of future use. They were typewritten. The sender must know that type could be traced to a particular machine; he obviously did not care. But there might be other facets.

Later that day he sought out Tony Marchant in the House of Commons and raised the subject of Gordon Chesfield again. They were sitting at the bar waiting for the division bell when Clarke said, "Tell me about this burglar chappie who went to Hull."

Marchant had to search his memory among the more pressing items of the day. "Scott. There's nothing else about him except that he was once a cat burglar. I told you all there was to know."

"You said an ex-intelligence chief sent him up there. I've been wondering why."

"What's your interest, Walter?" Marchant had almost forgotten the earlier incident and the promised introduction to the delectable Susan had not yet occurred.

"I told you. Chesfield was an old friend."

"One it's best to forget, old chap."

"I telephoned Susan before lunch. Will you be around at six. Or is Madge down from the constituency?"

Marchant gave Clarke a dirty look. "Below the belt, old boy. Six will do fine."

"I'd like to contact Scott. Could be interesting."

"Police don't think so. I believe his name is Willie and if he's not in the phone book, ask me again."

Halliman laid the photograph down on the table. He had met Scott for lunch in Rules just off the Strand. They sat in the quiet, refined interior in the knowledge that Scott's followers were outside. The two men had arrived separately, although both knew that they had been linked.

"Victor Anthony," Halliman said, firming his military mustache. "Sounds like two Christian names, but in fact Anthony is a derivative of Antopolov. Grandparents emigrated from Russia toward the end of the last century. The name was anglicized by Victor's father as far back as 1930. Victor was born in 1940. Political history far right of center. Became a member of the National Front some years ago, stayed in the organization for a while, and was imprisoned for two months due to his violent behavior at one of their demonstrations. The day Kate Mooney took this shot he was visiting Mervin Soames."

"So the right-wing stuff is a cover?" Scott asked.

"Yes, we've known that for some time. Even when I was still in office. But he's difficult to nail down. Certainly a back-room boy. Behind-the-scenes organizer."

"As far as murder?"

"That wouldn't worry him." Halliman toyed with his Dover sole. "It would seem that the block at the Home Office does not go as far as the Minister, and I'm reluctant to approach him at this stage. Anyway, I can manage without him, but it's interesting."

"Are you saying that someone in the Home Office has an interest in clamming up?"

"Not at all. There are plenty of bureaucrats flexing their muscles. Somebody is probably doing somebody else a favor on the old boy network and sees no harm in it. After all, I have no official status."

As Halliman did not enlarge on the issue, Scott continued to eat his veal, although discussions of this kind over a meal generally ruined it. "I'll have to go back to Hull," he observed after a while.

"To see Soames? He won't be forthcoming."

"To see Garry Fuller."

Halliman lowered his fork very slowly. He gazed across at Scott. "And you call *me* devious?"

Scott grinned. "I'll need another visitor's pass. Will Home Office block that?"

"They'd find it difficult after already granting one. Leave it with me."

"If it's difficult, I'll have a word with Bulman; they won't block the police."

"You think he'd want you to go?"

"I'm bloody sure he would."

Halliman pushed a piece of paper across the table. "That's the address you wanted."

Scott read it without touching it. His pulse quickened. It was the address he had stolen from the detective agency.

Scott took his tail with him back to Hull Prison. On balance he believed it better that they knew where he was going. It was one method of stirring things up. He had told Bluie to get a message through to Kate Mooney of his impending arrival and for her to take detailed shots of his tail since they would show themselves more clearly once he was inside.

He was again lucky with the weather, with the exception of a nasty, biting wind coming down the estuary off the east coast. He parked behind Kate's blue van and winked at the drilled out hole as he went past. After the usual herding in, he managed to select the same table as before in the visiting room. He had studied a mug shot of Fuller before leaving London.

When Fuller came in he appeared much older than his photograph. He was on the short side, wiry, with a hangdog look on a hatchet face and a disgruntled curl to his lips. At first glance Scott put him down as a troublemaker, yet his prison record suggested otherwise. Deep brown eyes scanned the room as he approached, and Scott rose quickly to make himself known.

"Scott?"

"That's right. Glad you would see me."

Fuller sat down while Scott obtained tea and biscuits from the small bar. "Thanks," said Fuller as Scott returned. "I don't think we've met before, so what's on your mind?"

"We did meet. Briefly. Years ago. I couldn't have made much impression."

"Don't piss about. Get on with it." Fuller stirred his tea.

"Why the hurry? Do you get that many visitors?"

"I don't need them. You came up for a purpose and I want to know why. Simple. You were on the creep, weren't you? I mean, you'd feel at home here?"

"I haven't done a job for years. But I still keep in touch with some of the boys. I was up here visiting not long ago."

"So I heard. Did that have anything to do with Inky taking a dive?"

"I wouldn't hurt Inky."

"*Someone* buggered up his home life. After your visit. Anyway, do you get to the point or do I finish my tea and push off?"

"The word is that Chesfield was topped in his cell; you'll have heard that more often than I."

Fuller sneered. "You've lost touch. Anyone spouting that kind of crap would finish up the same way."

"I'm not talking of open dialogue and you bloody well know it. I'm talking of whispers, oblique looks, understanding."

"You working for the fuzz?"

"I could never work for the fuzz. Ask around. I was hoping to do you a favor. But now I've met you I'm beginning to change my mind. You're a creep. And this is where you should be."

Fuller's eyes narrowed and biscuit crumbs dropped from his petulant lips. "Okay. So we don't like each other. Now get on with it."

"You don't like Mervin Soames, either, do you?"

Fuller spilled his tea. He wiped his mouth on his sleeve, eyeing Scott viciously. Too late, he said, "Soames is nothing to me. I hardly know him."

"Is that why you thumped him during a demo and then swore it was a copper?"

"Where're you getting this crap? You *are* working for the fuzz. Only they could have told you that."

"If they'd told me I wouldn't have believed it. You've got fuzz on the brain. You're like a certain type of Irish who blame Britain for everything they cock up."

Fuller looked over his shoulder at the guard standing by the far door. He turned back and tapped the table hard with a forefinger. "I've had enough of you. I still don't know why you came. If . . ."

"The word outside is that you made the arrangements for Chesfield's topping."

"*I what?*" Fuller half rose, realized how much he had raised his voice, and sat down quickly. He glared at Scott, hatred oozing out. "What are you trying to fix on me, you bastard?"

"I'm trying to help you." Scott flashed a warning. "Keep your voice down, the screws are watching." He knew that he now had Fuller's attention; there was no risk of him walking out.

"The bloody fuzz are trying to fix me."

"The bloody fuzz don't believe Chesfield was topped, so they can't be. But if Soames opens his mouth again they might begin to take notice."

"What do you mean? Soames? What's the lying bastard said?"

"He had a visitor the other day who brought back the possibility that you were hired to set up Naylor or Brooks or both for the murder of Chesfield. How many visitors have you had since Chesfield was brought here?" Scott already knew the answer, for his strategy depended on it.

Fuller became defensive. "A couple. They're not important." But they both had strong political leanings. Fuller was so violently sold on his beliefs, so warped in outlook, that fellow travelers were the only people likely to visit him. His wife had divorced him ten years ago after proven brutality from him.

Scott watched the sinewy fingers clawing at the table. "Could they have political links by any chance?"

"What is this? What's it to you?"

"Answer me first."

"No. What the hell has politics to do with Chesfield?"

"You should reverse that." Scott pushed his chair back, the sound carrying down the hall. "Well, if they weren't involved in any extremism, you're probably in the clear. Don't worry about it."

But Fuller was worried. His lie could easily backfire.

"You're saying that Soames has passed the word that I set up Chesfield?" Malice poured from Fuller.

"No. I'd have had to have heard them talk. I'm saying that the party who visited Soames came back and mentioned that that was what Soames said. People listen to these things."

"I'll fix that lying bastard. If it takes me the rest of my stretch, I'll nail him.

Scott gave him time to think it through, ready for the question he knew must come.

Fuller raised his cup, saw that he had finished his tea, and banged it down again. He glared suspiciously at Scott, but his thoughts were still largely on the man he had always detested. "What's your interest? Why would you come up here to spin something like that? I'm nothing to you."

"That's right. I wouldn't give you the time of day. My interest is Chesfield. I know his old man. And it's important to him that someone goes to the wall for his son's murder. If he thinks it's you, he has enough money and clout to nail it on you. That doesn't worry me either."

Scott reflected for a while, keeping Fuller on the end of the line of distrust and uncertainty. Nobody knew better than Scott the frustration that could build up in prison when something needed to be tackled outside. The hopelessness of not being able to come to grips with a problem directly could send a man off his head and sometimes did, particularly with highly emotional issues.

"I'm trying to help Chesfield. I don't believe in easy options. If Soames did send out word like that, why would he do it?"

"He'd do anything to get at me."

"But would he go so far?"

Fuller thought it over. "It has to be that. He's stirring."

Scott conceded the possibility and then said, "There is a chance that he set the thing up himself. Maybe after Inky left he got a bit scared. If he became worried he might start spreading his risks. To push suspicion your way would be tempting. And useful. If he's involved, he's the bloke I want."

When it had sunk in, Scott added, "I came here to help you, not for your sake but for Chesfield's father. I couldn't care less what happens to you, Fuller. But I do care that if Soames fixed something and is trying to squeeze through the door before it jams on you, then he should not get away with it. If he does, you're in deep trouble, mate. Be lucky."

7

Scott left the prison and walked over to the blue van. He knocked on the rear door but guessed that Kate Mooney would have seen him through the spy hole. She opened the door and he said, "I'm Willie Scott," and ducked to climb in.

"I know," Kate replied. "I've got you on film."

Scott smiled. "As long as it's not one of your usual variety."

The dark haired Kate eyed him provocatively. "With you, darling, I wouldn't even put a film in the camera." She offered a devastating smile. "Freebies."

Scott lowered himself onto a small canvas stool. "I'm tempted, Kate. You're as dishy as they say. But there's this girl I'm about to marry, and a baby to come."

"In that order?" Kate asked cheekily. "I've never broken up a marriage in my life. I reckon I've saved a few though."

She eyed him again, pouted. "Pity. Here you are right on the spot and there's a mattress."

"I'd need a book of instructions these days, Kate."

"Not with me, you wouldn't. I offer an action course and a replay. Still, in view of what you say, I suppose the baby will be plastic."

They laughed and Scott could easily see how Kate lured her men; and at the moment she was in denims and well covered.

She turned back to the mounted camera and peered through the view finder. "I suppose you realize you've buggered everything up?"

Scott made no comment.

Kate continued, "I've just missed some of the visitors leaving, but apart from that the party tailing you, who arrived in the red Citroen, now know what I'm here for. You've blown me, Willie. And you've blown yourself as being the one who put me here."

"I know. It doesn't matter now, Kate. You can wrap it up."

She turned, saw that he meant it, and immediately started to dismantle the camera and tripod. It was gloomy in the van; a certain amount of light came through the sliding opaque glass panel separating the driving section, and a circle of light appeared in the side of the van as the camera was withdrawn. Kate worked deftly, and soon there was nothing to be seen of her camera gear except the two packed cases. She squatted on the mattress. "I use this while I'm waiting for the visitors to arrive."

Scott nodded. "Send a bill for the full week."

"You've got what you wanted?"

"I think so. They were good shots, Kate. They helped. I'll thank Bluie for passing you on to me."

"What else could that fairy do with me?" Kate sounded aggrieved. She noted that Scott was thoughtful and was about to leave. "I hope you knew what you were doing when you showed your hand just now."

"So do I, Kate." Scott reached for the door handle. "I'm just about to find out. Thanks again."

Kate shrugged. "Makes a change. If I can help you again, in any way . . . ?" Her wide-eyed expression left the offer double edged.

Scott climbed out.

Nicolai Gorkin was slightly confused. He could not fully grasp why Kransouski should be used for an issue that should surely be under his own auspices. He understood that Kransouski knew something of the man Scott, but he himself could just as easily have dealt with it, and far less expensively. The first account from the Hammerton Detective Agency had been presented for payment. Not directly to the Embassy, of course, but to one Peter Goring, who was insisting on paying cash. The amount was astronomical, full of fat capitalist profit.

Kransouski had arrived at the Soviet Embassy with two other delegates from the Polish trade mission, ostensibly on a courtesy visit, and quite openly. While he sat opposite Gorkin, he was aware of an increasing frustration, but he was not the type of man to show it, nor to show anything much. He had expected the bill to annoy Gorkin, but he had obtained results, and that was what he had been sent to do.

Gorkin was wearing a poorly made Russian suit. Kransouski had already bought an English one, Regent Street off the peg, but he was an easy man to fit, and he carried his clothes well. He said pointedly, "I told you before that I can only offer substandard service unless I know precisely what I'm looking for." He was speaking for the tape recorder in Gorkin's drawer.

"I understand your feelings, General. Meanwhile, may I have your report." Gorkin waved the account. "Something that might justify this."

"Scott went to Hull prison. We don't yet know who he saw, but that will come. Afterward he reported to a van outside the prison. The men watching quickly picked out the viewing hole in its side. It seems that a woman was photographing anyone who entered or left the prison. It would also seem that she got what she wanted, as the van has not been seen since." Kransouski waved a deprecating hand. "There'll be another bill for that small service."

"Was she photographing visitors?"

Kransouski was irritated. "Of course, visitors. The prisoners do not come out on view."

Gorkin held back an urge to grab Kransouski by the throat; his question was not as stupid as it had sounded. "For how long had she been doing it?"

"We haven't been watching her, but it might have been for a few days. Part guess, part local inquiry, which, of necessity, had to be guarded."

"Thank you. That's most useful."

The tone of dismissal surprised Kransouski. "Is that all you want to know?"

"That's all. Continue to watch the man Scott."

"My orders to watch Scott come from General Rogov, comrade. I do not require your endorsement. My report will go direct to the General." Kransouski coldly stood up.

"As will mine, comrade." Gorkin was smiling vindictively.

Nicolai Gorkin met Victor Anthony in the reptile house at London Zoo in Regent's Park. These meetings were so rare that he had only met Anthony once before. He disliked such meetings intensely. The risk was enormous because MI5 knew that he was Moscow Center's Resident, and therefore would have him under surveillance. It had meant the tedium of deception, the use of other men he preferred not to expose in order to block or draw off his watchers; just to meet one man for a short time. Notwithstanding all this, he had to see Anthony personally.

The dim lighting of the reptile house was ideal for the meeting, but it was necessary to step into the open to be able to speak freely. They strolled together toward the Russian bear pit, neither consciously aware of the irony. The zoo on this cold autumn day was far from full; there was ample space to stand side by side at the railings.

"How did you get on at Hull?" Gorkin asked, looking down into the pit.

Anthony had expected something more than this after the summons. "I gave a report to John. Full detail."

"I've read the report. I want your own words."

Anthony was annoyed that his carefully constructed full report needed clarification.

When he had finished, Gorkin asked, "Was there a blue van outside the prison?"

"A blue van?"

"Think. Think most carefully. And take your time."

This alarmed Anthony. Gorkin was here for this very special and unusual meeting, yet he seemed to be asking unnecessary questions that must be more important than they sounded. "I think there

102

was," he replied at last. "I mean, I wasn't looking for one. I seem to remember . . ."

"Did it have on the side in white letters Jessop's Collection Service?"

Anthony did not like the way the questioning was going. There somehow seemed to be a sinister undertone. He was not absolutely certain that he could recall the van. He felt the disparity of his position. Gorkin did not particularly look his part, and appeared to be shabby, though not as shabby as Anthony himself. But Gorkin carried immense power, and through his own increasing unease Anthony realized, perhaps for the first time, that if Gorkin became awkward, he himself had no one to turn to. He had not felt so vulnerable before. It seemed that Gorkin wanted confirmation of this bloody van, so humor him. "Jessop seems to stick in my mind. I can't remember the rest."

Gorkin turned his head to stare directly at Anthony.

"Where was the van?"

"Outside the prison." That was easy enough. "The letters were white. I remember that." Gorkin had already told him.

"Good. Thank you, Matthew."

His code name. Anthony ran a finger around the inside of his collar. It was not supposed to be like this. He could not understand why he felt so uncomfortable. He was sweating around the collar, yet it was cold and beginning to drizzle. The bear started to climb his pole, to the amusement of the onlookers. Anthony saw the controlled power of the beast, the huge jaws, and the strong claws digging into the wood. He would hate to be down there, he reflected. Yet the bear had taken his mind off Gorkin. He said, "Is that all you want?" But when he turned, Gorkin was not there. He swung around to see the Russian walking away, raincoat collar untidily turned up, hands in pockets, shoulders hunched. Anthony was glad to see him go; he much preferred to deal with John, whom he had got to know quite well over the years. Removing his glasses, he absently polished them. He decided to get value for his money and headed back toward the reptile house.

Scott had warned Maggie that his movements might become erratic, and he had put Charlie Hewitt in charge of the office. But

Maggie wanted to be more involved, which meant she was not only worried, but intended personally to keep an eye on him as much as she could. There were occasions when this could be advantageous. A man and a woman together seldom drew attention, whereas separately they might. So it was with Maggie that Scott took a taxi to Kensington to be dropped off near the house of Peter Goring.

Embassy land. Apart from Park Lane, Kensington and Knightsbridge probably commanded the highest property prices in the whole metropolis. It brought back memories to Scott. Expensive apartments had burglar locks and spy holes and alarms. The penthouses carried iron grids to cut off the picture windows from the balconies at night, and skylights here were a burglar's nightmare. He smiled to himself. It had not stopped him nor, apparently, had it stopped others; the crime rate was still increasing.

The street he was watching was off the wide, busy stretch of Kensington High Street. Adept at finding cover, even in daylight, Scott had opted for the simplest protection. A bus stop was almost opposite the street in which resided Peter Goring, and the angle was sufficiently wide for the house to be seen from the bus shelter. Maggie and Scott simply stood there and waited.

That morning Scott had telephoned the Hammerton Detective Agency on behalf of Peter Goring, had given them a coded reference number he had copied from the agency card, and had instructed them to call off their men until further notice. Before picking up Maggie later that evening, he had done an elaborate check to ensure that he was now free of surveillance. The ruse would work until Kransouski caught up with it.

Maggie looked stunning, and Scott was well aware of the envious glances cast at her. They stood arm in arm in the bus line, letting others pass them when a bus pulled in.

After three quarters of an hour, Maggie was sorry that she had come and began to ease her feet in her shoes.

"I told you to wear flats," Scott said.

"But you don't even know that he'll come," Maggie protested.

"You need patience in this game, love. I could wait all night. The two best times are early morning and evening. If he's there at all." He looked down at her, saw her try to smile. "Shall I call a cab? You go back and leave me here."

"No. I'll stay."

"Good girl. Knocks the romance out of it though, doesn't it?"

They were talking almost in whispers, the line having grown around them.

Twenty minutes later, Maggie protested, "You're breaking my fingers, darling."

Scott had not realized how tightly he had grasped her hand. Kransouski had appeared on the steps of the house. He was not arriving, but leaving. As Scott eased his grip on Maggie, she followed the direction of his gaze, alarmed at the effect on him.

"I don't recognize him."

"It's him."

"Now I can see. Like that, he reminds me of Sir Stuart."

"They have a lot in common, believe me."

"He's kept his looks, though."

"He's a sadist. You've forgotten too much. He could smile as you died in agony." There was so much feeling in Scott's voice that Maggie realized that there must be a good deal he had not told her about the Russian.

They lost sight of Kransouski as the lights changed and the traffic roared across to cut off their vision. "Come on," said Scott. "I just wanted to be sure. Now I know where I can find him."

Maggie strode out beside him, distressed that Kransouski had made such an impact on Scott, whose jawline had tightened like a clamp, eyes uncharacteristically hard. Scott had been shaken and that did not happen easily. Her hand was numb in his grasp. At the moment, it was doubtful if he was wholly aware of her presence.

The atmosphere of hate was seeping into the room like creeping gas. The television screen flickered. The film was entertaining, yet concentration began to waver as furtive glances were cast from one to another.

At first it was difficult to know how it had started. One moment there was a reasonably satisfied audience of prisoners watching the screen, and within the hour a restlessness had slowly spread through them. Afterward, one of the guards described it as uncanny, almost supernatural, as if the devil himself had come among them.

Further recollection suggested that it started from the time Garry Fuller came into the room and noticed Mervin Soames sitting there. It was already known among the men that these two did not like each other. Generally, they kept clear of each other. Normally Fuller, having seen Soames already seated, would have gone into the other television room to watch another channel.

This time Fuller not only sat down, but got as close to Soames as he could. From that moment he did nothing but glare balefully at Soames, and soon the feeling of malevolence began to penetrate.

When he finally caught Fuller's stare, Soames suddenly went cold. The pair had always exchanged contemptuous glances, but this was entirely different. This was loathing coupled with an implicit, but deadly, threat. There was total menace in Fuller's unrelenting expression, and others began to notice. One or two of those near to Fuller left the room. And Fuller was able to move two chairs nearer to his enemy. In spite of efforts to resist, Soames frequently turned his head; Fuller's mind must have snapped.

Someone told Soames to stop fidgeting, but the reason for his increasing unease became clearer as time passed. No normal person could silently blaze hatred for so long and so unwaveringly. Soames wanted to leave, but he had always considered himself superior to Fuller in every way. However, the longer he sat, the faster his confidence ebbed. He began to sweat.

There was nothing Soames could do in the television room, no retaliation he could make. Neither he nor Fuller were popular with the majority, who did not consider them to be real villains. The situation was getting worse. Fuller was now leaning forward, as if to will Soames into some action he would regret.

Soames left and was relieved to get out of the room. He leaned against the corridor wall and had hardly begun to relax when he felt Fuller's hot breath on his neck.

"I'm going to kill you, you scheming bastard," Fuller whispered.

Normally Soames would have laughed off such bravado, especially from Fuller, but there was a terrible menace to it.

"Your time's up, Soames. I'll choose my moment. Just as Naylor chose his. You tried to fix me. Well, I have friends, sonny boy. I know what happened, and you're going to drop for what you tried to do."

"I haven't tried anything, you stupid bugger. What are you prattling about?" Why was his voice shaking; it was only Fuller he was talking to.

Fuller cunningly swung his back to the guard farther down the corridor. He leered at Soames, eyes narrowed and vicious. "You're on borrowed time, Soames. I know all about it."

Soames, about to grab Fuller by his scrawny throat, peered over Fuller's shoulder to see the guard looking their way. Fuller said icily, "Try it and I'll do you now." He moved his arm, and when Soames looked down he saw that Fuller was holding a crude blade embedded in a rough wooden handle. Soames knew of Fuller's wife-beating record, but this was another person, a demented man filled with hate and obsession. Before he could say any more, Fuller moved off, the knife miraculously gone. Soames was left with a feeling of horror; Fuller had not been bluffing, but what had triggered him?

Back in his cell, Soames tried to think it through. It was clear that Fuller knew about Chesfield, and that was enough to dement him. He now badly needed another visit from Anthony, but visits had to be regulated. He had three weeks to wait, and that was going to be a very long time with Fuller acting like a pathological killer. But at least Anthony was there as a lifeline, even if he had to wait. After that someone would get at Fuller.

Kransouski had nobody with whom to discuss his problems. Gorkin had pushed unhelpfulness too far for him to be acting on his own initiative. So Gorkin was under orders to reveal nothing of the real issue to Kransouski. Perhaps there wasn't one. When he reflected on that, he could not accept that General Rogov would uproot him from Bucharest just to organize the surveillance of Scott, unless there were deep roots to the whole issue. And if Kransouski, with his length of service, and his loyalty never in question, could not be permitted to have a glimpse of that issue, then it had to be of major importance.

There was nothing more Kransouski could do about Scott. The matter was under control. He rang the Hammerton Detective Agency because they had not rung him as was usual, each day at five P.M. He did not expect a director to ring, indeed he preferred no continuing relationship with any particular person; all he wanted was a report on time. When he was told that he had canceled the service earlier that day, Kransouski went cold. Would Gorkin go so far?

What had the man sounded like? The person answering the phone found the clerk who had taken the morning call, but it was difficult for him to remember the timbre of the voice. The caller had said he was speaking for Mr. Goring, had quoted the address and telephone number, and had asked for the account to be sent for final settlement.

"Was there anything distinctive about the voice?" Kransouski persisted.

"Slightly foreign. Very slightly."

There was no answer to that. Kransouski himself had a slightly foreign accent. He explained that there had obviously been a mistake and reaffirmed the original arrangements.

Afterward he sat back wondering who would action such a cancellation. It had been bound to come to light. Surely Gorkin would not be so crude. Why should it be done? Who could possibly benefit?

Kransouski's hands slowly went to his temples. Scott? How could it be? Kransouski felt sick. If it was Scott, then he would know who had put the tail on him and also this address. And he wanted Kransouski to be aware of this. Had he known from the beginning?

Kransouski was now satisfied to be acting alone. If Scott was so well informed, then Rogov must provide another course of action. He believed he knew what that would be.

Victor Anthony put on the kettle and searched for another jar of instant coffee. The apartment was untidy, yet it possessed a messy sort of charm. It was clear that Anthony's interests were diversified, hobbies changed, as if one subject was never sufficient to hold his interest. Yet among the confusion was a basic artistic tendency toward quality.

It was true that he easily tired of current interests and would switch to something else, applying himself wholeheartedly to it for as long as it held him. A product of a broken home, he had hated both his father and mother long before they went their separate ways. Family strife and blame for much for which he had not been guilty had forced him to be a secretive person from a very early age. Burying his opinions and openly covering them with others had never been a problem to him.

Anthony's one consistency had been his political opinion; that had not wavered over the years. He believed he had covered his views from all except those very few he wished to know them, for only by so doing could he serve them. He possessed the kind of blind fanaticism that could only deepen when opposed. He did not want another side to the story, for that way lay confusion.

Up to this time he had encountered no psychological problem in following his set course. And he was not wavering now. What concerned him was a pattern of events that might suddenly raise eyebrows. His visits to Soames had, in his view, been too frequent. Since Chesfield had died, he had called too often, yet he could understand the need to present a normal front for a while. Soames was coping. It was time to sever the link.

This attitude was supported by Gorkin, whom he knew as Peter, calling the panic meeting at the zoo. Peter was big time, and the subject matter had appeared to be small stuff. Anthony still felt uneasy about the meeting. He had been trusted with the most serious of projects, a trust well founded, and now he felt he was being excluded in some way. What was this about a blue van? What did it matter? Peter had given the impression that it involved a threat of some kind. Anthony needed to speak to his usual contact, John, to have this out. As if the thought was plucked straight from his head, the telephone rang and John was on the other end of the line. That was unique. John never telephoned. Drops, cut-outs, all the standard procedures were used, but not a telephone.

John wanted to pick him up on the Embankment opposite the Savoy Hotel back entrance in one hour exactly. A yellow Ford Cortina R registration. Another panic meeting. Something was going wrong; Anthony hoped that John could tell him what. John had been helpful all along the line, and had not been ungenerous.

Anthony finished his coffee; an hour was a close call. He left the apartment wearing denims, the universal uniform of the uncaring, with an unbuttoned anorak flapping over the top. The breeze ruffled his fair hair.

Untidiness did not extend to unpunctuality. He was waiting on the Embankment five minutes early. An intermittent breeze came off the river and carried the double hoot of a tug pulling barges. The water slopped at the stonework below the parapet, and across the river Festival Hall sprawled like a hybrid monument.

John was a few minutes late and profusely apologetic, explaining the problems of the traffic. As Anthony climbed in beside the slightly built Russian, he was surprised by the concern. John was normally unflappable and cool-headed; he did not apologize for anything. Now he seemed to be flustered.

They drove toward Westminster and the disdainful chime of Big Ben. The majestic spread of the Houses of Parliament produced the illusion that the buildings were far older than they really were. They crossed the bridge in silence, passed St. Thomas's Hospital, and continued toward Kennington. Anthony was surprised. Usually they had a brief meeting somewhere and that was that. The briefer the better.

John smiled a little nervously. "I'm sorry about this, Matthew. I hate driving in London. It is the one thing that is likely to throw me off my balance." He did not take his gaze from the road.

Anthony thought he understood. It explained John's fluster. "Where are we going?"

"Into the country. I want you to meet someone." John shot a glance at Anthony and then riveted his gaze back on the road, his gloved hands too tight on the steering wheel. "Would you prefer to drive?"

That made Anthony feel a little more important. John always managed to make Anthony feel an integral part of the whole Soviet machinery, even when being clinical about some point. "You're doing all right."

"No, really." Another glance, almost a plea. "I hate this bloody driving."

Anthony laughed. The "bloody" had sounded so funny. No foreigner, not even an American, can express bloody as the British do; there is an inflection that is difficult to imitate, whether soft or overstated. Anyway, John was pulling in.

They changed places and buckled their seat belts. John expressed relief. "I'll tell you where to go." He pulled a map out and folded it to a section. "I don't really need this, but I must be sure." He smiled warmly. "You drive much better. I drive on my nerves."

Anthony smiled back. It was difficult to imagine John with nerves. He wanted to raise the meeting with Peter, but thought he had better not. Like John, he preferred to be single-minded and found it difficult to talk seriously when concentrating on traffic.

Under John's direction he drove past Lambeth and Brixton, good propaganda areas for them, and then onto Streatham and Croydon, and beyond into open Surrey countryside. He enjoyed the driving. And the company. John and he had always been comfortable with each other.

Directions became intricate and the massive sprawl of a largely decaying London had long faded from sight and mind. Surrey was beautiful, spoiled only by the intense belt of snobbery that enfolded it. So mused Anthony as John gave him his final direction.

The trees were golden brown, more than half their leaves already down to form a crunchy patterned carpet under the wheels. The breeze kept the leaves spiraling, and birds flew among the foliage at various heights. The two men left the car on the edge of the woods and started to walk down a track that was difficult to find.

"Why so far out?" Anthony asked as he followed John's almost jockeyish figure.

"He lives here," John answered without turning. "A case of mountain to Mohammed. Nearly there."

John stopped and Anthony came panting up behind him. John turned and he was holding a gun. "I'm sorry, Matthew. But I know you will understand. You've always been a dedicated servant."

Anthony could not believe what he saw. He had always trusted this man. He felt himself choking in fear. He stood panting, eyeing the gun and the man who held it, and who he now realized he had never really known.

"But I've always been loyal," he protested. He could hardly speak through the dryness of his mouth.

"I know you have." John appeared ridiculously benign. "But these things are sometimes necessary. It's a pity that we can't take the risk."

"What risk for God's sake?"

"If you haven't worked it out, I certainly haven't the time to explain. Take my word that it has to be done."

Anthony's gaze fastened solely on the gun. It was small and appeared so stupidly inadequate. He was facing what he believed to be the danger and was on the point of making a run for it when he was seized by each arm. He opened his mouth to scream, but a solid gag was thrust between his teeth. Only then did he realize that it was not to be the gun, and that he had missed what little chance he might have had.

The two men held him while he kicked. They let him spend his energy while John put his gun away. As Anthony struggled, he tried to push the gag out with his tongue. His struggling grew weaker, but he was still alive and was still not sure what they intended to do. Perhaps they were simply trying to frighten him. But he had done nothing to deserve it, and this terrified him most of all.

His strength was going. He was not a powerful man, and he was beginning to sag between the two men, who had no problem in holding him. John received a signal from one of the men and stepped forward, but kept to one side and clear of Anthony's lashing feet. The two men partially lowered Anthony so that it was almost impossible for him to kick out with his legs bent under him. John pinched Anthony's nose and cut off the air.

Anthony struggled like a maniac, his head going from side to side in sheer terror and his glasses flying off. He was already largely spent, and his movements tailed off quite quickly. When he collapsed, they lowered him gently, and John still retained a grip on the nose. Afterward they made quite sure he was dead and awkwardly removed the gag. One man retrieved the glasses and jammed them in Anthony's pocket.

John wiped his hands on a handkerchief. "I must get back," he said, glancing at his watch. "You know what to do."

As John went back to his car, seemingly unaffected by the coldblooded silent killing, the two men lifted Anthony's body and carried it through the woods to a small, unused chalk pit. They tossed the corpse over, then one man climbed down after it while the other went back to a nearby car; he returned carrying two cans of gasoline and followed his colleague into the pit.

Anthony was drenched with gas, his open eyes unaware of the

stinging fuel being poured into them. When the cans were empty, the two men climbed up to the ridge where one of them opened a box of matches, jammed most of them between the tray and the box, lit them, and dropped the flaming box down. Anthony exploded in a huge burst of flame. The two men went back to their car where they changed into spare shoes, carefully dropping the chalk-coated ones into a carrier bag that would later be burned. They then brushed all chalk marks from their clothing, each helping the other.

8

NICOLAI GORKIN NEEDED SOMEONE WITH whom to discuss matters, but there was nobody above him in Britain, and Moscow, despite the excellent lines of communication, seemed suddenly remote.

Two men had been killed, always a reluctant step whatever the circumstances, but Anthony had formed a link that could possibly have led back to Gorkin himself. That was understood. The trail back was now dead. But time was passing and nothing had come of it until he received the message that now lay on his desk. The request to be patient, to someone who had taken years to set up various networks, at first seemed ludicrous, and in some ways it was indeed so. But Gorkin's patience held out longest when he pulled the strings himself and knew precisely what he was doing.

In this particular matter he had no control, and yet he had twice sanctioned killing for it. He had to go over it again and again to try to persuade himself that he had so far done the right thing. And General Rogov had agreed. But his position remained weak because he was in the hands of an outsider whom he had never met in spite of all efforts to trace him, and whose note now lay on his desk. He had accepted promises believing them to be genuine and hoping that in the end it would be well worth the wait.

Gorkin was a hard, dedicated, and highly experienced man. A carrot was no good to him unless he knew who held the stick. On this one occasion, he had taken the carrot without that knowledge, but he had not been guided by wishful thinking; there was no such thing in his profession.

Evidence of a bizarre nature had been produced for him, not the kind that would normally be expected. And yet, in its way, it was more solid than the accepted form. And no money had yet changed hands except in one minor respect, so his risks were not financial.

He gazed at the note again. How could he track down the sender? The question was always with him. To discover his identity was to gain direct control, and that was what he must achieve. He ignored the insistent buzz of his intercom while he tried to work out an effective trap.

Walter Clarke had repeatedly tried to do the same, but the only trap he had sprung had tragically misfired. Undeniably, he was dealing with an extremely cunning and relentless person or organization. He stared at his desk, and felt the loneliness of his apartment.

The nature of the attempted blackmail was obviously political, yet because of the method of approach, he had held the feeling that a foreign power was not directly implicated. Recent events, however, had made him wonder again. It was as though he was being pulled in opposite directions at the same time. And he didn't know how to react.

All he could do was to wait, for he had no means by which to communicate. There was perhaps one possible action he could take; it would be unorthodox and risky, but he could see no other course. He would have to be very careful, but it was surely worth a try.

"Come on, "I'll buy you a drink."

Scott stared up from his desk at the unbelievably benign figure of Detective Superintendent Alfred George Bulman. The "Alfred" was never used; Bulman hated the name. There was a smile on the moon face and an unmistakable twinkle in the heavily creased, deep-set eyes. Scott sat rooted; it was difficult to accept the change in the man.

"What's the matter?" Bulman asked pleasantly. "Afraid to be seen with me?"

Scott shook his head. "*Nobody will believe me when I tell them. That's what's griping me. George Bulman offered Spider Scott a drink. Jesus.*"

"We've both grown up, Spider. Bury the hatchet. I'm a good copper and you were once an 'honest' villain. They don't come like that any more. Come on, I'll make it a large one."

As Scott came around the desk, he called an instruction to the tireless Lulu. Before he reached the door, he casually asked Bulman, "Where's Fairfax got to? I've been trying to raise him for three days."

"He's gone away. Asked me to keep an eye on things."

Scott stopped at the door. "*Gone away? Where?*"

"Jamaica, I think. Needed a break."

Scott stopped with his hand on the door handle. "You saying he's run off and left me carrying the can?"

Bulman appeared slightly pained. "You've got *me* to lend you a hand."

"Jesus, I've got a tail outside. Doesn't he care? He lands me in it and then buggers off."

"Let's get that drink. You can complain on the way."

They left the office and turned toward St. Martin's Lane. A wedding was taking place in bright sunshine at St. Martin in the Fields. The wedding group was posing for the cameras between the huge pillars at the top of the steps. Morning suits and expensive dresses; gray top hats and splendid bouquets. A crowd watched at the foot of the steps, swelled by the lunchtime office workers.

Scott and Bulman stepped into the busy street to skirt the crowd. "We could have lost our tail then," Scott pointed out as he jumped back from an approaching bus.

"Your tail, Spider. I haven't got one. You want to get rid of them?"

"Let them stay. They need the practice." They were struggling against the thickening crowd.

"I mean permanently."

"How can you do that?"

"The agency is licensed. I can point out that it will be in their interests to refuse this particular client."

"They'd tell you to get stuffed."

"Not with the yarn I can spin them."

Scott led the way through the double doors of the pub, which was already filling. They eased their way to the bar, and Bulman called for two large Teachers. "On expenses," he explained to Scott with a grin. "Don't want to destroy my mean bastard image."

They struggled with their drinks to a position by the bottle glass windows. Scott was just tall enough to see through the plain glass above the opaque. Almost immediately he noted one of his followers outside stepping back against the bustling human stream. When he turned around he noticed that the ex-copper Barber had come into the bar.

"Well?" Bulman demanded.

"Pulling them off? I pulled them off myself for a bit, but as they're back, Kransouski knows that I know. To hell with it, make it difficult for him."

"I'll see to it."

"He'll try another agency."

"I'd deal with them, too."

"He'll put his own mob on, then."

"You can handle them; they're bum. Cheers." Bulman raised his glass.

Scott gave a wary "cheers." He could not get used to the new image of Bulman. A helpful Bulman. That was difficult to swallow. "Is that what you called about?" he asked suspiciously. He could clearly see the balding patch beneath the sparse hair combed forward. The change in Bulman came in many forms.

"No. That's just a favor. It can be bloody annoying with a dog pack on your tail." He gazed around, sweeping up Barber across the crowded room with barely a glance. He lowered his voice as he said, "I think you're right about Gordon Chesfield. I've changed my mind."

"So the police will reopen?"

"I didn't say the police. I said *I've* changed my mind."

"You *are* the bloody police."

"Yes, well, it's a private opinion. It had to be Naylor. You've been stirring it up there. Well, to be honest, Fairfax filled me in before he left. Soames has requested a transfer to another prison. Reckons his life's in danger."

"Will he get it?"

"Dunno. I think he should stay. Something might break, and if Fuller does top him, it will be no more than he deserves." Bulman sipped sparingly at his drink, gazing up sagely at Scott above the rim. "We might eventually get Naylor, although if everybody up there keeps his head it's doubtful. The best way is the method you used. Sow suspicions among them. I can help stir it by fiddling a transfer for Brooks to another cell. That will leave Naylor worrying his guts out as to why, and he's nowhere to run."

"There's more than that behind it."

Bulman shrugged. "We'll never get the bastards who set it up. Soames won't talk because he'll be done if he does, by us or by them. He'll either get killed or spend the rest of his life inside with enemies. Naylor won't talk anyway. And the real culprits will be behind diplomatic privilege, but give them their due, they've tidied up. Victor Anthony hasn't shown his face for a couple of days."

"Can't you start a search?"

"It's not worth it nationwide. Ties up far too many coppers. Somewhere, sometime, some poor sod will stumble over what's left of him. I hope it won't be a girl." Bulman drained his glass and pointedly passed it to Scott. "Let's just assume he's dead."

"That's that, then," Scott said, disappointed. "They get away with it."

"I didn't say that," Bulman objected. "I wouldn't say a thing like that. Now, are you just going to stand there or are we going to drink? Make it a triple, Spider, it'll be murder getting to the bar again."

"For an English girl you are not bad at all." Claude Denise reached for his shirt.

"Thanks for nothing, darling. You've finished then?" Gloria sat up in bed, hands covering large breasts in a strangely ironical act of modesty. Pay time was over. It was back to nothing for nothing

119

time. She swung shapely legs over the side of the bed and reached, in turn, for bra, panties, and tights. She slipped on her dress before she stood up. A smiling, partially dressed Denise came around the bed to do up her zipper. He gave her a last caress, which she resisted but would not have had she realized that he could have turned ugly at the rebuff. Fortunately, Denise was in a good mood.

Gloria combed her blonde hair and repaired her makeup. She slipped on high-heeled sandals, aware that Denise was watching her all the time. He was beginning to give her the creeps. She reached for her handbag as he said behind her, "You think I will take the money back?"

She could see his reflection in the mirror and noticed a leer that had not been there before. "If you tried that, darling, I'd scream the house down and sling this through the bloody window." She held up a heavy gold compact.

"I believe you would," he agreed, amused. "So you had better go before I try!" He was smiling again, pulling his trousers on.

Gloria collected her coat from the back of the door and gazed around the room. "Is this the best you can do? I'm not used to crummy places like this."

He pulled up his zipper and took a jacket from the back of a chair. "We all know what you're used to, eh? All ceilings look the same, cherie, from where you stare at them." As she opened the door he added, "Come again. My money is better than the room. And I'm an expert lover." He was laughing as she closed the door behind her.

When Gloria had gone, Denise smartened himself, using the mirror she had used, having to stoop to comb his hair. He was tired of the room and of the area. Time and again he had considered going to a first-class hotel and enjoying a luxury he much preferred. It was a matter of self-discipline; he would certainly exercise it for the sake of self-preservation and in order to destroy the one person he hated deeply. Hotels meant registration.

He moved one end of the bed aside and kicked the rumpled rug away. Using a jackknife, he eased up a floorboard. The Colt automatic was still there, together with two packs of cartridges. He checked daily. He replaced the floorboard, put back the rug and the bed. For a few moments he stared down at the hiding place, his face screwed with indecision. He hated leaving the pistol there, and would much prefer to take it with him. That was particularly true now. There was a strong sense of assurance about a gun, a backing for strong dialogue of the kind he was about to engage in.

Denise went to the nearest call box and rang Walter Clarke, M.P. There was no answer from the apartment. He rang the House of Commons. It was evening, but the House might well be sitting, and if Clarke were in the chamber, he would not be called out. Denise left a message with a girl who purported to be Clarke's secretary that a Monsieur Dumain had called. Monsieur Dumain from Amiens. He would ring Monsieur Clarke at home at nine that evening. No, he would not leave a number.

Denise was willing to gamble that, provided Walter Clarke received the message, he would somehow contrive to be at home to take the call whatever the importance of the government debate.

When Denise telephoned precisely at nine, Clarke was there. And from the speed with which the call was answered, he was there solely to receive it. His voice was controlled, nevertheless. Not for the first time, Denise felt a begrudging respect, but hate would quickly override it. He gave a number for Clarke to call in precisely one hour and made him repeat it. He hung up before Clarke could say anymore. The fish had to be brought in carefully.

Denise caught an underground train to Waterloo Station. He had a snack in the bar and a small cognac. At ten minutes to ten he went to a short row of phone booths in the station, lit a Camel cigarette, and waited. At this time, most of the booths were empty. At three minutes to ten, he entered the right-hand end booth as he saw two girls approach searching their handbags for coins.

Clarke called on time, as Denise was certain he would. It was the Frenchman's turn to answer quickly. "Dumain. I want the minutes of yesterday's defense meeting of the Joint Chiefs of Staff or I will release the first bulletin. You have less than two days from midnight tonight. You leave it at the left luggage at Waterloo Station in a Marks and Spencer carrier bag, and you telephone the following number at fourteen hundred the day after tomorrow, and you give me the claim check number. The telephone number is—"

"But I'm not in defense, for God's sake . . ."

"The number is . . . *listen to me.* You make a mistake and it will be the biggest of your life. Well, perhaps the second biggest. Now take this number down." Denise gave another phone booth number, this time at Paddington Station. He hung up as Clarke started to protest again.

Denise stepped from the booth. This was the testing time. Clarke would have had time to call in the police to check the location of the number. Denise would not have given it had he believed that Clarke would do that. But it was necessary to have confirmation of one's own judgment. Clarke was going to be a difficult fish to land; he would fight all the way to the pot. Denise moved away satisfied that nobody was with him. The war was now really on, and he believed that he had just won a major battle.

Willie Scott suffered an apprehension he had not had for a very long time. It was a kind of creeping warning that gave him a slightly sick feeling in the pit of his stomach. It was made worse because he could not quite pinpoint its cause. He knew his visit to Hull had produced an interest in him from old enemies, and that he had skated on thin ice up there, but he did not believe that was the cause of his anxiety. Being satisfied that Naylor had killed Chesfield was far removed from proving it, and, like Bulman, he did not think it ever would be proved. So in spite of his involvement, he did not see himself as any great danger to anyone. Not yet anyway.

But Scott did not ignore intuitions. They had served him well. By the time he reached home that night, he realized that Bulman had moved very quickly against the Hammerton Agency; his tail had gone. So at a time when he should be feeling happier, he had become far more cautious.

He greeted Maggie with a huge hug. "It's good to see you, love," he murmured into her ear.

Maggie stood back from him. As he reached for her again, she said quietly, "I can't go. I'm due no holiday and I'm not going to call in sick." She leaned forward to peck him on the cheek.

He stared at her. Why was it he could never fool her? "Now you've raised it, I think it a good idea."

"There," she claimed in triumph. "I'm not going. I like my job, and I'm not ducking out unless you can give me a very, very good reason."

"You could be in danger."

"Over this Chesfield business? Don't be silly. The person you think did it is already in prison."

"There's much more to it." Scott pleaded, "I've got a feeling that it's about to get out of hand."

"Darling, it always seems worse when you don't know quite what you're worried about. If I was away I'd be sick wondering what was happening to you."

It had always come down to this. He tried not to overplay by keeping his voice down. "They might try to get at me through you. They know it's my weak spot."

"They? Kransouski? So I'll not take lifts or candy from strange men. I'm not stupid."

"No." Scott held his arms out to implore her. "But you close your eyes because of me when you should be keeping them open. Please, love. Speak to George Bulman. He'll be around about nine."

"*George Bulman?*" Maggie held her hands over her ears as if they hurt her. "You hate him. You'd never have him in the house."

Scott shrugged. It was difficult to explain. "He's changed. We've all changed. He's filling in for Fairfax."

Maggie flapped her arms helplessly. "He's a better reason for my going than the one you've given me. I don't know anything anymore." Maggie gave Scott a perplexed stare before entering the kitchen. Scott was well aware that he had failed to persuade her to leave.

Cancellation of the arrangement came with the evening's telephone report. Don Hammerton, managing director of the detective agency, made the call personally. Kransouski listened attentively, knowing that he was hearing a string of lies.

"Well, sir, for one thing your account is still outstanding. It was agreed on a weekly basis and 25 percent in advance."

Gorkin was a fool, reflected Kransouski. Holding up the money only drew a focus. "I'll see that it's paid by tomorrow. It will come by hand."

"It's not only that, sir. We are tying up too many men on one operation. And there's another thing. The police have been seen with Scott and some of our men are ex-policemen. It raises a risk of recognition."

"What you are saying is, that no matter what I say or what I pay, you can no longer accommodate me?"

"That's about it, sir. Perhaps in a week or two . . ."

Kransouski hung up. Pressure had been put on the Hammerton Agency. Scott did not have the power. The police did. And a Detective Superintendent Bulman had been seen with Scott. The name stirred in Kransouski's mind, but he was certain that he had not met him at any time. There were other agencies. He reached for the yellow pages; he would call the next morning, for by now they would be closed. It concerned him that he had no immediate coverage of Scott's movements. And it worried him that pressure had been brought to bear.

By noon the next day, Kransouski realized the extent of that pressure. No main agency would take him as a client. All said the same thing; they had not the men available for a conscientious round-the-clock surveillance.

The blockage made Kransouski thoughtful. He would have to call on the help he had first used. This did not now seem so objectionable. The men were neither good nor sufficiently well practiced to fool someone like Scott, but Scott had known he was being watched, even by the more expert Hammerton staff. So why should it matter anymore? Let him know. It might unnerve him.

Kransouski caught himself in mid-smile. Unless Scott had changed character completely, he would not be unnerved so easily; he might even enjoy it. Perhaps it was time to come face to face with Scott.

Maggie had poured drinks for them, but it was taking her time to get used to the friendly liaison that now seemed to exist between Scott and Bulman. She did not trust Bulman, although he had certainly mellowed from what she recalled of him.

Bulman produced a stapled list of Gordon Chesfield's friends and acquaintances. He glanced uneasily at Scott, then at Maggie, trying to avoid looking at her legs, and waved the list. "People we know that Chesfield knew. I've been looking into their backgrounds over the last few days. A few have skeletons but nothing significant. Did Bluie come up with anything?"

"Rang this afternoon. Not a whisper about Chesfield. Anywhere."

Bulman scanned the list, flicking the pages over slowly. "Nothing here either that matches the gay theory. There are one or two, but there is no evidence of any affair with Chesfield. On the contrary, he rarely saw them. But he did deal with them, usually by letter or telephone, in business."

"So the list is useless?"

Bulman smiled crookedly. "That depends on what it hides. When you look into people's backgrounds, almost always there are one or two surprises. The question is, what link is there with what happened to Chesfield, and why did he murder Duncan Seddon, a man it would seem that he had not previously known. There's no evidence of blackmail at all."

Bulman waved the sheets. "There is one man here with a fascinating background. I don't think it adds anything, and it probably confuses, but it's worth relating as a matter of interest. Walter Clarke, M.P., Minister at the Foreign Office. Future extremely bright. In a recent poll he was picked as the most likely to become Prime Minister during the next decade. Young as politicians go."

Bulman folded the sheets and placed his head against the back of the chair to gaze at the ceiling. "He was born prematurely in the middle of an air raid on Amiens Prison in February 1944. The raid was ours, to release prisoners from jail who might be forced to talk to the Gestapo. Hundreds escaped and a good many were killed. So were some Germans. The mother died, having given birth in the freezing cold in a bombed-out house. She was shot, apparently to save her from further suffering. The resistance group that found her took the baby and the woman friend who had helped the mother. The baby survived, obviously, but it was touch and go at the time."

"How could they place the parentage?"

"That was never in doubt. The mother was Paulette Dumain, a young, passionate resistance worker who was shacked up with a dashing young English captain who had been dropped in France to help the resistance. He did well, too. Survived two years before capture. Paulette was also captured. The raid did not save her, and he was one of those who was injured during it. He was recaptured and released after the war ended.

"His name was Gerald Clarke, son of Colonel Austin Clarke, a peppery old devil who lost an arm at Ypres in the First World War. Gerald knew that Paulette was pregnant and that the child was his once he caught up with the news. He was shattered over Paulette's death, particularly the way she died. It was apparently very much an affair of the heart. Like you and Maggie."

"Obviously he found the baby."

"The baby was kept by a girl called Jeannette Renore. She was the one who helped at the birth. With the aid of her own mother, to whom the resistance took her, she raised the child until Gerald Clarke finally caught up with her. Jeannette was able to tell him exactly what had happened.

"There was an unfortunate twist to it. An American officer named Stacey was one of the escapees. He had the bright idea of dressing as a German officer and simply strolling away. It didn't work out that way. He found Paulette and Jeannette and helped them as much as he could. One of the French resistance who came on the scene thought that he was a German and shot him, leaving him for dead. But he didn't die. He suffered and his story is almost as bizarre as the other, but he survived. So far as I know he's still alive."

"What's this got to do with Chesfield?"

Bulman jerked himself from reverie. "Nothing. It's simply background to one of Chesfield's friends. They were at Oxford together. Close at one time but inquiries show nothing sinister."

"Presumably Captain Clarke brought the baby back to England with him?"

"His father, the Colonel, apparently bust a fuse. He didn't want any grandchild out of wedlock and despised his son for it. He moved heaven and earth and spent a ton of money, which he could well afford, on trying to disprove the parentage. But it was too cut and dried. There was no funny business and Clarke knew Jeannette and her family very well. They were much respected. She was a brave girl. In fact, she was awarded the Legion of Honor. So was Gerald Clarke."

"And absolutely nothing to do with Chesfield?" Scott asked again.

"How can it be? Where or how Walter Clarke was born has nothing at all to do with anything. There were press articles after the war. Made good copy. They looked for scandal but there was none, except the out of wedlock bit. Doesn't matter these days."

"Makes your nose itch, doesn't it?" Scott observed.

Bulman riffled the sheets. "It's all been out before."

"Even so." Scott intertwined his fingers and leaned forward. "Kransouski. Walter Clarke—he could be a top-priority target."

"Kransouski came over *after* the event. My guess is he came to keep an eye on you, his old enemy, who went to Hull and started to stir things up. In spite of him once having you tortured, you still beat him, and he'll do anything to get back at you. Anyway, Clarke would take a hell of a lot of bending. My check suggests that there's nothing strong enough. If there were compromising photos, he's the kind to order a dozen copies and insist on them being framed. And money wouldn't do it; he was left a bundle. He has no wife for them to lean on. Funny business."

"Was he close to Chesfield?"

"Not in recent years. They did meet occasionally, but their closest liaison was at Oxford. And I repeat that it stood up to inquiry. I can't see a connection. There are too many bloody big gaps."

"But your nose itches, too?"

"That could be through lack of booze." Bulman fiddled with his empty glass hoping that it would catch Scott's eye.

Scott took the hint and poured fresh drinks. "You going to poke around some more?" he asked.

"I'll go to Oxford. See what's been missed." Bulman stared critically at his fresh drink. "Would you go to America for me?"

Scott almost dropped his glass. "America? Where's that?"

"I know this is your turf and that you prefer to eat your continental under Maggie's magic touch. But don't kid me. You're a travel agent; you've been around."

"Who pays?"

Bulman ran a finger around his collar. He avoided looking at Scott. "I dare say I can drum up expenses. Provided that you get yourself a discounted ticket through your business."

Scott struggled to find a word sufficiently strong.

"Look at it this way," Bulman said reasonably. "I can go to America and you can go to Oxford. But you'd be out of your element among the dons."

Scott glanced toward Maggie, who refused to help him. "Where in America?"

"Just over the pond."

"To see this bloke Stacey? Is it worth it?"

"That's why I suggested a discounted ticket. If we do the job, we do it right. A lot of legwork will be wasted." Bulman stood up, convinced that he would not get another drink. He drained his glass, studied it to see if he had missed a droplet. "We're in business then?"

Scott felt a trace of warning. He had to remind himself of old encounters with this man. "Why me? Why not your own crowd?"

"Well, I think Fairfax would prefer it to be nonofficial. Perhaps he doesn't want the word to get around."

"But Fairfax keeps telling us he's retired. And he's pushed off at a crucial moment."

Bulman reluctantly put his glass down. "He has retired. But his mind hasn't. I think he's pushed off to confuse the Home Office. He didn't enjoy being baulked by them after the service he's given to the country."

"All right," Scott agreed. "I've got some clearing up to do first. A day or two. My visa's okay."

"Good." Bulman held out a hand. "Be strange working together. Always wanted to study your M.O."

They shook hands to cement the agreement, and Bulman said goodnight to Maggie. When Bulman had gone Scott said, "While I'm over there, you'll have to go away."

Maggie did not reply. She was sitting straightbacked and tense, as if she had seen a preview of the future.

9

CLAUDE DENISE WALKED SLOWLY FROM newsstand to newsstand, buying a newspaper at each. He went down to the men's room and reappeared moments later. He crossed to the entrance of platform two then moved along to the doorway of the FOTO FAST shop, almost opposite the baggage claim office. Walter Clarke was standing by the advertising triangle, halfway between Denise and the baggage claim office.

Clarke could not stay there all day. Unless he had made arrangements, he would have to get back to the Foreign Office or the House, whatever his duties demanded.

It did not matter anyway. When Clarke had deposited the Marks and Spencer carrier bag another man had joined him at the counter to leave a suitcase; that man had received the claim ticket following directly after the one Clarke had taken. An hour later the same man had returned claiming to have lost his ticket but was able to give the number and a description of the bag. Denise had already received the typesheets and had mailed them off.

Intermittently Denise had called at the station to see what action Clarke might take. That Clarke was making such a hash of observation did not surprise him. And it indicated that Clarke was still reluctant to call in help. He stiffened. It belatedly occurred to him that there might be another reason. Not quite so sure of himself, he watched Clarke for a little longer, then left the station.

Walter Clarke accepted that what he was doing was futile. And yet what else could he do? The man who called himself Dumain would have worked it all out, and yet on the basis of "you never know," Clarke was compelled to make what effort he could. He could have used an agency, but he was too well known.

So many people had been to the counter that further surveillance had become impossible. Clarke had decided to leave when he saw a woman approach, fumbling in her handbag. She stood in front of the counter, her back to Clarke who could not see what she received.

Suddenly she turned and he saw that she was holding a Marks and Spencer bag. He broke into a run, realized that he was behaving foolishly and immediately slowed to a quick walk. He approached side on as she headed for the exit next to the video library. Unable to stop himself Clarke raced forward again, stretched out a hand to grab the woman's arm then saw that she also had a small attaché case and a second carrier. He was almost sick on the spot. Instinctively he knew that the carrier was not his.

The woman saw him only at the last moment and thought he was about to attack her. She reeled back, case held in front of her like a shield, eyes wide and mouth opening to scream.

Clarke halted at once, red-faced and feeling stupid.

"I'm so sorry," he blurted out. "I thought you were somebody else. I'm so very sorry." He backed away flustered and confused, and desperately hoping that he had not been recognized from one of his television appearances. He turned and headed for the nearest exit.

Outside the station he leaned against the wall. He still felt sick from shame and shock. For an awful moment he thought a passerby was about to ask him if he was all right, and he pulled himself together quickly. But he was shaken.

What a mess. What a bloody amateurish thing to do. His own inadequacy struck him most. A boy scout would have done better. He chided himself ceaselessly. What would he have done if the carrying bag had still been there? Grabbed it? So why put it there?

Struck the woman if she had struggled? The episode made him shiver. He would have tried to follow her, he told himself. But that was more easily said than done. Anyway, he had panicked.

He did not even have the satisfaction of knowing that his blackmailer had missed the incident. In his tormented mind, everyone at the station had seen it. He sought the taxi line and tagged onto the end, knowing that if he did not do better he was doomed. He needed help.

Claude Denise reached his room and was annoyed that he had been so hasty in sending off the parcel. He sat on his bed and thought of Walter Clarke waiting at the station. Suddenly the image gave him no comfort. Clarke might well be an idiot when it came to surveillance, but in other respects he could be very sharp. Denise wondered if he had for once underestimated his man. He tried to recall the contents of the documents. They had all been photocopies and certainly related to military matters, figures, plans, and prospects, but really they had been mumbo jumbo to him. Yet he had satisfied himself that they related to defense. Perhaps he was worrying too much, but he was finding it increasingly difficult to remain cool.

Naylor was worried; not to the point of desperation, for it was unlikely that that could happen to anyone as coldblooded as he. He had taken an opportunity to see Soames and to remind him that Brooks wanted hush money. He satisfied Soames that Brooks knew nothing that could be used as evidence, but by fixing him with a sum of money, slipping it into his account or a numbered account abroad, it would keep him both happy and quiet; it would also, of course, implicate him.

Since then two things had happened to Soames. Garry Fuller was being increasingly intimidating. Soames had tried to speak to Fuller, to get him into a reasonable mood in order to find out what was really troubling him, but Fuller would not listen. Soames could be clever with words and Fuller knew it. Fuller had no intention of being talked out of what he increasingly believed.

Soames's application to the governor for a transfer to another prison had been refused. The great difficulty was for him to put up a convincing case, but if he told the governor that Fuller was waiting for an opportunity to kill him, he would have to state why. Fuller would be interviewed, and God knows what he would say. Soames had repeatedly gone over it. He was in a trap. Perhaps, eventually, Fuller would calm down, but there was no sign of it yet.

The second thing that had gone wrong was the nonappearance of Victor Anthony. Surely if he could not come, another contact would be arranged? With some considerable concern, Soames began to feel that the contact had been withdrawn completely. He was on his own. He could cope with that, he was satisfied that he had been paid for his part, but now there was no way that he could arrange for Brooks to benefit. And that could be dangerous.

He tried to explain to Naylor that the contact had failed him. Naylor did not believe him. Soames pointed out that he was in danger as well as Naylor if Brooks started to talk; Naylor reluctantly accepted this. But meanwhile, Brooks was agitating. So far, Naylor had curtailed him with threats. And now there was talk of separating them. One of the guards had tipped Brooks off that he was to be accommodated in another cell. Suspicion, fear, and threats grew. And Soames found himself a center of attention.

As Kransouski strolled up St. Martin's Lane, he refused to open his umbrella for a mere drizzle. He swung the umbrella like an Englishman and his bowler hat belonged to the City of London, yet there would always be an air about him of old St. Petersburg. He announced himself to Charlie Hewitt with the barest trace of accent.

When Kransouski stepped into Scott's office, Scott was already standing, not from politeness but in physical readiness. His middle desk drawer was open, a heavy bone ruler close to hand.

It was difficult for Scott to believe what he saw. How many more old friends and enemies was he destined to meet? Kransouski greeted Scott gravely with the slightest of bows, propped his umbrella against the desk, and carefully placed his folded gloves on top. He did not offer his hand, for he knew that Scott would refuse to take it. He smiled coldly, opened his jacket wide. "No gun. No weapon of any kind. And no strings, Mr. Scott. You can safely close your drawer and put away whatever it is you were ready to strike me with."

It was as though they were meeting after the shortest of partings instead of a gap of years. Scott closed the drawer and the two men sat down simultaneously, warily eyeing each other.

"You haven't changed, Willie. Not at all, except perhaps for a little extra weight."

"I got a lot of exercise running away from your goons, Boris." Scott had no idea what Kransouski's first name was; he had thought of him as Boris from the outset, and the Russian had not corrected him. "How's Fyodor?"

"Alas, dead. I'm surprised you remember him."

How could he forget; Fyodor had tried to kill him more than once. "You've worn well," he acknowledged reluctantly. "As this can't be a social call, why not get to the point."

Kransouski gazed around the office without wrinkling his nose, but giving an impression that he should. "You have not done too well in all these years. That's a pity."

"I've done a bloody sight better than if I'd been in your eternal prison camp, matey. Now get on with it. Sadistic bastards like you have a bad effect on me."

"You're very unforgiving, Willie." Kransouski shook his head regretfully, and Scott had to remind himself of what he had suffered at this man's hands. "You were always a brash young man," Kransouski added, "but you are direct."

"That must be tough for you when you're used to so many lies."

"I thought we might be of help to one another." Kransouski's cool eyes did not leave Scott's. "Let's not hedge. I've had you followed. We both know it. At the moment you are roaming loose, but I can still provide a team, not polished, but capable. You would know but that would no longer matter."

Scott was amused. "You want me to save you a lot of time and money and for me to provide you with a daily report of my movements?"

"Why not? Wouldn't it be better than chasing through the Civil Service Stores every time you wanted to lose my men?"

Scott smiled, shaking his head in disbelief. "You want it typewritten or longhand?"

"Willie, I've had you under surveillance, but I have not the slightest idea why. I have absolutely no inkling of where it is supposed to lead."

"So who do you report to?"

"You know I won't answer that." Kransouski waved a finger. "You were trapped by your own people once. Perhaps it's happening again. But this time, it is happening also to me. I don't like it. And you already know the feeling."

"So?"

"Why have I been asked to keep an eye on you?"

"How the hell do I know?"

"But you must know that what you have done has aroused interest. Can you not tell me that much?"

"I must be going crazy. You're honestly expecting me to help you? Do you realize the trouble you've caused?"

"Come now. I've livened your day. You've discovered you're as sharp as ever you were."

"Now you're lying. I reckon it took me two days to suss you out. I'm slower. Look, this is going to lead nowhere. It was stupid of you to come."

"Perhaps." Kransouski remained quite still, hands lightly clasped, shrewd eyes steady. "You know the feeling when operating on misinformation. That is what is happening to me. It's possible that it's also happening to you. We might need each other, as unlikely as that sounds. Think about it. I haven't been used in this way for many years. So why now? Because I once knew you? That was a long time ago. I don't think you've operated for a long time either. Isn't that a strange coincidence?"

"I'm not operating now," Scott insisted. "I did a small favor for someone. That's it. Finished. My business is here."

"Which will account for your absence from it so often? Willie, why the photographs at Hull? Why is that place the focus?"

Scott thought about it. He took his time. "Are you saying that you don't know, or are you trying to get confirmation of what you already know?"

Kransouski recognized that this was no time to lie. Scott was as skilled with lies as he was. And there was no need. "Something is going on here of which I have no knowledge. I have asked for it and have been refused. For telling you that alone I could be shot."

"I'm not running a tape and you know it. You're not risking anything." It was a mental toss of the coin. There could be advantages in telling Kransouski, or it could go the other way. Scott gave up reasoning and followed his instinct. "We believe a man called Chesfield was murdered in Hull on the instructions of your crowd. The inquest said it was suicide. A Home Office inquiry concluded the same."

"And they put you in to tap the grapevine?"

"Nicely said, Boris. That's my job exactly."

Kransouski was silent for quite a while. He seemed to be perturbed, his eyes unusually reflective. He reached for his umbrella and placed both hands on top as if he needed the support. "You will understand if I say that your claim is ludicrous. We would never stoop to murder in your country, particularly in circumstances so bizarre."

"Of course not," Scott said drily.

"Who and what was this man Chesfield?"

"You do your own homework. Ask the bloke who's holding out on you. Now what do I get in return?"

"Do you know why this man died?"

"No idea, and it's not my business. It's one you've got away with. Be grateful. I'm still waiting for the mutual help bit."

Kransouski nodded slowly, but he was deep in thought, stooped forward over the umbrella. "There is no information I can give in return because I have none. But I will stop the surveillance."

Scott was immediately suspicious. He had not really imparted information for a return, he could not trust Kransouski that far, but in order to cause dissent and distrust among the Russians. Kransouski's offer surprised him and he tried to see beyond it. "I'll know if they're there," he stated simply.

"Who better?" Kransouski rose slowly, for once showing his age. He straightened, gazed reflectively at Scott, but his thoughts were elsewhere. "Now at least I know why I was designated to observe your movements."

"And now you know what a waste of time it was." But as

Kransouski crossed to the door, Scott was not as confident as he sounded. He wondered if he had made a mistake; Kransouski had offered too much too soon.

Nicolai Gorkin refused Kransouski's request to see him at the Embassy. In his view, they were meeting too often. He considered that Kransouski was in danger of breaking his Polish trade delegation image, and that could implicate Gorkin himself. Of necessity, Kransouski had to attend the various trade meetings and this involved traveling to the industrial midlands and the north.

After a factory visit in Sheffield, Kransouski met with one of Gorkin's men. They sat side by side in a limousine, the glass partition closed behind the chauffeur.

Kransouski's request was quite simple. "I want some women trained in surveillance," he told his stone-faced companion. "Not many. I don't need a team operation, one woman at a time provided they are frequently changed."

"A woman would be noticed," Gorkin's man pointed out. "Particularly if she's attractive."

Kransouski hid his irritation. "A *man* would notice," he replied patiently, "although I doubt that you are able to provide a bevy of beauties. If you have any, you keep them well hidden."

"I'll pass the request on."

"It's not a request. You do as I say. My orders are from Moscow. And to allay your puerile doubts, it's not a man I want followed but a woman." Kransouski turned his head, smiling thinly. "A woman being followed might be sensitive to a man's presence, wouldn't you say? Particularly if he's attractive."

The message was in the obituaries column of the *Daily Telegraph*. It took Claude Denise a little time to work out the simple code in order to extract the telephone number, day, and time that he should call. He was now used to this method of contact and it suited him well, for it worked and it kept the two parties apart. It was now three days since he had sent the parcel to the agreed address, and the response was faster than he had expected although he scanned the *Telegraph* daily.

The call was scheduled for the day after publication, and if that failed, for two more consecutive days at the same time. Phone booth to phone booth. He approved. Only once had the number been busy, and he had waited for several minutes. As an ultra precaution, he used a different phone booth each time, and well away from his living area. Nor did he leave it to chance; he always plotted his booths in advance and checked that they had not been vandalized, which was why he chose the better districts.

Kensington was one such area, and it amused Denise that it was so close to the Soviet Embassy. He dialed the number exactly on time. The voice that answered was thick with accent, but the man understood well enough and was able to make his point slowly. After the usual identity skirmish, the voice said to Denise, "The documents you sent are useless. They are over two years old."

Denise gripped the telephone in fury. In his anger he replied in French. "Don't lie to me, you fool. And don't try that again."

The voice patiently repeated, "Over two years old. The information is accurate, but we already know it. Your man has tricked you."

Denise thought furiously. "If you are right, he won't have tricked me for long." The blood was racing through his brain.

"It would be much better if you let us handle this directly. We are skilled at it and you will not lose by it. It will save you a great deal of trouble."

"Oh no you don't. The control is mine, and it stays mine. Only that way can I be sure of a fair deal." Denise wanted time to think and a telephone call would not provide that time.

The voice observed in its tortuous English, "We already know who the man is. We agree that he is valuable, but it will not work like this. You will never get the best out of him."

The doubt and the challenge restored some of Denise's shattered calm. "You might think you know who he is. It won't help you at all. Leave it with me. I'll make contact in the usual way."

More quickly, the voice said, "Don't destroy it. Use patience. These things can take time."

Denise replied brusquely, "I know how to handle it. I've produced something, haven't I? He's already committed himself, even if it is old stuff. And I'm not just taking your word for that." He hung up and some of his earlier fury returned. Clarke had made a fool of him. The big temptation was to make Clarke pay dearly for that.

Well, Clarke would eventually, very dearly indeed, but the Russian was right. Keep cool, as difficult as that might be. He told himself again that it was a game of nerves he could not ultimately lose. There could only be one loser. As Denise left the phone booth, this basic thought enabled him to come to terms with a temporary setback. He had known that it would not be easy. And as a last resort he held the means to destroy Walter Clarke.

Denise went to the West End Air France office and booked a flight to Paris for the following day.

She ran a hand over his chest. "You're dark," she said, "and muscular." Her long, painted fingernails splayed out toward his chin, and she lifted her head from the pillow to gaze at his face. "You exude strength, darling. Everything about you. You must use the Parliament gym a lot."

"No. I play squash a lot. And tennis when I can. And I played second row at Oxford."

"Is that rowing?"

He smiled, captivated by what he saw, but filled with humiliation and apprehension at what had just happened. "Rugby football," he explained. She had told him not to worry, that these things could happen. Well it had never happened to him before, and he was worried sick. He gazed at her; she was ravishingly beautiful and eager for him, even now after such disappointment.

He took her and kissed her and knew that it would be even worse than before. He broke away, panting and frustrated because he did not understand what was happening to him. And Susan was not one who was slow to help.

"Leave it," she said softly, touching his lips with her fingers. "It will make it worse if you try too hard."

"God Almighty, I shouldn't need to try at all with you."

He sat up and she placed her head on his shoulder. "What's on your mind, darling? What's worrying you?"

He put an arm around her. It was crazy to be like this. "Worrying?"

She lifted her head. "This is not physical, it couldn't be. I know you too well. Walter, something's on your mind."

Was this his future? Was this how it was going to be? He kissed

Susan lightly on the forehead. God forbid. He had not heard from Dumain for days, and he had been scanning the newspapers far more than duty demanded.

The problem was lack of knowledge. Dumain was an unknown quantity. If he could put a face to him, a character, he would know better how to deal with him. Yet he had no regrets in having taken the course he had. It was vital to test the strength of the opposition, even if it meant ruin, but if he really believed that he would not have taken such a step.

"You're miles away," Susan observed. "And I don't take that as a compliment."

Oh God. He turned to her. "Forgive me. You're quite right. I *do* have something on my mind." He smiled at her. "Otherwise I'd have to be raving mad, wouldn't I?"

"I hope it's not another woman, my darling."

Clarke began to laugh quietly. "If only it were so simple." His laughter grew until it became almost wild and uncontrollable. And as he laughed, tears began to prick his eyes, the tension flowed from his body, and she felt him begin to respond.

Willie Scott's common denominator with the gangster Rex Reisen was his belief in his own country. His car was British, and he would fly nothing but British to New York. He had nothing against the others, but at all levels his sense of loyalty was virtually indestructible.

Before leaving for Heathrow Airport, he had contacted Detective Superintendent George Bulman with a personal plea to keep an eye on Maggie while he was away. Maggie had refused to budge from the apartment. Bulman had promised to have her protected so far as he could. They both knew that police protection was thin to any determined person. It was the best that could be done.

As the 747 took off, Scott sat in tourist class, still worried about Maggie. His feelings had been growing stronger since he had seen Kransouski. He reclined his seat and stretched his long legs. Bulman had refused to pay for first class on Concorde, and had been alarmed when Scott had explained that discounted tickets required proper application forms, which took time to approve. Public funds had provided a full fare, and Bulman would have to justify the cost. The fact that he could merely pointed out to Scott that there were probably aspects of the case that Bulman was keeping to himself.

Scott had positioned himself in the middle row of seats. He hated flying, and by sitting well away from the windows he could try to forget the emptiness outside. This was odd because he had a strong head for heights no matter how far from the ground as long as he was directly connected to it. He paid for the headphones and watched the film, trying to forget the vast, deep stretch of the Atlantic Ocean below him. Which raised another oddity because he was a superb swimmer.

Scott was well aware of his complexes. There was nothing he or anybody else could do about them, but they contributed largely to his charm and his unpredictability. He was not at all sure why George Bulman had not elected to go to New York himself, unless he felt that official police presence would have to be cleared and that official interest was best kept hidden. Meanwhile, Scott drank more than he should and ate everything that came his way, anything to fill in the time and to help him stop wondering how this huge monstrosity of a plane stayed up.

After they landed at Kennedy and gone through customs, Scott took a cab to Brooklyn. It was some time since he had visited New York, and he had an affinity for it, as most townsfolk do. He chatted with the cab driver as the place unfolded in white and brown patches and the buildings grew as they progressed. It was strangely colder than London.

General Lorne Stacey lived in a Victorian house that rested in one of the quiet old spots of Brooklyn. The house was big but hemmed in, and somehow Scott felt that an American general should have something much grander, a ranch or something out West.

Scott paid off the cab, gave a wink to some watching children, and climbed the steps to the big front door, which had an old-fashioned bell pull. He yanked the chain and the peals were like a fire alarm from inside.

"Mr. Scott?"

It was as though the man had been waiting behind the door. He wore baggy slacks to cover a noticeable paunch, and he was shorter than Scott had expected. Blue eyes smiled from a chunky face that

140

was topped by an unruly mass of graying hair. A loose, canvas jacket partly covered an open-necked check shirt.

"General Stacey?" Scott was not sure.

"Did you expect me in uniform?" Stacey held out a hand and Scott increased the pressure of his own before his fingers could be crushed. "The uniform wouldn't fit me now anyway. Come in. You're on time. Dump your case in the hall."

Scott followed the stocky figure of the general down a hall passageway; a door was opened for him to enter. It was a large bright living room full of old and comfortable armchairs with an ashtray next to each one. The vague smell of tobacco suggested the general smoked a pipe. Tapestries hung on the walls, and a cabinet contained old china. Scott realized that he was eyeing the place in his old capacity. He saw no security locks on the windows, no alarms.

"Sit anywhere. I've got it fixed so that I don't get too fond of any one chair." And then shrewdly Stacey asked, "You think I should be wired up?"

Scott sank into a chair, still looking around. "You've got some good stuff. You should take care of it."

Stacey sat opposite Scott and pulled out a pipe. "They know me around here."

It's the ones who don't you want to worry about. People talk. Believe me, I know."

"You're a cop?"

"I was a burglar." Scott grinned. "I'd like to take a look before I leave. At the stuff. Then I'll tell you how to protect it."

Stacey laughed loudly. "I like you. You don't pull punches. But this is not what you crossed the Atlantic for. By the way, have you eaten?"

"On the plane. I'll probably go back tonight."

"Like hell you will. I have many good friends in England and have had too many good times there to let you get away that easy. Tonight we go to Manhattan and do the town. I can still drink and eat like a horse. I hope you can. Now tell me what you want to know." Stacey lighted his pipe as he listened to Scott relate the story of Gordon Chesfield's role as an accessory to murder and his subsequent demise.

Stacey did not interrupt at any point, but when Scott had finished he asked, "So you're chasing up the background of anyone this guy Chesfield knew? Walter Clarke being one of them. You a cockney?"

"Not quite. Outside the hearing of Bow Bells. I don't think I talk like a cockney."

Stacey waved his pipe. "I'm losing touch. Without being offensive, why is an ex-con looking into the background of a British Foreign Minister?"

"I was asked to do it."

"Who by?" As Scott hesitated, Stacey blew out a stream of smoke and added, "Look, I was in the OSS, forerunner to the CIA. I was bound to ask."

"Then you'll have heard of Sir Stuart Halliman?"

"Stu? Heard of him? I know him. *He* sent you?"

"Indirectly."

"But he's out of the game. Like me. Retired."

"He can't get used to the idea."

Stacey was watching Scott closely. "That's him all right. Clever. We had a few words from time to time. Awkward cuss."

"No comment."

"Okay. Sit back and I'll tell you the story of when I put on a German uniform, which hung like a sack, and thought I could just walk away from trouble."

As Stacey talked, Scott built up another picture of the man: younger, courageous, determined. Scott's gaze slipped to a photograph on top of a bureau and guessed that he was seeing Stacey as he had appeared forty years ago. The general was still forceful, and as he unfolded his story, he became slightly animated. It became clear that he had lost some good and brave friends at that time, and that this was an occasion to remember them. Scott had a glimpse of a period in recent history that he had only read about or seen documented on a screen. The man facing him, who was digging into memories that would always be there, had been an active part of that scene, and his descriptions were graphic. Scott felt the cold and the snow and heard the first cries of a tiny baby who was to live against all odds.

A silence followed Stacey's recounting of the prison bombing and the breakout, and his pipe stayed steady in his hand while he slowly brought his mind back to the present. And then he said, "We read of different reasons for that bombing now. It was unfortunate because many of our own were killed, but the prison walls were weak and the goddam bombs were skidding off the ice and ricocheting right through them. But hundreds escaped, and I was one of them in spite of being plugged." He rubbed his stomach. "Still plays up in this weather."

"So Walter Clarke was the baby?"

"Well, the baby became Walter Clarke. I knew his father well. Good man. We worked together in the field. It was tragic that Paulette Dumain should have died like that. It was brutal, but perhaps necessary. The Germans were searching everywhere."

"And there were no problems that you know of?"

"About the baby? Jeannette Renore took care of it. None better. It all worked out in the end. Clarkey caught up with his son and took him to England. Grandpa Clarke was the problem. He didn't want the baby in the family. An oddball, the old man. Hated the French. Claimed that he had personally been at war with them all his life. Blamed them for everything that went wrong. He wasn't liked. His wife tried to divorce him, and Clarkey would have left home but for the child and for the inheritance he would one day receive." Stacey drew on the neglected pipe before it went out. He fiddled with a box of matches. "Young Walter's done well then? Being earmarked for even higher honors. A pity his father didn't live to see it."

Scott said nothing. Stacey was still recounting, bringing events up to date.

"I'm surprised you've come all this way to find out about him. You could have looked up Jeannette Renore in France. I believe she's still alive, although the last I heard of her she was sick, in a nursing home."

"Perhaps they want a rounded picture. Everything they can get hold of."

"Well, nice as it is to meet you, you've wasted your time. In spite of the strange background, it's all cut and dried. I met young Walter a few times after the war. He was a bright boy, full of promise even then. The only person he resented, was afraid of even, was his grandfather. They never got along together at any time, although his grandmother cherished him. I think she's still alive, too. She was a good deal younger than her husband, but she must be getting on." Stacey pointed the stem of his pipe at Scott.

"You must know that. Easier from there than here."

"I know nothing at all."

"Well that figures, if it's anything to do with Stu Halliman. How many more have you got to look into?"

"Three or four," Scott lied. "They're the easy ones."

"And is any of this going to help?"

Scott took the warning; Stacey had a right to be skeptical.

"I doubt it. I'm very grateful for what you've told me but I don't think it will add a thing toward Chesfield's murder."

"Who says he was murdered?"

"I do. And he was."

Stacey inclined his head. "There's no answer to that. You've got a tough one. Two murders and nobody knows why?"

Scott resisted the prompting. He had said nothing of Russian involvement, but the mention of Sir Stuart would produce its own thought waves in Stacey's mind.

"By the way, did you ever find the missing dossiers or identity tags?"

"No. I never found out who took them. The group scattered once Jeannette settled the baby in. I hope they were used sensibly."

Stacey rapped his pipe on a glass ashtray, and Scott considered it remarkable that both pipe and tray stood up to the treatment. "Ever approached Manhattan over Brooklyn Bridge at night?"

"Once only."

"What did you think?"

"It's like approaching another planet. A galaxy of lights. Nothing like it back home."

"No. Well, you've plenty we like to see. Have a short nap, then a shower, then we'll go out. If I can think of anything else, I'll tell you."

Two hours later, while Scott was absent, Stacey went to a small book-lined study at the back of the house and pushbuttoned a telephone number. When he was answered, he said, "Is Jim Cernik back from lunch?" Stacey smiled. "Now, now, we all know Jim

144

makes a point of getting back by four. It's General Stacey. Put me through."

When Cernik came on the line, Stacey exclaimed, "Jim? Lorne. Small job for you. Do a rundown on an English guy called Scott. Willie Scott. Ex-con. Base, London. Says he was sent by Stu Halliman; yes, that old devil's still around. I must go see him some time. Dig as deep as you can and go back as far as you can. Check description. Height, six feet plus. Weight, about a hundred and ninety. Eyes, gray. Hair, dark. Says he was a burglar. And find out through London what he might be doing currently. There was a cop in one of those gray areas between Special Branch and MI5 who officially operated for the Metropolitan Police out of Scotland Yard who might be helpful. George Bulman. He was a detective chief inspector the last I heard, but that was a while ago. Let me know."

Stacey went to his desk, opened a drawer, and took out a flat tobacco tin. Inside was a military button. He clasped it in his hand and closed his eyes. Vivid memories came back to him, as if the button had magical qualities. He opened his fingers. The button needed cleaning; it was the only souvenir of the German uniform he had worn over forty years ago.

10

GEORGE BULMAN FELT CHEATED THAT he was not in Oxford by his own academic efforts. His background had not encouraged such scholastic ambition; his father had been a sergeant major in the king's African Rifles and had wanted Bulman to follow suit. Eventually Bulman had seen the police as a perfect compromise.

In the period when he had first run into Scott, he had suffered the effects of false rumors and malicious gossip, from both jealous colleagues and revengeful villains. Stories were spread about the way he had gained promotion to detective sergeant, and innuendos were cast about some of his arrests. These were some of the dangerous assertions that had reached Scott at that time, and above all things Scott detested bent coppers.

The truth was that Bulman was, and always had been, a first-class detective. He did not always go by the book, but he had never discarded it. In this sense, he had many of the traits of his old enemy Scott; he was unorthodox but was not given to physical violence. And that was used by some as indicating cowardice. Bulman would always confess to being a coward, but those who really knew him also knew the impossibility of the claim.

George Bulman, realizing the disadvantage of his background, had set out to improve his mind, and in so doing had accumulated a mass of information, much of it useless, on topics ranging from Communism to poetry. He could quote verse with genuine feeling.

He had not wanted to visit the colleges, his reasons deep-rooted but obscure. He would feel out of place and cheated. And yet he would have liked to tread the same ground as Roger Bacon, Sir Thomas More, and even the once Chancellor, Oliver Cromwell. It brought home to Bulman all he was not, and all he would like to have been.

So he met Professor Julien at the rounded corner of the Bodleian library, and from there they walked toward the Clarendon building and the Bodleian extension. They made a good pair; Bulman was wearing his smartest overcoat and had brushed and lacquered his hair against the stiff breeze. Professor Julien had a torn pocket in his shabby raincoat, and his flamboyant tie was badly knotted and askew; his sparse hair pointed everywhere in a series of flattened spikes. He was lean and stooped and looked half starved.

"It is very good of you to see me, sir." Bulman did not quite bow. "I had to make sure you were the right person."

"I may not be." Julien pecked at his words quickly, but each was distinct. "I did know both men well when they were undergraduates. The police have already asked, you know."

"I know, sir. I'm sorry it's cropped up again. All I want . . ."

"Look, can't we pop in for a drink?"

Bulman peered ahead to the pub, which seemed to be hiding between two buildings. He could not read the sign. "Won't we be overheard?"

"Not at all. You do drink, don't you?"

Bulman was already calculating his expenses. He nodded weakly.

The professor led the way. The bar was small and smoke lifted to the blackened beams. It was half full, although it was not yet twelve thirty. The young barmaid spotted him, gave him a wink and a nod, and Julien opened a door at the side of the bar and went through. It was a tiny nook, just a small table with two rough benches, and the two men had it to themselves.

Bulman developed a new respect for the professor. Almost

before they sat down, the barmaid brought in a pint of best bitter and placed it in front of Julien, with a plateful of sandwiches.

"Same for you, sir?" The barmaid switched her bright smile to Bulman, who could only nod in awe. "Chesfield and Clarke," Bulman prompted when the barmaid had gone.

"There's little I can tell you that has not already been said." Julien bit into a sandwich, then swigged his beer while he was still chewing. Bulman was fascinated and took his pint from the barmaid as she came in.

"Cheers," Bulman said, knowing that if Julien spoke now he would choke himself.

"Walter Clarke was brilliant," Julien said, scattering moistened breadcrumbs. "Do have a sandwich. Ham or egg." He pushed the plate across. "And Chesfield was a toiler rather than bright, but he did work hard."

Bulman had resigned himself to an intermittent recitation caused by chewing and beer swigging, but he knew the value of patience.

"They were good friends." Julien frowned, his long jaws now in perpetual motion. "And it was difficult to understand why, for they were poles apart. Clarke was a scholar and an athlete and did everything with flair. Chesfield played no games well and rather hated playing them at all."

"Was there any funny business between them" Bulman asked cautiously.

"Committing buggery, you mean?" Julien wiped his lips in a quick action, as if it interfered with his drinking. His eyes were piercing above the glass rim. "This keeps cropping up. The answer cannot be changed by repeating the question." He put his almost empty glass down.

"I've consulted others about this," Julien continued. "Those who knew them at the time. We've discussed it in depth. At times it has seemed that the police would like to prove such a relationship when none apparently existed."

"Apparently?"

"Who can be absolutely sure? If such a relationship was there, then it was never uncovered. Personally, I don't think that there was anything like that between them."

"But you did say they were close, sir."

"I said they were good friends." Julien suddenly bellowed for more beer and Bulman fumbled for his wallet. The barmaid entered with two pints, and Julien ordered a large pork pie, which left Bulman wondering what happened to the calories.

"I've thought this over many times. I'll accept your inaccurate interpretation of what I said. They were close. You are quite right. It was rather a one-sided affair as I recall. Chesfield doted on Clarke. It's not uncommon at that age. Clarke was dashing, a pacesetter, and had a brain in him too. Chesfield set his sights on that image. He hero-worshipped Clarke. If he was inclined to be effeminate, so far as I know it stopped at that. In his eyes Clarke could do no wrong. And Clarke tolerated him for quite solid reasons.

"Clarke had a grandfather whose home he lived in and who was totally intolerant of him. Underneath the self-assuredness Clarke could be quite sensitive. His periodic brashness was a cover for his own uncertainties. I'm quite sure of that. Clarke had to prove himself, and he was fortunate enough to have the ability to do so. He drove himself hard, and he always had a soft spot for Chesfield, which most of the others did not. Perhaps he saw in Chesfield, who had a dominant father, something of his own problems, which he could overcome, and which poor Chesfield could not."

Julien was chewing more slowly now that the pork pie had arrived. He ignored the knife and fork and broke the crust from the meat. "Chesfield would do anything for Clarke."

"*Anything?*"

Julien looked up. "Do I detect a sinister innuendo there, Mr. Bulman?"

"Straight question, sir. What's your definition of anything?"

"I'm not being drawn on that one. You know very well what I meant."

"I see. You're telling me not to read too much into it?"

"I'm doing no such thing. It's an expression, no more, one you have undoubtedly used yourself without literal meaning. Chesfield doted on Clarke. I have said so. Whether that feeling continued after graduation I have absolutely no idea."

"Would idolized be too strong a word?"

"That would be a fair description. I've seen it often enough over the years. It usually levels out with the idolizer later wondering what on earth he ever saw in his hero. I'm making the point that there is nothing unusual in that sort of thing."

"Except that Chesfield comes across as a lonely, rather unpopular figure, in whom only one person was willing to show real interest."

"He was not unpopular. He was not harassed in any way that I recall. I would be inclined to say that most students were indifferent to him. His father had a lot of money but that was not in evidence with the son."

Bulman expressed surprise. "His father seems to be very concerned for his son's reputation now."

Julien smiled cynically. "For his son's reputation or for his own, Mr. Bulman?"

Having received his cable, Bulman met Scott at Heathrow Airport and drove him back to London.

"Fancy a cup of tea in my office?" Bulman asked as he pulled onto the M4.

"I never enter any nick voluntarily."

"The tea's not much good either," Bulman said. He drove expertly, without effort. "So how did you get on?"

"Interesting bloke, Stacey. I should think his background is worth at least one fat book. He put a check on me."

Bulman smiled. "How d'you know?"

"I was listening at his study door while he thought I was in the shower. It'll come to you. Your name was mentioned."

"Well it was bound to be, wasn't it? I'm the only one with any bloody brains. I'll deal with it when it crops up. We don't want the Americans treading all over the place or they might bump into the Russians and figure things out."

"Figure what out?"

Bulman told Scott what he had learned at Oxford the previous day. "Something or nothing, but at least it gives a new slant. Tell me what happened over there."

Scott told him, then said, "Why didn't we go to this woman Jeannette Renore first? She knows more about Clarke's birth than anyone."

Bulman was aggrieved. He slowed down as they hit the heavy traffic at Uxbridge. "Stacey assumed we know it all. We don't. You'd better go and see Clarke's grandmother."

"You're mad. It will get straight back to Clarke."

"Maybe that won't be a bad thing. All we can do is stir."

"We?"

Bulman ignored the challenge. "Fuller is dead."

"*What? Fuller?* Do you mean Soames?"

"I mean Fuller." Bulman never turned his head while driving, his visual concentration total. "It seems that Fuller pushed Soames once too often, and Soames picked up some scissors in the tailor's shop and plunged them straight into him. Fuller died on the operating table. Soames has been charged."

Scott sank back. He had paled. "God," he said quietly, "I've done that. They should charge me."

"Don't talk balls. They already hated each others guts. You planted a seed to stir. A good one. That was no excuse to murder. Normal people don't react like that. Fuller was always looking for an excuse, any excuse to get back at Soames. He wouldn't have killed him, he was all piss and wind. Anyway, your seed hadn't grown anymore. Fuller must have known that if Soames had done the dirt, he would have heard about it before now."

"It wouldn't have happened but for me. That's a fact, George." Scott stared ahead, seeing little of the chaos surrounding them.

"You shook the carpet from under a pair of first-class bastards who deserved each other. Soames would have coped with Fuller's threats if he hadn't been guilty of murder. That's what made him burst; fear of what Fuller might say. The screws were beginning to notice. Soames murdered Fuller to cover another murder." When Scott remained silent, he added, "I don't know how to cope with a bloody villain who has scruples. It's not right. Now snap out of it and look on the bright side."

"I don't see one."

"Soames is tucked away from the others. Murder charge. Maybe he wanted to be removed from the likes of Naylor and Brooks. Maybe Naylor was putting pressure on him or Brooks was putting pressure on both. Soames had lost contact with Victor Anthony, who is still missing. And Fuller was making bubbling noises around his ears. There will be witnesses to Fuller's threats. Soames didn't panic. He would have thought it out. When he's found guilty of murder or manslaughter, he'll be moved."

Bulman tapped Scott's leg. "Naylor will be sweating now. Soames going up for murder might find an argument for asking the other one to be taken into consideration. He'll get life anyway. What can he lose? If he does that he'll have to finger Naylor." He chuckled. "We might get a Red mention yet. Never know your luck."

But Scott sat there feeling that he had started it all. Whatever Bulman said, it would not have happened if he had not seen Fuller and fed him lies, whatever the justification.

"For Christ's sake, if it makes you feel any better, send a wreath and go to his bloody funeral," Bulman burst out. "I'm not losing sleep over the violent bugger. Killing is part of their nature. If it was part of yours, you wouldn't be sitting there feeling sorry for yourself. They're beginning to run. That's what I wanted from the beginning."

Scott bit as Bulman had intended. "You? You've only just come into it."

"Don't give me that. Who do you think set Fairfax onto you? I needed you. At that stage I knew you wouldn't give me the time of day. Do you think I could have pulled off what you did at Hull? They wouldn't have given me anything up there."

"Are you saying Fairfax isn't abroad?"

"The last I heard he was on Moor Park Golf Course trying to improve his handicap."

"You bastard. You bloody rotten bastard. You stinking piece of fuzz. Old Bill . . . I'll fix you . . ."

Bulman slipped out of lane. "That's better. That's the Spider I remember so well. Don't choke on your tonsils, lad." He closed his ears to Scott's curses.

Kransouski put Maggie on a loose lead. The women designated to watch her had strict instructions not to follow if Scott was with her; and if at any time Maggie gave signs of suspicion, they were to drop right back, give up until later.

All Kransouski wanted to do was to monitor Maggie's day-to-day movements to see what pattern they made, to judge how often she was alone and where, and how long she spent at the apartment without Scott. Were there particular days when Scott was late getting back from the office?

Scott's weakness was Maggie, and Kransouski, with the foresight of an old campaigner, wanted to be ready to pounce if the need arose. He was prepared to torture her and, if it became necessary, to kill her. He would do that, too. Scott was a difficult man to handle, and Kransouski would manage in any way he could.

He did not see his preparation as being beyond his assignment. His job was to have Scott watched, and that had become impossible to do effectively, and his report had stated as much. In the back of his mind was the need for his own protection. He had not liked the open way he had entered the country, even if thinly disguised. General Rogov well knew that he was known here no matter how long he had been away. If everything went well he would survive, but if it did not, then it would be his head that would be offered on a plate to cover up for Gorkin and his men. And there would be no trade-in if he survived to be imprisoned. Kransouski had no doubt of this; he would have used the same tactic.

What he could not break down, because his movements were channeled as a trade delegate, was the whole underlying issue. Scott, the prison, Detective Superintendent Bulman, the dead man Chesfield, and Nicolai Gorkin. He missed having the facilities that Gorkin enjoyed, yet he was left with the feeling that Gorkin was not himself wholly aware of what he was involved in. Kransouski had never felt so shackled. But if it became necessary to take Maggie Parsons, he was confident that truth would come out in a flood.

Bulman was forced to pay the price for deceiving Scott into operating with him. As much as Scott hated flying, he preferred that to facing an elderly lady, who some said was ailing, about her highly successful grandson, whom she reputedly thought the world of. It was left to Bulman to tackle her, which he could do officially—a prop Scott would be denied.

Scott left London in rain. The plane plunged through the nimbostratus into the dense layer of cumulonimbus, the thundercloud pressured above it. If he could have stepped out he would have, but he remained locked with the other passengers in a propelled cylinder that was being tossed around the skies.

To his immense relief, the plane eventually belly-landed on top of the cloud, and then, all too slowly, climbed away from it. The plane rode above the cloud as far as the Alpes Maritime, and suddenly there was no cloud at all. Sunlight cascaded off mountain-tops into valleys, lightening and darkening them, and ahead was the incredible blue of the Mediterranean. They came in low over the sea to land at Nice Airport.

Scott took a cab to the Clinique d'Azur, which lay on the upper slopes above the quaint, clustered old harbor town of Villefranche, just three miles away. The palm-ridden band of the Promenade des Anglais, the sea reflecting white lights beyond it, was cluttered with cars and coaches to remind him that in England it was autumn and cold, and here he could already feel the heat around his collar.

As the taxi climbed, he had a better view of the sea and the yachts, and the calming effect of them made him realize just how screwed up he was. He could handle villains and one-time shad-owy people like Stacey. They had never worried him, but now he felt he was about to intrude into someone's life.

The sea sank below him and the horizon extended almost as if he were flying again. Rich subtropical foliage thickened as they climbed, and drooped over the retaining walls to encumber lush trees. The taxi turned into a drive and wound upward, gravel warning of its approach.

The Clinique d'Azur unfolded like a holed sheet, white and seemingly full of arches. Potted plants, full of color, lined the long pillared terrace. As Scott left the taxi with his suitcase, the silence was almost physical. If peace were a criterion to cure, it would be found here. He paid off the driver as a nurse approached him, white uniform, stockings, and shoes. Scott hoped it was not so white in heaven, where momentarily he almost believed himself to be.

He understood the smile but not the smooth flow of French. "I'm sorry, love. I'm English. I telephoned from London."

The nurse answered in French and indicated that he should follow her. He felt out of place in the rich, quiet atmosphere of the large pink-washed foyer. There was no hospital atmosphere about the place, but he supposed that was really what it was, no matter how elite. There was a friendly feel, but it was not on his own earthly level. The smiles seemed to be professional, but really it was he who was out of context.

He waited by a long reception desk that gave the illusion of being a hotel desk, with its tourist brochures and racks, maps, and colored postcards. The receptionist gave him a quick smile while the nurse went off to fetch someone else, her low, rubber heels silent on the Italian tiled floor.

Scott came to terms with his feelings and took a more professional interest in the clinic. A child could break in, he thought. He could see no wards and presumed they were in the huge extension that he had glimpsed at the back as the taxi had come in. There were two offices marked private; he could understand that well enough. He saw nobody who appeared to be a patient, but perhaps he was thinking in the wrong terms. Not everybody here might need treatment. A doctor walked past with a stethoscope dangling from his pocket; that was the only medical instrument Scott was to see.

A sturdy, middle-aged woman came bustling through the opaque glass doors at the rear of the foyer. Gray hair coiffured high on her head, hands in the pockets of her white coat. She smiled warmly at him.

"M'sieur Scott?"

"Yes. Was it you I spoke to on the telephone?"

"No. But your inquiry was passed to me. Because I speak English," she added, smiling again.

"Better English than mine. I'm sorry I don't speak French."

"Shall we sit over there?" She led the way to a wrought iron table with cane chairs around it. As she passed him, he noticed the blue name tag pinned to her coal lapel, and the inscription Dr. M. Belime. They sat down and she asked, "What exactly is it you want, Mr. Scott?" Her eyes remained impartial.

"I explained on the telephone. I would like to see Jeannette Renore. Just for a few minutes."

"I understand that your telephone call was to ascertain whether Madame Renore was here, only."

"And that I would like to see her."

"That was not passed on to me." She gazed coolly at him. "If you
156

asked to see Madame Renore and someone here approved, they should not have done so. Madame Renore sees only her son, and even then she does not recognize him. She is very ill."

Scott had not expected it to be so bad. "Are you saying that I can't see her?"

"Are you a relative?"

"I'm a friend of a friend. I merely wanted to ask her a couple of questions. I don't think what I have to ask would upset her. It's about something of which she should be very proud."

"About her resistance days? Are you a journalist?"

"I could pretend to be one, but I'm not. Something happened during the war, something very much to her credit, which she knows about more than anybody else. Her knowledge could unlock a door for someone else, someone she would undoubtedly want to help, and who but for her would be dead."

Dr. Belime appeared to relax a little. "She was awarded the Legion of Honor for what she did during the war. But any mention of that time could have a disastrous effect on her. *If she were to understand what was being said at all.*"

"I'm told that she speaks excellent English."

"That is not what I meant. Her mind is—numb. She has shut out the world. She is happy looking at and tending the garden. Her sight is good, her hearing adequate. But she suffered a trauma sometime ago, and there is no sign yet of recovery. In her strange way, she is happy as she is. She wants no intrusion. I think she deserves her peace, however limited that might be. Don't you?"

"Of course. But how can you know I'd destroy that peace? I might even help her. It could be the jolt she needs." Scott spoke persuasively without convincing himself.

"Because I am her doctor, Mr. Scott. You must respect my judgment."

Scott shrugged in defeat. "I do, of course. Although doctors can be wrong."

"Are you a psychologist?"

"You know I'm not. Your English is too good for me to try to trick you."

Dr. Belime smiled, and Scott realized he had struck the right note.

"Couldn't I just see her?"

"Will you promise not to speak to her?"

"I'll only speak to her if you say so."

"You did not specifically ask to see Madame Renore, did you? You perhaps thought you would be refused?"

"Maybe." Scott stood up, leaning forward to catch the doctor's arm as the chair toppled back when she rose.

"You are a strange mixture, Mr. Scott. I'm sorry I cannot be more helpful. But the patient must come first."

"I understand. It's a pity, because a couple of days ago, I stayed with a very dear friend of hers, an American general called Stacey, in New York. He knew her well during the war. It was his idea that I call. I suppose I can't even tell her that?"

Dr. Belime hesitated, as if the high rank presented another dimension. "They were real friends?"

"They were both in Amiens prison when the RAF bombed it in 1944. They both escaped." Observing the measure of the doctor's indecision, Scott added, "Couldn't I just offer his love to her? In your presence?"

Dr. Belime gazed thoughtfully at Scott. "You are a determined man. And you are persuasive. Perhaps passing on someone's love will do no harm." She took Scott by the arm. "Don't misconstrue this as a mark of affection. I don't want you to leave my side." She took him through the opaque glass doors into a stark, white corridor with rooms off of it and a blank door at the end. They went through this door into brilliant sunshine.

Low buildings spread laterally from them so that there was little or no incline to reach them. Beyond the buildings the gardens spread upward in a series of terraces, with two lots of stone steps picking their way haphazardly through the blooms and multicolored shrubs. At the end of the central building, almost opposite where they were standing, was a wide, concrete path that wound upward in a design that took the slopes more gradually than the steps. At intervals were terraced areas with benches where patients could rest. The concrete path was wide enough for wheelchairs to pass.

Now Scott could see the patients. Some were fully dressed, others in dressing gowns. They sat or walked through the grounds, and they were of all ages.

"If ever I'm sick and can afford it, this is where I'll come," said Scott with feeling.

"Those on the higher ground have a wonderful view of the whole coastline. And that is where I'm taking you."

Scott reversed position and took the doctor's arm as they mounted the right-hand set of steps. There was an iron rail on one side and a rope one on the other.

Jeannette Renore sat in a wheelchair facing the sea with her tired eyes screwed against the lowering sun. As the light pierced the foliage, it formed broken shards across her sagging face. She was alone and gave no sign that she had heard anyone approach. Her thin hands lay motionless on each arm of the chair.

Indicating that Scott should stay back, Dr. Belime approached openly. "It's Marie, Jeannette. It will be too cold for you as soon as the sun slips behind the hills. How are you?"

A wrinkled hand came up to cover the eyes from the sun and the head tilted slightly to get a better view of the doctor, but there was no verbal response.

"I've brought someone to see you. He has a message from an old friend of yours." Dr. Belime signaled Scott forward and Scott was aware of Jeannette's eyes switching slowly to him. When he saw the eyes, he thought they were dead. It seemed to him that Jeannette stared without seeing, but that could not be so. There was an almost total lifelessness about her, and yet the hand, the head, the eyes had all moved. But it was as if their power were running down.

He stepped toward her and glanced at the doctor, who, after hesitating, gave an almost imperceptible nod. "I was in New York," he said, "and I met Lorne Stacey. When he knew I was coming to France, he insisted that I drop in to give you his love."

Jeannette's eyes livened at the mention of Stacey's name. She stared at Scott more acutely, but still said nothing. It was difficult for Scott to reconcile this wreck of a woman with a heroine who had received France's highest accolades. What had happened to reduce her to this? It was impossible for him to determine whether she had once been attractive or ugly or ripe with personality. The nurses had done their best, combed her hair, added some cosmetics, but there was nothing from Jeannette herself.

Jeannette's response had interested the doctor, but Scott kept his word and added nothing. He looked toward the doctor, who was gazing thoughtfully at Jeannette. Dr. Belime glanced at Scott, who was not sure what to do.

Afterward, Scott swore that the doctor nodded. More than that, he was certain that her eyes gave their own message. In effect, she had given him a signal having been encouraged by Jeannette's reaction so far.

Scott said, "I came from London to see you. While I'm here, is it possible to talk to you about Walter Clarke?"

He had spoken quietly, even apologetically, and Dr. Belime gave him no indication of disapproval.

At first there was no reaction at all from Jeannette. Her hand still shaded her eyes, which were gazing at Scott. Then her expression changed, at first slowly, then dramatically. She half rose from her chair and stayed in that position. Her eyes suddenly glared and her mouth opened to let out a terrible scream that rose above the terraces to scatter the birds in a great noise of flapping wings. And then she collapsed back in her wheelchair and her head sagged forward, her arms dropping to her sides.

11

D R. BELIME DASHED FORWARD, SHOOTING Scott a withering
look, and she called out in rapid French as she reached Jeannette,
who showed no sign of life.

Scott was rooted. Nobody could have expected so dramatic a
reaction, and that included the good doctor, who was now frantically waving Scott away. He could not simply leave the scene; if he
had caused Jeannette's collapse, then he wanted to know what
would happen to her.

A nurse came running up the steps with a tray and a syringe, and
Scott saw the doctor shining a torch in Jeannette's eyes. He went
slowly down the steps, sick at heart and wondering what other little
surprises he might perform that could affect people so. He told
himself that had he believed there was the slightest risk of Jeannette
reacting as she had, he would not have mentioned Walter Clarke.

Two nurses dashed past him carrying a stretcher between them.
He reached the buildings. Both patients and staff were staring at
him as if he were a leper, and he felt wretched and bemused. Yet
beneath his misery was the repeating query of *why*? He had
somehow to find out.

The two nurses descended with Jeannette strapped to the

stretcher; noticing the way they were going, Scott moved away. Behind the stretcher came Dr. Belime, bustling and anxious and studiously avoiding Scott, who she must have seen. Scott tagged on, a little distance behind, into the rear buildings, down a long corridor with private wards, until Jeannette was hustled into one of them. Scott did not enter the room, but he gazed through the circular glass window to see Jeannette put to bed and Dr. Belime take her pulse. He assumed that Jeannette was still alive.

He wandered back to the reception foyer to await news. His suitcase was still by the counter. He paced up and down, watched by a concerned receptionist who had heard the scream; everyone had heard it.

After a while he moved over to the iron table and sat to stare out of the window. He was seated sideways, an arm along the back of the chair. He tried to imagine what made Jeannette scream as if she were in the last throes of mortal agony.

The sun sank and the subtle hidden lights of the foyer came on before Dr. Belime came back. She crossed to the reception desk, then caught sight of him. "I would have thought you'd have gone by now, Mr. Scott." Her voice was cold and accusing.

He came toward her. "You know that there was no way I could have expected that to happen. You didn't yourself."

"Just the same, you had better go. The damage is done."

"The damage was already done. I triggered what was already there. What happened to her in the first place?"

Dr. Belime took Scott out of earshot of the receptionist and stopped by his bag, staring down at it. Her face was strained. "I don't intend to discuss a patient with you. Please go."

"I'll go when I know how she is."

"She's quieter. I've put her to sleep. But I cannot possibly say at this stage how she will later react. We have to wait. That's all I can say. And you must not see her again. The shock could kill her."

Scott picked up his bag. "You did give a sign for me to go ahead, you know. Don't make me the scapegoat."

Dr. Belime's shoulders sagged and her brows rose in a gesture of acquiescence. "There is no scapegoat. But what you said devastated her. God knows what her mental condition is now or will become."

"But will she be all right?" Scott persisted.

"I don't know. Her heart is weak. Mr. Scott, there is nothing to stop you telephoning as often as you like, and we will report her condition."

"Okay. Give her my . . . No, better not." Scott turned to the door. Behind him he heard the quick, soft tread of Dr. Belime hurrying away.

He walked down the winding drive. The bag was heavy and the slope acute, and it was difficult to see. Rhododendrons and yuccas brushed him as he kept to the edge. He could still distinguish the sea from the shore, but lights were increasingly pinpricking both. It was so tranquil. Yet the scream still filled his ears. A car came crunching up the drive; he moved into the shrubbery, blinded by its lights.

For a while he could not see at all, but when he continued down the slope he gradually picked out swaying mast-top lights. Out in the harbor a cruise ship was strung with colored bulbs.

Scott found a top floor room in a small pension on the higher ground at the back of town. He showered and changed. In the small dining room he ordered a meal with difficulty and wished that Maggie was with him. She could be practical when necessary, and right now he wanted the comfort of her, and of her advice. He realized he was feeling a little sorry for himself, but that was because he was floundering emotionally. His feeling of concern was much stronger for Jeannette Renore. Even without the scream, a very brave woman having been reduced to a cabbage deeply moved him.

After the meal he trod the cobblestones of the charming harbor town and went down to the quay. It was fresh now, to him ideal; to others taking in the pleasantness of the late evening, too chilly. For a while he watched the boats rocking against their moorings and listened to the gentle lapping of the sea. He looked at his watch. It was far too early for what he wanted to do, and he did not want to pass the time drinking; he would need his reflexes unimpaired.

He returned to his room, opened the old-fashioned window, and gazed down into complete darkness. But he had taken stock the moment he arrived; he knew what was down there. He lay on the narrow bed, feet overhanging the end, and dozed with hands clasped behind his head. When he had rested, he examined his feelings. He was nervous, and that was quite different from being keyed up. He could not recall being nervous before an operation, however important.

At half past midnight he changed into his track suit, sprayed his hands and fingers, and opened the window again. He eased himself onto the sill, already doubtful that his muscles would stand the strain after such a long layoff. He reached for the rainspout at the side, gripped it and pulled to test its strength; it was the old-fashioned variety and solid.

Scott swung over, pulling himself one-handed at first with the intention of grabbing the spout with both hands and foot crawling down the wall to the ground. His heart leapt as he found himself slipping at speed, hands burning from friction. With immense effort he stopped the slide, then clung grimly to the spout, knees and feet locking on to it.

The strain was enormous, but he hung on grimly because a drop could kill him. After a while his panting eased, and he began to descend, canvas shoes gripping the brickwork, hands around the spout. His muscles creaked, and he found the pain crucifying.

He reached the ground and steadied himself against the wall, filled with self-disgust and aches and pains. In the darkness he made a smile of self-derision; he could have gone out by the front door, but he did not want to be seen by the other guests; he wanted it to be believed that he was still in his room. His hands burned and he realized that their protective coating was already off. Confidence battered, he moved off over the cobblestones.

Villefranche is full of narrow alleys and winding streets. He had no difficulty in keeping out of sight. He reached the main street, traffic much reduced now, and chose his moment to lope across to the other side. After a while of following the road line, high banks rising above him, he found the street that led to the clinic.

It was pitch black up here, the climb steep. Scattered lights from villas spread up the terraces, and the silence was almost complete.

Scott took his time. When a car came speeding down, he had plenty of warning to step into the shrubs while the headlights swept out to sea like searchlights. He continued on until he found the driveway.

He stepped off the gravel drive into the shrubs. It meant mount-

164

ing the terraces one by one, but it was safer and quieter. When he reached the clinic he crouched for some time. The building was mainly in darkness, but here and there dimmed lights showed, and ahead of him the reception area glowed prettily with subdued and hidden lights. He moved around to the back of the building, still keeping off the gravel.

When he reached the rear wards into which Jeannette Renore had been carried, pale blue night lights were ghostly through some of the windows. He had no problem in opening a door that had no security lock. He closed it behind him.

Confidence returned. He went along the corridor with private rooms on either side. The glow of the blue night lights reflected eerily on some of the round observation windows, but others were dark. There was a dimmed bulb each end of the corridor.

Footsteps approached from the other end of the corridor, a sound so muted that most people would have missed it. Scott chose a room without a night light, opened one of the double doors, and stepped inside. Behind him was shallow regular breathing. He remained quite still, staying by the door.

The footsteps stopped before they reached him. A door opened quietly and Scott waited. A minute or two later the footsteps resumed, and it was clear to Scott that a nurse was peering through the observation windows in turn. He drew back, heard the footsteps go past, and from that surmised that only the dimly lit rooms drew attention. The footsteps went back again and faded. Scott timed two minutes before stepping out.

Jeannette Renore's room had a night light. Scott peered through and prayed that he would not disturb her. He pushed the door gently and stepped in. The ethereal glow gave the strange illusion that Jeannette was levitating above the bed.

Each side of the bed was a small cupboard. On top of the one nearest to him was a telephone and a glass of water. Jeannette lay on her back and at first he thought her eyes were open and staring, but it was a reflection of the blue light on her lids. Her arms were inside the sheets and her mouth was slightly open as she breathed heavily. As he stepped nearer, he noticed her lids were fluttering, and she began to murmur and move restlessly. With some despair he thought that she might be suffering a nightmare.

Dropping to his hands and knees, Scott crawled forward. The

drawer of the cupboard stuck when he tried to open it, and the cupboard rattled. He stopped at once, watching the pale face on the pillows. Jeannette's lips were moving.

Scott steadied the cupboard with one hand and eased the drawer out with the other. There was a book whose title he could not read, and which had a pristine appearance, as if it had never been opened. Removing it quietly he held it by the covers and let the pages hang down. Nothing fell out. He replaced it and opened the cupboard door to find nothing but the medical apparatus of the bedridden.

He crept around to the other side of the bed. In the drawer he found a small case, which he opened. A medal lay in its recess, and Scott sat back on his heels. If an award for gallantry was so near to hand, it could not be the war itself, or her valiant part in it, that triggered her distress. This somehow put Walter Clarke in a separate category from the war. He stared at the medal, then at the twitching face of the heroine who had won it. From what he had learned about her, Jeannette Renore had suffered severe torture during the war; she had seen killings and she herself had killed. None of this could have had any serious effect on her with the medal here to remind her. He closed the box and carefully put it back. He had found something relating to her past, but it was not what he wanted.

He had just closed the drawer when the door opened. He dropped flat at the side of the bed. There was no shout, no scream, and he lay there sweating with anxiety. Someone was moving the other side of the bed. Something metallic rattled, and he supposed it was an instrument tray. Perhaps the nurse had seen something of Jeannette's distress and had returned with a treatment. When Scott peered under the bed he saw white shoes and stockings.

The sheets were adjusted and the nurse came to the foot of the bed. Scott remained still. Something clicked and he belatedly identified the sound as being the clipboard containing the medical data being put back on its hook.

A door opened. With horror Scott realized that it was the slatted door of the built-in wardrobe that was directly behind him. Hangers were moved along a rail and then stopped. The door closed. There was complete silence, as if the nurse were standing and staring at his back. Footsteps again, unhurried. And then the room door opened and closed.

Scott restrained the immediate impulse to move. When he finally did, it was to roll gently onto his back. He raised his head cautiously. The nurse had definitely gone. He stared at Jeannette, who seemed to be far less troubled.

The job was not done. He needed something far more informative than a gallantry award. He moved toward the wardrobe and opened its doors.

There were few clothes there, but they did indicate that Jeannette was sometimes well enough to wear them. Scott went through every pocket and, from old habit, felt along the hems and the lapels. There was nothing to find. Underwear and blouses were in one of a line of drawers; so were handkerchiefs and other personal items. A handbag was in one of the drawers, but it was empty. It seemed that even money and feminine items like cosmetics and perfume had been removed. There was nothing, not even a letter or postcard, as if nobody cared anymore. Or as if she wanted to lose identity for reasons of her own.

Scott looked back at the bed. There was nothing he could do to help her. He pushed the room door, peered out, and left.

He went the way he had come, not wishing to be trapped in the confines of the clinic. Reaching the front again, he had a little more difficulty with the main lock before slipping into the foyer.

Although dimmed, there was adequate light, and here it was a rose-colored glow, almost like a photographer's darkroom. He unlocked the nearest office marked private. There was one large desk in the room, and comfortable chairs. A Menez bronze of a pelican with a fish in its mouth was a centerpiece on a low marble table. He tore his mind away from the superb sculpture and quickly assessed that there would be nothing in here for him. What he wanted would not be found in desk drawers.

An interconnecting door was unlocked and Scott went through. This would be it, he reflected. A more utilitarian office with three desks and two typewriters. And filing cabinets. Ten minutes later the sum total of the gain from his risky break-in was the address of Jeannette Renore in Paris. There had been figures on the file which he could not interpret, but he guessed that they represented the payment for her expensive sojourn in the clinic, probably settled regularly by a banker's order. Jeannette Renore was not poor.

The house was in Hampshire with a trout stream bubbling through part of the grounds. It was said that Capability Brown had planned the extensive estate with its lake and gentle slopes, and judging by the resulting beauty, Bulman thought the claim could well be true.

Martha Clarke took him out onto the huge terrace at the rear of the house in spite of the blustering and biting gale. Dried brown leaves crackled as the wind scattered them, but still Bulman could appreciate the vista of rolling lawns, which was totally enhanced by the magnificence of the trees, even though most of the leaves were down.

They sat in a recess of the east wing by the side of an extensive rectangle of a fish pool. Water lilies spread out in huge leaves, under which multicolored fish were lurking.

"Are you interested in fish, Mr. Bulman?" Martha Clarke had caught the direction of his fleeting glance.

"Oh, very," he said, "colorful creatures."

Martha smiled. "You don't have to humor me. They are new to you, aren't they?"

"When you put it like that, ma'am, I suppose they are. A long way removed from the one goldfish I kept in a bowl as a kid."

"That's a cruel way of keeping them, my dear."

"It was all my parents could afford. I'd watch it for hours." Bulman was amazed at the sharpness of Walter Clarke's grandmother. For a woman in her eighties, Martha Clarke's mind and sight were incredibly clear. Age was given away by her appearance, but even that had a regality he could only admire. She came from a section of society he often despised, but it would be difficult to despise this woman.

Martha's posture was superb. Her clear eyes commanded, yet Bulman sensed that she was a woman who led by example rather than position. He could not help but like her. She wore an old topcoat against the wind, but even that hung on her like a couturier's garment. Her white hair was gathered in a bun at the back, but in spite of this and her sometimes severe expression, there was an air about her that was essentially feminine.

"If you look carefully," she said, "you will see a variety of koi, shubunkin, comets, and black moors, chocolate orandas, and red-caps among the fantails. All beautiful specimens."

At first Bulman thought she was listing the varieties of specimen plants in the garden; then he realized that the names were species of fish. "Beautiful," he agreed.

"Yes they are. I hope you have not come here to harm my grandson. If you have, you can expect no help from me and every obstruction."

Bulman guessed that Martha Clarke could be very obstructive, indeed, if she was so minded. "It's a routine line of inquiry, ma'am. We're following up the background of all Gordon Chesfield's known friends. He's the man who died recently. Your grandson is just one of many. We're eliminating them one by one."

"I remember that young man. I met him several times, but he lacked Walter's qualities. A dreadful business. He must have been so desperately unhappy to do such a thing to himself."

"Nobody really knows why Gordon Chesfield killed himself. Checking on his past and on those who knew him is a painstaking business. But it has to be done if we are to uncover the reason."

"I thought that was straightforward. The lad simply could not face the trauma of prison life or come to terms with what he had done."

Bulman felt himself to be under close scrutiny. "We are not satisfied that Chesfield killed himself for those reasons. And some of his friends are of the same opinion. So we dig deeper and try to discover if there is some connection with one of his friends or acquaintances that might somehow have led to such a tragedy. We are not trying to implicate anyone, but merely intend to find a clue to help unravel an intriguing mystery."

"I can't see how I can possibly help you."

"All I want is a little background on your grandson."

"Then you should get it from him, Mr. Bulman."

"I should think he's seen enough of policemen, and he certainly won't want any more traipsing after him around the House of Commons. Anyway, he's a very busy man. We simply have to finish our inquiries some other way."

Martha peered down at the pool. There was a flash of red and blue as her reflection scared a fish. "Don't take me for an idiot, Mr. Bulman. I may be old, but I'm not stupid, yet."

"No ma'am. I wouldn't try to fool you."

"Tell me, what kind of trouble is young Walter in?"

Bulman knew that this was crunch time. He could blow it or succeed. "He's in no trouble with us. But like it or not, he was once a very close friend of Chesfield's. I just wondered if there is some sort of link that could help us."

"Do you *think* that Walter might be in trouble?"

Bulman shook his head slowly. "With respect, Mrs. Clarke, you've twice raised the possibility. Your thoughts appear to lean more in that direction than mine."

"Mr. Bulman, you're trying to be too clever. Please state precisely what you believe, or I must ask you to leave, which would be a pity. I don't get much in the way of interesting company these days."

"I'm sorry you feel that way. I just need to know if there's the possibility of anything in Walter Clarke's background that could remotely throw any light on Gordon Chesfrield's death. Bits and pieces, ma'am, from any source." While he spoke, Bulman couldn't help wondering why the old lady was so defensive about her grandson.

As if reading his mind, Martha Clarke said, "I don't want him hurt in any way. You must be aware of the circumstances of his birth. He not only lost his mother, but discovered the tragic, horrible way in which she was killed. That has affected him badly. He's had a great deal to put up with, and I don't want the press resurrecting the past.

"That couldn't hurt him, could it? He would get everyone's sympathy if that happened."

"He does not want or need sympathy, Mr. Bulman. He's left all that behind him. He's made a success of his life through his own efforts and does not want his life disturbed by the past. He is totally honest, and I mean by anyone's standards."

"You're very fond of him, ma'am. Did your husband feel the same way?"

Martha eyed Bulman coldly. "What have you heard?"

"I heard that your husband did not like or accept him."

Martha sighed. "That is true. My husband lived by his own

values, and I admired him for that, but he would be considered hopelessly old-fashioned now. He did not like the fact, and could never accept it, that Walter was born out of wedlock. That was the attitude of his times."

"I can understand if he had not accepted the mother. But the child had no say in the matter. Couldn't he accept that premise?"

"He was unrelenting. We argued about it, but he would not compromise his principles, not even for me."

"Yet Walter was brought up here."

"Yes, at my insistence. I could not desert a child, particularly when my son loved *his* son, who, after all, was a love child."

Bulman knew the tide had turned. In spite of Martha's instinctive protection of Walter, he felt that she wanted to talk about him.

Carefully, Bulman continued, "Was that the only reason your husband did not like Walter?"

The old eyes flashed. "What precisely do you mean?"

"Did your husband acknowledge the child as your son's?"

"That was never in doubt. The heritage was unquestionable. My husband not only accepted that heritage, but it was one of the issues that made him so obdurate. If he could have disproved that branch of the family tree, he would gleefully have done so. God knows, he tried hard enough. But I did understand and even respect his feelings."

Bulman said cautiously, "Did any of this have any effect on Walter's feelings? I mean, if your husband made his thoughts so 'clear, couldn't that have undermined Walter somewhat? It couldn't have been very pleasant to be rejected by his grandfather."

Martha suddenly snapped from a reverie. "What can that possibly have to do with Gordon Chesfield's unfortunate death?"

Bulman appeared to be embarrassed. "I'm sorry. I overstepped the line between useful inquiry and personal interest. It is such a fascinating story. I really am sorry, ma'am."

"Young Walter was sufficiently strong to cope. Of course he was hurt, but he had his father and me to rely on. And in spite of his attitude, his grandfather did show some charity on occasion. He used to take his grandson on long walks. They both loved the countryside."

And fed him with what, mused Bulman, who now believed he

would get no more. The truth always seemed to be just out of reach. He accepted that Martha was not lying; it was not in her character, although she might if she thought it would help Walter. But there was a barrier she would not cross, and Bulman knew there was something about the relationship between her husband and young Walter Clarke that would remain locked away. It lay with Walter to fill in that blank, but Bulman could not see him being very forthcoming. He rose and held out his hand to help Martha to her feet.

Denise pulled into the side of the track, easing the car into the tall hedgerow. In this part of the country there was virtually no risk of another car approaching, but he had left just sufficient room if one did. He climbed out and walked slowly up the slight incline, the hedgerows blocking his view. The sky was clouding up, but there was little threat of rain. He passed wheel tracks to his left and remained on the main track for some minutes. He did not hurry, but when the barn roofs came into view, he stood still to listen for any sound. All he could pick up was the far-distant clatter of a tractor. He continued to walk.

The farm was run down, verging on the derelict, and Denise knew that very little was grown here now; just enough to justify occupation. An open, corrugated-roofed barn faced him, and beyond it, two smaller barns with holed roofs. Some distance beyond them was the cottage. There were clothes flapping on a line. Denise circled slightly so that there was always a barn between himself and the cottage. As he drew nearer, he made his approach more obvious to the man who was working alone at a small smelting plant in one corner of the main barn.

Denise called out softly, "Nabih. I got your message."

The slightly built Algerian turned in surprise and waved. "It was good of you to act so quickly."

"I just happened to be in Paris. You were lucky." Denise felt the heat from the brick-cased furnace as he approached. On top of the furnace was a large iron cauldron with a lip, and at the side were molding trays. Above was a rough, pulley attachment to a beam that Nabih used to pull in order to tilt the cauldron when he wanted

172

to pour. The whole apparatus was crude but functional. A chair was positioned in front of an upturned orange box, on which was a flask and a mug.

"What's in it?" Denise asked as he drew level with the Algerian, who wore a thick kitchen apron around his waist. The brown eyes smiled. "Lead."

"Lead? Why?"

"There's always a demand for lead. It's in short supply."

"So how do you get so much?"

"Old roofs. Churches. Demolition jobs. People want it for all sorts of reasons. These days the wealthy cover their atomic shelters with it. Stops radiation. I melt it down to mold it into manageable blocks."

Denise nodded understandingly. "You're always up to something. What's your problem, Nabih?"

The Algerian peered into the steaming cauldron and wiped his small hands on the apron. "Money. I made a bad investment."

"A man with your talents should never be short. And I paid you well."

"I know. It's only temporary. I need a loan for about three months. I'll pay it back, of course."

"How much?"

"A hundred thousand francs should cover it."

Denise whistled. "That's an awful lot. That's not living money. That's paying off debts money."

Nabih smiled sheepishly. "As I said, I invested badly."

"Gambled, you mean."

Nabih shrugged. "That amount is petty cash to you. I'm not asking for extra. Really. I will pay it back."

Denise made up his mind quickly; Nabih had spoken carelessly. If the Algerian knew that a hundred thousand francs was petty cash to him, then he probably knew who Denise really was.

"Where's your wife?" Denise asked.

Nabih looked surprised. "In the cottage. She knows better than to interrupt me when I'm working. Will you help me?"

"Of course." Denise dipped a hand inside his jacket, drew out a gun, and smashed the barrel across Nahib's forehead. The Algerian fell and lay huddled as he collapsed on top of himself.

Denise pulled Nabih up, held him awkwardly, and rammed his

173

injured forehead against the rim of the cauldron. It was important to leave a suggestion of what had happened with blood and skin traces. He then heaved Nabih head first into the molten lead, the legs hanging outside the cauldron as it tilted. A huge shudder, like an immense electric shock, ran through the body once, and then it was still. An air bubble painfully pierced the surface of the lead.

Denise used a handkerchief to pull forward the chair. He angled it against Nabih's legs and then pulled the rope forward to drop the loose end in the lead. It would appear that for a reason known only to himself, Nabih had stood on the chair to pull the rope and had lost his balance. Perhaps the cauldron had been difficult to tilt.

Making sure he kept the line of vision from the cottage blocked by the barns, Denise went back to his car, coldly reflecting that he should have dealt with Nabih a long time ago. Once in the car he drove swiftly back to Paris.

Willie Scott took an Air France flight from Nice to Paris, found a second-class hotel in the rue du Caumartin, and booked a room for the night. Once he had dropped his bag in his room, he wasted no time. He studied a tourist plan of Paris in the hotel lobby and noted that it was a good distance from the Opera District, where he now stood, to the avenue Hoche near the Arc de Triomphe.

The last time he had used the Metro, he had ended up at the wrong station, so he decided to walk. For a man whose sense of direction was finely tuned while self-propelled, his senses always seemed to desert him when he placed himself in the hands of others. It was what he called the loner syndrome.

He went north up the narrow stretch of the rue du Caumartin. It was late evening, the light was poor, but direction was embedded in his mind. The tail end of the rush hour traffic made itself heard around him, and he enjoyed the frenetic bustle, as he did in any big town. At the top of the Caumartin he turned left into the long stretch of the boulevard Haussmann, and imagined he was in Oxford Street.

No journey like this was wasted with Scott. He observed as he went; turnoffs, pedestrian density, traffic build-up, shops, office blocks, the depth of doorways, and buildings that could be climbed without aid. As he recorded this information he knew that even if his muscles were not in trim, his mind had completely adjusted. He was back in business.

There was no hurry, and he kept within his natural stride. He did a check on being followed as a matter of routine and was satisfied that he was on his own. When he reached the junction of the boulevard Haussmann and the avenue de Friedland, he took the right-hand fork into the rue du Faubourg. At the avenue Hoche he turned left and halted around the corner.

Scott stood with his back to the wall. He tried to quell the sensation, but the old urge was back. This was burglar land. Not quite so plush as the avenue Foch the other side of the place de Charles de Gaulle, but plush enough. He fought back the feeling, surprised that it should still be so powerful. He pondered on the objets d'art and paintings that lay behind some of these walls: Faberge, Monet, Cezanne, and others. He could feel them around him, impervious to the movement of hurrying people, of speeding cars.

He broke his mini-dream and continued on, turned left and then right, and was brought back to reality by the splendid old building that had been converted to modern apartments. There was more than one entrance of double shatterproof glass doors with huge bronze handles. The block was too big to accommodate voice-box security. But inevitably there would be a concierge.

Scott stood on a lower step, his back to the doors, and glanced over his shoulder. He located the inquiry desk to the right of two elevators. A uniformed porter stood behind the short counter. The porter would well know that Jeannette Renore was not at home.

It was a long time before the porter became occupied with a man and a woman. The porter was turning up a timetable; Scott ran lightly up the remaining steps and opened a door just sufficiently to slip through. He headed away from the desk to the stairs to the left of the elevators; made no sound as he crossed the lobby. Once on the stairs without having raised a shout from the porter, he knew he was clear.

It was a hard climb to the eighth floor, and he took it slowly, resting now and then. He reached the floor and followed the arrow pointing to the section he wanted. Number 806 was no different from the other doors he had passed. They all had spy holes in them, and they were all waxed pine.

He roamed the floor, found the metal exit door to the fire escape; it was locked by a bar that could not be manipulated from the outside but was easy enough to open from within. He opened it and mounted stone steps that led to another door that opened onto a flat, low-walled roof. There were two sets of fire ladders looping over the wall to the rear of the building.

Scott examined the roof area thoroughly to find it sectioned off according to which wing of the block it served. He peered over the edge in various places. The streets appeared to be narrow from up here, the traffic slow-moving. When he was satisfied, he returned to the eighth floor, locking up as he went. He stopped outside Number 806, examined the two locks. Both were burglar locks, but he doubted that there was an alarm, and could detect no external trace of one.

Scott rang the bell; he had to make sure the apartment was empty. When the nape of his neck prickled, he knew that he was being watched through the spy hole. He had heard nothing move inside. He stood there innocently and after a time rang again.

Had he not been tuned up he might have missed the faint sound of a door chain being removed. The door opened and he was face to face with Claude Denise.

12

SCOTT DID NOT LIKE DENISE on sight. He had met too many hard cases not to recognize one now. The Frenchman was good-looking, seemingly fit, and almost as tall as Scott himself. Ostensibly the image was good, but there was something about the eyes and mouth and an overassuredness that warned Scott at once. It made him briefly wonder what the Frenchman was thinking about him.

It was a strange, protracted, silent encounter, with both men appraising each other in unspoken suspicion.

"Oui?" The inquiry was casual.

"That's about all the French I know," Scott replied in English. "Do you speak English?"

Suspicion hardened in Denise's eyes. "What would you do if I didn't?"

"Ah! Thank God for that. Good English too. I'd use the sign language, mate." Scott was smiling good-naturedly. Before he could continue, Denise asked, "And what would your sign language demand of me?"

"Are you Mr. Maurice?"

"Maurice? No."

"I didn't think you were. I would expect him to be older. Anyway, is he in?"

"There's no Mr. Maurice here. You have the wrong place."

Scott pulled out the slip of paper with the address on it. He stepped back to check the door number. "This is Number 806 isn't it? And this is 58 to 68 rue du ..." He stumbled over the address and then passed the slip to Denise.

Denise stared at the slip, then at Scott. "This is the correct address, but there's no name on it. Are you sure the name is right?" He was studying Scott with far more interest now.

"I don't need a note of the name. That's the one thing that can't be wrong. He's an antiques dealer. Specializes in small enamel boxes. Has a personal collection that never sees the light of day. I understand he has the best collection of Faberge and Battersea around. Does that ring a bell?"

"None. Shouldn't you go to his shop?"

"This sort of bloke doesn't have a shop. He's a dealer's dealer and his stuff is small."

"I don't know the name. I can't help you. Where did you get the address?"

"A mate of mine in London. A dealer."

Denise eyed Scott's clothes down to his shoes. "You collect these boxes? They are costly, no?"

"Bloody costly. No, I don't collect them. But I know a lot about them. I buy for a wealthy client." Scott's gaze slipped over Denise's shoulder, but Denise was too well positioned for him to obtain a good view, and the door was only half open. "I'm sorry to trouble you," he said and turned away.

Denise said, "Check with the hall porter. Maybe the number should be 608 or something." And then, as Scott was halfway to the elevators, he called, "Are you a cockney?"

Scott turned. "Everyone says that except a cockney. No, I'm a Londoner."

"Have a drink before you go. I can practice my English."

"Your English doesn't need any practice. Everyone here speaks it better than I do. Look, I must find this character Maurice. A quick one?"

It was a rich person's apartment, as Scott expected it to be. And it was masculine. Nowhere could he see evidence of Jeannette Renore. The leather armchairs and settees, the glass-topped tables, the free-standing ashtrays, were a man's selection. There was infinite comfort, but severity too. The window drapes were expensive but too dark and plain. Scott noted the type of window and ran his gaze along the latches.

Denise waved Scott to a seat and crossed to a modern, glass-backed bar that appeared to have been lifted straight from a small club. "Whisky? Beer? Or something French?"

"I've led a sheltered life; whisky will do fine, thanks. A little water, no ice."

"Ah, the ice; an American habit."

"Kills the taste of the Scotch. When were you last in England? You speak English too well not to have spent some time there."

Denise was behind the bar pouring the drinks. "I'm often there."

Denise brought the whisky over, with a coaster. He returned to the bar to fetch his own and took it to a small, modern escritoire. He sat down behind it, facing Scott, and rummaged around until he found an address book whose pages he flicked through. "No Maurice, I'm afraid. Thought there might be one in here, but there's not. Bon appétit." He raised his glass and sat back.

Scott steeled himself; although he could not see it, Denise had left the desk drawer open. If the apartment were anything to go by, Denise was meticulously tidy. Scott tried to dismiss the notion that he was being overcautious, but with characters like the Frenchman, he would always be. What was in the drawer that Denise wanted near to hand? "Cheers," he said a little late. "Good Scotch. If you're not Mr. Maurice, who are you?"

"My name is Paul Dumanier. I'm in the wine business, which is one reason why I visit Britain so often. You're drinking more of the stuff over there these days."

"Not me," Scott smiled. "Britain grew great on beer and beef, and the beef is now beyond a lot of people."

"But you personally must do well as an agent for what will be very expensive objects d'art?"

"When I can find it. It's all in America now." Scott was satisfied that Denise had detained him to find out more about him, and that led him to wonder why. He came back to pondering about the open drawer. The man who said he was Paul Dumanier reminded him of a psychopath he once knew; completely rational, likable even, until he killed. Why did Dumanier want to know about him?

They talked on and Scott recognized that both were fencing with some experience. Had Dumanier been inside? It was a fleeting thought, but it communicated. If he had a gun in the drawer, it meant that he did not trust Scott but wanted to squeeze what he could from him.

Scott finished his drink and stood up. "I enjoyed that. Thanks a lot."

"Won't you have another?" Denise had a hand below desk level.

"No time. Nice pad you have here." He had almost said drum, and if he had he believed that Denise would well have understood the criminal slang. "The wine business must be booming."

Denise rose but remained behind the desk.

"Business is okay. I hope you find your man."

An atmosphere had sprung up between them as if neither believed a word the other said. They were still fencing and it became uncomfortable. Denise was edgy, his gaze darting and puzzled.

Scott reached the door unhurried. "See you. Next time you're in London pop into the Duke of York in Dean Street after six. I'm often there."

"I'll do that." At last Denise left the desk, but he made no effort to write the name of the pub down, as if he accepted that he had just heard one more lie. And he had not once asked Scott his name, as if he knew that that too would have been meaningless.

Scott took the elevator down. He felt uneasy about the encounter. Denise meant nothing to him, but he was living at the address listed as Jeannette Renore's. He supposed it unrealistic to expect the apartment to remain empty.

He reached the lobby and crossed to the porter. He produced his slip and said, "I was given this address for a Mr. Maurice and discover it is the wrong one." He spoke slowly in English.

The porter picked up the gist, looked at the slip, and shook his head. "Il n'ya a personne de ce nom ici, M'sieur. Not here, Maurice, no."

Scott looked disappointed and gave his thanks. He left the building. Ten minutes later Denise rang down to ask the porter if Scott had called to check on a Mr. Maurice. They were fencing to the end.

Kransouski was worried by Scott's absence. Scott had driven off with Maggie, who had driven back alone. At least it was now easier to keep an eye on her without Scott around. But a man with a probing mind like Kransouski hated being kept in the dark. He felt like marching into the Soviet Embassy and wringing the truth from Gorkin, or at least as much as he knew. In Gorkin's position he would have handled everything quite differently, and with infinitely more flair. He wondered how the man had ever been appointed as London resident.

One of the women watching Maggie had reported another presence. Someone else was keeping an eye on her, but in a more obvious way, and from this Kransouski concluded there was a bodyguard.

He was now concerned that his small female band might be picked off for soliciting. They were instructed to be doubly careful. Yet the development pleased him. If Maggie was being guarded then Scott and the detective Bulman must consider that she must know something worth protecting. With luck he might wind this up under Gorkin's nose.

Willie Scott went to Orly Airport the next morning. He had not booked a flight but expected no difficulty. When he saw Denise at the reservation counter, he stopped in his tracks and then backed away. He had been about to join the same short line. He did not think Denise had seen him, but he hung around the entrance to get a better idea. When he saw Denise check his luggage in, he went outside and caught a cab back to town.

He returned to the hotel and rebooked his room. Between lunch and dinner he rested, and at 10 P.M. took a cab to the avenue Hoche; he paid it off near the Royal Monceau Hotel.

Scott did a thorough casing of the apartment block. It was a good time, with the streets far from empty. The rear of the building was much quieter, little more than an alley. To try the fire escapes with people still around was out of the question, and the rear and tradesmen's entrances were closed and solidly locked. In the back of his mind was the possibility of Denise returning the same day.

He went back to the doors he had used before and crossed to the desk. A different porter was on duty, and Scott changed his tack quickly. Between them they surmounted the language problem. Scott told the porter that he had been looking for a Mr. Maurice the previous evening and had been told that nobody by that name was in the building. The porter confirmed this to be so.

Was there a similar name? The porter checked his list. No. Nothing like it that he could find. The nearest to Maurice was Mortier, and that was not very similar.

"Mortier? Which apartment?"

"Two fifty. In the next wing."

"That cannot be him. *Non possible*," Scott managed. He offered his thanks and went straight to the next wing. As he crossed the lobby to the elevator he called out to the porter, "*M'sieur Mortier. Deux cent . . .*" The porter nodded and Scott entered the elevator and pressed the button for the eighth floor in the knowledge that the porter could not see the indicators from his position behind the counter.

He climbed out at the eighth, located the fire door, and went up onto the roof, which he crossed to climb over the parapet to the other wing. Below him was Denise's apartment.

Scott had ruled out trying the front door. There was a limit to the equipment he could bring from England, especially with metal detectors at the airport, and the locks on Denise's door were too professional for scratch treatment. There was also the risk of a neighbor approaching. He grasped the rails of one of the fire escapes and climbed over.

These old slabbed buildings were full of footholds to a man with his techniques, and they also offered shallow ledges at various heights like the rings around a Georgian decanter. He used one of the ledges to climb along. It was not at an ideal level. With feet splayed wide he had a complete foothold and the strain was limited. He pressed against the wall, hands above him, obtaining fingertip grip on the stone slabs.

He suffered a wave of nerves. He could look down without

danger of vertigo, but the fall would be fatal if he slipped. He edged along making sure he did not lean back.

He reached the area of Denise's line of drawing room windows. He stretched up to grab the stone sill and found sufficient hold to risk leaning back to line up the run of the windows. He moved on a little more, checked, and was satisfied.

He tested a toehold on the slab above the ledge, took his weight on his hands, and levered himself up. He went up one more slab and could now rest his forearms along the sill.

Adjusting his balance, Scott pushed at the window he had selected. He felt the minute give and knew that he had the right one. With one arm remaining on the sill, his toes tucked into the crevice below, he started to push hard at the window with the flat of his hand. He repeated the pressure on the narrow framework and kept a regular motion going until the frame began to vibrate.

He could see the catch through the glass. With constant rhythmic pressure on the frame, the lever began to move, taking the least line of resistance. When it swung just clear of the catch, he obtained a fingernail grip under the frame and pulled the window gently toward him. When there was sufficient gap, he put his hand through and opened the window wide. Scott adjusted his position and pulled himself into the room, breathless and aching but satisfied. He turned the screw on the lower bar to hold the window in position to stop it from banging. Most people leave the lower bar screws loose so that the window opens and closes more easily.

Using a pencil flashlight sparingly, he crossed the room, entered the hall, and checked the front door locks. They could not be opened without a key, but the fact that the chain was off suggested that Denise had not returned. Scott checked every room to make sure the place was empty.

The apartment was larger than he had imagined, with two double bedrooms, a fair-sized dining room, and a study equipped with a typewriter, word processor, and small copier. The well-fitted kitchen held a row of le Creuset pans hanging from a long shelf.

Satisfied, Scott went back into the living room, pulled the cord of the heavy drapes and switched on the lights. He went first to the escritoire. All the drawers were locked, but he had little difficulty in opening them, and he could take his time. He discovered he was right about the gun; a 9mm Beretta lay to one side of the center drawer. He examined it, took out the magazine, and pulled back the breech. A round flew out. The magazine was full, safety catch off. A highly dangerous weapon ready for instant use. He carefully put it back as he had found it.

His lack of French was a handicap, but he was looking for anything that might contain the name of Jeannette Renore. He searched systematically, replacing all papers as he found them. There were two small, delightful pieces of modern jewelry that he enjoyed seeing and regretted replacing. They suggested that Denise entertained women here.

In the bathrooms were female toiletries, and on the bedroom dressing tables expensive perfumes and cosmetics. No traces of powder suggested daily help, or that Denise might not have entertained recently. There were women's clothes hanging in one of the built-in wardrobes, but not in the room where Denise hung his clothes.

This was a small pointer that puzzled Scott. Could the women's clothes belong to Jeannette Renore?

He found a wall safe at the back of the main bedroom wardrobe. He pushed the clothes along the rail and switched on the interior lights. It was an old-fashioned tumble-lock safe, but heavy and solid; without a key it would need explosives to blow the lock out.

Scott cursed himself for being so ill-prepared, but he was not on his own turf and had not expected to find himself in this situation. He turned the handle on an off chance, and the door swung open. He was not surprised to find it empty. What immediately caught his attention was that the lock had already been blown.

Scott examined it closely. Even with the closet lights on, it was not easy to see detail in the back of the wardrobe. He used his flashlight on the front of the safe door, closely examined it and then the lock. He was certain that the metal plate over the keyhole had been blown off and later fixed back on; it was still buckled but had probably been partially flattened out with a hammer. The lock itself was a shambles, the spring in pieces, the bolt shattered and loose by the ruptured tumbler. The whole unit needed pulling out and replacing, and Scott could now see the buckling around the bolt.

It had been an expert job and executed as he would have done it: a rubber sheath filled with plastic explosive kneaded through the keyhole so far; detonator inserted; wax applied to seal off the explosive; wire from detonator to a light socket and then switch on. Scott was impressed that just the right amount of explosive had been used.

But would Denise blow his own safe? Yet Scott could somehow not accept the idea of Denise being burgled and the safe left as it was; not someone as meticulous as the Frenchman appeared to be. Scott closed the safe, rearranged the clothes, and slid the wardrobe doors across.

After a room-to-room search, looking in places a layman would probably ignore, Scott found nothing that referred to Jeannette Renore nor anything that bore the name of Paul Dumanier.

He went into the kitchen, old memories stirring. He searched the bread bin, pushed a skewer into a half loaf of bread, then opened the washing machine and tumble dryer. He found items in both.

There were small bundles of index cards, some covered in writing, some typewritten, all in German. A name, often difficult to read, was on the top left of each card. Each card was numbered with a signatory at the foot of the reverse side, and had a faded photograph at the top right-hand side. Among the bundles were more identifiable items: identity tags. Scott himself had once worn the same type.

He took the whole lot into the study. The large room was really an office with its desk and typewriter pushed to one side of it. The word processor and the copier rested on metal cabinets designed for them. He had already searched this room thoroughly. It bore out what Denise had claimed. There were leaflets and price lists on wines. There was evidence that some of the wine circulars had been run off on the copier, a small, modern "chip" variety, which Scott now plugged in.

While the machine was warming up, Scott found cassettes in the cabinet beneath, and he clipped one on. When it was ready, he photocopied every card and identity tag, arranging them in rows to fit the space. He switched off, put the cassette back, pulled the plug out, and wound the wire, placing the coil where it had been before. He took the original cards and tags back to the kitchen and placed precisely the same ones in their respective machines.

As hiding places went, the machines were an old-fashioned concept, *but they were a villain's hiding place.* Scott felt that the cards might have been in the machine for some time, and this led him to believe that while they had initially been hidden there, their importance must have waned or Denise would have put them in a safer place. Scott made sure that the copies were secure inside his shirt and decided he could learn no more here. He had not even established that Jeannette Renore had ever been here.

He switched off the lights, opened the drapes, and went back to the window. Climbing out was easy. When he closed the window he gave the frame one big thump and the catch partially fell back. It kept the window closed; it was enough. He was relieved when he reached the fire escape.

When George Bulman asked for an appointment with Walter Clarke, the Minister of State for Foreign Affairs suggested the House of Commons. There was a solidness about the place that Clarke felt he needed. They went out onto the terrace for more privacy. It was chill and the seats were slightly damp, which discouraged most M.P.s, although a few of them were leaning on the parapet watching the motion of the gray river.

Clarke led the way down to the most secluded end and said, "I gather it's about Gordon Chesfield. I thought that unfortunate affair was buried with poor Gordon. Do you realize how many times the police have seen me?"

"You and many others, sir." Bulman was dutifully apologetic. "I'm sorry, sir. There are still one or two things that are puzzling. I don't think we'll ever find the answers, but I've been designated to try. Did you meet with Chesfield shortly before his crime?"

In an exasperated tone Clarke said, "I've been asked that so often that it's beginning to annoy me. *No.*"

Bulman appeared uncomfortable. "Another friend of yours said that you did."

"Oh? What's his name?"

"There were several of you. A cocktail party at your place about six weeks before the crime."

"Yes, I remember that. What's that got to do with anything?"

"Bear with me, sir. You did say that you had not met him."

Clarke frowned. "Let's get this straight, Mr. Bulman. You said, *shortly before.*' To me that means a day or two. You also said, '*meet him.*' I don't consider a party means meeting anyone in any purposeful way. I hardly spoke to him, and when I did it was trivia. I often throw parties. But I would not describe any of them as meeting people in a way that could be of any possible help to you." He shot Bulman an angry glance. "You're not suggesting I withheld information?"

"Of course not. But if you forget one thing, you could possibly forget another."

"Mr. Bulman, *I did not forget.*" Clarke held up a hand. "Look, I know you have your job to do. But the party was meaningless. It can add nothing to your inquiries unless you want to include a few risqué jokes to your repertoire." He smiled wryly. "It did not enter my head to mention a party at which Gordon Chesfield was only one of many guests. We've seen very little of each other over the past years; the invitation to him was for old times' sake."

Bulman sighed. "Well, thanks for telling me. It would have helped had I known before, if only to prevent harassing you. I agree that the party adds nothing to the cause of his murder."

"*His murder?*"

"I don't think he committed suicide. I know that was the coroner's verdict, but I don't believe it myself."

Clarke gripped the edge of the table. "*In prison?*"

"It's happened before. And it will happen again."

"Why?"

Bulman smiled disarmingly.

"The answer to that could be the clue to everything else. Frankly, I haven't the slightest idea. I'm sorry to waste your time, sir." Bulman stood up and watched a pleasure boat steam past a pair of barges. "Must be cold out there for sightseeing."

"Why did you go to see my grandmother, Mr. Bulman?"

"I'm sorry she told you."

"She was bound to. What made you disturb an old lady?"

Head down, Bulman wandered over to the parapet. He turned slowly, leaned back, hands on the stone.

Clarke came toward him, glancing up the terrace to ensure they were out of earshot. Bulman raised his head to meet Clarke's accusing gaze.

"Well, sir," he said heavily, "I just felt that you would not want to talk about the painful circumstances of your background."

"What have the circumstances of my background to do with you? Or anyone else?"

"Nothing in the ordinary way. I've been looking into the backgrounds of anyone who knew Chesfield reasonably well. Like it or not, I still want to know why he engineered a murder and was later murdered himself. You have no priority in my inquiries, but they have to be made, sir."

"They should have been made to me, not to an old lady. It's unforgivable."

"I was trying to protect your feelings, sir. And, I might add, save your time."

"Yet you're here again, still not satisfied. Did you think I'd say something different from my grandmother?"

"No, sir. I think you are reading too much into it."

"Perhaps. But I don't care for the way you work, Mr. Bulman. I've had enough. I've nothing further to tell you, except that if you try something like that again, I shall ask the Home Secretary to have a word with the Commissioner of Police."

Bulman pushed himself away from the wall. "Perhaps you should, sir. I'm sure he'll give it full attention. Good day." He walked away, watched by Clarke, until he had disappeared through the door.

Clarke took up the position by the parapet that Bulman had vacated. His problems were multiplying. That morning he had received a copy of an article from a little-known provincial French newspaper raising a query regarding a British M.P. No name was mentioned, and the short article was obscure as to intent; but to Clarke the purpose was all too clear. If a larger newspaper picked up the story, the probing would certainly begin. The article had come through the mail with a typed English translation to make sure that Clarke did not miss the point. At the foot of the translation was a postscript: "That's for passing useless papers. The next time your name will go in together with a detailed exposé."

Well, he had taken a calculated risk. And so had the blackmailer, who clearly had not panicked. There were no further demands, but Clarke knew that these would soon come from the man who called himself Dumain—it was a cruel, but obviously deliberate, twist to use his mother's name. Yet he was no longer even sure it had been. He had finally been forced into a corner from which he could see no way out.

He wondered what Bulman had extracted from his grandmother, who was, thankfully, unaware of his present pressures. He recalled the walks his grandfather had forced on him, and the subtle, yet constant, undermining of his confidence. The old man had not wanted him in the family; he had known that from early on. But nobody had been aware of the way the old boy had worked on him at every opportunity.

At first, when he was very young, much of it had passed him by, except the obvious dislike his grandfather bore against him. But as he grew older, the insinuations and comments made deeper marks, until he had finally run to his father in an attempt to quell his fears and unhappiness. He had been too young to anticipate the result. His father found the memories too painful and did not want to be reminded that Paulette had been shot dead. Nor did he want to be reminded that nobody had made the effort to get her to a safe place and at least *try* to save her life, as they had her baby's.

His father's reassurances were too brief for Clarke, but he never asked for clarification again. The doubts about his mother had perhaps always been in his mind—after all, he had never known her—but they were so cruelly exploited by his grandfather that eventually the reluctant explanation his father had offered him began to fade from Walter Clarke's young mind. More often than not, he considered that Paulette Dumain had not been his mother at all. In adulthood he could look back and see the irreparable damage a wicked and cunning old man had done to him, but the scars still remained, and his father, by dying prematurely, had denied him any last hope of sorting out his doubts.

Whatever happened now, Walter Clarke could not quell the uncertainties that had been so assiduously implanted in him. He knew that his grandfather had looked into his background. Given present developments, it now seemed that the old man had been right in the substance of his tauntings, and it even made some sense of his own father's reticence.

The horror of what was being suggested terrified him. Even his grandfather had not gone so far. He could remember lying in bed weeping, unable to sleep, with only his grandmother to turn to. But her comfort had been from love for him, a powerful tonic, but not one that could provide the answers he needed. If his mind was disturbed as a child, then on the issue of his birthright, it had now become completely scrambled.

Walter Clarke turned to watch the river, the turgid current a physical reminder of his own inner turmoil. He left the wall and slowly walked back to the doors of the terrace. He resolved to do what he always had done when pursued by his private demons; he would lose himself in his work. It was the only way he could carry on. He smiled bitterly to himself; friends and colleagues believed his drive to be born of ambition. If only they knew that its power source was desperation.

13

WHEN SCOTT REACHED HOME, MAGGIE clung to him as if he had been absent for years. She had been worried; for him and for herself. Yet, he still could not get her to visit her parents.

Over a delayed dinner she sparkled and he let her talk, knowing that she was unwinding and that she was untypically relating trivia. She'd had her hair done, and her eyes were bright, her features animated. "I'm babbling on, aren't I?" she said at last.

"Like a favorite record, love. Keep going."

"*You* talk while I catch up on eating."

He looked at her plate. "You've managed to do both. The sweet and sour was great."

She asked seriously, "Do I look *normal?*"

He laughed. "How d'you mean?"

"Well, I think I'm being followed by a woman. She crops up now and then and has caught my eye."

"Butch?"

"I think so. Plainly dressed."

"Has she attempted any contact?"

"No. She must be admiring me from afar. It could be just coincidence. You know, you catch someone's eye and from then on you keep bumping into them."

"That's probably it. Keep an eye on it though." He was worried. *Women* used as watchdogs?

Bulman called an hour later and Scott produced his photocopies.

"All in German except the identity tags. Can you sort them out?"

"How did you break in?"

"I didn't say I did."

Bulman raised his brows in doubt.

"That's the trouble with you coppers. You watch too many films and TV. You see these blokes with block and tackle and gadgets that stick on walls and beating alarms that wouldn't fool a kid. Where do they put all this stuff? In a car? In the dead of night? With the police having the powers of stop and search? You know Old Bill has nothing at all to do at night but stop the isolated car. Keeps him awake."

"Then how did you manage before?"

"I carried a cranium saw in my jacket lapel. And sometimes an umbrella to shake out and catch the ceiling rubble as I cut. I never carried anything I couldn't manage on a bicycle." Scott smiled. "I'm telling you in front of Maggie because she knows it's over."

Maggie made no comment and went into the kitchen. She leaned against the door with her eyes closed. The men had been making light of it, but she knew better; there were undertows in this affair that none of them really understood, and they could gush out to swamp them.

Scott said, "I think she's being followed. By women."

"Women? Who'd think of that? Kransouski? Keep away from you but keep an eye on Maggie? You know what that means?"

"Yes. I'm worried sick. I can't budge her."

"I can't spare more men than I've provided, Spider. Upstairs won't go for it."

Scott shrugged it off for the moment. "Can you do a rundown on Dumanier with Interpol?"

Bulman made a note. He put the photocopies in a pocket.

"What about Clarke?" Scott asked.

"He's an enigma; a bit of a crypto man. There's something there even if it's not connected with the case. There's so much funny business about his past that I'm beginning to wonder if he is who he purports to be."

"Jesus. A ringer?"

"I dunno. It won't be easy to prove. He's already threatened me with the Home Secretary, and if I can't produce something, then he can sink me. I can't continue an official investigation without some very sound foundation."

Scott tensed up. He examined his feelings closely. Bulman was sitting like a benign Buddha, his expression relaxed, his thoughts hidden. "Why are you looking at me like that?"

"You've already done a couple of useful break-ins."

Scott felt the chill down his back. "Are you asking me to break into Walter Clarke's place? You must be mad. If I were caught, I'd be back inside and they'd throw away the key."

"You're too good to be caught."

"How come I've done so much time then?"

Bulman waved a hand. "That was always *after* the event. You were never caught on a job. Were you?"

Scott did not answer. He did not like the warnings flashing through his mind. "Are you setting me up again?"

"I didn't set you up before. What good would it do?"

"Anything to save a high-ranking politician from exposure. If he's being blackmailed and has threatened you with the Home Secretary, we're treading hot coals. What chance would I stand?"

"I can make it easier for you. Get a bit of attention diverted and turn a few blind eyes."

"I don't like the feel of it."

Bulman waited. His timing was excellent. "But you'll do it?"

Scott was about to agree when he saw a white-faced Maggie standing in the kitchen doorway. "No," he said quickly.

Catching Scott's gaze, Bulman turned around. Maggie was scared at what she had heard, but she was also blazing angry; her hand crept down to cover her womb. Bulman felt as if he had been caught with his hand in the till. What made matters worse for him was the discovery by two schoolboys the previous day of a charred body in a chalk pit in Surrey. The pathologists were working on the few remains that could be transported. Although it was still too early to know, the belief was that Victor Anthony had been found. The Russians were playing for high and long-term stakes, and were killing the evidence as they advanced. It was as well that neither

Maggie nor Scott knew the grotesque way Anthony had died. If Chesfield had been permitted to live, Bulman considered he would have had all the answers by now. Except, perhaps, who Walter Clarke really was.

Bill Hahn studied the cable. He took it over to the window, as if the morning light coming in from a dull, rain-splattered Grosvenor Square could enlighten him further. The name of Willie Scott was on the fringe of his memory. Somewhere, sometime, he had heard of it.

Hahn had been stationed in London for four years. He had belonged to the service for almost thirty years. In a way, he had been put out to seed. He would progress no further than being head of London station, but he was well satisfied. It was good to reach retirement among his English friends, even if he was foraging in their backyard. He crossed to the desk and pressed the buzzer. When his tight-skirted secretary came in, he asked her for all the information she could find on Willie Scott.

When Hahn received the file, he sat down and went through it, reading details only when necessary. He continued studying the file between telephone calls and coffee, and finally laid it flat and pressed a switch on the intercom.

A pugnacious man of medium height came in, his aggressiveness lightened by eyes that seemed to smile perpetually. He carried himself as if he were about to throw a punch with no malice behind it. He was about ten years younger than Hahn, who said, "Sit down, Hank." And then, "Willie Scott?"

Hank Miller's face suffered a series of changes. "What exactly are you asking?"

"Anything you can tell me."

Miller noted the file on the desk and said, "I guess you've got it all there. He made monkeys out of us. A long time ago, though."

Hahn resisted a smile. "Not so long ago that you still remember?"

"You don't forget that sort of guy. He had a lot of luck. And a lot of talent." Miller indicated the file. "In there it will tell you that he was a cat burglar. The anomaly of Scott was that he was the kind of burglar you could safely leave your house keys with. If he liked you." Miller grinned ruefully with recollection. "I was working with Joe Harvey at that time. Joe has left the service, but he'd bear me out."

"What sort of work did they give to him?"

"You mean the S.I.S.? Political. They could trust him. His word was his bond. He was also a natural patsy; they would try to use him and then make sure he took whatever rap was going down so that nobody was embarrassed and so that someone took the blame to satisfy everyone else."

Hahn tapped the file. "But he didn't take the blame, did he?"

"That's where the luck came in, although he made some of it."

"Well, it's not the first time ex-cons have been used in this way. How far up the tree does his political use go?"

"All the way. I don't know his case histories, of course, only the one I was working on, but that was top level, someone close to the Prime Minister."

"So if I tell you that this same Willie Scott flew to New York to see General Stacey about the details of birth of the present British Minister of State for Foreign Affairs, you'd read something into it?"

"I'd read a helluva lot into it. I don't think Scott's been used for years. Not that I've heard about. Walter Clarke? Jeeze. We'd better start looking over our shoulders. Warn Washington, clamp down on exchanges. Think of Burgess, McLean, and Philby all together, and then double it."

"Don't jump the gun, Hank. We've taken precautions. There's something else. A detective called George Bulman, who seems to fit into no identifiable police pattern, has been helpful on occasion. The old quid pro quo. Another deceptive guy. He doesn't look or act like a cop. Most of his enemies feel sorry for him until the cuffs go on. Anyway, General Stacey, through Langley, asked him for information about Willie Scott." Hahn sat back, watching Miller closely. "You know Bulman?"

"I know him personally. Whisky swigging enigma who should be on the stage. And he can't be calibrated; I've tried. On his day, he'd make Dean Martin look like a teetotaler. Hollow legs. He's a crafty devil."

"Who does he *actually* work for?"

"He works for George Bulman. He's good, and some of his colleagues hate him for it."

"But he's helped us?"

"Sure. If it suits him. Nothing for nothing with George."

"That's what he came up with on Scott. Nothing. Said he was an ex-petty thief who was once used by MI5 about a decade ago. Using him was a grave mistake. Scott is unstable and unpredictable and has disappeared from all known scenes. Exit. Forget him."

"George Bulman might say that genuinely. From what I recall, they hated each other's guts for reasons I don't know. You wouldn't expect Scott to like a cop."

"People sometimes change."

Miller made no comment, wondering where it was all leading.

"So you believe Bulman?" Hahn pressed.

"I didn't say that. You're talking of two very cagey guys. Bulman mentioned that Scott had been used. That's true."

"Come on, Hank. He'd know that we'd know that much. Something stinks here. If Bulman is holding out, I want to know why. If for some reason Walter Clarke is a risk, I want to know. Dammit, he's on the inside of foreign affairs and acts as a liaison with our people all the time. I want you to look into this. Use all the resources you need."

Miller saw part of his past. "Just how far do you want me to go? I might have to tread on toes. It could ruin the special relationship between us and Britain. It could end up like a multimagnified international Watergate, with my neck on the block."

"What's the matter? Are you scared of this guy Scott? I'll tell you what you do; you make subtle inquiries with S.I.S. about Walter Clarke. Tell them we've received some disinformation and don't rate it, but thought they might like to know. No detail. That should get them off their butts and stir things nicely, and you would naturally expect any spinoffs. Or have I got to do it myself?"

"No, no." Miller held up his hands in surrender. "I'll deal with it. Just look after my wife and kids when the shit hits the fan."

"If it's at all possible, I'd like to go to Washington with you, sir."

The Foreign Secretary peered up at Clarke and adjusted his spectacles. It was rare for his subordinate to call him sir or to be so formal; they had a good working relationship.

"I need you here, Walter, while I'm away. What's the matter?"

"I want the break. I just feel I must get away from London for a bit."

The Foreign Secretary pushed some papers aside. He was vaguely amused, eyes owlish behind the lenses. "You don't have to go to Washington for that. Just leave town and keep in touch with the ministry. Wouldn't that do?"

Clarke had known it would be difficult. "The Washington trip offers advantages to me. And I would like to get out of the country for a spell."

The Foreign Secretary smiled. "Are you in trouble? Too many late nights and too many women? I thought you were going steady with young Susie what's her name. Got one tucked away over there have you? Oh, Walter."

"I wish I could explain. Just now I feel pressure and need the break. It wouldn't disrupt anything, would it?" It was dangerous to admit pressure, for it implied that he might not be up to the job.

The Foreign Secretary still took the request lightly.

"It would spend more of the taxpayers' money. I'm always being accused of taking an entourage wherever I go."

"I'll pay my own fare." Clarke could feel himself handling it badly.

The Foreign Secretary took off his spectacles and laid down his pen. "What's up, Walter? What's the problem?"

"I suppose it will sound trite if I say that it's personal."

"In your position, a personal issue is something of a luxury. You're entitled to your privacy, dear boy, but if that encroaches on your work, I feel obliged to ask you why."

"It's really nothing to do with work, although it would seem that I'm asking for time off from it. That's not true, though, because I would expect to work in Washington."

"As you haven't really told me a thing, I suggest you might have been studying my style too closely. There are times, Walter, when a political answer is not the right one. Look, if it's something you'd rather not talk about, why don't you simply push off to the continent for a few days?"

Because the trip must appear to be official or Dumain will see the obvious ploy of playing for time, and Dumain would not concede more time. An official trip abroad was different. It would provide a little more breathing space.

Clarke said, "All right, there is someone there I want to see."

"As badly as that?" And then, casually, "No security problems are there?"

Clarke was blank-faced; as he allowed it to slowly dawn on him for his Minister's sake, he ejaculated, "Good Lord, nothing like that. My emotional wires are crossed. It will be quite simple to untangle them; Washington would give me the opportunity."

"You should get married, you know. Steadies you down. Better image."

If ever he found his true heritage, he might. Meanwhile, he wanted nobody intruding on fears that must be conquered. And he worked too hard for marriage. "Remaining single didn't hurt Ted's image. He finished up Prime Minister."

"Indeed, but he kept a respectable profile. You seem to be becoming involved on too many fronts."

"Lloyd George, then." Clarke managed to laugh with it.

So did the Foreign Secretary. "Don't try a Lloyd George on us, Walter. News travels too fast and wide these days. Give me a day to think it over."

Bulman gripped the receiver tightly as Scott came on the other end. "Spider, I thought you should know, I've had to take the watchdogs off Maggie."

"*What?* Leave her exposed? You can't do it."

Bulman felt wretched. "It's not my idea. I argued for you, but was told in no uncertain terms that we need the men elsewhere. There's nothing I can do. I'm sorry."

"Thanks very much. You know she's in danger."

"Then get it through to her. Send her away for a bit."

"Whose idea was it?"

Bulman dared not tell him. "I'm not the bloody commissioner. I have to do what I'm told."

"*Since when?*"

Bulman heard the click as Scott hung up abruptly. He glared at the receiver and dialed another number. "Well, Sir Lewis, I've told him."

"Good. We need to hasten things along."

"You know that Kransouski made a mess of it when he went for Scott before, so you're putting Maggie on the line and making it easy—for them. Scott will go berserk all right, and he'll dig, and if he runs to form, he'll produce. But he may not get Maggie back, and you know it."

Bulman put the receiver down slowly; his chief had already hung up.

Clarke glanced at the slip he had obtained through Tony Marchant and pressed out the number. A woman answered, cultured voice and well modulated. "Is Mr. Scott there, please?"

"He's at the office. Who's calling?"

Clarke hung up a little breathlessly. He was not at all sure that he was doing the right thing, but he could see no other course open to him. He had to admit that he was now operating from a position of desperation. The French article, as seemingly innocuous as it had appeared to be, had shaken him. True it was innuendo in a sheet nobody with sense would take seriously, but it showed a willingness in Dumain to carry out his threat.

Clarke had no alternatives other than submission or a search for his blackmailer, and he had already tried the latter with disastrous results. Who could he ask to help? Which friend could he trust to that extent? He knew what they would say. Go to the police. And that was the last thing he could do. That was the beginning of the public launching of his problems.

When he considered that, Clarke reasoned that he might just as well fight his blackmailer to the last. That way he could live with some faint hope; the alternative offered none at all. And now he was about to try a compromise, and he would have to tread carefully. But he could not cope alone anymore. He needed help, and he had no recognizable aid at hand except, perhaps, this one last, highly desperate measure. He had never felt so cut off and lonely as he did now.

It was worse than the nights he had spent alone as a child thinking, and with his imaginative flair, believing always the worst; crying, longing for someone in whom to confide, someone who would really understand. And now his nightmares were on the verge of coming true, and they were far worse in reality than they had ever been in the dead of night, when he had cried out in his sleep.

He shook off the black reverie. It was becoming more difficult to do. His meeting earlier that morning with the Foreign Secretary had almost been a giveaway. A child would have lied better. Friends would soon notice that he was not himself, if they had not done so already. He picked up the receiver again, pressed the numbers.

A woman answered again, not like the last one, cheerful with a southern accent. He asked for Scott and refused to give his own name.

Scott accepted the call. Clarke said, "Mr. Scott, have you your own line? I don't want to discuss what I have to say through a switchboard."

"Who are you?" Scott had the terrible feeling that he already knew.

Clarke did not give an answer and said instead, "If you'll give me your direct number, I'll ring you right back and tell you."

"I can ring *you* if you prefer."

"Oh, no. May I have your number?"

Clarke jotted the number down, released the telephone bar, and immediately called Scott on his own line.

"Scott."

"I'd like to meet you. There's something I want to discuss."

"I still don't know who you are."

"If I tell you, do I have your word that you'll keep it to yourself?"

"Sure. But how do you know my word is worth a monkey's?"

"Because I've done my homework, Mr. Scott. Your word?"

"Okay, you have it."

"My name is Walter Clarke. I'd like to see you some time this evening, if that's possible."

"Walter Clarke? The M.P.?" Scott felt it necessary to go through the motions of surprise. "You can meet me here after hours. Say six thirty?"

"I'd rather not. Can you . . ."

"A restaurant then? Any choice you like, provided it's your call." Scott was deliberately forcing Clarke into his first admission.

200

"I was about to say that my face is fairly well known. Television is a double-edged sword. I'd rather not be recognized. I suggest . . ."

"You mean you don't want to be seen with me?" Scott interrupted.

"That's perfectly true, but it has nothing to do with *being* with you. I'm quite sure that is a pleasure I will enjoy. I live in Sloane Square. I can send a taxi out to bring you here a little later than the time you suggest. The House is likely to sit latish. Say nine o'clock?"

"That's a bit late. I have responsibilities of my own."

"If they are in the form of the delightful lady I spoke to when I rang your flat, then I envy you. I really can't make it earlier. I do realize that the request is mine, but it's terribly difficult for me."

"All right. I hope you won't be wasting my time. I'll get my own cab. If you're in the directory, I'll look you up. Nine o'clock, your place."

In his office, Scott kept his hand on the receiver and gazed at the opposite wall, idly thinking that it needed repainting. He could not believe that Walter Clarke had called him; he had refused Bulman's request to break in, and now the opportunity was being presented to him.

Keeping his word would be no problem. He would not even tell Maggie, and certainly not Bulman.

Later that evening, it was not easy to explain to Maggie that he had to go out. He always told her where he was going. He left her worried and unhappy because she knew he was keeping something from her. All he would say was that he was meeting someone and would do nothing illegal.

Outside his block he took the opportunity of checking whether the place was still being watched; he found it clear. Maggie had not seen the woman again, and there was no one that Scott could pick out in the darkness. But since Bulman had removed his men, Scott had been deeply concerned.

Scott went to the main street and waved down a cab. He felt terrible leaving Maggie alone, but the temptation to meet Clarke was too strong.

Clarke's apartment was connected to an entry phone; his name and apartment number appeared in a metal frame by the box. Scott rang, announced himself, pushed the door as the buzzer went, and entered the building to take the elevator to the third floor. Clarke's door was ajar. Scott called through the gap.

"Come in."

Scott went in and closed the door behind him. The lock was standard, which surprised him.

The drawing room reminded him slightly of the one in Paris. It was sizable, but the furniture was in much better taste. Modern comfort mixed with older, interesting pieces. It was just a little too club style with too much leather.

Clarke was standing, waiting for him, with a drink in his hand. He was a little shorter than Scott had expected, but he possessed a sportsman's shoulders, and his features were strong. The dark hair was already beginning to gray. Scott guessed that they were of similar age, although Clarke might appear to be a little younger if the strain showing around his eyes were removed.

"What will you drink, Mr. Scott? It's good of you to come."

"Whisky, please. Equal water, chilled if you've got it. No ice."

Clarke turned to a drinks tray, putting his own glass down. "I don't mean to be impertinent, but you look anything but a burglar."

"I'm not."

"I'm sorry. Of course. That was presumptuous of me." Clarke crossed the floor with a generous drink. "Do sit down. It doesn't matter where."

Scott sank into sprung leather; he could smell the faint tang of polish on it. "Cheers." He sipped his drink; it was potent. He said, "If I drink this too fast, I'll miss what you have to say."

"It's too strong? Would you like a sandwich or something to sop it up?" Clarke seemed concerned that he had made an elementary error, for he needed Scott's full attention.

"Don't worry. I'll take it slowly."

Clarke sat down, drained his glass, then placed it on a side table. "I won't beat about the bush, but before I say anything important, may I ask your indulgence once again. I don't want what I'm to say to go beyond these walls. Your word will be good enough."

Scott was tensed up. He could imagine the heart searching

Clarke must have endured before arranging a meeting like this. "If it involves violence or breaking the law, I don't want to know."

"Nothing like that. I know that you have been called in to look into the death of Gordon Chesfield. He was a friend of mine. I know that in certain circles you are very highly rated, and in human relationships, you are a man of high integrity. I've discreetly used what avenues there are to do a check on you. Otherwise, you would not be here. If this sounds underhanded, it is only because I had to be sure of you as a person to approach. I can promise you that anything I have to tell will not repulse you or make demands on your conscience."

Scott noticed the way Clarke's fingers were clawing at the arms of his chair. "Then you have my word. You don't have to worry about me, drunk or sober."

Clarke showed obvious relief. "I'm being blackmailed, Mr. Scott, and I don't know which way to turn. I must find the blackmailer before I am ruined. It's my only chance."

"I take it that you don't want anyone to know the nature of the blackmail, otherwise you'd have gone straight to the police?"

"Precisely. I have done nothing of which I am ashamed, and I have done nothing in my life to warrant any form of blackmail. It's important to me that you know that I'm not covering some crime or indiscretion. Which must leave you very puzzled, but it's true. I am open to blackmail through no fault of my own. That is the truth. Will you please help me? I have nobody else to turn to. I can back you financially for whatever you need to do."

14

"I BELIEVE YOU WERE THE last to leave the party, sir."

"Who told you that, Detective Superintendent? It's a malicious, unfounded lie." "Happy" Harrison was quietly laughing. "I'm never the last to leave any party. And if I am, I wouldn't remember. I'd be carried out. Well, laid out to rest. What's the point of all this?"

"A load of rubbish, sir," Bulman replied easily. "It's finished so far as I'm concerned. But those above me with more brains than perception, and totally without commonsense, insist that I interview each person who was at the party to discover when he or she left and whether anyone can recall when Mr. Chesfield left."

"It was stag. No women. Disappointing really, but the drink was good. Always is at Wally's."

"Wally's?"

"Walter Clarke. Sound fellow. Good host. I don't think I was the last to leave. I seem to remember seeing a pair of legs overhanging the arm of a chair as I left the room."

Bulman could see why Harrison was called "Happy." The man refused to take life seriously, but it went deeper than that. His wife had died of a brain hemorrhage two days after their wedding. It took Harrison nine months to recover in a nursing home, and he had never faced life seriously since. More tragically, his cynicism was all that carried him through. Bulman knew this, and that Harrison was the one most likely to talk, simply because nothing mattered to him.

"Anyway," Harrison continued. "Why the hell is this being raised again? We've all been through it. You can read our statements. Might be fun."

"I've told you why, sir. Someone upstairs isn't satisfied. It's like digging a hole and filling it in again and then digging it again. Waste of time. Humor me, sir, please."

"You don't look the type who needs humoring. Look, it's midday, opening time. Would you like a drink? Or don't you drink on duty?"

"I drink at any time, sir, on the premise that a policeman is always on duty; if he weren't allowed to drink during it, then we'd all be on the wagon. A large Scotch, if you don't mind, sir. These routine jobs are thirst-making."

Harrison widened his smile. "I like your style. Life stinks. Enjoy the best parts. Here you are. Never let me be accused of being mean with drinks. Can't stand mean drinks."

"Nor can I, sir. Cheers." Bulman turned to the window. "Not a bad view."

"If you say so. I must admit I've seen it in every hue, and when the outlines are fuzzed, it's quite splendid. Chesfield was not the last to leave, if that's what you need to know. I've already said so."

"That's what I thought. It was a waste of time checking."

"But he might have gone back later."

"*What?*" Bulman turned his head sharply.

"I'm not saying he did. But he might have. If I wasn't the last to leave, I was certainly close to it. Chesfield's Daimler was still parked up the street, and I believe he was in it."

Bulman stepped away from the window. Both men were standing, as some men prefer to do when drinking. "Was this in your original statement, sir?"

"Come, Mr. Bulman. You must have read it before calling here." Harrison gazed thoughtfully at his drink, flabby features verging on the debauched, eyeballs pink-tinged with angry red capillaries.

His body was going the same way as his face. "There are many reasons why that bit is not included."

Harrison gazed around as if looking for a suitable chair, but he remained standing as he said, "In the first place, the original inquiry came as a total surprise. And I still don't think Chesfield's presence at the party had the remotest connection with what the poor fellow did soon afterward. Seeing the car had not fully registered at the time. I couldn't say on oath that it was his, or that someone was in it. But with you chaps calling, asking a lot of silly bloody questions, the old brain begins to tick over and bits and pieces come to mind."

"Have you reported this since?"

"I couldn't see the point. As I've said, I can't be absolutely sure. You know how it is. When I first *thought* I saw the car, it was just a fleeting impression, meaningless. We were all well over the limit. He might have been sleeping it off. Anything. I might have been so far gone that I dreamed it. Afterward, the more I thought about it, the more I believed that it was his car and that he was in it. But you know, Daimler Sovereigns aren't uncommon around Wally Clarke's manor."

"But you *think* it was his car?"

"Yes."

"Why are you telling me now if you weren't prepared to report it before?"

"That's a good question. There are policemen and policemen. Some produce a notebook and ask questions with the monotony and automation of a litany being recited in church. Some drink my whisky with great appreciation and give the impression that what they say is a lot of nothing, but in fact they are deeply, deeply interested. Anyway, I like the way you hold a glass. But I still wouldn't have gone out of my way to report it, and it still might be total rubbish initially born of a euphoric alcoholism."

"Now you're sorry you mentioned it?"

"Not a bit. It won't make a bit of difference."

But it could, Bulman thought, it could.

Kransouski studied the cable. He decoded it a second time to make sure that he had got it right. It was the first direct communique he had received from General Rogov since leaving Bucharest. It had been routed through the Polish Embassy in a code that Rogov had supplied; it was a priority "for his eyes only."

His elation was quelled by a secondary feeling of extreme caution. He read it through yet once again, left the Polish Embassy, and headed for the Soviet Embassy, his long legs striding out with uncharacteristic speed. He could not wait to see Gorkin's face. The cable was in his pocket. It should have been burned before leaving, but he wanted to misunderstanding; he could destroy it under Gorkin's nose. He swung his umbrella like an off-duty guards officer.

When he entered Gorkin's office, he needed only one glance to see that Gorkin already knew. Hostility flared across the desk at Kransouski, who could now revel in it.

"When are you leaving, comrade?" Kransouski had difficulty in keeping the satisfaction from his voice.

"I'm catching tomorrow's plane. I wish you luck."

Kransouski laid his umbrella provocatively along the desk top. Gorkin was standing behind the desk as Kransouski said, "It cannot be pleasant to be recalled."

"You should know," Gorkin replied with venom.

"My instructions are to take over from receipt of the message." Kransouski ploughed on remorselessly. "So move aside, comrade, let me get the feel of my chair."

Gorkin swallowed and left the desk. "The drawers are already cleared. I did not want carrion birds picking over the pieces."

"Sit down, dear fellow." Kransouski indicated the chair he had previously used. "We have a lot to get through between now and your flight tomorrow."

"It won't take long." Gorkin sat down. His sullenness showed, but there was an underlying doggedness about him.

"If it won't take long, then it's worse than I thought. You must be a total failure here. I want the complete details of all networks, projects, everything there is to know that came under your unfortunate auspices."

"You won't get them, comrade. My instructions are clear. You are taking over in one respect only. You are not my long-term replacement, but a stopgap for one job. The rest will remain under my subordinate here until someone is officially nominated to take over from me. Meanwhile, you can use this office and the resources open to you, which I will outline before I depart."

Kransouski controlled his feelings, which had almost run away with him. "Who is your subordinate here?"

"That is classified information. You do not need to know. The Second Commercial Secretary will act as intermediary for anything you might need to put into action. If you look under the empty file in front of you, you will see my explicit instructions received last night." Gorkin was striking back effectively, and with the satisfaction Kransouski had enjoyed only moments ago.

Kransouski read Gorkin's directive, which had also come from Rogov. While he read, Gorkin went on, "You are project director. Just one project."

Kransouski waved the message. "One project that you failed to complete. One project so important and yet so badly handled that you have been recalled."

"General Rogov refuses to acknowledge the problems I have faced. We have had to kill twice in order to protect a potential mole who could become the most important of all time."

"*Potential* mole?"

"You sound like Rogov. If we had not severed the two links, our man would be exposed by now, and the opportunity wasted.

"I repeat, *potential* mole?"

"He's not under our direct control. Another person has convinced us that he can handle this man. He has provided limited proof. It's a matter of patience. Nothing new.'

"You've killed twice for something you haven't got? Something in the hands of another party? Someone you haven't traced? No wonder you've been recalled."

"Don't trade on it, comrade. Your seat may not have time to get warm. Both killings were justified; they have left our interest intact. In spite of your sneers, you'd have done the same. Indeed, having studied something of your record, you would most probably have left a death trail of much larger proportions.

Kransouski inclined his head. This show of ill-feeling was a luxury he could not afford. He wanted as much as he could get from Gorkin, and to antagonize him too much might result in important and deliberate omissions that could send Kransouski on the same route back to Moscow. "Who can be so important?"

"Walter Clarke. Minister of State for Foreign Affairs. Highly tipped as future Foreign Secretary and, at his present rate of progress, eventually Prime Minister."

"I apologize, comrade." It was time to be contrite. "I had no idea it was so important."

Gorkin appeared somewhat mollified. "We can't rush it. We were contacted some months ago by a man who is in a position to blackmail Clarke, and men like Clarke do not give in easily. He was probably being hooked long before we were approached. It takes time with such a man, but he's wriggling now, and there are only two ways he can eventually go. He can retire at the height of an extremely promising career, which will bring its own barrage of questions and could even bring down the government, or he can succumb to blackmail. And when that happens, I've no doubt that he will believe that he can control his output, and eventually dispose of his blackmailer, but it will be an act of final desperation. Once begun, he's in for life. There will be no way back."

"But he hasn't yet begun?" Kransouski asked tentatively.

"Yes, he has. He passed over some out-of-date defense papers. They are useless. He's still wriggling, you see, but it was a positive step. We are very near."

Kransouski whistled quietly. "I don't like the idea of someone else holding the strings. He approached us for money, presumably? What's to stop him selling to anybody?"

"Nothing. But once we have the first genuine leak from Clarke, via this intermediary, we will then hold the power to blackmail Clarke directly."

"The intermediary wouldn't like that. He would expose Clarke for whatever it is he holds over him."

"He would not know. We can still pay him for what Clarke gives him. The thing is, we would have direct control, push Clarke for information that *we* wanted. We would always express our satisfaction to the blackmailer, whatever rubbish he might hand over."

"And meanwhile track him down and discover what this precious hold is?"

"We're already doing that. It's not easy in a foreign country, and it's too hot to pass freely among our network of British friends. He's cunning. He boasted to us that he provided Clarke with a dupe; someone Clarke would believe was his blackmailer and who would be easy to find. He claims that man was Duncan Seddon, who was murdered by a man hired by Gordon Chesfield, a friend of Clarke's. There was always a risk that Chesfield might break down and talk. If that had happened, we would have lost Clarke forever."

Kransouski reflected that he was right about Gorkin's recall; the man should have been found. There were still so many unknowns in this operation, and that worried him. "Have we any idea of what this man has on Clarke?"

"None. We've been through Clarke's background. We've checked with our positive vetting man in MI5, who himself is in some danger at present; we might have to whip him out. But there's nothing. He's had plenty of women, committed the odd indiscretion, but that's all, and it's not enough for blackmail."

"It's all very odd, isn't it. Obviously something is being missed."

"I think the answer lies somewhere in his birth."

"His birth? How?"

Gorkin related the story as he knew it and added, "It all checks out. There's nothing additional we can find. Walter Clarke is no saint, but neither is he a fool, and he's a strong character. We just don't know the answer."

"We would if you had found his blackmailer."

"That's true. But as I've pointed out, if the blackmail is successful, which I believe it's about to become, then the reason will no longer matter."

But it will, comrade, it will, Kransouski reflected. It was vital to know the hold the blackmailer had over Clarke, for it worked. It was a pity he had been unable to make a deal with Scott, who could have used his underworld contacts to ferret out the blackmailer. Perhaps that was still possible. Kransouski smiled for the first time since entering the office, which was now his.

"I've no change on me, Spider. Get 'em in, will you?" Bulman had forced his way to the bar, and having found a gap, he was putting on an act of searching his pockets for money.

"One large Scotch, please, love," Scott called to the overworked barmaid.

"Are you not drinking, Spider?" Bulman asked in surprise.

"No, you're not, you mean bastard."

"Do you realize how little a copper earns?" Bulman was genuinely put out.

"If he's anything like you, he *earns* nothing at all. I don't know what he's paid, if that's what you mean."

"Don't be like that, Spider. I really have lost . . . ah, I've found it. I was sweating there for a bit." He called across the bar, "Make that one large and one single, love. Mine's the large."

"I don't drink singles, George."

"Oh, all right. Two doubles, love. Sorry he's messing you about."

"How is it," Scott asked reasonably, "that you've not done time?"

They fought their way out of the crush to the bottle-glass window. It was still crowded, but they found a spot.

"Speaking of time," Bulman observed, peering over his glass, "that's exactly what you'll be doing if you go on acting behind my back."

Scott raised his glass. "What are you going on about?"

"A visit to our Wally is what I'm going on about. Your visit."

Scott stiffened. In quite a different voice he asked, "Have you had me tailed?"

"Without you knowing? You would have lost your touch."

"So what's the rubbish you're talking?"

"When we've finished these, I think we'd better go to the square and talk. It's too crowded here."

They crossed to Trafalgar Square and leaned against the balustrade opposite the National Gallery. They overlooked the square and the fountains, and the area was surprisingly full for a chilly day. The corn vendors were as busy as in summer, and the pigeons came in on cue for the street photographers.

"We weren't watching *you*, old cocker, but Clarke."

There was no way Bulman's men could have seen him enter Clarke's actual apartment, so Scott said, "You're talking bull."

"I thought you'd say that." Bulman fiddled in an inside pocket. "One of those special cameras. Infrared or something. Looks like you."

212

Scott took the snapshot from him. "Could be anyone." He handed it back.

"There was also the personal description." Bulman put the photograph away.

"From your men?"

"Trained coppers. Observers, Spider, old son."

"What the hell would I be doing there?"

"That's what I asked myself. Oh, I almost forgot the voice." Bulman pulled out a miniature recorder. "Hold it up to the ear, the volume's not strong. One of those directional mikes. *Very* good they are."

Scott switched it on and held it up to his ear. He switched off and handed it back. "It could be anyone's voice. Any Londoner."

"But this one announced himself as Scott to the entry phone."

"I thought it was Trott. Sounded like Trott. Not me."

"Swore you to secrecy, did he? Your loyalty is to me, Spider, old son."

"My loyalty to you finished when you left Maggie hanging yesterday."

Bulman had his hands clasped before him as he gazed down into the square. Scott envied Bulman his gloves; it was cold and damp. With the traffic grinding past behind them, the two men appeared no different from the late tourists being used as pigeon perches below them. Up beyond the National Gallery, a chained man was trying to escape from a sack while his colleague endeavored to rally interest from a thinning audience. Close to them a pavement artist was retouching chalk portraits the earlier rain had partially erased. The scene was so normal.

"You're gonna get yourself killed," Bulman said as if he were talking about the weather. "I know all about your code of conduct, but this is different."

"Why?"

"Whatever your commitment to Clarke, even if you haven't made one, he's placed you in a position of no return. He must have admitted *something* to you or you wouldn't be so bloody reticent. This man is fighting for his whole future, Spider. He hasn't called in the police to help him, which means he doesn't want the police to know what he's up against. But his problems might be much more serious than that, and I think they are. If you get him off whatever hook he's on, where does that leave you?"

"You've cracked, George."

"You know I'm right. You finish up by knowing what the black-mailer knows, and that makes you equally expendable. You'll go the same way."

"What's this about blackmail?"

"It's all that's left. If the police find out, that's one thing; they have massed backing, and he can't knock off the whole force. But if you find out on your own, that's your lot, mate."

"Are you saying that he is really capable of killing?"

Bulman gave Scott a sideways glance. "As I think it's your life we're talking about, I feel bound to say that I think he's already had very effective practice."

"Are you serious?"

"I've spoken to him recently. Officially. And I've spoken to his friends. I mean it."

"Then you know more than I do. It's you who's not sharing information."

"I've nothing more than a growing conviction that I can't even voice to my superiors. You see, I trust you, Spider."

"You've every reason. Don't press me on this, George. You won't get anything out of me."

"You're being a fool. If you can't consider yourself, think of Maggie."

"I think of her all the time. You didn't. I can't see her as a problem to Clarke in any way. Our aims are the same, yours and mine, so drop it."

Bulman struck the balustrade. "I can't understand you. You've lost your edge. You've always survived by sensing danger." He followed the flight of a gray pigeon. "Nicolai Gorkin has been recalled to Moscow."

"Who the hell's he?"

"He's in Kransouski's old position., And Kransouski has taken over again. I could be castrated for telling you that. Kransouski will take the easy way. For God's sake, act your age, Spider."

"Why would I help Clarke, assuming that he needs it?"

"Because you're a sucker for a sob story. And by so doing it, it could lead you to what we're after anyway. The crunch is what happens then."

Scott turned around to face the National Gallery, his elbows propped behind him. "You say you trust me. Fine. If I open my mouth to you, you'd never be able to trust me again, would you? But thanks for the warning, George. It's where I always finish up, isn't it?"

Bulman's warning had not been necessary. From the moment Scott had agreed to listen to Walter Clarke, he had realized the trap he had walked into. Sometimes it was the only way to get anywhere. The knowledge did not stop the back of his neck from prickling, and the sensation had been there when facing Clarke.

As the two men stood together, facing opposite directions, both were aware of the pattern that was forming. At last some motive was showing through, but there was still the massive question of why any of the events should have happened at all.

Bulman made one last attempt. "I haven't told you we found Victor Anthony, the guy who was Mervin Soames's contact and paymaster. The pathologist is still not certain how he died but he did manage a positive identification, which was remarkable considering he had only bits of charred remains to poke about in. Of course, he might have been burned to death, but that would have been noisy." Bulman turned his head to see how Scott was taking it. "That's how you could finish up, Spider. Burned to ashes in a chalk pit."

"Thanks, George."

"It's true. Duncan Seddon killed by Bert Smith, who was set up by Gordon Chesfield. Chesfield probably killed by Naylor. Fuller killed by Soames. Victor Anthony killed by the Russians, who almost certainly set up Soames to set up Naylor, to get Chesfield before he opened his mouth. There may be others we don't know about. The loose head in this violent pack is probably an unknown blackmailer, and the power pack that motivates the whole shebang is most likely Walter Clarke. Well, at least we've got that far. The big question is, who will be considered the next danger to whatever it is they're trying to cover? Who's next for topping?"

For two nerve-wracking days, Kransouski thought he had lost

contact with the blackmailer for good, and all he could see was a death trail that led nowhere. Once he knew that he was in charge of just one project, surely the most important one, he knew why Rogov had appointed him. Kransouski had a pistol at his head. He was being given a second chance. Rogov had decided that the events leading up to success had been amply handled by Gorkin, but that matters needed speeding up. Kransouski had the right kind of ruthlessness to do it, and a second chance with no immediate hindrance from Moscow would spur him. He also had good knowledge of one of the participants. If he failed, it would not be Bucharest he would return to.

His detachment from the Polish trade delegation had been openly managed; most of the group had already returned to Poland, so the cover was already breaking up. He was transferred to the Soviet Embassy as a temporary helper in the trade section.

For three days the same death announcement had appeared in the *Daily Telegraph* without response, and this worried Kransouski considerably. Claude Denise took up the call on the third, and what would normally have been the last, day. Kransouski's man, passed on by Gorkin, had been instructed that a face-to-face meeting was imperative. When Denise made the call, he refused a confrontation, whereupon his contact gave another number to be rung the following day, so that Denise might speak to someone in a more senior position.

Denise was disgruntled. He was still smarting from his partial failure to deliver the goods, but he was reasonably satisfied with the article he had paid a small-time journalist to publish in France. Clarke should be malleable by now. Now the Russians were being awkward. He had little alternative but to speak to someone higher up the ladder, but it irritated him. There was always something cropping up, but he consoled himself that with so many factors involved, it was, perhaps, inevitable. And waiting should make success that much more satisfying.

Kransouski had refused to be drawn into the Soviet staff habitat. It was too easy for MI5 to keep an eye on him. His present address would naturally be known to the British, but one of the reasons he insisted on staying there was that it was easier to leave undetected. There was a back way, but the apartments consisted of three buildings joined together, so, effectively, there were three entrances and three exits, and also side windows where there was a gap between the block of three and the next dwelling. There were other ruses he could use.

In fact, he left openly with a colleague who had his car parked outside the building and who drove. The usual nonvalid diplomatic plates were up, and the car was easy for anyone to follow. The time was six P.M.

It was a good time. The traffic was rush-hour thick, and the pace was slow. In Oxford Street, in an impossible snarl up, Kransouski climbed out, skipped through the traffic, and entered Selfridge's main doors. It was a late-closing night.

There were so many entrances to the massive store and so many places to lose himself that all he need do was to move as fast as the shoppers would let him.

He went to the rear of the store, past Miss Selfridge and the parking lot pay desk, and out into the one-way street. He went along Wigmore Street, which ran parallel to Oxford Street, with the intention of continuing the long walk to the Oxford Circus underground station. He was lucky. A cab pulled in to disgorge a passenger, and Kransouski's umbrella shot up like a royal command.

He hated performing in this way, and wasn't even certain that MI5 people were following him. It was policy to assume that they were. He could afford no mistakes; his head was on the block for the last time.

At Trafalgar Square there was more congestion. Kransouski paid off the cab and crossed Cockspur Street to head toward St. James's Park. He crossed the wide stretch of the Mall, at the end of which could be seen the broadening lights of Buckingham Palace, and entered the park.

It was by no means deserted. The many paths through the park, beautiful even in darkness, were full of office workers taking shortcuts to bus stops and underground stations. Kransouski went deep into the park, crossed the bridge to the other side of the lake, and then, starting from the St. James's Palace end, began to count the benches on the left-hand side.

He stopped at the third bench and sat down. At this time all the benches were empty and passersby were in too much of a hurry to notice him. The seat was damp and he adjusted his raincoat. It was wet and cold and dusk, and an ideal time for a meeting.

It was another twenty minutes before Denise arrived. He had been standing under a tree with a good view of the bench, and he had seen Kransouski approach. For the next fifteen minutes, he spent his time trying to determine whether Kransouski had brought help. There were no loiterers that he could see. Beyond the lake and the weeping willows the dimmed headlights of the Mall traffic reflected off the wet road surface.

Denise's feet were damp in the grass, but caution was his byword. He did not like meeting like this, but when he had rung the second number, the Russian, presumably the one waiting for him on the bench, had been adamant. No meeting, no deal. Peddle your wares elsewhere. The game is over. Denise was not used to this sort of treatment. In the beginning, they had leaned over backward to be nice to him and had always been careful not to offend him. This man had been assertive from the moment he had answered the phone. Denise had almost hung up, but had quickly realized that had he done so, he would have had to ring straight back, unless he wanted to be left floundering.

Denise came up behind Kransouski, trying to get a good view of him. He was within two feet when Kransouski said, without turning his head, "You'd better sit down. You'll find the seat slightly less damp than the grass."

Denise came around the bench and sat quite close to Kransouski, with one arm along the back of the seat. "You are James?"

"I am. Who are you?"

"Harry. That's not the name I used before."

"If we're to do business, it's the one you'll use from now on."

"The other man was careful. He used a code sequence. I don't like your lack of security."

Kransouski laughed. "I'm James, you're Harry. That's all we need. What do you want extra? A buttonhole? A copy of yesterday's *Times* folded upside-down under the right armpit? Harry, you are under new management. With what you boast you have to sell, you are of no use to the Americans, who have a close ear to British affairs anyway. The Chinese still don't know what they want and haven't any money. Small, arrogant states like Libya would pay you much more, then dispose of you once they tired of the game. Only we are reliable. That is a fact. And we look after our own."

"I don't need your protection."

"One day you might. It will do you no harm to know that it is there. You are French?"

"That won't help you. Why have you insisted that we meet like this?"

"Because we're getting nowhere. In future, we will tell you what we want and you make sure your man delivers." While Kransouski talked, he took stock of Denise, who he was certain was wearing a wig; the heavy mustache might also be false.

Denise was bristling with anger. He did not like this slim, aristocratic man who was so sure of himself, and who made him feel inferior. "I don't need your money. I don't need anybody's. Don't talk to me like that again."

"Oh, come now, don't be so touchy, Harry. This is business, and so far it's lacked a business attitude. I talked of protection. You might be surprised to learn that we've already protected you. What we now want are results. We've taken grave risks on your behalf."

Denise snarled in anger. "What risks you've taken were to protect yourselves. You want what I have to offer and you protected *my* source. But let me tell you, James, what happened to Duncan Seddon will happen to you if I have any more of your bullshit. I could blast a hole in you now."

Kransouski glanced down and saw the tip of a silencer through the opening of Denise's coat. He had suspected from the outset that a gun was pointed at him. He had learned something about the man since they had started talking. Harry was evidently free of money problems. His motive was undoubtedly power or some personal, twisted satisfaction in manipulating, which made him highly dangerous and probably unstable. The gun and the anger showed too clearly the violence in the man. Even so, it was not yet time to be conciliatory. Quite firmly Kransouski said, "I've faced a gun many times, Harry. It does not intimidate me. Shoot if you want to. There are plenty of witnesses. Even with a silencer, someone will hear at so close a range. Your wig and your mustache won't protect you for long." Kransouski smiled and leaned forward to indicate that if he was shot, he would fall onto the path and attract maximum attention.

Denise was bemused. His cunning did not so far match the Russian's, and he felt a grudging respect for him. His anger slowly abated.

In a much more friendly tone Kransouski added, "Let's face it, if you kill me you will have the enormous and completely unrelenting weight of the whole KGB after you. We cannot allow that sort of thing to go unpunished. Even if Scotland Yard got to you first, I think you will admit that a prison would not stand in our way."

"I've killed before and I am still around." Denise spoke less emotionally now. He had to regain control.

"I'm sure you have," Kransouski replied pleasantly. "And efficiently, too. But not one of us. There is no country where you could hide, and why waste your life running? Now let's get down to what really matters." Kransouski was careful not to be patronizing. The Frenchman had a hair-trigger reaction, yet beneath it Kransouski detected a hard intelligence; he would not easily sabotage his own efforts. Another thing Kransouski had learned was that Denise was not a political animal. There was no suggestion of political rapport. It was an unusual case. It was time to be open.

"Walter Clarke is a marvelous find and I am sure that you can do with him all that you have claimed. I know it takes time. It often does. Clarke is a strong man, so your grip must be exceedingly tight on him to have made him produce what he has."

"He tricked me. I have made him suffer for that. The next time I ask he will deliver."

Kransouski avoided asking how Clarke had been made to suffer. "There's a full cabinet meeting in three days time. Instruct him to provide the details of that meeting. Once he provides that, there will be no further problem."

"He's not in the cabinet. That will come later."

"I realize that. We don't want him to endanger himself. But he is very close to cabinet ministers. It shouldn't be difficult for him to pass on what will be discussed on foreign affairs. We're not asking him to steal the minutes, but to discover what happened in his own field. Most of it he'll be told anyway. We need a strong hook to start with."

Denise was thoughtful. He objected to being told what to do; yet when he thought it through, he realized that however self-assured the Russian might be, without control of Clarke he could achieve nothing. "This could have been agreed on over the telephone," he said as a face saver.

"Perhaps. But we've now met and I fully accept that you can produce the goods. You are a positive man. The telephone does not show that sort of detail. Also, you have met me. I think we understand one another. Payment will be prompt, I assure you."

Denise was peering into the distance as he stood up. It was clear that his hand was still on the gun.

Kransouski smiled. "Don't worry. I would not have been so stupid as to bring support with me. This matter is between you and me. But before you go, have you heard of a man called Scott?"

"Scott? No. Why?"

"He's poking around."

"What does he look like?"

Kransouski gave a very accurate description. Denise went cold. He quickly pushed the safety catch on the gun. "Has he a London accent?"

Kransouski caught the concern. "Yes. Have you met him?"

"I met a man of that description in France. Quite recently."

"Is that where you live?"

"That's not important. He was looking for someone else. An antiques dealer."

"Scott has a great eye for objects d'art. He knows as much as many dealers and more than some."

"Give me more detail."

Kransouski related some of Scott's mannerisms, the slow grin, and minor details such as the wideness of the eyes, the often self-effacing manner, and the cleanliness of his nails, with the large half moons. And as Kransouski dug into his memory, he became more certain that Harry had met Scott. Now he knew where Scott had disappeared to for a few days.

"Is this man a problem?" Denise asked.

"He's far more dangerous than the police. He is not bound by their regulations and is answerable only to himself. He often operates outside the law with the knowledge of those who cannot."

"What would be his interest? Money?"

"Not always. Have you run into him in London?"

"No. He can't know where I am here."

"But he found you in France." Kransouski could not accept the possibility of the meeting being an accident. Scott was further ahead of the game than he had believed.

Denise reflected that Kransouski, in spite of his outward control, was shaken. And he, too, was rattled. He had been suspicious of the tall stranger almost from the outset. He had regained some of his stature in front of Kransouski. Somehow matters had evened up. The Russian had shown himself as vulnerable after all. He had to be careful how he answered, though. "It might have been easier for him in France than here. Nobody knows where I am here."

Kransouski recovered a little. He now knew what to do. He said, "You might already have considered the need to change your address here. You don't want Scott on your trail."

"Moving is no problem. Are you afraid of this man?"

Kransouski smiled wryly. "I respect Scott. I wouldn't underestimate him."

"If I see him, I'll kill him."

"It will come to that. But we need to know what he knows. Meanwhile, there's another way. I said we look after our own. Is there a telephone number that will raise you immediately?"

"You know there's not."

Kransouski knew that he would have to leave it at that. Harry had recovered some initiative. Scott must be dealt with.

15

"I'M NOT PLEADING ANY MORE, love. I'm telling you. Tell your boss your mother is ill. You've got to leave here now. I'll drive you to the station and put you on the train."

Maggie sat on the edge of the bed. Scott was *scared* for her. She knew it was largely intuitive with him. It was no use her asking him why, but she could not help saying, "This started out as a favor to find out if Gordon Chesfield was murdered. How has it reached the stage where you want to pack me off?"

Scott sat beside her and put an arm around her shoulders. "It's the way it goes, isn't it? Do this for me, love. I'll help you pack."

"I can't go tonight. It's not playing the game. I'll go to the office in the morning and arrange my work. I'll be back for lunch." Maggie was close to tears. It was not going away that distressed her, but all that it implied. "I'm letting people down by doing this."

"I know. They'll cope." He kissed her on the cheek. "You'd better call your mother now."

Maggie reached for the bedside phone, her face drawn. "Oh, Willie, when will it stop?" She forced back tears. "I thought we were finished with all this. Now look at us."

He held her close. He could not remember feeling so bad. If he could have safely opted out then, he would have done so, but it was never so simple. There was no way he could put a sign up to convince others that he had retired from the game.

"I'm sorry," he said. "God I'm sorry. You look after that nipper of ours while you're away."

George Bulman telephoned Scott the next morning just after Maggie had left for the United Nations offices. "The photocopies turned out to be dossiers of allied prisoners of war in Amiens prison in 1944."

"They'd be the dossiers General Stacey told me about. And the identity tags. Do they help us?"

"The Surete are running them down now. We don't know how many are still alive. Give Stacey a call tonight and ask him if Paulette Dumain and Jeannette Renore were among the ones he took out."

"He's not likely to remember after so long."

"He might; he was a trained field man."

"What about the tags?"

"American, British, French, one Dutch. They don't add a thing as yet."

"So we've got to wait on the French police."

"They won't sit on it. I have a friend in the Surete who'd make Sherlock Holmes look like an ad for pipe tobacco. I'm worried about Maggie, Spider."

"She's leaving after lunch. I'll see her on to the train myself. Anything else?"

"One or two of these dossiers were starred on the reverse side. Just a little inked-in asterisk beside the name of the interrogator, which is something else the Surete is running down. I had a word with one of the retired S.I.S. boys . . ."

"You mean Fairfax," Scott cut in.

"He seems to think that those who carried that mark were collaborators. Others were deliberate plants among the prisoners. A lot of that went on. Some will still be around, and they would not be at all happy if they knew the dossiers existed."

"Maybe they already know. This bloke Dumanier may be blackmailing them. Those with money anyway."

"You got the impression he doesn't need the money."

224

Scott shrugged. "Whatever turns him on."

"Has the similarity struck you," Bulman asked thoughtfully, "of Dumanier and Dumain? They come over different in the pronunciation, but on paper they're close."

There was no speculation that either was willing to make. At last Scott said, somewhat apologetically, "By the way, you can forget about me and Walter Clarke."

Bulman sounded relieved. "You thought it over and you turned him down?"

"I'm saying no more."

"If you have turned him down, he's not going to like the fact that if he's being blackmailed and he's told you so, that you're around to pass it on."

"He need not worry."

"But he will. Sometimes you're unbelievably naive, Spider."

"Maybe it's just an impression I give."

"Just remember that he might be fighting for his entire future. His life. If we're right, he's not going to be fussy about what happens to you or anyone else who poses a threat to him."

"What have you come up with?" Hahn asked.

"May I sit down?"

"Sure. You must be feeling your age as well as looking it."

Hank Miller ignored the barb. He sank wearily into a chair. "I haven't had a lot of time. I feel as if the referree is giving me an odd clout while he's behind me. Both MI5 and MI6 have stonewalled. They know nothing. Scott is a private citizen. He does not work for them and they have no control over him. They've no idea what he's up to."

"You believe them?"

"Perhaps the first two parts. But it's difficult to swallow that they've no idea what he's up to. They expressed no interest when I mentioned that he'd flown over to see General Stacey."

"None at all?"

"You know how it is with those plum in mouth so and so's. Really? How odd? Nothing to do with us, old boy. Bull. I discovered one thing though, but you might already know. Nicolai Gorkin has gone back to Moscow. The word is recalled. Kransouski has stepped into his place, whether temporarily or permanently I don't know. Kransouski was here with a Polish trade delegation, but he's an old KGB man. Very experienced. On the face of it, it's bona fide. A trademan filling another trade position."

"Yes, I know all that," Hahn admitted.

"Did you know that Scott and Kransouski are old antagonists?"

"Yep."

"Then I'm wasting my goddam time."

"So far. Why don't you have a word with Scott?"

Miller started to laugh. "Sure. He's every reason to remember me. He'll love that."

"Cut it out, Hank. I want to know what's going on. What do you think you're here for?"

"To spy on my friends. Unless we can put a tail on Scott, we'll get nowhere. Even then, he can lose a tail in his sleep."

"What about putting one on Kransouski? Or Walter Clarke? Or Detective Superintendent George Bulman? Wouldn't you think they're all heading the same way?"

Claude Denise caught the first flight to Paris and went straight to his apartment off the Avenue Hoche. He wasted no time. He checked his desk. He had an acute eye for detail and believed he would know if anything had been moved even slightly. It was this fastidiousness that Scott had noticed.

Denise was quick to note that one window handle was not quite in position. Instead of pulling it down the rest of the way, he opened the window and looked down into the street. It was difficult to believe that anyone could get in that way. Even so, he did not think that he would have left the handle halfway closed. He always checked everything before going away. He closed the window.

The carpets revealed no marks. Everything was in position. He examined his study, even the position of the plugs of the word processor and the photocopier. And then he checked the washing machine and the tumble dryer. Everything was in correct order. Even someone as exact as he could not possibly remember the precise position of the dossiers. They appeared not to have been disturbed.

He returned to the study and pulled out the cassettes from the cabinet. Again, it was almost impossible to judge whether any of the paper had been used.

Denise sat down opposite the offending window catch and gazed thoughtfully at it. It had been the only minute telltale sign, and he could not be sure whether it meant anything.

There was nothing in the apartment to incriminate him, and it was not what might have been found that worried him. The possibility of someone being on his trail was another matter altogether. The dossiers would raise eyebrows, but there was no reason why he should not have them. And those that really mattered were in a safe place.

He went over to the telephone and dialed the Clinique d'Azur in Villefranche. "This is Jean Renore. Connect me with Dr. Belime, please."

He heard the announcement go over the speakers and assumed that the doctor was somewhere on the grounds. He waited impatiently.

"M'sieur Renore?"

"Ah, doctor. I will not be able to get down for a while. How is Madame Renore?" He immediately detected the hesitancy of the reply.

"She's as well as can be expected, m'sieur."

That wasn't the answer he had received last time. "Is there something wrong?" Again there was hesitancy.

"She had a slight turn for the worse, but she is slowly getting back to normal again."

"Normal?"

"Normal for her, m'sieur. There is no fundamental change."

"I'll call you before I come down, but it might be a week or two. Has she had any visitors?" The silence was too long and he knew what the answer would be.

"She had one visitor a few days ago. A friend of someone who knew her a long time ago."

"That would have been nice for her. She doesn't often have a woman friend calling. Not these days."

"It was a man."

"Oh? Did he give a name?" He noticed that the answers were coming faster now the commitment had been made.

"An Englishman named Scott. He did not stay long."

"An Englishman? Did he talk to her?"

"You know Madame Renore cannot talk, m'sieur. It is unlikely that she ever will."

"I just thought he might have cheered her up. I think I know the man. Rather tall?"

"Yes."

It was clear that Dr. Belime did not want to talk about it, and there was no point in pressing her. Denise thanked the doctor and hung up. My God, the Russian was right. Scott had tracked him. His ego was badly jolted.

Denise caught an afternoon plane back to London, went straight to his apartment, and packed. He took the gun from under the floorboards with the two magazines and tidied the room before he left. The rent had been paid in advance and there were still two weeks to run; the landlord would have no complaint.

The message that Maggie Parsons was leaving at lunchtime to visit her sick mother was relayed to Kransouski by mid-morning. One of the typists in the United Nations London headquarters had telephoned her contact, who had passed the message on. It gave Kransouski little time to move.

Kransouski hated rushed jobs. He checked back to discover the time Maggie was likely to leave and then made his arrangements. At twelve o'clock Maggie received the message that Willie Scott would send a mini-cab to pick her up just before one. On the way back the driver had been instructed to stop at a liquor store, where she was to buy a bottle of the best champagne they had to bring with her.

The message warmed Maggie. The champagne touch was typical of Willie, she thought. He must be pushed or he would have bought it himself and kept it as a surprise. Nevertheless, she was puzzled why Willie himself had not telephoned. She rang through to the switchboard operator who had taken the message. The girl was busy and the conversation was intermittent, but finally Maggie gathered a reasonably coherent picture.

Willie Scott had arranged for the mini-cab company to make the call because he would be out of town most of the morning. The driver who had phoned had confided to the operator that he should have made the call much earlier, but he had been delayed on another job and would have his work cut out to get there in time. If he told Maggie this, she might have given him trouble. The operator had agreed to pass on the message partially to save his face and partially because "he sounded so upset."

Still doing what Scott would have wanted her to do, she called home. There was no reply. She then called his office, and Charlie Hewitt told her that Scott was not in. This bore out the being out of town assertion. She still had clearing up to do, a mass of work in a short space of time. There was no time to do further checks, and in any event, there was nothing really to make her suspicious. She had done the checks because later Scott would have asked her if she had. By one o'clock she was in a flurry. She gazed around the office, grabbed her coat and bag, and went down in the elevator.

There was the usual lunchtime snarl-up. A driver of an old red Ford Escort was arguing with a traffic warden and looking toward the building at the same time. He saw Maggie hesitate and called out, "Are you Miss Parsons?" When she acknowledged, he said, "Climb in." And then to the cop, "I told you. My fare. Have a heart." But the cop defiantly slipped a ticket on his windshield.

"Sorry about this, miss," the driver said to Maggie as he opened the door for her. "It's been one of those days. Everything's gone wrong." He smiled wearily. "But you got my message okay or you wouldn't be here."

As Maggie climbed in she said, "We've got to stop at a liquor store on the way."

"I know, Miss. I've had strict instructions on that." He closed the door and climbed into the driver's seat. As he pulled out, Maggie noticed the glass screen behind the driver. It struck her as strange on a mini-cab. Taxis were different; in them she would expect one. Nor was there a sliding panel so that she could talk to the driver.

Maggie had qualms. It was a sharp, sickening reaction that struck her in an instant and deepened as she took further stock. She could see through the windows, the traffic, people hurrying, buildings, they were all there, but the definition was somehow poor. Not quite fuzzed, but rather as if the glass needed wiping. She called to the driver without response. Then through her fear she began to feel ridiculous. What would she say to him?

Then she noticed that there was nothing with which to open the doors and nothing with which to lower the windows. The internal levers had been replaced by steel plates. She began to panic and hammered on the glass partition. The driver did not look around. Really scared now, Maggie began to scream and strike at the window near her.

She was frustrated at seeing people so close, some gazing at the car as they waited to cross the street, yet they seemed not to notice the frantic pleading of Maggie and her frightened face pressed close to the glass. It was then that Maggie felt sick and she heaved. After a while she steadied. She had disgorged nothing on an empty stomach, but the deep feeling of sickness remained as she grasped the truth. The windows were one-way glass. She couldn't be seen and she could not get out.

By half past twelve Scott was certain that something was wrong. He did not sense a trap of any kind, but he did not accept that Bulman would keep him waiting this long. Something must have happened. Up to that time he had not been too worried about Maggie; he had left a note for her. There would still be time to have a late lunch and a little celebration before seeing her off on the train.

His old Jaguar was parked outside the tall brick pillars of the Clarke's estate. The massive wrought iron crested gates were closed. It would be easy enough to open them and to drive in, but it might take time to convince old Mrs. Clarke that he must use her telephone for an emergency. There were many reasons, apart from the old lady's probable awkwardness, why he did not want to do this. He did not want Walter Clarke to find out. And if Scott went in, he might destroy whatever Bulman had in mind for this visit.

Scott paced the narrow country lane outside the gates. The property was totally isolated, but the village was only two miles up the road. It would be quicker to telephone from there. He checked his watch. The meeting was supposed to have been at twelve. A three-quarters of an hour wait was long enough. He must ring Maggie to ask her to wait for him.

He climbed into his car, recalling the details of what had happened as he drove off. The telephone had rung soon after he had reached his office."

"Mr. Scott?"

"Yes."

"Ah, glad I caught you, sir. This is Detective Sergeant Haldean. I work for Mr. Bulman. I've a message from him to ask me to call you as soon as I got in. Can you meet him at the Clarkes's place at twelve, midday?"

"Which Clarkes's place?"

"Sorry, sir. The country house. Outside the gates."

"Why didn't he ask me when he called earlier?"

"There you've got me, sir. I don't know where he is, which is not unusual. He left a scrawled message that has taken me time to decipher. If you know his handwriting, you'll know what I mean, sir."

"Where are you phoning from?"

"Scotland Yard, sir. Oh, and if you do meet him, will you please ask him to contact me? I've got several messages and one or two are urgent. I'll be here all morning, so you can tell him to use the quick way."

"What does that mean?"

Haldean chuckled. "It's a joke between us. He has a direct line, sir. If he's out and I'm in, I answer it. If I'm not here, they won't rupture themselves next door to answer this phone. They swear they never hear it, but we can hear theirs. Otherwise, calls for him should be routed through the Yard switchboard and they'll pass it through next door."

"What's the direct line number?"

"Oh, Mr. Bulman knows it, sir. If he doesn't by now, he never will."

"I might need it."

"I don't think I should give it to you, sir. It's unlisted."

"I'll explain to him. Just give it, Sergeant."

There was silence, and then, with obvious reluctance, Haldean called the number out.

Five minutes later Scott called the number back.

"Mr. Bulman's office." It was Haldean's voice.

"Just checking," Scott said drily and hung up. He then called Scotland Yard's main number. "Have you a Detective Sergeant Haldean up there?" He waited while the name was checked; the confirmation came back. "Does he work with Detective Superintendent Bulman?"

"Who are you, sir?"

Scott gave his name and address and telephone number, thinking that if they pressed the computer button his name would come up with his form to give them room for conjecture.

"Yes, he does, sir."

And now Scott drove at top speed to the picturesque village to locate a telephone. There was a kiosk outside the village post office–general store. He went into the store, exchanged some notes for a pile of silver, entered the phone booth, where a saddled horse was tied to the railings next to it, and called his own number. When there was no reply, his breathing became awkward. He began to fear the worst.

He called the number Haldean had given him and again there was no reply. He called the normal Scotland Yard number and asked for Detective Sergeant Haldean.

"D. S. Haldean."

As soon as Scott heard the voice he realized he had been conned. "This is Willie Scott, Sergeant. Just in case you've changed your voice, you didn't call me earlier this morning by any chance?"

"No, sir. Mr. Bulman's been trying to get you. He's right here. I'll pass you over."

On the way back to London, Scott drove in a cold fury. He was contained, but was too taut, his movement of the steering wheel a little too jerky. His face was grim, his eyes cold. For the first time in his life, he had to rely on George Bulman as a friend. They had worked together on this and had shown concern for each other. The gap between now and the years they had been bitter enemies had healed many wounds, many attitudes between them. They had both mellowed in that time, but even working with Bulman had not convinced him that he could trust him. They had got along much better than either could have expected, but that was all.

Now Scott had to put his complete trust in Bulman and the strange thing was, the feeling he had was that Bulman would work as frantically as Scott himself. His concern for Maggie over the telephone had been no act.

"Spider," Bulman had said heavily, "leave it with me. Get off the bloody line and get back here quick and don't worry about speeding tickets." He had hung up before Scott could reply.

Scott was having difficulty in remaining cool-headed. His body was responding to the needs of driving, but his mind seemed to take off on its own. He wanted to weep at his own failure. He blamed himself for falling into a trap, and then blamed the life of honesty he had led over the past years that had blunted his sharpness. His nose had let him down when his instincts were most needed. A police siren started wailing somewhere behind, and he increased his speed.

16

GEORGE BULMAN HAD THE NUMBER Scott had given him
checked out and it came as no surprise to find that it was in an
apartment in Victoria where the owner was away. A further check
revealed that the owner was actually abroad with his wife and was
not due back for another week. The owner was not in Special
Branch or MI5 files, but almost certainly he was a fellow traveler.
His use was finished and there was no point in taking it further.

In the meantime, Bulman arranged with the Serious Crime
Squad to raid the premises off Kensington High Street. Because of
the spread of the buildings, the three entrances and the rear exits, he
needed a good number of men, some of whom would be armed.
Less than an hour after Scott's telephone call, police squads arrived.
The buildings were sealed off back and front. Uniformed police
were used to keep the gathering crowds back.

While this was happening, Scott arrived at Scotland Yard, and
for the first time in his life, he entered a police headquarters
voluntarily. When he asked for George Bulman, it was discovered
that he was out. He curbed his impatience while he asked where.
That question entered the realms of official secrecy, and Scott
almost had the sergeant who was dealing with him by the throat.

"This is a kidnapping," he yelled. "Where is he?"

"I've no doubt he's acting in your best interests, sir."

The unflappability forced Scott to rage, *"For Christ's sake. Where is he?"* And then it dawned on him that George Bulman would not want him around while he operated. He ran from the huge building, climbed into his car, pulled out amid a blare of horns, and drove to Kensington, where Kransouski lived.

He ran into traffic problems on the approaches to Kensington High Street. The police had hastily erected diversion barriers, and cones and were directing the traffic away. He was tempted to step out and leave the car where it was, but the traffic was already in a state of chaos. He took a diversion, could find no parking spots, and was forced to use somebody else's reserved space. He left the car and ran back.

When he neared Kransouski's place, it was clear what was happening. He had seen this many police only during crowd disturbances. The street had been sealed off and emptied of people. Police and patrol cars were in position. Scott fought through the crowd and, aided by his height, could see the mass of activity around the houses. Men and women who were clearly residents were arguing with police outside the house; some were gesticulating wildly.

Scott was eager to get through the police barrier, but he realized that Bulman wouldn't thank him for it, and Bulman was quite clearly doing his best. All Scott could do was to wait. Oh, Maggie, he thought. Maggie, Maggie. Kransouski was the type to register screams on a decibel scale to see how many phons he could obtain. It was best not to dwell on it.

It was almost two hours later when an untidy, dejected Bulman came into sight. He appeared defeated. Scott tried yelling at him above the crowd; he struggled nearer to the barrier. "GEORGE." Scott waved his arms.

At first Bulman seemed not to notice, then he spoke to a uniformed policeman who hurried up and helped Scott through the barrier.

"She's not there," Bulman said as soon as Scott was within earshot. "I don't think she ever was. We've torn the place apart, every room, every cupboard, every basement and boiler room. He knew

236

what he was doing, the bastard." Bulman gave an instruction to his men to wrap it up. Patrol cars started to move off. The barricade was partially dismantled, and some of the crowd, sensing police disappointment, began to drift away.

"What now?" Scott asked. He felt sorry for Bulman, who would be answerable for what he had done.

"There are men out searching 'safe houses,' those known to us anyway. Kransouski himself is not here. But it was him. It couldn't be anyone else. He has motive and knowhow." When he saw Scott's misery, he added, "It's back to legwork, routine, the solid, patient stuff."

"Can't you pull Kransouski in?"

Bulman shook his head. "He's a diplomat now. You and I know he did it, but there's no way we could convince anyone else. It wouldn't surprise me if you receive a ransom demand to convince everybody it's for money."

"I've got no money. It wouldn't hold up."

"The wrong people have been snatched before, Spider. Kransouski will cover it up, but maybe he's not even worried." Bulman gazed around at his disappearing men. He ignored shouts and fist shaking from two of the inhabitants of the building who were standing on the steps. "Where's the nearest pub? God, I need a drink."

They walked together toward a dismantled barrier and stepped through the thinning crowd.

"I suppose there are just fancy restaurants around here," Bulman moaned, but his comment was a cover for his chagrin.

They found a pub, and Bulman bought large whiskies without thinking. When they'd settled and acclimated themselves to the cigarette smoke and the surrounding banter, Bulman observed, "All he wants is a hold over you, and with Maggie he has it. It's the bloke who's putting the screws on Wally boy he really wants. It seems to me that K is dealing through another party, and he won't like that. He'll find out who and why, dispose of your man, and take over." Gazing mournfully at the floor, he went on, "Having taken the extreme step of snatching Maggie, I have to say that puts you both in a very difficult position. It's the big one he's after, Spider. I know you're depressed enough, but you must face it."

"I know the form. There's no way I'll accept it as inevitable. If he's taken over, then he knows as much as his predecessor. For him to have done this, I must have come nearer to the blackmailer than I realized. *And Kransouski must know it.* He wants me to find him for him."

"If I know K, he'll have met him already."

"If he's dealing with the bloke I met in Paris, Kransouski wouldn't risk a tail on him. The whole thing could blow up. But I'm not working for the Russians, and inquiry would show that I hate their guts. I'm his best bet. It's got to be the Paris bloke."

"Okay, I'll get onto that too."

"If you find him, don't pull him in. Let me know."

Bulman said hopelessly, "I've got nothing to pull him in for. Clarke won't help us. And he's not likely to confess." Bulman laid a hand on Scott's arm. "I'll do everything possible for Maggie. Nationwide. I'll keep in touch."

"Can you let me know quickly how it was pulled off? They must have conned Maggie somehow."

"It'll probably be on my desk now. Things are moving while we're here. I'll get back and get the whips out."

It seemed that the stairs had been widened somehow. The color of the walls had been lightened and watercolors of British birds were at head height all the way to the landing to illustrate the interest Rex Reisen had in nature. At the top, two of Reisen's men, neither of whom Scott recognized, searched him apologetically, as if Reisen had warned them to show him respect.

The waiting room had been improved; leather armchairs and a long glass-topped, brass-framed table was in the middle. On it were copies of the *Financial Times*, *Country Life*, and *Tatler*. Scott remembered the former, but the other two were later refinements. At any other time he would have smiled. Reisen's type of investment would not be found in the pages of the *Financial Times*. He did not sit down. There were no windows in the room, and he suddenly found it claustrophobic. He was reminded of being in a prison cell, which he realized was ridiculous among this opulence. He could feel the sponginess of the pile beneath his feet.

He tried to keep his mind detached from Maggie, but it was

almost impossible. So far nobody had heard anything. There had been no contact of any kind, and Kransouski would well know the value of silence; it made those who were waiting squirm.

Scott was shown in. Again the decor had been changed, to a terrible pink floral arrangement, and the huge desk was placed differently, with a good oil painting of the queen hanging behind it. The bright green carpet was top quality, but the general effect was just as disastrously tasteless as Scott remembered.

The light from the window gave the small, pinch-faced man who had risen an ironic halo that clung close to his cropped head. The dark eyes were shining and friendly, but they could change in a second to something more chilling. Reisen was not a great deal bigger than a jockey. He smiled to show new teeth and held out his hand in welcome.

As Scott took the hand and accepted the real warmth of the welcome, he noticed that the rumors about the Union Jack having been switched from a chrome to a silver stand were false; the new pole looked like solid gold, and it would not be nine carat.

"Take a pew, Spider, old mate. I can't believe it's true." Reisen waved a cigar almost as long as his face; he hated cigars but believed they created an image. Scott noticed the flower boxes on the outside of the window sill, where Reisen used to keep his second set of accountancy books.

"You haven't aged, Spider, old cocker," Reisen continued. "How do you do it?"

"Silicone job and a hairpiece," Scott joked in return.

Reisen laughed, only half understanding. They chatted about old times; Scott bore with it because he needed Reisen's help, and Reisen always presented himself as one of the boys. When Scott raised the matter of the new faces at the top of the stairs, Reisen thought back and recalled that the two Scott would have remembered were both dead. He did not say how they had died.

At last Reisen said, "What's the problem? You back in the game?"

"Not the creeping game," Scott replied carefully. And then he lied, "I've had to keep straight over the years for reasons you'll well understand, Rex. Not easy."

"You were the best, Spider. Shocking waste of talent." He glanced at the flag. "But we all have to make sacrifices for the old country, eh! I even pay my taxes now." Which meant that he paid some. "Come on, Spider, what's gone wrong?"

"They've got Maggie."

"*Your Maggie?*" Reisen's cigar had stopped halfway to his face. "Who's effing got her?"

"The Russians. They're holding her against me."

Reisen sank back in the wing chair, which almost engulfed him. "They've got your Maggie? The rotten bastards shouldn't be allowed in the country. What d'you want? The bloody Embassy burned down? We can take care of Old Bill, son."

At any other time Scott would have had difficulty in not laughing, which could literally prove fatal. He knew that Reisen meant exactly what he said. Reisen had always solved his problems by using extreme methods. If there were a problem he could not understand or cope with, he would remove it. "That won't bring Maggie back, Rex. I want her. We can deal with them later."

"Do you know who actually snatched her?"

"A character called Kransouski. He's venom."

"Kran . . . wasn't he the bastard. . . ."

"The same one."

"He's still here? he should have been kicked out."

"He did go. He's back. Behind all this, they're out to undermine a member of the government."

"High up?"

"Dangerously high."

Reisen drew on his cigar and eyed Scott disconcertingly. "It's like your past life shooting before your eyes. Shit. I'll fix Kran what's his name if you tell me where he is."

"He'll have taken safeguards. And I must make sure I can get Maggie back first." Reisen did not like his suggestions being shot down, however reasonably, so Scott added, "I agree with everything you've said. I feel as deeply as you do, Rex. I'd like to burn the bloody place down as well. But first we get Maggie back."

"Can this bloke Kransouski be persuaded?"

There was only one way Reisen could mean that. "Maybe. If it comes to it. Is Knocker Roberts still around?"

"Knocker? You two were inside together, weren't you? He's still with me. But he's slowed down, Spider. You remember that

240

mashed up side of his face that looked as if it was filled with wire wool? He had a grafting operation on it. I reckon it's made it a bloody sight worse, but there you are. He's still strong though, a bull."

"Give him my regards."

"He always had a soft spot for you. I think you helped him in stir."

Scott agreed. Roberts was a psychopath, but he had once saved Scott's life. "What we want is the word spread around." Scott pulled an envelope from his pocket. "There are a dozen recent shots of Maggie here. It would help if you can run some off. Pass them around to the boys, newsstands, cab drivers, you've got outlets all over the place. The fuzz have learned that Maggie stepped into an old red Ford Escort. She was seen by a colleague and a traffic cop. The cop slapped a ticket on the windshield. There's the number of the car. It's a start. They've either burned it out, or it's tucked away in a garage somewhere. Not necessarily in London."

"I've got provincial contacts." Reisen took out a photograph. "Lovely girl. Never knew what she saw in you." And then, icily, "What are the fuzz doing in this? We don't want them in the way."

"It was inevitable. Without them I wouldn't have the car details. In the envelope is also a description of the driver, for what it's worth. There's one more thing, Rex." Scott sat back wondering how Reisen would take what he next had to say. "I've no money to pay for all this."

Reisen's expression changed very slightly. The dark eyes were still bright, but now they were hard. A long time ago Scott had likened Reisen to a gun with a too finely balanced trigger; a jerk could make it explode. It was never possible to know which way Reisen might jump, but he was the only man outside the police who had the facilities to organize a search in depth; in fact, in many ways his resources were far better than those of the police. He could reach dark corners the police would hesitate to tread. And his net could be cast wide. "Is Fairfax in this?" he asked reasonably. The smoke from the cigar was like a piece of string hanging above the ash.

"He's in there somewhere. But because Maggie is personal to me,

I can only get police backing. He won't finance a deal with you while the police are operating the same search. I'm here because we go way back and because I've more faith in you than the police." Scott pointed to the flag. "Maggie or not, that's what it's all about. With her back and the pressure off me, I can finish the job."

"Okay, Spider, old cock. We'll sort out the cost later."

Scott felt immense relief. Reisen would move fast. As an act of homage and one that he knew would please Reisen, Scott stood up and touched the flag.

Reisen nodded his approval. "Eighteen carat," he said somberly.

They met as they had met before, in the darkness of St. James's Park with homegoers providing a moving screen.

Denise came straight to the point. "I want to know where Scott lives. I want him out of the way for good."

"So do I," Kransouski replied easily. "I'm trying hard to locate him, but I'm quite content to let you finish the job if that's what you want. Otherwise, we'll do it ourselves."

"I can't understand why you haven't found him."

"It's not so easy for us here. Some of us are watched. Of course, there are ways and means of avoiding this, but it does cramp us at times. We are working on it through friends."

"You had better not try to locate me through friends."

Kransouski glanced down to see if Denise had brought the gun with him again. He could see nothing, but it was best to assume that he had. "It's not the same thing. Scott can be a danger to our arrangement. We've *got* to find him. I am fully aware that if we tried to find you, our deal would be dead. Neither of us wants that to happen."

Kransouski clasped both hands on the handle of his umbrella and continued. "I think we've reached rapport, you and I. I know you're suspicious and so would I be from where you are sitting. It's all a matter of priorities. I'd be a hypocrite if I said I have no interest in knowing where you are. Of course I'd like to know. But I'd be an absolute fool if I upset you to the extent that you took your wares elsewhere. I need what you have, and I agree to your terms. That is established but it needed repeating. I might also add that if I am stupid enough to lose you through some folly of my own, then I am accountable to Moscow. They don't take fools gladly there either. I think we understand one another."

Denise said nothing, so Kransouski added, "Keep your suspicions, Harry. It is healthy. I can swear that I have nobody trying to find you, and if somebody disobeyed my orders he would not be seen again. That's how seriously I take our relationship."

"Okay. But I shall be on the lookout."

"I trust you will be."

"Won't Scott be in the telephone directory?"

"Along with hundreds of others. He varies his first name, and I'm not even sure that Scott *is* his real name. The directory won't help you."

"Where does he work?"

Kransouski smiled. "He used to work on the wealthiest homes. Don't worry too much about him. I'm sure that he won't know where you are here. There's no reason why he should find you. I'm certain that we will find him first."

Bulman had his direct line and his switchboard phones to his ears when the door crashed open. As soon as he saw the uniformed lanky figure of Deputy Commissioner Sims he knew that he was in trouble. With hands still holding the telephones, he gave a warning glance to Detective Sergeant Haldean, whose desk was against the wall. Haldean had turned when the door had opened, and he too recognized the signs. Sims was breathing fire, his eyes blazing with anger. Haldean rose, discreetly squeezed his way past the Deputy Commissioner to leave the office, and closed the door behind him. It was rare that he felt sorry for George Bulman, but he did now.

Sims signaled frantically for Bulman to put down the telephones, but Bulman shrugged helplessly and continued to talk into them in turn. It would make no difference what he did. When eventually he replaced the receivers, he could see that the delay had done nothing for Sims's fury. He sat back and waited for the blast.

"My God, you've overstepped the mark on occasion, Bulman, but this time you've blown it. Clear your desk, you're suspended as of now."

"I'm entitled to know why, sir."

"*Why?*" Sims could hardly contain himself. "You raid diplomatic quarters with the heavy mob and you ask why? God man, you didn't even consult anyone."

"They're not diplomatic quarters."

"Don't split hairs with me. They may not be registered, but that block of three houses contains only diplomats. Nobody else. They're bawling their heads off down there. The Commissioner has already had a personal visit from the Soviet Ambassador, and Moscow is screaming for retaliation. There's hell to pay over this. We haven't a leg to stand on. How dare you make a decision like that on your own? And you've involved the Serious Crime Squad. God, we're going to have trouble."

"The Squad is not involved. They took my word that the premises had no diplomatic immunity even if some of the residents did. The rest are fringe agents and semidiplomatic staff the Soviets don't really need except to keep us occupied. Kransouski snatched a girl, and he's holding her somewhere. I had to move fast. I'd do it again."

"You won't get the chance. When the PM hears about this your feet won't touch the ground, so get out before the balloon really goes up. You've asked for this."

"Sure. So did the girl, I've no doubt. Why don't we lick their shoes? Or better still, print an apology?"

"Don't make it worse for yourself, Bulman. I'll get someone in here to take over."

"With respect, sir, you will find that beyond your brief."

"Does the press have this story?"

"How can a raid like that escape the press? It'll be splashed over every sheet. Girl missing. Soviet premises raided. And I'll tell you something else; if the Russians could put a clamp on our press, they'd do it right now. They don't want it publicized. They'll clamor behind the scenes, but that is all. *They're bloody guilty.*"

"You mean to say you haven't requested a D notice?"

"No, sir, I have not. If you want censorship, you see to it."

"Out, Bulman, now." Sims reached for a telephone. "I just hope it's not too late."

Bulman grabbed his coat from the hook behind the door.

"Your sense of concern over the girl touches me deeply, sir. Still, as long as we keep those Soviet bastards happy, that's all that matters."

Sims demanded a number through the switchboard, then said to Bulman, "You self-opinionated fool. You don't even know they took her. You're probably as right about that as you were about the raid you organized. Out, damn you. And stay out."

"Suspended on full pay I take it, sir?" Bulman said, and slammed the door as he left. He had taken only a few paces down the corridor when he turned back and opened the door again. Sims was issuing urgent instructions for a D notice. When he put down the phone, Bulman said sweetly, "Just one more thing, sir. While the Russians are rupturing their vocal cords and the Home Secretary is making profuse apologies before the P.M. sends him to the Tower, you won't forget to mention the high-powered radio equipment and the codes we unearthed, will you, sir?" He closed the door quickly, before Sims had a heart attack. Haldean appeared in the corridor. As Bulman went past him he clapped the sergeant on the shoulder. Neither man spoke.

17

T HE DAY OF THE RAID Walter Clarke left for Washington with
the Foreign Secretary and his entourage. He was withdrawn and
had great difficulty in raising a smile for the press before boarding
the Concorde at Heathrow. When the Foreign Secretary queried
Clarke's moroseness, he received the explanation of a mild stomach
upset.

Clarke was more worried than he had ever been. The man who
called himself Dumain had telephoned the previous night demand-
ing a report on the next cabinet meeting; Clarke knew that this time
there was no way he could hedge. He could either produce or face
exposure. Dumain would not allow him to prevaricate any longer.
The running was over. Even if Clarke reported the whole affair to
the Foreign Secretary, which would also mean the Prime Minister,
it was not a course for survival. And a thwarted Dumain would
publish anyway. The final trap had been closed.

There were a few days stay of execution due to his visit to
Washington and the fact that the next cabinet meeting would take
place in the absence of the Foreign Secretary and himself. There
was no way he could avoid the meeting after that, and if he tried the
worst would happen. He took nothing but whisky and black coffee

on the journey over the Atlantic. His future as he had seen it was finished.

Denise read the report of Clarke's departure to make sure he had been told the truth. He foresaw something of what might happen next, and he decided to follow his instincts. He had not been completely misled by the Russian. He accepted that his new contact was too professional to do anything obvious, but would try just the same. The Russian needed to possess the influence Denise wielded over Clarke and would inevitably attempt to obtain it. But the Russians were merely a tool. Once Clarke was passing significant information that would be turned over to the Russians, Denise would then betray the fact to those who mattered, and Clarke's destruction would be complete.

It was as though his blood was overheated. He had not felt this excited since he had killed his half sister and the Algerian. It felt good to demoralize someone, get him on his knees begging for mercy, but it was never the same as total destruction. It was good to make an intelligent mind suffer, but the adrenalin rose that much more quickly when he could actually see the life being squeezed from someone.

What had made Clarke more of a challenge was this silent defiance: he had *not* begged for mercy or offered easy substitutes such as money. From the beginning, Clarke had accepted what Denise had provided, and had tried to fight his way from the corner into which he was hemmed. And yet the ultimate result had been obvious to both men. Clarke had failed to find a miracle, and Denise now knew that the final stage was at hand. The exhilaration was almost unbearable.

Denise could neither sleep nor keep still. Everything was poised as he had planned. It had taken longer than he had hoped, but that would only make it better on the day. Meanwhile, he did not believe that Scott could not be found. The Russian had been too obtuse about Scott, and Denise perceived why. He would kill Scott while Clarke was away.

Scott gazed at Bulman, unsure of his own feelings. The news that Bulman had brought with him had both stunned and deeply affected him. Everything was going wrong. His anguish over Maggie was partially muted by his concern for Bulman. "Suspended?" he repeated. "For trying to find a kidnapped woman?"

Bulman studied the bottle of whisky that Scott had placed, with a glass, on a table beside his chair. The bottle remained unopened, as if Bulman needed to prove that in crisis he could do without the stuff. He shrugged. "People like Sims get hysterical if it comes to rocking the diplomatic boat. They're not all like him. But we didn't find Maggie and that made the difference."

"Did you expect trouble over the raid?"

Bulman was drawn to the bottle, but his arms remained stretched along the chair. "I don't suppose I thought about it. Anyway, Kransouski had been at the Embassy and apparently had done his normal shift before and after Maggie disappeared. I told Sims and I'm telling you, I'd do it all again."

"For Maggie?"

Bulman appeared embarrassed. His craggy face turned away, as if he could not face Scott, but he replied, "I owed you."

"That was ages ago."

"Maybe. And maybe, too, if I'd have got my way then, you'd have still been tucked away inside."

Scott did not know what to say. He was deeply touched, and it affected him the more because the feeling came so much as a surprise. "Thanks, George. But you're out of a job."

"It's all under control. It was on the move long before Sims showed his face. The wheels are turning and I've got friends who'll keep me posted. Don't worry. I can operate on suspension. It's better in a way. I'm not tied down with other jobs."

"I've had a word with some friends, too."

"I thought you might. I don't want to know."

"And Walter Clarke left for the States today. Are your men still watching his place?"

"Not while he's away, but Sims would have stopped that as a first priority anyway. Keeping tabs on a Minister? He wants to make Commissioner, God forbid."

"Then I'm breaking in tonight. It will help keep my mind off Maggie, and maybe I'll find something to pry this thing open."

Scott went to a West End florist, bought two dozen assorted roses, and attached a blank card to them. He called a cab and went to Walter Clarke's apartment block. There were two women listed on the nameplate beside the entry phones. He rang the bell of the first one. There was no reply.

It was mid-afternoon. Scott preferred to work in darkness, but without a front door key, he was forced to operate in daylight to gain entry to the building. He tried the second name and received a response.

"Mrs. Walker?"

"*Miss* Walker, yes."

"I have a bunch of flowers for you. Interflora."

"Flowers? Who from?"

"I don't know ma'am. The card is sealed."

"Bring them up."

The buzzer went and Scott headed for an elevator. He got out at the third floor and rang the bell of Miss Walker's apartment, keeping the roses in front of his face."

Miss Walker called out, "Leave them in front of the door, please."

Scott did not blame her. Flowers were an old entry trick, and he preferred that she not open the door anyway. He left the roses outside, turning while he bent down so that she would miss his face through the spy hole as he straightened. He went up the stairs to Walter Clarke's apartment. He opened Clarke's door with one of his skeleton keys, entered, and quietly closed the door behind him.

His first priority was to make sure the rooms were empty. Clarke was bound to have a cleaner, but generally speaking, domestic help operate during the morning. He then looked for an alternative means of exit and found a precarious one through the bathroom window, which had a rainspout running down the outside wall.

Clarke had been careful. Possibly due to the fact that a cleaner almost certainly let herself in, there were no ministerial or government papers to be found anywhere. But for some personal letters, unrelated to politics, it would have been difficult for anyone without prior knowledge to guess Walter Clarke's occupation, until Scott found two copies of *Hansard*.

He searched minutely. After an hour, the ground-floor buzzer rang. Scott waited. The ring was repeated, prolonged this time. Someone did not know that Clarke was away, or was trying to establish that the apartment was empty. Scott peered down through a gap in the drawing room's net curtains, but the angle was wrong. After a while he continued with his search.

Some time later the telephone rang. It pealed out as if it would never stop; three minutes can be an eternity. Scott knew the techniques. They were obvious ones but could be effective. He believed that whoever had rung the bell had also telephoned. As a precaution he wedged a chair under the front door handle; it would give him time to get out the other way if someone tried entry through the door.

At five o'clock he sat down at the kitchen counter to think over the problem. There might be nothing to find, but he doubted that. He had discovered some keys, one of which might be a safety deposit key.

As Scott sat pondering, he looked into his own past and wondered whether he had forgotten too much. But when freedom is at stake, the lessons remain, even if response to them has been slowed. Scott felt he had broken through the rust layers. He was now operating as he used to do: calmly, methodically, and with considerable experience.

He had more than ample time, for he had no intention of leaving before it was dark; he would leave long after rush hour. He wanted the occupants to settle down for the evening, either out or in, before leaving. He did not want to be remembered by anyone in this building. He briefly thought of Miss Walker trying to work out who could be so stupid as to not have signed the card with the roses, and then he started work again.

He found the safe behind a ladder bookcase. There was no need to move the case, and by taking out one shelf full of books, he was able to see the safe quite clearly. He laid the books down on the carpet.

The space between the shelves was about a foot, and the width of the bookcase twice that much. The safe door was about ten inches square and would open comfortably within the shelf space.

It was awkward operating through the shelf gap and difficult to get his head close to the door. Scott went back to the kitchen and found a tall glass. He pulled out a wad of plasticine and kneaded it around the open rim of the glass; then he pressed it onto the safe near the dial. The glass acted as a crude stethoscope, the sound blocked in by the seal.

It was slow, tedious work. Even with the glass suctioning on the safe door, the glass had to be kept in place; it became irritatingly tiring. When the telephone rang again, Scott jumped, his concentration ruined. He started again. There was now a pattern to the telephone calls; they had become hourly on the half hour. The calls were making Scott uneasy.

The safe took much longer to open than he had expected, and the light was fading. He did not want to pull the drapes until it was really dark, but in preparation he had already padded a bath towel along the bottom edge of the front door.

Finally he heard the last tumbler fall, and the safe door swung open. The depth of the safe was no more than the width. Some papers had been folded over in order to get them in. Before touching anything, he memorized the position of the contents. He then took them out layer by layer and spread them, top to bottom, on a low table.

The very first layer contained what he was looking for. A dossier, similar to those he had found in the Paris apartment, was there with translation in English clipped to it. There were letters written in German and French with translations, and there was a document of commendation signed by Hitler. There was also a press cutting from a French newspaper or magazine, and, again, there was a typewritten translation. Scott started with the dossier.

He was not sure at what time he rose to pull the drapes and to put on the lights. He did not even glance at his watch. Time had suddenly become unimportant as the content of what he was reading made its riveting impact on him. Long before he was finished, he became desperately sorry for Walter Clarke, yet he realized the dangers that went with the sentiment.

One by one, Scott read every item. Each document, letter, or article was a photocopy, and Scott guessed that they had been done on the machine he had used in Paris.

There was no such convenience here. Clarke's study was small and cramped, and there was not even a typewriter. Scott got down to the job of making notes. The general data were easy enough to remember, but names and certain sections were too important to try to memorize.

It was past nine o'clock before he had finished, and he was late to realize that the telephone calls had stopped. He placed all the papers back in the safe, locked it, and put the books back in order.

He went through the rooms to check that everything was as it should be, and the moment he was satisfied, his mind flew to Maggie, although, whatever his preoccupation, she was always there. It was agonizing to think of her. He decided to wait until half past nine before leaving, so he rang Rex Reisen.

Reisen was not in his office, but someone answered. When Scott gave his name, he was quickly given the number of one of Reisen's clubs. Scott rang again and was put through.

"Where've you been? I've been trying to get you," Reisen shouted into the telephone.

"You must have something." Scott was almost afraid to speak.

"I don't sit on my arse doing nothing. We traced the car. As soon as you mentioned it, I had an idea who'd have pulled that stunt. Freddie Bannen. Red Freddy. Sometimes called the Banner. Runs a mini-cab company. And a lot else. Has messenger motorcycles and can produce drivers with crowd control experience. They were used during the Brixton riots, directing the rioters away from Old Bill. Walkie talkies, the lot. Probably had a hand in those up north as well. Right bastard. The car has been used before for a snatch to raise money, but not for some time. Registration plates don't mean a thing; he has a stack of plates from old bangers. Are you listening, Spider?"

Scott found he was trembling. All he could say was, "Go on, Rex."

"We didn't waste time looking for the car at first. It turns out it's out in the sticks now anyway. Tucked well out of sight. The fuzz won't find it. We went straight for Freddie. We gave him the old witch's treatment by putting Knocker onto him. If he survived he was guilty, and if he croaked he was guilty." Reisen laughed at his own crude joke and Scott kept silent. Scott wanted to know what had happened to Maggie, but he had to endure the build-up that Reisen obviously enjoyed so much, and the result of which had filled him with immense satisfaction. His gesture, as helpful to Scott as it appeared to be, was also the resurrection of his own image, which from time to time he felt needed a boost.

"Anyway," Reisen went on. "Red Fred survived. Just about. Nothing wrong with him that a decent orthopedist can't fix." He laughed again. "I hope the poor sod has health insurance."

"And Maggie?" Scott ventured nervously.

"Oh, yeah. Well, Freddie took her out of town and she was then handed over to a couple of goons out in the sticks, and they took her off in another car."

"He doesn't know where?"

"Right now he doesn't know his own name. And don't feel sorry for the bastard because what he's just had was overdue. Besides, it gave Knocker some well-needed practice. But there was nothing more left in him, Spider. What he had, we wrung out've him."

So far, no further. Scott felt the huge disappointment grow. He could not complain. He said, "Surely the cops know about this character Freddie."

"Oh, sure. They've had him in and out over the years. But this time he went to earth, and they didn't know where to look. We have better black hole connections, old son. We eat *three* Shredded Wheat. It took no time at all to find the stirring bastard."

In spite of Freddie's obvious critical condition, Scott felt obliged to say, "Thanks, Rex." And then, "What happens next?"

"How far do you want to go, cocker? We've gone halfway. Kransouski is the bloke who knows. Do you want him lifted or not?"

"That won't be so easy to do."

"Old Bill watching him?"

"Bound to be."

"If this is for queen and country, can't you fix it? Get 'em to miss a duty or two? Won't take us long to do the job if the coppers are looking the other way."

Scott was silent for too long.

"Do you want it done or not?" Reissen demanded.

"I don't want what happened to Bannen to happen to him."

"Don't be so bloody fussy. Okay, I'll tell Knocker to use one hand, but if you want your Maggie back, that's the way it's gotta be. Now do we, or don't we?"

254

"Do it," Scott said. "Just one thing. I'll have to talk to . . . I'll have to fix it. I'll ring you later tonight or early tomorrow."

"Done. See you, boy."

Scott put down the telephone. He felt weak. The only way he could justify himself was by thinking of Maggie and what she was now suffering. She would be terrified, and Kransouski was well trained in terror. He had to convince Bulman first; suspended or not, Bulman was still a copper.

Scott made sure he had his notes, switched off the lights, and pulled back the drapes. He stood in the darkened room for a while, a reflection of the town lights cascading through the windows; then he went into the hall. He looked through the spy hole before opening the door, then took the elevator to the ground floor and let himself out.

It was the time of night when the dinner crowds had broken up and had gone on to pubs or clubs, and the theater crowds had yet to turn out. Scott walked to South Kensington underground station for the Circle line. He was still lost in thought. The apartment would be unbearable without Maggie, with all her things around him. Everything there would remind him of her. Being half-crazed with worry was something he could partially shut out, particularly while he worked, but the apartment would suggest her actual presence. He considered whether he should go back or not. He needed to see Bulman anyway.

He was also worried about Reisen. When Reisen believed he was flying the flag, he could go berserk and expect to get away with it, believing he possessed a kind of national immunity while, in his view, he operated for the crown. Yet Reisen was right. The police would not solve this one. Apart from any other reasons, they would be treading on egg shells, working with one hand tied behind their backs.

As he sat in the three-quarters empty subway car, totally immersed in his thoughts, he received his first pinprick of warning. It came out of nothing; a spark that flared in the gloom of his mind. Suddenly he knew, without actually having seen, that he was being followed, and that this was different from the other times because with the knowledge came a sense of danger. Slowly he looked up and stared around the car.

18

T HERE WERE PLENTY OF EMPTY seats. A group of youths at one end of the long coach were looking for trouble and swinging from the straps. Scott scanned his way down the opposite side of the car, across the gap to the next compartment.

Weary eyes suggested late nights at the office. Two over made-up teenage girls ogled him suggestively, and he felt pity for them. One or two elderly people stared at the ad opposite them. There was a central core of nondescript types, both men and women. Scott's gaze switched to his own side of the coach, and, through the glass, he saw the shoes at the far end.

The legs stuck out or he might have missed them. He had last seen the handmade pair of shoes in Paris. The man's face was behind a newspaper, but just above it Scott saw the top of the head. The hair was the wrong color. He was not put off by this. He himself had worn wigs often enough. He moved his feet noisily, as if to stand up, and immediately the paper was lowered, and hard bright eyes glanced toward him.

Scott rose and moved down the coach to sit next to the man with the newspaper, which had shot up again to screen the face. One of the man's elbows was on the armrest, and Scott deliberately pushed it off to make way for himself. There was no response; the paper remained where it was. It was then that Scott was sure. He put out a hand and deliberately pulled down the paper.

"Well, well," Scott said. "Paul Dumanier. You won't have forgotten that you gave me a drink at your place in Paris. How's things?"

The hard eyes tried to stun Scott into silence. "You have made a mistake." The paper came halfway up again. "That is not my name."

"Well, I don't suppose it is. Dumain perhaps? Or isn't it that either?"

Denise kept his voice down, aware that one or two people were staring. "I do not know you and you're beginning to make yourself objectionable." Denise's jaw was clamped, the muscles protruding at the joints. He was blazing angry.

Scott leaned across and touched his arm. "Come on, Paul. The wig is bloody awful, the cheek pads are crucifying you, and the mustache doesn't match the hair. The only thing that's normal is the gun in the shoulder holster. Right-handed I notice. But you wouldn't shoot me now, would you? On a subway train?" Scott briefly gazed about him. "Too many for one magazine to knock off. You'll have to wait until we're outside."

Scott's jibing tactics had completely unsettled Denise. The hands holding the newspaper were bunched, the paper screwed into them. Scott continued, "Why did you keep ringing at Clarke's place? Did you see me go in? Take a chance of flushing me out? Oh, by the way, I change at Paddington. It's the nearest I can get on this line. You want to tag along? I'll return your drink at my place."

Denise made sure the newspaper covered his face from the other passengers. He turned his head, eyes hard with fury and hate. "I'm going to kill you, Scott."

"Aren't I trying to help you do it? So Kransouski told you my name, did he?"

"Who?"

"Ah! So you don't even know who you're dealing with. Uses a code name, does he? Tom, Dick, or Harry? No, he'd keep one of those for you. Too common for him. Tall, aristocratic? Looks as if he's served in the British Coldstream Guards? I see I'm right. Watch him, Paul. He's a treacherous bastard. Right now he's using me to find you, but if he'd have tagged along he'd have got us both."
258

Half turned in his seat, Scott was watching Denise closely. The Frenchman had lost some color and did not know how to deal with the situation. He could not kill Scott with so many witnesses; he would have to wait. Yet he had learned something from Scott, and other doubts had been confirmed. When he turned to face the Englishman, he poured out his malice, willing Scott to back down. He could not understand the mildness of the gaze, almost humorous, the relaxed posture. He began to wonder if Scott himself was armed, as both hands were now in his pockets.

"I accept your offer of a drink," Denise said at last.

"Good, old mate. For reasons I can't explain now, it won't be possible to knock me off in my own pad. Just take my word for it. We'll have a chat. I mean you must be worried sick about what I might have found at Clarke's place. Don't worry. I won't tell Kransouski. Do you want me to spell that, by the way?"

While Scott had been talking, he had been taking note of the stations. The train had stopped twice since he had joined Denise, and the approaching station was Bayswater. As the train slowed and the platform began to slide past, Scott said, "Next one. Paddington." But Denise was trying to keep behind his paper shield again.

The doors slid open. Denise steeled himself as he had done at each stop, but Scott was relaxed, feet out and crossed. Suddenly Scott scooped his feet under Denise's and kicked them up. Denise fell back in his seat, newspaper flying but still firmly held in one hand as Scott rose quickly and stepped over Denise's straddled legs. In three long strides, Scott was at the doors as they closed. He just managed to get his hand through the gap and pulled one door back to worm his way out. He released the door just before Denise reached it.

Denise was mouthing through the door, scratching at the glass, newspaper trailing, as Scott ran for the exit. When Scott reached the street he found the nearest doorway and sank back into it. After a while he realized that Denise had not managed to get out. Only then did the tension ease. It had taken a lot out of him to put on his uncaring act.

He rang Bulman from his apartment. It was by now half past ten. Bulman had gone to bed early after the disappointment of the last two days. Bulman made no protest; he dressed quickly and went over to Scott's place. It was Bulman who found the note on the mat behind Scott's front door. Scott himself had missed it in his relief to get home and his need to telephone Bulman.

The sealed envelope contained two typed words in the middle of a single folded sheet of notepaper: "AN EXCHANGE." That was all.

"Mailed in Croydon," Bulman observed. "He wouldn't risk a hand delivery. Nothing incriminating. We know what he means, and that's all that matters. It won't trace back to K, and Sims won't have him picked up with all the political furor."

"He could almost have had it tonight," Scott said bitterly. "I met Dumain."

They sat down and it was then that Scott noticed the edge of pajamas under Bulman's trousers. Scott told him what had happened and afterward he said, "I toyed with the idea of grabbing a cab to Paddington and picking up his trail from there. But I wouldn't have made it, and there's never a taxi when you need one. And he might have caught the next train back to Bayswater."

"Spider, I'd move out of here. He knows you've been to Clarke's; he'll want you dead quick. He's only to look you up in the telephone directory."

"The flat is in Maggie's name. So is the telephone number."

"Does he know about her?"

Scott shrugged. "I don't know. In any event, I've got to draw him to me or go out and find him. We both know the form."

"The only difference is, he carries a gun and you don't. He'll go flat out for a kill, Spider."

"By then you'll have the details, too, so he'll have to kill you as well. He can't kill the whole bloody police force."

"The whole bloody police force isn't going to be told. If it's really dicey about Clarke, I've got to be sure of my facts before I tell anyone. So what did you find?"

"It's grim," Scott replied, pulling out his notes, "and terribly sad, an impossible situation from Walter Clarke's viewpoint. I now understand why he didn't report the matter and why he was so desperate to approach me." Scott riffled through his notes and got them in order.

"It boils down to this," he said. "Paulette Dumain was not

260

Clarke's mother. Nor was Captain Clarke his father. There was a baby all right, but whether the child survived or died, I don't know. Walter Clarke is Jeannette Renore's son. She gave birth five months after Paulette Dumain. Jeannette was a brave woman, there is absolutely no doubt of that, but her award for valor was ironic. She was a traitor and had been almost from the start of her resistance work. A good many resistance fighters in Amiens prison were there because of her treachery. To make it look good, she had to join them in jail; but there was another more personal reason.

"For some time Jeannette had been the mistress of a man called Werner Hochricht. Hochricht was the Gestapo's second in command in the area; he operated to a large extent from the prison. He was known as the Butcher. He tortured to death many of Jeannette's colleagues, and he left others useless, maimed in both mind and body. His final death list is impossible to estimate, but it must have been phenomenal.

"Jeannette was kept well away from the torture chambers so that she would not hear the horrific screams of her lover's victims. Paulette Dumain, who was herself a true patriot, a real daughter of France, kept her company. The two were friends, but Paulette had no idea to the last that Jeannette was a traitorous bitch. Presumably, all prisoners were taken from their cells and tortured individually, so it would be no problem for Jeannette to simulate pain and agony after having had a passionate interval with Hochricht.

"In fact, both women had been in prison for no more than four months, but the finger must have been pointing at Jeannette before that, which tells us almost certainly why she was brought in. She was invaluable to the Nazis and managed to escape with others during the R.A.F. bombing raid on the prison. That would have been ideal for her. Heroic escape and back among the true resistance. If she were ever picked up, there would be no problem.

"We'll never find out who put a bullet through Paulette's head. It might well have been a merciful killing, but the dossiers and ID tags General Stacey lifted were almost certainly taken by Jeannette. Her own was among them, and it had the special asterisk to indicate the status of collaborator. But she had more than that attached to the card. In Hochricht's own handwriting was her real dossier, her antiresistance activities, her acts of 'bravery,' and the date of the baby's conception according to a German army doctor. She was pregnant for three months before the bombing. Hochricht would have wanted to get her out before it showed that she conceived in prison."

During Scott's narrative, Bulman had remained absolutely still. He had not expected anything as far-reaching as this. "So Walter Clarke is the illegitimate son of a Nazi mass murderer and a traitor who sent many of her colleagues to their deaths, but who holds the highest French decoration for valor. Have I got it right?"

"According to what I've read, that's it. Could *you* live with it in his position?"

Bulman shook his head slowly. "It's not his fault. But fingers will point. People will say the evil must show itself through the genes. If he had the pluck to stick it out, the first harsh political decision, the first sign of no compromise, and it would all start up again. He's in an impossible position. He would be under pressure from most of his colleagues to resign for the sake of party and country, in that order. Yet it's worse than that. If this gets out, it will be worldwide. The French will expose Jeannette. A national heroine rotting away in a Riviera clinic. Relatives of the victims of her treachery and Hochricht's sadism will start banging the garbage can lids. There might even be a show of sympathy for Clarke, but it would not last long. Sooner or later the suggestion would come that he knew, and tried to keep it hidden. Poor bugger."

"His only hope lies in no one finding out. Dumain would have to be silenced and the original documents destroyed."

"Would you like to take that responsibility?"

Scott was silent. He stood up and paced the room.

Bulman said carefully, "It can never work. Not ever. He's finished. And before you feel too sorry for him, bear in mind that his friend Chesfield was murdered."

"*Because of him?*"

Bulman clasped his hands behind his head and gazed at Scott. "I've thought a lot about it, particularly since being thrown on the scrap heap. I discovered that Clarke threw a party. It seems that Chesfield went back when it was over. My guess is that in the early days of blackmail, Dumain hired Duncan Seddon to dummy for him in such an obvious way that Clarke would soon track him

262

down. At that stage, Dumain would want to know how far Clarke would go, and he must have had a shock when he found out. Clarke spins a yarn to his old mate Chesfield, who, we are told, loved the man. Chesfield acts for him, hires Bert Smith, and Seddon is killed. Perhaps Clarke himself didn't think it would go so far. Maybe he simply wanted to scare the man he believed to be his blackmailer. He certainly underestimated Chesfield's devotion to him and what he was prepared to do, and Chesfield died because of him. An unnecessary murder, since what I learned about Chesfield showed that there was no chance of him betraying Clarke. Clarke might even have believed in the suicide. For a time, anyway."

Scott stopped pacing and looked down at Bulman. "We've found the blackmail motive and we know who's doing it. Whatever happens, Dumain must be stopped and the stuff destroyed before Kransouski gets it. At least give Clarke the opportunity to resign with dignity. He's bright enough to start a new career."

"What's the hard evidence of all this, Spider?"

Scott handed over the batch of notes. "You can go through these, but I'll tell you about the stuff I couldn't bring. There's Jeannette's complete dossier, detailing her real and cover-up activities, with evidence of the baby's conception. There is a delayed birth certificate in the name of Walter Clarke dated three months after the actual birth of Paulette's baby. A deliberate compromise date, you could say, between the two births. There are letters between her and Hochricht showing that she had a son at that time. But there is no birth certificate for Jeannette's child, nor mention of its later existence. My feeling is that Paulette's baby died or was even, later, killed when the opportunity to do a switch occurred. Jeannette lived on a remote farm with her mother, who died a few years after the war. The letters are conclusive of parenthood and of the association, which is, of course, authenticated in Hochricht's own dossier on Jeannette.

"Then there are old postwar press clippings detailing Hochricht's massive crimes. None of them mention his death, and he might still be alive. If he is, he'll be tucked away somewhere in South America. Judging by the letters, which are handwritten, some in German, some in French, but all with typed English translations attached, there is no way Jeannette could have later married

Hochricht. He was on the run after the war anyway, and the passion had probably lost steam. But she would have to explain her baby away some time, and she found a way of covering up. Everyone knew she was looking after Paulette Dumain's child. She secluded herself for long enough to get away with it. If both children had lived, there would have been no more than five months between them. Given the difficulties of the times and the postwar years, late development of Jeannette's baby could then be explained. It's all there."

Bulman joined Scott by the window. "You know, the seed of uncertainty was already in Clarke's mind. His bloody grandfather cast doubts on him right from the beginning, and he never let up until he died. I don't think it was based on real doubt; I think the old boy was a malicious, bigoted bastard. When the chopper came down on Walter Clarke, the doubts were already well planted in his head."

"I'd like to get the original documents," Scott mused, almost to himself.

Bulman glanced at Scott suspiciously. "To destroy?"

"To get Inky Peel to have a look at them."

Bulman looked thoughtful. He said, "I'll have to report all this. I can't sit on it."

"You have only my word and my notes. You'll accept that, but will your bosses? I'm an ex-con. Sims won't believe you anyway."

"Sims is my boss only on police matters. Why do you want to hang on?"

"To give Walter Clarke a break. He doesn't seem to have had any."

"All right. I've enough reason for hanging on for a bit. It can't be long, though. There's one person I must tell, but he'll sit on it for me. You must face up to the fact that if Dumain thinks you've found out, he'll expect it to become official, and that will nullify his blackmail. He won't like that, Spider. He'll come gunning. I can't give you protection; I'm out in the cold. And so are you, mate. Dumain will salvage something, if it's only revenge."

"I know," Scott said. "One thing more before you go. Have you anyone tailing Kransouski?"

"I did have. I can't tell you if he still has one."

"If he has, can you pull them off for a bit?"

Bulman looked troubled. "Jesus. Don't tell me. I'll see what I can fix."

"I want Kransouski."

The Russian operator explained that Comrade Kransouski would not be in until ten thirty that morning.

"You get in touch with him and tell him I want to speak to him now."

The operator, who had been struggling with his own English, could hear the angry breathlessness from the receiver. He would have hung up, but there was an authoritative insistence about the man whose French accent had broadened heavily with emotion. "Who is calling?"

"Tell him it's Harry. And I'll phone back in exactly one hour."

Tom, Dick, or Harry, Scott had said, and it only made Denise the more furious to realize that he had been right. From now on he would listen to nobody but himself.

When he telephoned back in one hour, he announced himself as Harry and demanded to speak to Kransouski.

"This is madness," Kransouski complained. "Get off the line and give me a number to ring you."

"You talk to me now or . . ."

"*Or nothing.* Calm down and give me a number. I'll ring you in a matter of minutes." The fact that Denise had obtained his name was enough for Kransouski to realize the seriousness. Something had gone drastically wrong, but he would not discuss it on the Embassy telephones; he accepted the worst where MI5 and official lines were concerned. He left the Embassy, taking his umbrella with him, and he marched up to Kensington High Street.

Two of Reisen's men were standing by the corner of "Million-aires' Row"; they identified him from the description Scott had passed to Reisen. They looked at each other as if they could not believe their luck. They had already learned that Kransouski had arrived at the Embassy by car, although they had been advised that he liked to walk. Perhaps he knew that he was in possible danger. Yet here he was hurrying, long strides, swinging the umbrella, impervious of anyone around him, as though he had the weight of the world on his mind.

The two men had also been lucky in being so close at hand. Armed police who protected the embassies down the "Row" had a nasty habit of summoning local police on their radios when they spotted loiterers. The surveillance had been done from across the street, and even then they had to change often and be extremely careful. A window was needed for men using binoculars, and Reisen was working on it.

One of the men immediately crossed the busy street and gave a signal to a van with its rear doors open, as if it were about to be unloaded. The van had been there since early morning and arrangements had been made for space that evening and the following morning. It had been accepted by Reisen that snatching Kransouski would have to be done nearer his residence than the Embassy. Meanwhile, they were trying to plot his movements.

The van driver closed the doors and climbed into the cab. One man followed directly behind Kransouski at a distance. The morning crowds were out, early shoppers and late office workers. The conditions were ideal for tailing, and Kransouski seemed to be totally preoccupied.

When Kransouski entered the nearest telephone booth, his immediate follower believed he was setting some sort of trap. It was never this easy. The van driver was frantically signaled and he pulled out, trying to find a break in the traffic in order to make a U-turn.

Kransouski entered the booth, laid some coins out on top of the box, and dialed the number Denise had given him. Meanwhile, Reisen's man approached the booth and turned his back to it, as if waiting his turn to use it.

Denise was waiting to answer. "Kransouski?"

"How did you know my name?"

"I met Scott. He broke into Clarke's. I followed him from there, but I lost him later."

Thank God, Kransouski reflected. "It's too dangerous to use my name openly. I'm James and don't forget it."

"You're anything I like to call you. Do you realize that Scott could blow everything?"

266

"You don't know Scott. If he found anything, he won't go running to officialdom unless he's sure. He's not a friend of the law. And the policeman he was working with has been suspended. But I agree it is desirable to know what he found."

"*Desirable?* He's got to be stopped now. Don't you realize that everything could be ruined."

"Of course I do. But losing your head will make it worse. I have a way of stopping Scott from saying anything at all, whatever he knows. And I'll attend to it as soon as you are off the line."

"You attend to what you like. I want Scott's address. Either you give it to me now or the whole deal is off."

Kransouski thought quickly. Denise was verging on hysterical. He would have to give him the address. And he would have to keep Scott alive until he had what he wanted from him. If Scott had the full story, Maggie could be used to extract it from him. That would mean that the finding of Denise would lose immediate urgency.

"I'll release what I have to the press," Denise threatened viciously. That was another problem to be solved. Kransouski realized that he would have to come out in the open with Scott and make a quick deal. "I'm looking through my address book," he complained. "Hang on." Kransouski pulled out a small diary and flipped the pages near the receiver so that Denise would hear. He did not need a note of Scott's address. "Here it is." He called the address out slowly and then started to repeat it, but halfway through Denise slammed his phone down.

Kransouski replaced the receiver. Denise was mad. Scott must be warned. It was an ironic decision to make, but Kransouski felt that while he held Maggie, Scott would respond favorably. He turned up the telephone numbers at the back of the diary. He was checking the coins on top of the box when the door was pulled open and a tough, but quite well-dressed, man asked aggrievedly, "You going to be long, mate? There's a queue 'ere." He thumbed another figure behind him.

"Just one more call," Kransouski apologized. "A short one."

"You've made your last call, mate. Pick up your change."

The tone was still amiable but the man's expression had changed. Kransouski stared down at the long blade of the knife and then up at the bleak, challenging eyes. The booth was cramped even with the door half open. The man outside conveniently covered the door gap.

"What do you think you're doing? I'm a Soviet diplomat."

"And I'm Flash 'Arry. I know who you are, sport. Now be sensible. I've very strict instructions about you, and I do what I'm told. Any trouble from you and you'll get this blade straight in your guts or your kidneys, depending which way you're facing. My mate here has a gun, so one of us is going to get you. Right?"

"But you've made a mistake. I can't be the man you want."

"If you're not, it will soon be cleared up, old son, so don't fret. We'll return you right here. *Soviet* diplomat, did you say? What's that?"

"Russian." Kransouski was putting on an act of fear, but his mind was working fast.

"Russian. You bastards cause enough trouble, so don't rile me any more. There's a blue van right outside this booth. Just get in the back and be a good diplomat. Okay? I would enjoy pig-sticking you, so don't tempt me."

A change in Kransouski's eyes must have warned the man. Without knowing what, he sensed that something was about to happen. With his free hand he thumped Kransouski under the ribs. Kransouski gasped, but the blow had been partially softened by his topcoat. The knife came up under Kransouski's chin to straighten him and the fist went in again.

The man held on to Kransouski as he doubled forward; he called out, "Charlie, the poor bugger's been taken ill, let's get him back home."

The two men bundled Kransouski across the pavement to the stares of passersby, but they kept up the banter and made sympathetic noises and pushed Kransouski into the back of the already open van. Kransouski was recovering fast. He fell on his knees, but when he turned he was facing a gun with a silencer, and above it, a crude face that bade him try. The first man went back to the booth to collect the umbrella and the loose change on top of the box, which he casually pocketed. He climbed in the back with the others. It had all been so unbelievably easy.

19

HANK MILLER DID NOT REPORT to Bill Hahn until just before lunch. He expected trouble, for the message had been classified as urgent.

Hahn looked up. "I'll buy you lunch," he said. "Where do you usually go?"

Lunch on Hahn? Miller reasoned that he was being sent back to the States and Hahn was trying to soften the blow, in which case a condemned man was entitled to a last request. "I'll go wherever you usually go." Hahn considered himself a gourmet; let him dig deep, Miller reflected.

"Okay. Have you seen Scott yet?"

"No, but I intend to today. I had to fly to Scotland. There was some trouble on Polaris. I'm just back."

"Of course. Well, forget Scott. And Walter Clarke. Forget the whole thing."

"Why, what's happened?"

"Put it all out of your mind. It's dead."

"What about Washington? Clarke is out there now."

"I understand it's under control."

"Whose control? The Company's or the Firm's?"

Hahn hesitated. "We're not involved, but you won't get a memo on it. Come on, I'll buy you the best lunch in town."

"You trying to buy me off with a lunch?" Miller asked good-humoredly. "I'd drop it for nothing."

"No," Hahn said as he reached the door. "I'm trying to educate your taste buds. It'll be down to expenses."

So now it won't taste the same, Miller reflected as he followed Hahn out of the door.

Scott called Reisen at his office. "Is Knocker free, Rex?"

"What do you want him for?"

"To watch my back for a day or two."

"So they're after you? Well, let me put it this way. A certain gent offered himself up this morning. He pulled the net around himself. At the moment Knocker is interviewing him. Do you want me to take Knocker off?"

Scott's pulse raced. "You've got him? Christ. No, keep Knocker there."

"The guy's resisting. He's had some practice, so it might take a little time. I've told Knocker to leave some pieces for you and that's slowing it down a bit. Where will you be?"

"Here, at home." He wanted to thank Reisen, but the sudden image of Knocker Roberts with Kransouski made the words stick in his throat. He hung up, relieved that Reisen had managed to snatch Kransouski and worried sick at the outcome. If it meant getting Maggie back at Kransouski's expense, he had no qualms. He had seen Kransouski operate. And Knocker Roberts, too.

George Bulman came over at lunchtime, bringing fish and chips for them both. "I'll pop them in the oven, Spider, they're getting cold." He took them into the kitchen and turned the oven on. Scott handed him some plates.

When they were back in the drawing room, Scott produced a bottle of Scotch and half filled the glasses.

Bulman raised his brows. "Something to celebrate?"

"Kransouski's disappeared. The way I heard it, he gave himself up."

Bulman spluttered over his drink. "I haven't heard a thing." Bulman reached for the telephone. He punched out the numbers

270

with his back to Scott. The exchange was so low key and mumbled that Scott could only catch an odd word. "It's not news yet," Bulman said when he had finished.

"You sure?"

"My source is sound. Maybe they don't know he's missing. So you're waiting for him to talk?"

"Someone is. The sooner the better."

"Well, that certainly sounds like good news." But Bulman's unspoken question was, what had happened to Maggie meanwhile, and were there any instructions out on what should be done to her if Kransouski disappeared?

"I can't raise a thing about Dumain or Dumanier or whatever his name is. I've been on to my Surete pal in Paris. What he needs are fingerprints, of course."

"If he calls here, I'll get them for you."

"If he calls here, you get out bloody quick. By the way, I hope Kransouski doesn't croak. He's not a young man. We'll all be inside if that happens."

"It worries me, too, but if that's what it costs to get Maggie back, I won't worry for too long."

"You're expecting Dumain, aren't you?"

"In his position, I'd be out looking. He'll find me."

"You want me to hang around?" Bulman grinned wryly. "I've got time on my hands."

"You're in enough trouble. Don't worry."

"I do worry, Spider. Because for once you're not coming clean. That man is dangerous. He's handled Kransouski, and he's got Walter Clarke climbing the wall. He's indirectly responsible for getting Nicolai Gorkin sent back to Moscow. He's kept out of reach and he's playing a very peculiar game. Don't underestimate him, Spider."

"I know what sort of bastard he is."

"Yeah. Well, knowing and handling are two different things."

After Bulman had left, Scott went up to the roof and tested the fixing of the rainspout that ran past his bathroom window. It was solid and the brackets were well embedded. He tried the spout further down by kneeling on the sill of his bathroom window. It was not the best time to try; the streets were busy and anyone who

271

happened to look up might see him. He then took the elevator down to the boiler room and collected a coil of rope that he kept with his bicycle.

The rope was not long enough to tie to a roof fixture in order to make a cradle, which he would have preferred to do, but he believed that he could cope. He did not think that Denise would risk coming in daylight. He removed all the window locks but left the retaining bars, which governed how far the window could be opened.

Scott had to wait for darkness before he could take his next step. With the lights out he climbed from the bathroom window to the rainspout; his knee gripped it. Then he tied the rope firmly to the nearest bracket above the window and made two loops for footholds. He made a pulley arrangement so that he could vary the length of the rope. He brought the two ends back with him to dangle over the bathroom window sill. He then took all the windows off the catch so that a push would open any one of them. He pulled the curtains across and switched on the drawing room and kitchen lights.

He went around the apartment to ensure that he had gone as far as he could with preparations. Then he made himself a sandwich and coffee and took them into the hall and squatted behind the door. Scott was back to doing one of the things he did best: waiting.

The evening stretched out into night. Sometimes he would rise, always silently, and stretch arms and legs. He had taken the cup and plate back to the kitchen and had put them in the dishwasher, but he had left both living room and kitchen doors wide open so that he did not lose contact with the front door.

At eleven o'clock he was still there and had fallen into a state of mental blackout. He closed his mind to everything except sound. At half past eleven he put out all the lights, as he would normally do. At midnight he was still there, shifting position now and then but never carelessly. At no time did he think of stopping his vigil. He would not consider doing that until after the period of deepest sleep, which is about four A.M., and he would stay for at least another half hour after that.

Two o'clock passed without him showing signs of impatience. Any fidgeting he did was noiseless and merely to ease his circulation. That nothing had happened did not surprise him. At half past two he heard the first sounds; he was immediately fully alert. There was the faintest scratching around the lock.

He hurried to the bathroom, opened the window wide, climbed on the sill, slipped his feet in the loops, leaned out, letting the rope take the strain on the stack, reached out to close the window, then removed his feet from the sill and swung over. The bracket and the pipe took his weight. He pulled on the rope and rose above window level; he then wound the rope around the bracket to stay in position.

He was not comfortable but was ready for quite a long wait.

Denise opened the front door expertly. He gently pushed it but the chain stopped it from going further. So Scott was in. Sliding bolt cutters through the gap, he cut the chain and waited for a reaction from the tinkle of the links as it fell apart. He put the bolt cutters back in his belt under his jacket, and took out his Colt with the silencer attachment. Slowly he pushed the door right back against the wall where Scott had been sitting. The closed living room door faced him. Denise shut the front door quietly.

He opened the living room door, standing to one side as he pushed it back, and produced a pencil flashlight, avoiding the area of two other doors he was able to pick out without its use. The room was empty, as he expected it to be. After searching the bedroom, he continued on to the kitchen and the bathroom and the small dining room. The apartment was empty.

It was then that he recalled the door chain, which could only be applied from inside. Denise began to prickle at the back of his neck. He went back to the bedroom, looked under the bed, inside the built-in closet. There was nowhere else to hide. He stood in the middle of the room, pivoting and swinging his gun. Scott had to be here.

Denise felt a faint draft and thought he saw a curtain move; then he distinctly heard a rattle behind the curtain. But the curtains were not floor length, and there was nowhere behind them to hide. He carefully lifted the corner of one. There was less than six inches between the curtain and the window. He noticed that the windows were unlocked and that that had caused the rattling. He was uneasy and extremely edgy, ready to fire at anything. He checked the windows in every room. They were all unlocked. Every one of them, not opened on their bars, but simply unlocked.

Denise knew he had been tricked but he could not understand how. His skin was crawling. He had moved expertly, found every hiding place, and yet nobody was in the apartment. He examined the windows again. Why were the locks missing? He could see where they had been screwed to the wooden frames. True, he was five floors up and security was not such a problem, but Scott was a burglar and he would know better. The retaining bars could keep the windows closed, but they could be easily opened just the same. If Scott had served time, perhaps he could not tolerate the feeling of being locked in.

Denise went around the windows in turn, pushed them open, and looked out and down, sideways and up. Scott had flattened himself against the wall on the far side of the rainspout, and it was dark. Denise then reasoned that either Scott had found a way of putting the door chain on from the outside, or he had somehow left by one of the windows, in which case he might be waiting outside ready to shoot Denise as he left. It was a psychological disadvantage; Denise could not conceive that Scott would not be armed in such a situation.

He had never experienced fear. He had seen and enjoyed it in others. Even now he did not feel it, but his degree of unease was something new. He locked the front door, then moved a chair to back onto the living room wall, which faced the hall door, sat down, and decided to wait. The living room windows were in view; he was level with the bedroom and kitchen doors. Scott had to come sometime.

Scott had no idea how long Denise would take, but he was able to put himself in the Frenchman's position. The man would be puzzled, but would he finally leave or wait? He did not think that Denise would lose his nerve, even if he were rattled. Scott decided to move when it became increasingly difficult to remain as he was; his arms and legs were aching.

Using the rope as a pendulum, he pushed himself away from the spout and swung over to the sill. He pushed the window open very slowly, ready to swing back at the first warning. He crouched in the gap of the open window and noticed that the door had been closed. Retaining a grip on the rope, he stepped onto the carpeted floor. He pulled out a clasp knife and reached back to cut off a good length off the rope. He undid the foot loop and then weighted the end of the rope by tying a large knot.

Scott well knew why Denise had closed the door and guessed that the others were closed too. Opening doors could make noise and produce drafts. But it did indicate that Denise was waiting.

Knowing that his life depended on it, Scott knelt at the door and depressed the handle. As a matter of old habit, he always made sure that handles and hinges did not squeak. On hands and knees he crawled through to the bedroom to satisfy himself that it was empty. The door that led to the living room was designed to open toward him; it was located on the wall facing the hall door. He did not know that Denise had his back to the same wall. At the other end of that wall was the kitchen door.

Scott depressed the handle a fraction at a time, and when it was fully down, he held it there. Maintaining his grip, he half flattened himself and pulled the door slowly inward. When there was sufficient gap, he slowly released the handle and made sure it went back all the way. Now he flattened himself fully and inched forward. With his head around the doorway, he took stock.

Night sight had never been a problem; he had thrived at night. He saw Denise quite clearly. The Frenchman's head was down, as if he were asleep, but Scott knew that he would not be. The gun, unfortunately for Scott, was held between the knees, so that it was not clearly visible. It was necessary to get the gun up.

Scott withdrew into the bedroom. A coin would have served his purpose, but he had emptied his pockets of anything that might clink or rattle. On a bureau was a glass pot with some cuff links he never wore. He delicately picked out a stud and went back to the door, where he knelt just out of sight of Denise.

It was so utterly silent in the apartment that even the movement of the stud through the air might be heard. Scott waited until Denise moved his position slightly, then threw the stud at the hall door. It struck the frame, but it was enough; in the deep silence it was like a pistol shot, and Denise rose as though jerked forward.

The Colt came up and two shots, with no more noise than an air gun, went straight through the hall door.

Realizing that he had acted too swiftly, Denise was on his feet and racing for the door as Scott rose and swished the rope over like a bola, the weight of the knot encircling the rope around Denise's wrist. Scott pulled hard and Denise snarled as he lost balance on his way across the room. The gun went off twice more, plaster cascaded down, and wood splinters flew off from a ricochet.

With Denise unbalanced, the gun wrist held with tourniquet tightness, Scott kicked the Frenchman's legs from beneath him. As he fell, Scott held on grimly to the rope, which he pulled again. Denise screamed, and Scott hammered his heel onto the gun wrist until the fingers opened and the gun fell free.

Denise reared as Scott picked up the gun and struck him backhanded with the barrel. As Denise fell back, Scott cracked his jaw again, and Denise arched. Scott wasted no time. Keeping the gun in his hand, he unwound the rope, tossed the unconscious Denise onto his face, and rapidly tied his wrists behind his back. There was enough free rope to cut off and use to tie his ankles.

Scott sat back on his heels. He was panting but relieved. From the outset, he had known that he would have to get Denise very quickly or Denise would get him. He went back to the bathroom, climbed onto the sill, fetched the second branch rope with the remaining foothold, anchored it, and went back for Denise. He tied the rope around Denise's bound feet, and hoisted him onto the sill. He needed more rope, so he went into the kitchen and cut a length from an ordinary ball of string, which he looped loosely around Denise's neck. He tested the rope, then pushed Denise out of the window. Denise dropped slightly, and swung sideways, but before he crashed against the rainpipe, Scott checked him with the attached string, pulled him toward the window, and fastened the string. Denise now hung upside-down at an angle, his head at window level.

Scott waited for him to come around. It took longer than he thought it would, and happened in stages. Denise struggled at first, but as he gradually realized that he was not only tied but was dangling above the empty street, he quieted and tried to get sight of Scott. Scott gave a tug on the string, which resulted in a stream of violent invectives in French.

276

"Don't raise your voice or I'll drop you," Scott warned.

At the threat of being dropped, Denise became still. He was now fully conscious, and his deadly plight sank into his aching head. It was then that Scott realized that under the bravado, Denise was terrified. Was he scared of heights? Scott had seen those quickly forming sweat beads before.

Scott said evenly, "Listen carefully, you blackmailing bastard. Get it into your head that I believe all blackmailers should die in agony. The drop will break every stinking bone in your body, and there'll be time to reflect on it on the way down. You hear me? I want to know all about you. Your real name, where you're from, who you're dealing with. Where the original dossiers and letters are. You start now."

"You're wasting your time. You won't drop me. And you won't kill me."

Scott raised the gun, steadied his hands against the sill, aimed and fired. The bullet struck the rope, which jerked and sent Denise spinning. Scott steadied the movement by using the string. Denise was almost sobbing from fright. For the first time in his life, he was on the receiving end of terror.

Scott said, "There's a lot of crap in films about single shots severing a rope. There's too much give in a rope, too little flat surface. But you can chip away at them. Weaken them. At this range, even in darkness, it's easy. I can see where I've cut some strands. Bring your head up and see for yourself."

"You bastard." Denise's voice shook.

"I've checked the magazine. There are four rounds left. More than enough." He raised the gun again. "It's up to you, old son. You give me a rundown or you'll be scrambled on the street."

Walter Clarke went to his hotel room. His head was aching and had been for the last two days. He was due to return to England with the others the next day, and he was dreading it. He had won time from Denise, but had come up with nothing to help himself. His days in Washington had been busy and had helped to keep his mind off what awaited him in London. The evenings had been fully occupied, dinner at the White House the first night, a reciprocal at the British Embassy the next. Both occasions had been late.

Each time he had drunk more than he should. Once he was back in his own room, the nightmare began again.

The Foreign Secretary had again remarked that Clarke appeared to be strained, and to appease him Clarke went to a doctor. The visit did not diminish his problem, but he was able to obtain sleeping pills. He now found that he could not get through the night without them, and even then ugly reality would penetrate the drugged sleep. He would struggle awake sweating and compelled to take another pill to help quell the terror.

As he undressed now, he looked haggard. He really did not know what to do. He climbed into his pajamas and got into bed, leaving one side lamp on. He was afraid to try to sleep. He reached across to the bedside table for water and for the sleeping pills. His mouth was already dry from the liquor he had consumed. It seemed to him that no matter how much he drank, he could not get even mildly drunk, and could never stop the tentacles crawling through his brain.

He took two pills and swallowed most of the ice water. He sat up and waited for drowsiness to overcome him. Sleep eventually claimed him, but his face and hands twitched, and occasionally his legs would jerk as dread crept into oblivion with him.

His terror drifted into a lighter fantasy. He dreamed that his bedroom door opened and two men came into the room. He could only see fuzzed images with several outlines like auras around them; he knew they were men because of their voices. They moved very quietly so as not to awaken him, and he supposed they had come to pull up the sheet he had forced down the bed through restlessness. He thought he heard one of them murmur, "He's half done the job for us."

What job? Why half done? Clarke tried to pierce the drug that had claimed his mind. He must be hallucinating, yet somehow he found relief in it, and he stopped struggling against it. Something was in his mouth; that wasn't so good. And something soft was smothering him. He tried to struggle and then a grenade burst inside his head. He would not need sleeping pills anymore.

He was found mid-morning with a pillow over his face. Under the pillow was a Saturday Night Special still clutched in his hand, which had fallen away from the ugly mess of his mouth. Underneath the jagged cavity at the back of his head the bed was a bloodied mess, and it was this, mainly, that forced out the repeated screams from the chambermaid.

"You want me to go in with you?" Knocker Roberts sat beside Scott in the car.

"Perhaps you'd better. Kransouski might have lied." Scott glanced at the granite face of Roberts; Reisen had been right; the operation on Roberts's face had done nothing for him. Time had eroded an already rough skin to make it appear harder and meaner than Scott recalled. The very appearance of Roberts would scare most people, and he was at least as tough as he looked.

The street was ordinary, the house small but screened by well-matured shrubs and trees. The two men walked down the short drive to the front door. Roberts pulled out a gun.

Scott said, "If you use that, the whole neighborhood will call the fuzz."

Roberts was disgusted. "I don't need it. But as you say, that Russian bastard might have lied to gain some time. I'll finish him if he has."

Scott rang the bell. Nobody came. He rang again, prolonged. Roberts stepped back, ready to kick the door down. Scott said, "Hold it. I can open that window." He sprung the catch and climbed through, very wary. The room was badly furnished, small and empty. He carefully entered the hall and let Roberts in.

They searched the downstairs. It was empty, but the back door was unlocked.

"Skipped out," Roberts suggested. "Didn't like the look of us."

It was possible. According to Kransouski, Maggie was in the care of a woman. Checks were frequently made by telephone. Also, according to Kransouski, Maggie had not yet been touched; that would have come later had Scott failed to unearth Denise and to pass over the blackmail details.

They found Maggie tied to a bed upstairs. The windows were shuttered to dull any calls for help, but she was, in any event, gagged. She cried in relief as they untied her, and Knocker Roberts had the good grace to leave the room when she and Scott fiercely embraced. Roberts could not help wondering why it never happened to him, and a sadness crept into the brittle eyes.

On the way back to London, Roberts, who was driving, asked, "Shall I dump him on the Embassy steps?"

"The police would have you. Wait until night and you can drop him at an address I'll give you." With trepidation Scott asked, "Can he walk?"

"I don't know, Spider. He hasn't had a chance to try. You want to see him?"

Scott had seen the results of Knocker Roberts's work long ago; the memory lived vividly. He glanced at Maggie, whose head was cradled on his shoulder. Now and again she shuddered, and she was holding onto him as if she would never let go. He had no regrets about Kransouski, but seeing what Knocker had left of him was different. "No thanks," he said. "You tidy him up." Which would not be easy.

"How long can you keep him without charging him?"

Bulman looked wisely at Scott and said, "Sometimes I can't believe your naiveté. Particularly with your background. We've nothing to hold him on, and we can't *prove* blackmail with Walter Clarke gone."

"All I want is a little time."

"The original documents are due from Paris sometime today. There was a technical problem with the safety deposit people, but the Surete has acted like lightning over this. Once we knew Denise was Jeannette Renore's son, everything fell into place over there. Jeannette had a married cousin by the name of Jacqueline Denise who could not have children of her own. To avoid the possibility of incriminating speculation, an adoption for the baby was arranged long before it was born. They were turbulent, chaotic days, and by then the Allied invasion had started. Law and order was at a minimum. The cousin registered the baby as her own.

"Years later Denise found out that his mother was infertile. He probably wrung the truth of the adoption from her, and from that moment he went looking for his real mother. It couldn't have been easy. Jeannette had married a few years after the war and had drifted south. The marriage was a failure, and the husband pushed off after a couple of years, but Jeannette had a daughter by him.

"It seemed that Denise was hell bent on wrecking the family to which he rightly belonged. He certainly managed that. He killed his half sister, and from that point Jeannette went rapidly downhill. Denise was put away in a criminal asylum for some years."

"Do I get the time or not?" Scott demanded.

Maggie came in with a tray of coffee. Bulman gave her close scrutiny, but beyond being unusually quiet, she appeared none the worse for her experience. He reflected that the same could not be said of Kransouski, who had been stretchered back to Moscow with, strangely, no complaints from the Soviets. Scott pecked Maggie on the cheek as she bent over to place the tray. They were happy because there had been no need to put the wedding back.

"Of course you get the time. Denise is tucked away in a very special prison. When he gets out, he'll be in no position to beef."

"My fear is that he'll release his guff to the press just for spite. At least let Clarke stay dead."

"We can't stop Denise. All we can do is to send him back to France."

"What about trying to kill me?"

"You want to press charges?"

Scott shook his head. "I'll tell you one thing, though. Denise may have sung like a canary once he lost his nerve, but I don't think he told it all. I think he told me just enough so that I'd pull him back into the room."

Later that day Scott obtained special dispensation to take the original blackmail documents to Lennie Peel at Wandsworth Prison. By the strange influence of the still suspended George Bulman, Peel was given a cell of his own in the overcrowded prison while he examined the documents. It was strange, too, that George Bulman did not insist on calling in a handwriting expert, however technically qualified. Bulman knew, as Scott did, that there was no greater expert than a master forger.

Two days later Lennie Peel gave his verdict, and George Bulman invited Maggie, Scott, and Sir Stuart Halliman to dinner. Sir Stuart made his excuses not to attend, but he arranged champagne for them and sent Maggie a superb orchid. Bulman destroyed his image of meanness by taking them to the Mirabelle, a restaurant well above his income level, frequented by millionaires and those in high society. Scott couldn't help wondering who was paying. They waited for coffee before entering into the subject of Clarke in depth.

"How many of the letters were forged?" Bulman asked.

"About half. The dossier is genuine, and the handnotes are certainly Hochricht's when compared with the genuine letter. The forgeries are top quality, but it is these that give the damning information about Clarke's parentage. It's strong stuff. Very convincing."

All three were silent. It was Maggie who eventually spoke. "So Walter Clarke *was* Paulette Dumain's son. How dreadful. He need not have died."

Scott laid a hand over hers. "It's not so simple." He glanced at Bulman who took his cue.

"Maggie," Bulman said heavily, "there are points about this that we'll never know for certain. Denise has all the answers, but he's confusing fact with fiction. He's mad. We've had a shrink onto him, and I personally think what happened was this.

"We don't know what went on between Jeannette and Denise when he eventually caught up with her. He obviously unearthed the dossiers and letters. Why Jeannette kept her own dossier is difficult to understand. The others could have been useful to the Nazis had the war continued. Perhaps she kept hers initially as insurance against uninformed German capture. She probably hid them all. The letters are more understandable; most women cherish their love letters. She may have forgotten about them as life returned to normal, or she may have kept hers as some secret and highly personal penance. The forgeries that Denise later arranged to have done cleverly followed the same vein as the originals, but slanted away from the truth.

"When Denise got digging, he didn't stop until he had dug all the way. There was no safe hiding place from him. He probably killed his half sister because she found out something of what he was up to. All his plans were suspended while he was in the asylum, but he had plenty of time to build up an intense hatred for the child who had been cosseted for almost two years by Jeannette, who had kicked her own son out soon after he was born.

"After his eventual release, he would have wanted to trace Walter Clarke and get revenge. But the years of incarceration had provided him with cunning, and there was the plain matter of survival. He was brilliant in his way. From nothing he built up a highly successful wine business in the Rhone Valley. It took time, but his need for revenge never waned. At last, he had the money to search for Walter Clarke."

While Bulman sipped his coffee, Scott reflected on the wreck of the woman he had visited in France. "Jeannette must have known what her son intended to do. That must have been when her real trauma began. She had no defense he could not destroy, and it probably sent her over the edge. Denise had looked up his Nazi father's history because he sent press clippings to Clarke. The irony is that she probably looked after young Walter Clarke only because the resistance boys who had rescued her knew the baby was Paulette's; it would look good for Jeannette with what she had to hide to do so. And later, Denise would have been living evidence against her, had she kept him."

The mood around the table was solemn until Bulman said cheerfully, "I think you should know that my Surete pal told me that an Algerian master forger was found dead with his head buried in molten lead. It was about the time when you met Denise over there, Willie."

Maggie shivered. "I can't stop thinking of Walter Clarke. The poor man blew his brains out for nothing." While Maggie was speaking, Scott was watching for Bulman's reaction very closely, and was perturbed by the lack of it.

"Not quite for nothing, Maggie," Bulman replied. "He used his friend Gordon Chesfield, who died for him after Seddon was murdered and Bert Smith was put away for life."

Avoiding Scott's gaze, Bulman added, "Denise craved a birthright, and when he found it he wished to God he never had. He probably gets satisfaction from seeing his mother slowly rot away in a clinic. I'll have to let him go. He can't get the stuff published because I can now tell him we know which letters he's had forged. We'll keep all the originals. They'll deal with him over there."

"In the same way that we dealt with Walter Clarke?" Scott asked softly.

Maggie suddenly kept quiet. She knew what it meant when he looked like that, and with utter dismay realized that he was right. She felt cold.

"Willie, what are you talking about?" Bulman asked blandly.

"You know what I'm talking about."

Bulman called the waiter for more coffee. "You're a suspicious bugger. Sorry, Maggie. Walter Clarke started to die the day he met his grandfather. He drove himself through life trying to run from the doubts that man had planted. Clarke and Denise. It happened to them both in different ways. *C'est la guerre.*"